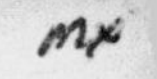

Loretta was born in Perth, the eldest of four girls. She enjoyed writing from a very early age and was just eleven years old when she had her first short story published in *The West Australian* newspaper.

Having graduated with a degree in Civil Engineering and another in Commerce, she was hired by a major Western Australian engineering company and worked for a number of years on many outback projects. She drew upon her experiences of larrikins, red dust and steel-capped boots for her bestselling novels *The Girl in Steel-Capped Boots*, *The Girl in the Hard Hat* and *The Girl in the Yellow Vest*. She is also the author of two rom-com novellas, *One Little White Lie* and *Operation: Valentine*.

She lives in Perth with her husband and four children.

The Girl in the Yellow Vest

LORETTA HILL

BANTAM
SYDNEY AUCKLAND TORONTO NEW YORK LONDON

A Bantam book
Published by Random House Australia Pty Ltd
Level 3, 100 Pacific Highway, North Sydney NSW 2060
www.randomhouse.com.au

First published by Bantam in 2014

Addresses for companies within the Random House Group can be found at www.randomhouse.com.au/offices

National Library of Australia
Cataloguing-in-Publication entry

Hill, Loretta, author.
The girl in the yellow vest/Loretta Hill.
ISBN 978 1 74275 737 7 (paperback)
Work environment – Fiction.
A823.4

Cover images: (woman) © Pando Hall/Getty Images; (construction workers) iurii/Shutterstock; (landscape) Wouter Tolenaars/Shutterstock
Cover design by Christabella Designs
Typeset in 11.5/15.5 pt Sabon by Midland Typesetters, Australia
Printed in Australia by Griffin Press, an accredited ISO AS/NZS 14001:2004 Environmental Management System printer

Random House Australia uses papers that are natural, renewable and recyclable products and made from wood grown in sustainable forests. The logging and manufacturing processes are expected to conform to the environmental regulations of the country of origin.

For Mum and Dad,
Your enduring love and faith in me has
always been my biggest blessing.
Thank you so much for all that you are.

Chapter 1

Emily

The head bridesmaid, a brunette in a long blue gown, rose from her chair and walked unsteadily to the dais with the studied clumsiness of someone who was completely wasted but trying very hard not to show it. After leaning on the lectern a few seconds too long, she unfolded a rather worn-looking piece of paper and placed it in front of her.

'Good evening, everyone,' she hiccupped. 'I'm Robyn Churchill, Lena's best friend. I've known Lena,' she squinted at the piece of paper, 'for f-fifteen years and – oh to hell with it.' She tossed the piece of paper aside and lifted one purposeful finger before slurring, 'The truth is, when Lena told me she was off to the Pilbara to be a proper engineer, I never thought she'd come back engaged. *Never.* Sunburned maybe . . . but planning a wedding? Ha! The thought never even crossed my mind.' She teetered a little and had to grab hold of the lectern. 'But you know, when I think about it *now*, I really should have seen it coming.' She patted her hair; the cream-coloured flower she was wearing now hung precariously from one bobby pin.

'After that day he spotted her swimming in her red bra and matching knickers, it was *blatantly* obvious that Lena was going to attract his attention.'

The bride, sitting three seats to the left of the podium, in a strapless satin gown with a crystal-studded bodice, covered her mouth with both hands and looked down at her plate.

'Good Lord.' Julia, who was sitting next to Emily at table number seven, leaned discreetly sideways so that she could murmur out the side of her mouth. 'There's one at every wedding, isn't there?'

Emily's mouth twisted wistfully as she studied Lena. While her old uni friend had appeared momentarily embarrassed, she was now looking across at Robyn with a sort of helpless affection. It was the kind of expression worn by a person whose cup of happiness was so full nothing could be said or done to empty it.

And with just cause.

Her new husband looked gorgeous. The groom was dressed in a smart black tux – its very cut a stark tribute to his masculinity. He cast his glowing bride a look so potent it made Emily's heart ache.

Is it wrong for me to feel resentful?

In their group of friends, Lena was never supposed to be the first one to get married. For starters, she'd only been dating Dan for a few months before he'd popped the question, and in the Pilbara of all places. Wasn't that like the most unromantic place on the planet?

Emily, on the other hand, had been in a committed relationship for five years. They'd owned a house together. They had a dog, for goodness' sake. His mum called *her* to find out what he wanted for his birthday. If anyone had been well and truly on the road to a happily ever after, it was her. Her fingers tightened around the stem of her wine glass.

How wrong were you?

In Trent's mind, it had clearly been a different story. Instead of the pulp-fiction ending she'd dreamed of, he'd gone with a very literary alternative.

Tragic symbolism.

The tragedy she got. What it symbolised she had yet to decipher.

Lifting her wine glass, she took a soothing sip. She had promised herself not to wallow in her misery tonight: there was too much to enjoy. A reunion with her engineering buddies, for a start. There were eight of them. Three girls – Lena, Julia and herself – and five guys, one of whom was her best friend, Will. She could still remember late nights spent in the Reid Library with this crew trying to finish a Structural Analysis assignment or, worse, a Mathematics one. They'd take it in turns to do the coffee run to the café downstairs. Then, of course, there were the toga parties and the quiz nights, the early-morning dancing at some club in Northbridge. If they were honest, they hadn't got through engineering individually but collectively. Each had needed the others to be responsible when he or she failed to be. They shared information, assignment answers and hangovers alike.

Graduating and entering the workforce had been a sobering period during which they all realised it was time to stand on their own feet. Now, if they were lucky, they caught up once a month instead of every day. In fact, if Lena hadn't decided to get married that Saturday, Emily doubted they would be catching up at all.

No, that's not completely true.

She would have made time for Will. Now that he worked in Queensland, she only got to see him every four or five weeks when he flew back to Perth to take his R and R. While they did text and email a lot, she missed having her best friend in town.

Smiling, she turned to the subject of her thoughts, who was sitting on her right. 'Now, when I ask you to be my maid of honour, you need to promise me to stay sober until after the speeches.'

Will returned her smile but shook his head. 'There is no way, this side of hell, that I'm being your maid of honour.'

She raised her eyebrows. 'Why not?'

He gave her a long look. Will might be her best friend but he invariably refused to do anything girly. No facials. No chick flicks. And no shopping together – though he had made a binding exception to that rule in the case of them needing something like a top-secret computer microchip available only from the Japanese black market. 'And then I'd expect you to be my Bond girl,' he insisted.

This was pretty funny, considering Will looked nothing like James Bond, though Emily suspected he would secretly like to. With longish brown hair, a short beard and black-rimmed specs, he was a lovable nerd who hadn't changed one iota since the day she'd met him, an eager seventeen-year-old with a passion for science similar to hers.

She couldn't help but notice that he still hadn't answered her question.

'Well?' she pressed him.

He was silent and for a moment she thought his expression was serious. Would he really not stand up for her at her wedding? She knew it was a little corny, but she'd do it for him. Then his expression cut to a jovial one: 'I think Trent would want me to be his best man. And, to be honest, I think I'd much rather be a best man than a maid of honour. No offence.'

She froze. *He doesn't know.*

She was so sure he'd been avoiding the subject till they had a private moment to talk. Why hadn't Trent told him?

'What's the matter?'

As she looked up to meet his eyes, she realised she couldn't blame Trent. She hadn't told anyone yet either. Telling people about her break-up made it real.

'Will, the truth is –'

But Robyn was now calling for everyone's attention. 'I'll need you all to charge your glasses!'

The moment to speak was lost as Julia passed her a bottle of white. At the front of the room, Robyn leaned over and plucked her own champagne glass from a table beside the podium, looked at it and then set it down again. 'I'm going to need some more grog in that,' she said to the bridesmaid called Sharon. A chuckle rippled through the crowd as Sharon complied.

Robyn raised her now full glass and rocked on the balls of her feet as she surveyed the crowd. 'There is no doubt in my mind: Dan and Lena make an exceptional couple. So in love, it makes you ssss-sick.' She looked down momentarily and with studied resolve clutched her stomach. A few seconds passed. Emily and the rest of the room held their breath.

But with a valiant smile Robyn looked up again, waving a hand in reassurance. 'What I'm trying to say is, there is no couple better suited or matched than these two. They are the ying and the yang, the head and the tail, the . . . well . . . you get the point. I just wish we could all be as lucky. Soooooo,' she lifted her glass unsteadily, 'I want to propose a toast.'

Emily and the rest of room posed at the ready.

'To red underwear.' Robyn thrust her glass in the air. 'May we all find a set!'

'To red underwear!' The wedding guests laughed and everyone drank.

As Lena got up to embrace her friend lovingly, everyone else returned to dinner and conversation.

Julia leaned on the table and said, 'How embarrassing. I thought her speech would never end. Where did Lena meet that girl anyway?'

'I don't know.' Emily shrugged. 'I don't remember her from uni.'

'That's because she didn't go to our uni,' Will informed them both. 'Lena met Robyn in high school.'

Emily rolled her eyes. 'Of course Will remembers.'

Will never forgot anyone or anything: he had a photographic memory. He remembered everything he read and had probably been the smartest guy in their study group. His honours were so first class they had wanted him to extend his thesis and apply for a PhD. He did so and was granted it.

'Well, I don't recall her.' Julia examined her fingernails. 'I have enough trouble keeping track of you lot.' She glanced across the table. 'So, where are you guys working now? Jake?'

'CPG,' Jake responded. He was a stocky guy with a streak of red through his dark brown hair. 'Just started.'

'Oil and gas,' Julia murmured. 'Not bad. I don't suppose you've had to sail to an offshore platform yet?'

Jake cracked his knuckles. 'I'm working on it.'

'And what about you, Caleb?'

Julia proceeded to go round the group and interrogate everyone on their current positions. She was very competitive and was always trying to compare their successes, particularly in a manner that elevated her own.

Julia believed, of course, that the footbridge she was working on was the most high profile. And maybe, in a way, it was, because it was going to be located in Perth's Kings Park. Therefore, it would automatically be heritage listed, built to last a hundred and fifty years and no doubt have some sort of cultural significance written on a plaque and placed beside it. But as far as Emily was concerned, Will had the best gig. Like Lena, he also worked for Barnes Inc, the biggest engineering company in the state. However, he was on a different project at a different location. And what a location it was!

The Whitsunday Islands.

The Great Barrier Reef.

Living in a resort.

And best of all, being part of the expansion of what was already the largest coal export facility in the Southern Hemisphere. Hay Point Wharf – she'd sell her right arm to see it.

But she didn't begrudge Will his success. It wasn't his fault he was super-smart and easy to work with. He deserved to be there.

Emily reached over and took a gulp of her wine, dreading Julia getting around the table and back to her. There was no doubt she was going to as she systematically made everyone give a breakdown of the projects they were working on. The moment came all too soon.

'Emily, are you still with Johns, Anstey & Carlton?'

Emily looked into her glass, studying the translucent liquid and wishing it were just a touch more potent. 'Yeah,' she mumbled and took a gulp.

'What do they have you doing?'

'Oh, you know, nothing worth mentioning.'

'Now you've tickled my curiosity.'

'Really, it's not that exciting.' She looked around, hoping for a waiter to show up or the band to start playing. Seriously, these people never did their jobs conveniently. 'I wonder when dessert's coming.'

Julia's eyes widened. 'Are you *still* doing that dilapidation survey?'

Crap. She'd forgotten she'd had a bit of a whinge to Julia about it over coffee four months earlier.

'Yes. There's a lot of buildings involved.' Emily wound her napkin into a tight rope and then looked up brightly, hell bent on a subject change. 'Has anyone spoken to Sharon, the other bridesmaid? She looks like an interesting girl. That husband of hers is so funny. Carl, isn't it?'

'Hang on a minute.' Jake exchanged a look with Caleb. 'So what's a dilapidation survey? What does that involve?'

Emily had been counting on the ignorance of graduates only two years out of uni. The last thing she wanted to do was enlighten them.

'It's actually a really important step in the pre-construction process, especially in high-profile areas like the city,' Will put in. She cast him a grateful look that was short-lived.

'But boring as hell,' Julia scoffed. 'I'm surprised she hasn't shot herself in the head yet.'

Trust Julia to elaborate. Oblivious to Emily's mortification, her ex-study-buddy turned to the rest of the group. 'You know how they're putting in that second tunnel under the city? Well, Emily here has to go check out all the buildings that will be sitting over the top of it.'

'Check out?' Jake repeated.

'She has to examine every room, floor and wall in every building and take a record of the cracks present in the structure so that her company has a snapshot of what they were like before construction. So when construction starts and the lawsuits start coming through, they can say, "No, sorry, those cracks were already there and not caused by us." '

The truth dawned on Caleb, a sandy-haired guy with freckles to match. 'Let me get this straight: you're counting cracks?'

Emily winced. 'In a manner of speaking.'

'That must give you the shits.'

The rest of the table burst out laughing at his unfortunate play on words.

Emily wanted to crawl under the table and die. 'I'm not just counting them precisely; I have to look at dents and water damage too.'

But nobody was really listening, except Will. 'We've really got to find a way to get your boss to give you something else. It's been way too long.'

She nodded. Thankfully, a few seconds later the table conversation moved on to something less close to the bone than her floundering career and Emily could concentrate on the after-effects of being the laughing stock of her peer group. The worst thing was she had stayed in that job for the benefit of her relationship. The company seemed to focus on Perth-based projects and she hadn't wanted to leave Trent to work out of town, especially when she thought he was on the verge of proposing. In her mind, she had been about to settle down, maybe even go part-time when they decided to have a family. What a joke!

She had sacrificed her career development for the man she thought was the love of her life. And he'd dumped her. How could she have read the signs so wrong? Her embarrassment about her career was only compounded by her poor judgement about Trent. Somehow she didn't feel like making the announcement that they were no longer together now. When she'd first arrived at the wedding, her friends had all remarked on his absence but she'd simply told them he was working late. Which, let's face it, was perfectly believable. As a lawyer, Trent worked horrendous hours and they were used to him only turning up sporadically to social functions. So there was no rush to set them all straight. She had a bit of time before the truth had to come out.

On the pretext of wanting to wish the bride and groom luck, she left their table shortly after the main meal. Luckily, she didn't have to follow through with her cover because the blushing bride and her handsome husband had been waylaid by one of those elderly relations no one has ever heard of but who always seem to resurface at weddings. Aunt Betty had Dan by the cheek and was saying, 'Well, I never thought I'd see the day.'

Emily escaped outside into the gardens, breathing in the fresh fruity smell of the nearby vineyard as her eyes adjusted to the dark. Lena and Dan had chosen to get married in the Swan Valley. They had a huge marquee set up on the lawn at Featherdowns Estate, right next to a giant circular pond with a fountain in the middle. The spotlights at the bottom of the pond made it possible for Emily to see her reflection in the rippling water.

Curly brown hair, brown eyes, a pert little nose. She looked a lot like her mother, which wasn't exactly a bad thing. She had always thought her mother was pretty, though not beautiful in the way that some girls like Julia and Lena were.

With a sigh she guessed somebody had to be average. And in this case it was her. Average engineer. Average looks. Below average love life.

She leaned over the wall and swatted at her own reflection.

'Hey.'

With a start she turned around, lurching back against the wall of the pond on one elbow. 'Will!' She put a hand to her chest. 'You scared me half to death.'

'What's the matter? Why are you moping around like the world has come to an end?'

She blew on her fringe. 'I wasn't moping.' At his disbelieving stare, she lifted her hand and pinched her thumb and forefinger together. 'Okay, maybe just *a little*.'

'Because of the fuss Julia made over your job?' He frowned. 'You know, with friends like her, who needs enemies?'

Despite herself she smiled. 'Julia can't help herself. I make her look good.'

'You're too hard on yourself.'

'You think so?' She cocked her head to one side. 'I can't help feeling like a failure.'

'Don't be ridiculous. It's just a job. You can change it. Have you spoken to Trent about it?'

'No.'

He sighed. 'Well, I hope you've at least given him a piece of your mind for missing Lena's wedding. He's been working weekends way too much lately.'

When she didn't respond, he added, 'Come on, they're just starting to bring out dessert. That'll cheer you up.'

She shook her head. 'I'm on a diet.'

His jaw dropped. 'Okay, now you're starting to worry me.'

She ran her hands down her size-twelve hips. 'Since when is slimming down a crime?'

'You don't need slimming down,' he said quietly. 'Besides, diets are dumb. I don't see how starving yourself can possibly be healthy.'

'Oh, I'm not starving myself.' Emily lifted her chin. 'This is a special diet. It's the magic bean regime, proven in the

US a billion times over. I bought the book and everything. It's actually not that hard to do and very flexible.'

'Really?' His flat tone clearly conveyed his scepticism.

'Absolutely.' Emily held up her hand in reassurance. 'Basically, what you do is eat nothing but legumes all day.'

'Legumes?' He made a face.

'Alfalfa, clover, peas, beans, lentils, mesquite, carob, soybeans and peanuts.'

'I know what legumes are; I just didn't think you did. Otherwise you wouldn't commit to eating them.'

'I will admit it is slightly challenging.' She winced. 'But if you're good you're allowed to reward yourself with your choice of a berry after dinner.'

'Just one?'

'Well,' Emily flushed guiltily, 'sometimes I have a handful.'

'You rebel, you.'

'Don't give me that.' Emily put her hands on her hips. 'This diet has been helping me feel stacks better about myself. And today is the first time since I started that I've had to break the rules, so it's no wonder I'm standing out here feeling depressed.'

'When did you start the diet?'

She hunched a shoulder. 'Yesterday.'

'Oh, Em, for goodness' sake. You don't need to lose weight. What's really going on with you? You've been acting weird all night.'

She clasped her hands tightly together and looked back at her reflection in the pond. 'They're kind of interrelated . . . You see, I need to look my best because . . .' she paused '. . . I'm . . . back on the dating market.'

For a moment there was dead silence before he said incredulously, 'You're *what*?'

She knew he'd be surprised. The last time they'd caught up, she'd been talking marriage and babies and now . . .

Emily swallowed hard. 'Trent and I broke up.'

'What? When?'

'Two weeks ago.'

'Why didn't he tell me?' He frowned. 'Why didn't *you*?'

Why didn't I?

Shame.

Shock.

Maybe the vague hope that the split was really just a bump in the road and one morning Trent would wake up and say he'd made a mistake. Two weeks later she had to concede he wasn't going to do that.

Emily hugged her arms as goose bumps broke out on her skin. 'Well, I knew you were flying back to Perth for the wedding and I thought, if he hadn't told you, I'd tell you then . . . now. Besides, I needed some time to get used to the idea before, you know, I made the announcement that I'm single again after five years.'

Man, I don't even know how to be single any more.

Will's face seemed to harden. 'What happened?'

Emily couldn't help it. 'To be honest, I don't know.' She felt her face crumple.

Will blinked at her, pushing his glasses up the bridge of his nose. 'Now we both know my love-life is a train wreck but even I can usually pinpoint the place where things went wrong.'

It was true. In the entire time she'd known Will, which was nearly two years longer than she'd been with his best mate, he'd been out with exactly five women. None of them had been on the scene for very long but there always seemed to be a legitimate reason for his relationship failure.

There was the copy-writer who'd annoyed the hell out of him by speaking all the way through every movie they went to see. And then there was a Korean girl who giggled at everything, even when it wasn't funny. After these two, he decided to go for an older woman – hoping for someone more mature in her outlook in life. And she was.

Unfortunately, so was her husband.

His last relationship had seemed the most promising. The female in question had been sweet, intelligent, pretty. All was going well until she asked Will if he wanted to join a cult with her and live in a commune so as to recapture the missing pieces of their souls.

Uh-huh.

Emily still hadn't found out what had happened to his first girlfriend, Sasha, with whom Will had been going out when they first met. But she figured that if Will had thought her 'viable' he would have said so. In fact, that was the difficulty: Will approached women in the same way he approached an engineering problem. Like a scientist. He dissected their personalities into parts and used the breakdown to decide how compatible they were with him. He had no belief in the old idiom 'Opposites attract' or that, given time, some idiosyncrasies could grow on a person. He even had his own theorem about conversation. More than three awkward silences and the relationship was dead in the water. It didn't help that his facial hair was too long to be fashionable and he refused to take an interest in his physical appearance. Usually only men in their fifties wore cardigans, a circumstance that Emily had been moaning about for years, to no avail.

'They're comfortable,' had been Will's argument. 'And they have pockets.'

'So do jeans.'

'Not nearly big enough for a calculator.'

Emily's lips twisted at the memory.

'So tell me how did it happen, then?' Will brought her mind back to her own relationship disaster.

'We went out for dinner, that really nice place I've been wanting to go to for ages. He said he had something to tell me.' She shut her eyes. 'I thought he was going to propose. And instead –' her voice wavered '– instead he said he wanted me to move out so he could start seeing other people.'

'Why?'

'He said that he felt we were stagnating and we'd been together too long and a whole host of others things I didn't quite understand, which he summed up with the age-old line: *It's not you. It's me.*'

Will snorted. 'What a chump. There's got to be more to it.'

Out of habit, Emily opened her mouth to jump to Trent's defence but to her dismay nothing came out. In confusion, she looked down. 'Do you think there's something wrong with me, Will?'

'No.' His tone was adamant.

'I think Trent was right about a few things.'

Will's brow furrowed. 'In my experience there are very few occasions on which Trent is right. I mean, he tries but even when we were kids he used to say the dumbest things.'

'Well, he did say that, you know, we were each other's first love and we hadn't really given each other a fair chance to find anyone else. He said he needed to do that before he could just settle down with me and I guess that is sort of a fair call. I mean, when you buy a car you don't just test drive one, do you? You –'

'Oh, for goodness' sake,' Will snapped. 'Did he give you that analogy too?'

Emily blushed. 'Sort of.'

'I'll have a chat to him.'

'No don't, please!' she responded, alarmed.

'Okay, okay, sorry, calm down.'

She sighed. 'When you think about it, you can't really blame him for wanting to check what else is out there. I mean, look at me.' Emily's gaze returned to her reflection.

Will was horrified. 'Are you referring to your weight again? Because if he said anything to you about that I swear to God –'

'Calm down, Will.' She was touched by his anger but laid a hand on his shoulder to stop him speaking. 'He didn't say anything. The truth is, my whole life seems to need a revamp.

I'm terrible at my job, I'm slightly overweight and now I'm living with my parents again.'

'Ouch.' Will winced. 'I mean, just about that last part. The weight thing is all in your head and I don't know how you can think that you're a bad engineer.'

'Well, I must be because my manager has never given me anything worthwhile to do.'

'That's not true.'

'Will,' she said pointedly, 'I *count cracks*. That's what I do. After five years of study I'm counting squiggly lines on concrete. Did you know this week I started in the basement of a twenty-seven-storey building? It was basically the parking lot and there I was with my notebook and camera and three hundred and twenty-two bays. Trust me, I *wanted* to slit my wrists.'

He grinned. 'Okay, look, maybe you're right. Maybe you do have a crap job. But that's not you, that's them. Why don't you quit?'

'And go where? Jobs at my level are pretty scarce right now.' Emily put her head on her palm. 'Do I really want to lose my boyfriend and my job all in the same month?'

'Well,' Will nodded decisively, 'you're right about one thing. Your life does need a bit of a revamp, or a fresh start. You need to get out of town and realise your potential. Why not come and work with me?'

Emily snorted. 'Yeah, why not?' she said sarcastically.

'I'm serious. They're advertising a position for a new graduate. My manager has already contacted head office about it. I could put in a good word for you.'

She could get out of town. Leave Trent behind, physically and mentally. Focus on her career. Reboot her life.

Move on.

It was exactly what she needed. She turned to him like a long-lost relation. '*Really*? You really think I could get a job in Queensland? With you?'

Will cleared his throat. 'Of course.'

She jumped up and down, fisting her hands in glee.

He rubbed the back of his head self-consciously. 'Now don't get too excited, it's not a done deal yet. I will have to ask first and they'll probably want to interview you and all that. I can give you a few tips, so you know what'll impress them.'

'I know, I know.' She wasn't worried. Past experience had shown her that when Will put his mind to something he got it done, no matter what it was.

'And there is just one other condition too.' He looked at her sternly.

'What's that?'

'No legumes!' He held out his palm to her, indicating they should shake on it. 'Have we got a deal?'

Emily ignored his hand and threw her arms around his neck. 'Queensland, here I come!'

Chapter 2

Will

It was five to seven and already the morning had taken on the hot sticky feeling that was Queensland's signature ambience that time of year.

Thank God for air-conditioning.

Will walked into the main office donga at Hay Point to the rush of cool bliss against his face. After pausing a few seconds to take in the state of the office, it really was all he had to be grateful for. The open-plan layout did little to contain the disorder. The desks were crowded. Workspaces overlapped. People and computers were crammed together, along with a light film of paperwork that seemed to blanket the place like snow. Drawings were pinned to the walls, and not just on noticeboards but around the windows and on cubicle walls as well. There was not an ounce of space unused. At least ten huge A3 drawing files sat on two layout tables in the centre of the room. Most of them were open. There was a bookshelf against the wall, but it was clear that the drawings were never put away and just remained permanently open for engineers to peruse on their way in and out of the office. The hooks by the door containing a bunch of dirty, yellow, high-visibility vests and hard hats seemed to indicate that this happened often. It was chaos.

Unpredictable. Stressful. He loved it.

In fact, there was really only one thing he loved more than his job. *Emily.*

A dark cloud descended at the thought. It had been so simple when she was forbidden fruit. Beyond his reach . . . beyond hope.

But now Trent had stuffed up either deliberately or accidentally. He didn't know, because his best mate still had not drawn him into his confidence. Not that he could talk. Trent would be stunned to learn that Will had feelings for Emily. He'd kept it a secret all these years.

How he rued the day he had introduced the two of them. It had been at a party. In hindsight he realised he'd been in love with her by then, only he hadn't admitted it even to himself. At the time of course he had been with Sasha, though their relationship was deteriorating. After he met Emily, it had started to dissolve slowly like salt in water. If things had worked out the way they were supposed to, he should have broken up with Sasha and then asked Emily out. But he was too slow, too confused. Trying to appease Sasha, trying to work out how Emily felt. He shouldn't have been surprised when Trent swooped in like an eagle that night and asked Emily out on a date.

Six months older than Will, Trent was bigger, better looking and more experienced with women. It was no wonder Emily had been swept off her feet.

Still, after he'd broken up with Sasha, he'd held out hope that their relationship would fizzle and die. Up until that point, Trent hadn't been interested in a steady girlfriend. Like a cruel twist of fate, Em was the one to finally make him toe the line.

It had been excruciating watching them. Going on holidays together. Buying a house. Getting that damned dog, which he assumed Trent must still have, as Em had not mentioned it.

Every milestone was like one more nail in the coffin that he'd built for his love.

They had all been friends for so long now. Too long to just declare himself.

He stood to lose two friendships, not just one. If he was going to make a play for Emily after all this time, he was going to have to do it very carefully, diplomatically and slowly.

And he was afraid, *very afraid*, that he had already made a critical mistake.

'Hey, Boy Scout, you're back,' the man at the desk next to his stated quite unnecessarily.

'Wow,' Will grinned. 'Can't get anything past you.'

The man everyone called Nova spun around in his chair, loose limbed and lanky, a grey-blond fringe brushing his eyebrows. He was fifty at least, but acted much younger. 'How was the big smoke?'

'Eventful.' He chucked his backpack under his desk and turned his computer on. The whir of the clunky motor gave no ease to his rattled brain. He shouldn't have made promises to Emily, promises he didn't know he could keep. His mind immediately pictured her waiting by the phone in anticipation for his call, though not for the reasons he often daydreamed about. The thought of disappointing her made his gut clench. She never directly asked anyone for help, but he knew this time she was really counting on him.

Emily needed a fresh start, a new lease on life. And to get it for her he was going to have to make a deal with the devil.

His fingers went into his hair, curled into fists and pulled at the roots. Will was good at a lot of things. Maths. Science. Finding cost-effective workable solutions to difficult problems. But confrontation was not his strong suit.

Everyone had a nickname on this site. He was called Boy Scout because he was always trying to please. Besides that, he was also considered the new kid on the block, the inexperienced engineer who had a lot to learn. Nova's real name was Joshua but Will had never heard him called that. Nova was his name, short for Casanova, because he was such a gun with the local ladies. Not that there were many. This project was situated on a deserted beach right on the edge of nowhere. To Will it signified beauty and hardship, pain and paradise. The wharf in all its magnificence could not compete with the splendour nature wrought on this coast. The Great Barrier Reef was just one natural wonder on their doorstep.

Another natural wonder in the area was their project manager. The man definitely incited awe if not admiration. He was the one person on site who didn't know his own nickname. Or at least no one thought he did, for his employees never said it to his face. They were all pretty much too intimidated to do or say anything much to their boss's face. Those heavy-lidded eyes of his were always so utterly *bored.*

But appearances were deceiving.

Mark Crawford might look like he was half asleep but he had the personality of a Venus flytrap. If you so much as twitched in the wrong direction, you would shortly find yourself swallowed whole. He enjoyed both the suffering and the torture of his subordinates. And Will had never observed him let the opportunity for either to pass him by. He was ruthless and unforgiving, and treated his men more like slaves than employees.

That was why they called him Caesar.

And now you're going to ask him for a favour. On what planet did you ever think this was going to work?

Will's computer pinged as he opened his inbox. Two hundred and twenty-nine emails had come in since he'd been on R and R. He swore and flicked his mouse.

'Okay, I can't take it any more. Spill it!'

Will jumped and then swivelled in his chair to discover that Nova was still steadily regarding him, his hands clasped lightly between his knees. 'I've been watching you crash, rattle and bang in that little space of yours like a bean in a tin can.'

Despite himself, Will felt his lips curl. 'Really?'

'You know you have. Tell me what the problem is. Is it in my area of expertise?'

Nova was a draftsman, but that wasn't his area of expertise. There were three things that Nova held the floor on:

a. Women
b. Booze
c. Women + booze

He had doled out many gems of knowledge and had pulled many a young welder, turner or fitter out of the doghouse.

'You tell me this is not about a woman and I'll call you a liar.' The draftsman's long nose twitched as though he had sniffed out the clue.

'This is not about a woman.'

'Liar.'

Will laughed. 'Well, I'm not telling you about it.'

'Then she must be special.' Nova smirked. Will pretended that he didn't hear but the draftsman was not fooled. 'A man loves to talk about his conquests except for the one that actually counts,' he said with a smile. 'That's the one they don't want to talk about at all.'

'Well, I've never been with this one, so you're way off.'

Nova studied him shrewdly. 'Aah. Not just *the one*. But *the one that got away*. Let me guess, you've got another chance with her.'

'Well if I do, it's a bloody long shot.' Will's mouth twisted as he allowed his gaze to wander across the room to the commotion in the kitchen. Ann Humming, a woman a few years older than him, was flittering around behind the dirt-marked counter, practically on the verge of hysteria. She was Caesar's secretary. She also appeared to be frantic as she opened cupboards under the bench and overhead, shutting them with a bang when she didn't find what she was looking for. She pulled open the fridge, gave the contents a frustrated onceover then slammed it shut again. Hand pressed to her heart, she spun around muttering, 'God help me. God help me. God help me. We're out of milk.'

'Uh-oh,' Nova said as he too followed Will's gaze.

Caesar always started the day with a cup of coffee. Specifically, one sugar, two heaped spoons of Robert Timms, hot water just boiled and a dash of milk that set the overall temperature of his beverage at a warm 80 degrees Celsius, which was, relatively speaking, 176 degrees Fahrenheit, 353.15 Kelvin and 0.8 atmosphere of pressure at sea level.

Nothing else was acceptable.

Caesar had the only office on the floorplan with a door. His morning beverage was delivered to this private abode when he arrived and was followed by one hour of silence.

No one, absolutely *no one*, was allowed to interrupt this sixty minutes of solitude. Nothing short of life or death, maybe not even that, would grant you entrance to his throne room during this time.

Gossip in the yard said that Caesar used this hour to dream up horrendous, unspeakable punishments for those who had crossed him. Will, who in general didn't have time for construction site myths and legends, was sure that Mark Crawford used it to field emails. As he had discovered himself only seconds earlier, the morning was rife with them. People always put off crisis to the morning and pushed bad news out the door in the evening.

Nova had once told Will that in all his thirty years of experience he had never worked on a job that was not losing money or time somewhere. He called it 'leaky tap' syndrome. It wasn't a matter of whether you had a leak, but where it was dripping.

Will glanced at the clock on the wall. Six fifty-eight am. 'He's going to be here any minute,' he said, watching Ann scurry about with her mouth open and her eyes wide, like a frog catching flies.

'Looks like,' Nova muttered.

Just then, the office donga door flung open and Caesar infused the room like a cloud of genie smoke. Tall, muscular, with a head of coarse black hair, he was an intimidating sight. Everyone stopped what he or she was doing to watch. Ann's hand shot out to grab the kitchen bench, clearly bracing herself against the onslaught that was about to ensue.

'Mr Crawford,' she moaned like one in pain. 'You're here.'

Caesar's eyes darkened. 'You know how much I hate it when you state the obvious, Ann.'

'Sorry, sir. Wasn't thinking.'

'Yes,' Caesar murmured baldly. 'You tend to do that more often than I like.'

Ann cleared her throat. 'The thing is, s-sir . . .'

'Yes, yes, spit it out.'

'It's your coffee.'

'What about it?'

'It's black.' She wrung her hands. 'You see, we ran out of milk. George forgot to put our order in and I didn't check the fridges last night,' she finished, breathless.

'Given it's George's job to make sure the kitchens and stationery supplies are fully stocked I'm not surprised you didn't check the fridges last night. Rest easy, Ann, this is not your fault.'

Ann breathed a sigh of relief. 'Thank you, sir. I'll have your correspondence waiting for you on your desk.'

'Excellent. And can you run out and buy some milk for the fridges?'

'Of course, sir. Shouldn't be a problem at all.'

'I'll have my coffee a little later this morning.'

'Can do, sir.'

'And, er . . . just one more thing, Ann.' He flicked a speck of fluff off the arm of his shirt. 'Fire George, will you?'

There was a full five-second silence before Ann finally gulped, 'I . . . I beg your pardon?'

He glanced at his watch and sighed. 'I just don't have time to do it myself, now that I'm running behind.' He tapped the face of his timepiece.

'Fire him?'

'Are you having trouble with your hearing, Ann?'

'No, sir,' she choked. 'It's just that it wasn't my intention to get George into trouble.'

'Yes, well, you weren't thinking. I do recall you mentioning that. There's no need to go over it again.'

Ann's hands were fluttering more rapidly now, the desperation evident in her face. 'What I should say is that I never meant to have him fired.'

'Really?' Caesar seemed mildly amused. 'Then you had best apologise to him after you fire him.'

Before she could reply, Mark Crawford moved past her and headed straight for his office. A second later the door was shut behind him with a snap.

Ann's hand flew to her mouth, her eyes boggling from their sockets. As she leaned back against the bench, Will knew the waterworks were not far off.

Oh shit.

Nova groaned beside him. 'It's such a pity there aren't more women in this office. They'd all be clucking around her like birds by now. Do you want to take this one or should I?'

'I'll do it. I think it's my turn.'

He nodded at a couple of other men who were looking askance at him and Nova. They inclined their heads with relief. After Caesar, the number-two item on every man's avoidance list was a woman about to cry.

Sticking his hands into the pockets of his blue Hard Yakka pants, Will got up from his seat and walked the few metres to the kitchen.

'Hey, Ann.'

'*Oh, Will*,' she wailed, her eyes dangerously shiny. 'I can't do anything right.'

'That's not true.'

'I'm useless at this job.'

'You're not useless. We all know what Caesar is like.'

She wasn't listening to him. 'I just got George fired but I should be the one on the chopping block.'

'George is not exactly a saint.' Will tried to console her. 'This isn't the first run of supplies he's missed so I wouldn't get too cut up about it.'

'Yes, but I can't fire him,' Ann moaned. 'I just *can't*.'

'It won't be too bad.'

'You really think so?'

'Well . . . yes,' he responded, encouraged by her brightening face – clearly it was the right thing to say. 'It'll be over with in a flash.'

'Then you should do it.'

'*What?* Me?' He cursed his loose lips. 'I'm a graduate.'

'Well, I'm just a secretary.' She put her hands on her hips, suddenly growing a spine at exactly the wrong moment. 'You've got seniority over me. It'll be nicer for him coming from you.'

'I don't think so.' It wouldn't be nice coming from anyone.

'Please, Will.' She clasped her hands under her chin. 'I'll owe you favour. Name it, anything!'

He was about to deny her, when he realised that he actually did need a favour. A rather big one actually. Emily's face immediately flashed into his head, distraught and hopeful. Why is it that he always ended up here? At the raw end of the stick with nowhere to hide.

He cleared his throat. 'I need a private moment with Caesar.' Even hearing himself say the words sounded scary.

Her eyes flared. 'Really?'

'Yes. Can you get me a moment alone with him this morning?'

'That's seriously what you want?'

He nodded.

'All right.' She tapped her chin. 'A parcel arrived today. I'll let you take it in to him when the hour of silence is up.' She pointed her finger at him. 'But you have to fire George.'

He sighed. 'Okay, it's a deal.'

He was about to turn and go when she stalled him. 'There's just one thing I think I should mention.' The tone of her voice worried him and he turned back slowly.

'What's that?'

'The parcel is from his wife.'

He blinked. 'And that's a problem because?'

Her voice lowered to the barest of whispers. 'Last week, I saw his wife's birthday marked in his diary and reminded him to give her a call. He told me not to meddle in his personal life and threw me out of his office – gave me the silent treatment for days. I was sure I was done for.'

He groaned. 'So they're not on good terms.'

'I don't know.' Her mouth twisted. 'But if I were you, I would ask whatever it is you want to ask him *before* you hand over the parcel.'

'Gotcha.'

She beamed at him. 'Will, I swear, you're the sweetest, kindest guy I've ever met. I don't know why you haven't got a girlfriend.'

She patted him on the shoulder as she chuffed off back to her desk. Why did women always think they were being complimentary by mentioning his 'surprising' lack of a partner? He found the observation more annoying than flattering. With heavy feet he returned to his desk, wondering how on earth he was going to fire George.

'You know, you've got to stop playing the knight in shining armour,' Nova observed dispassionately as he sat down. 'It's going to get you in trouble.'

You don't say.

'A simple "there, there" would have sufficed. That's what I was gunna go with.'

Will shrugged, a grin tickling his mouth. 'I wanted to mix it up a little, do something different.'

'Well, you certainly did that. What do you want with Caesar anyway?'

Will turned back to his computer, a move to hide his face. 'None of your business. Have you finished those temporary platforms yet? I've got scaffolders asking when they can have the drawings.'

He heard Nova grunt. 'You've been back ten minutes and you're already cracking the whip. I hope Caesar fries your balls.'

Will rolled his eyes. 'I'm sure he will.' He stood up. 'Well, if the drawings aren't ready I might as well go speak to George.'

'You make it sound so easy.'

Will didn't deign to reply, knowing talking about it would only serve to make him lose his nerve. He walked across the room and exited the main donga. George's workspace was actually in another of the temporary buildings. He was a peggy, so he didn't have a computer. His role was to run errands, collect supplies and clean where necessary. Will was unsurprised that he'd forgotten to buy the milk. Diligence wasn't exactly George's middle name. He tended to leave things to the last minute and, as he'd pointed out to Ann, had already been caught behind on more than one occasion.

Despite this, Will had no desire to fire him. First, he'd never fired anyone in his life, least of all a man ten years his senior. And secondly . . . well, George was a big guy. Who knew when that temper was finally going to get the better of him?

Unfortunately George wasn't in the other donga: he was standing outside it having a smoke and chatting with two others. One was a man they called Fish and the other a heavily set gentleman called Dipper. They both stood beside him, not smoking but definitely chewing the fat.

'Bream, whiting, flathead, mackerel and tuna. But no jewfish yet,' Fish was saying. 'I just don't understand it. What am I doing wrong?'

'You need to go further north to Mackay,' Dipper was saying. 'Near the marina. We'll go there next Sunday off – you and I?'

'Or we could go tonight?' George suggested.

'I don't like hunting at night.' Dipper shook his head.

Fish snorted scornfully. 'You're soft, that's what you are. Soft.' As he was finishing his sentence, he looked up to see Will approaching. Fish's eyes brightened, as though delighted by the distraction. Will groaned inwardly. He knew his eagerness was a bit of a running joke between the older guys. He was going to get a ribbing before they let him state his point.

'Well, if it isn't the little graduate come to say hi. Hello, Boy Scout! How you going?' Fish grinned. He wasn't exactly easy on the eye – greasy, knotty hair tied back in an untidy ponytail framed a hard face. While he was wearing the Barnes Inc uniform, he still managed to look like a homeless person. His shirt certainly hadn't seen a wash, let alone an iron, in a few days. His eyes, however, sparkled with all the alertness of one who knew the cut and thrust of construction like the back of his hand. Will hated to admit it, but he admired him despite his poor attention to hygiene and, indeed, social etiquette in general.

'Boy Scout.' Dipper inclined his head.

'You still got your city shine on you, young William? Haven't been out on the wharf enough yet,' George commented.

There was no way firing George was going to go down well. Better to do it in private. 'Could I speak to you, George? Alone.'

'Ho, ho, ho,' George rocked on his feet, 'hear that boys? I'm being singled out for a little one-on-one. Must be serious.'

'Er, yeah it is.'

'I'm listening.' The ignorant fool put out his cigarette by dropping it and stepping on it. 'Tell me now.'

Will bit his lip. 'Probably better in private.'

'This is private enough.'

'Are you sure because –'

George rolled his eyes. 'Yes, damn it.'

'Caesar is . . . letting you go.'

George's jaw dropped. 'What the fuck?'

'He's firing you. I'm, er, firing you for him. He asked Ann to do it but she was . . . she was busy.'

'Ann! Now that's just insulting. Why am I being fired?'

Will cleared his throat, shuffling from one foot to the other. 'He, er . . .' He lifted his head. 'He had a black coffee this morning.'

The men all stood there in stunned silence for a moment before Fish suddenly let off a bark of laughter and slapped George on the back.

'Well, fuck me. I think Boy Scout just slipped you a little arsenic, Georgie boy.'

George rolled his shoulder, angrily dislodging the hand. At this point, Will thought it best to get the rest out before George completely lost it. 'You've probably got the usual two weeks' notice. I guess if you ask the HR manager they will tell you for sure. I'm really sorry to ruin your day.'

'Ruin my day?!' The words burst from George's mouth like red paint splattering against a white fence. 'You good for nothing, two-faced little bastard! You tell Caesar –'

'Actually I think I'd rather you tell him,' Will shot back.

'That's it, Boy Scout,' this time Fish clapped him on the back, 'stick up for yourself. Not your fault. We all know what the devil's like. Truth is, a man needs to get fired from time to time. Keeps him honest.'

Will liked being manhandled by Fish even less than George did and discreetly stepped forwards out of arm's reach.

'Yes, well, we all know your reputation, Fish,' George spat. 'But I've never been fired in my life.'

'Barnes Inc hired me back on a different job.' Fish shrugged. 'Maybe they'll do the same for you.'

'Fuck that!' George grunted and stormed off.

Will breathed a sigh of relief. It was done. Now all he had to do was give Caesar his mail. He winced. What a morning!

He went back to his own desk, ignored as best he could Nova's demand for details and saw that Ann had left the parcel on his desk. It was a rectangular object in a brown tough bag that had been delivered via courier. The label on the back clearly stated that the parcel was from a woman.

Kathryn Mary Crawford of 13 Highgate Road, Subiaco.

'What was she thinking, eh?' Nova grinned before turning back to the drawing displayed on the two computer screens in front of him. 'Marrying that son of a bitch.'

Unfortunately, Will still had to wait another forty minutes before Caesar's hour of silence was up. The time was just enough for his nerves to wind as tight as a compressed spring.

Finally, the clock struck eight. He looked across the room and Ann nodded at him from her vantage point. It was now or never. He headed over to the lair of the tiger and knocked on the door twice. At first there was no answer, so he braced himself and tentatively knocked again.

'Come in,' a murky tone instructed him.

He opened the door and was immediately standing before a large white desk that was neither regal nor expensive yet made him feel like a minion come to beg for bread. Caesar's eyes flicked upwards from the paper he was signing, though he didn't lift his chin.

'Aah, if it isn't young William. To what do I owe the pleasure?'

'I, er . . .' He squared his shoulders and changed tack. 'Good morning, sir.'

'Not really but I'm sure you didn't come here to discuss that.'

'No, I . . .' He lifted the parcel in his hand, all at once grateful for its existence. 'I brought your mail.'

'I see. Who is it from?'

'I'm not sure,' he lied and held onto it, remembering Ann's warning. 'But there was something else I wanted to ask you too.'

Caesar stopped writing and looked up in silence, neither asking Will to continue nor saying that he couldn't. Will tried not to find this expectant stare unnerving.

'You see, I overheard before I went away that you were trying to get head office to send another graduate over here to help me out. And then I noticed that no one has turned up.'

'Yes, well, I believe the girl they had in mind didn't want to leave the Pilbara.'

'Lena Todd?' Will started.

'I didn't think it important to remember her name.'

'We're good friends. Went to uni together.' Will nodded.

'As happy as I am for you,' Caesar drawled, 'how does this concern me?'

'We . . . I have another good friend, also female –'

'No doubt.'

'– who would love to come here and work. We were in the same year at university too. She's currently working for a company in Perth but is not overly fussed with the work they are giving her and I thought –'

'William, William, William.' Caesar held up his hand. 'I see what you're doing, I really do. The problem with you is that you think I care.' He rubbed his chin with thumb and forefinger. 'Now as much as I hate to be the one to shatter your illusions, I don't. Now can I have my mail, please?' Caesar held out his hands.

'But –'

'Boy Scout, my parcel.'

Helplessly, Will placed the package in his hand and made haste to plead his case while he still had half a chance.

'It's just that it's so clear to me that we need more hands on deck and she would be perfect. She's very enthusiastic, very hard working and extremely eager to learn.'

But it was too late, for Caesar had turned over the tough bag and spied the name on the back. A muscle clenched in his cheek and there was a chilly silence. Will folded his arms tightly and looked up to see if icicles were forming on the ceiling.

'William.' Mark Crawford finally dropped the parcel on the desk, reverting sinisterly to his real name, his lips set into a hard line. 'I will not be mobilising your girlfriend to site. Another crane maybe or a couple more utes, even a pallet of bolts might come in handy. But not your girlfriend.'

'She's not my girlfriend.'

However, this statement didn't seem relevant to Caesar, who spread his hands and gazed heavenwards as though he were complaining to a higher power. 'Why is it that everyone thinks it's my job to improve their social life? This is not a holiday. This is not a picnic. I know the Whitsunday Islands are right next door but we're here to work.' His gaze returned to Will's. 'The whole point of working fly in, fly out, my friend, is that when you fly out you have someone to fly out to. Console yourself with that fact. Others are not so fortunate. Now, if you'll excuse me.' He closed a large foolscap file of correspondence and stood up.

'But –'

'We're done, William.' Picking up the parcel, he shoved it in a filing cabinet behind him and then locked the drawer. He reached for his vest on the wall hook. 'I'm going out.'

Will watched in resignation as his boss headed for the door. As luck would have it, however, as Caesar opened it, there was someone standing on the other side, barring his path.

Charlotte Templeton, Will noted, as he always noted whenever he saw her, was a very good-looking woman. Definitely the prettiest landlady he'd ever had. A little too old for him perhaps and when set alongside Emily she faded from memory. But he was sure other men would not have the same experience.

She was at least ten years his senior, with porcelain skin and wavy auburn hair – a classic Nicole Kidman lookalike. She stood there, hands on hips, foot tapping.

'So you *are* here!'

Caesar frowned warily, his hand still on the doorknob. 'What do you want?'

'Perhaps, Mr Crawford, if you had bothered to answer a single one of my emails or phone messages you would know that by now.'

As she took a few steps forwards, Caesar took a few steps back, as though her proximity was too close for his liking. Will watched with interest slightly mixed with satisfaction the way she shut the door and advanced on Mark like a spider picking its way across its web.

Unafraid.

Irritated.

And totally in command of the room.

Given the man she was addressing was Caesar, this was completely unexpected and definitely worth watching. She seemed to feel his eyes on her and momentarily looked up.

'Oh, hi, Will.'

'Er, hi, Charlotte.'

'This won't take a moment,' she assured him. 'So sorry to interrupt your meeting.'

'That's okay. We were done anyway.'

Caesar noisily cleared his throat. 'Ms *Templeton* –'

'Mr *Crawford*,' she responded just as imperiously, 'I have a number of items, a whole list in fact, which I need to discuss with you regarding the use of my resort, the primary place of accommodation for your men.'

'I can't discuss your list right now,' Mark returned tightly. 'I'm busy.'

'All right, can I come and see you tomorrow?'

'No.'

'How about after work?'

'No.'

'I could drop by your unit; it's not far from my reception office.'

'Definitely not.'

Charlotte's lips pulled into a thin line and her delicate hands were back on her hips. 'Then how am I supposed to address the issues I must raise with you?'

Mark's closed expression did not change as he shrugged into his safety vest. 'That's the thing. You're not.'

'But –'

'Ms *Templeton* –'

'Call me Charlotte.'

He seemed to baulk at her suggestion. 'Ms *Templeton*, if you are looking to raise your rates, you're barking up the wrong tree. I can't offer you anything more.'

'Now just hang on a second there –'

'Are you sure you only want a second?' he drawled dryly, snatching his hat from the corner of his desk and determinedly putting it on. 'In my experience it is always much longer.'

Charlotte looked furious and Will sucked in a deep breath, hoping she wouldn't, praying she wouldn't . . .

She did.

'*Mr Crawford*, I do not want your money. I do not want your disregard. And I most certainly do not want your mockery. What I want is respect! Respect from you and respect from your men for the services provided by Silver Seas resort. On numerous occasions I have asked your men for more care and I am constantly ignored. These units have been in my family for more than forty years and your men have inflicted more wear and tear on them in the eight months they've been here than they've experienced in their whole existence. Frankly, it's unacceptable.' She was practically panting by the time she came to the end of her impassioned declaration.

Caesar sighed. 'There, you see? More than one second. It was inevitable.'

Charlotte gasped. 'Do you intend to continue to make fun of me, Mr Crawford?'

'Was that what I was doing, Ms Templeton? I was under the impression I was listening to you with unprecedented patience.'

'Then I suppose it is I who should be sorry for having put you out,' she replied with a sarcasm that was completely lost on her opponent.

'True.' He nodded. 'Apology accepted.'

She opened her mouth to say something else but he waved a hand to stall her next rebuke. 'Oh, very well. I *suppose* I will give your "list of items" a onceover. Have it ready and I'll come pick it up after work on . . .' he seemed to pick a day at random '. . . Friday.'

It was apparent to Will that Charlotte seemed to be having some sort of internal struggle before she said with tight-lipped politeness, 'Thank you. What time should I expect you?'

'I have no idea,' said Caesar as he walked around her, opened his door and let himself out.

She turned on Will, who grimaced apologetically. 'That man,' she announced, 'wasn't beaten enough as a child.'

Will grinned. 'Well, maybe you'll just have to take a stick to him now.'

She gave him an answering smile. 'Maybe I shall.'

Chapter 3

Charlotte

It was Friday morning and Charlotte Templeton was desperately trying to get off the phone.

'So I'm going to the Port Pub in Mackay tonight,' said the male voice on the end of the line. 'You should come.'

'Er . . .' She fingered the cord. 'I have paperwork to do. Lots of paperwork.'

'Oh,' came the hesitant response, 'because I was thinking . . .'

Don't think.

'. . . that you'd love it. It's ladies' night.'

She'd hate it.

Apart from the fact that she just didn't have the time for dating, she wasn't interested in Jared, her plumber, that way. Not that there was anything wrong with him. He was certainly nice enough. *As a plumber*. 'Er, thanks for the offer but I think I'll have to pass.'

'You work too hard.'

He said the words like he knew her. The truth was he'd fixed her leaky taps and changed her showerheads twice.

He didn't have a clue what was going on in her head or how much baggage she had. If he knew, he'd be glad he'd got off lightly.

'Well, you know,' she tried to make light of his comment, 'running a business single-handedly is no laughing matter.'

'Yeah, you're one smart lady.'

Charlotte glanced at her watch. She was beginning to feel uncomfortable. Hopefully, he'd say goodbye soon and they could both get on with their lives. She glanced at the computer screen in front of her. She really had to get this invoice done and off within the next half hour. Not to mention the stack of other chores she had lined up for the day, as well as a meeting with the emperor himself at TBA o'clock that evening.

'Would you like me to come and service your hot-water system some time?' His languid tone broke her thoughts. 'It was looking pretty run down when I was there yesterday.'

Were they back to business again or was that a trick question?

Regardless, her hot-water system did need a service. Ever since Silver Seas had entered 'the slump' she had been letting things like that slide. 'Yeah okay,' she finally agreed. 'I'll give you a call about it later. But I really must go now.'

Thankfully he didn't protest and they rang off. Charlotte put the receiver back on the phone and sighed. It wasn't that she was against relationships exactly. It was just that she had two already that were taking up most of her time. A fifteen-year-old sister, whom she was practically raising, and a mum who needed almost twenty-four-hour care. Where was she supposed to put a boyfriend in that mix?

Besides the fact that Jared's double-pierced ears, neck tattoo and bleached hair with red roots didn't even slightly get her ticker counting faster. In fact he probably made her double her resolve to save herself the pain. She didn't have anything against the 'bad boy'. He just lacked that charismatic, irresistible something that . . .

Her thoughts dissolved as the lithe, masculine figure of Barnes Inc's notorious project manager sauntered past the reception window. He neither glanced in, nor paused, in that arrogant, dogmatic way that was only his. Even so, she couldn't help but crane her neck a little so that she could watch him manoeuvre that perfect arse of his into the driver's seat of a white ute.

Now that's what I'm talkin' 'bout. If only he didn't have the personality of a cactus.

'He's a bit of all right,' a voice cackled at her elbow. 'Don't suppose he's looking for a fling while he's in town.'

Charlotte jumped, nearly sliding off the counter she'd been leaning on so heavily and landing on the floor. She didn't like the direction her mother's thoughts were taking. 'Mum, you gave me a fright!'

The older woman who had suddenly materialised by her elbow ignored this remark. She patted her wiry, grey-streaked hair, watching the ute disappear in a cloud of dust. 'I'm calling dibs.'

'You're *what*?'

'He's mine. Hands off.'

'I wasn't –'

'Yeah right,' she scoffed, adding smugly, 'Gentlemen prefer blondes. And stop calling me Mum. I'm too young to be your mother.' And she removed a pocket mirror from her purse to examine her make-up, which had been applied with all the coordination of a five-year-old. Yes. Definitely having an episode.

Charlotte kept her voice light. 'It's not even seven yet. You should still be in bed.'

Her mother, otherwise known as Virginia Templeton, shook her head. 'I have business in town, Sarah.'

Sarah was the receptionist her mother had let go about eighteen years ago just after Charlotte's father had died. Sarah had been caught renting rooms to her friends for free. But that wasn't the most telling hint that the sixty-year-old was suffering from Alzheimer's disease. Despite the fact that she was carrying an old-fashioned handbag and had pulled most of her hair back into an off-centre bun, she was still dressed in her long pale-pink nightie, the kind that buttoned up at the front.

'Come on, Mum, let's get you some breakfast.' Charlotte came out from behind the counter and took her by the elbow. 'You haven't eaten yet, have you?'

Virginia pulled her arm away but looked slightly confused. 'Actually . . . er . . . I don't think I have.'

'Thought so.' Charlotte put up a plastic sign on the counter top, *Ring bell for service*. Spinning her mother in a complete circle, she walked her back through the door she'd come in by. It was also the entrance to their home.

They entered a cosy-looking living room. The decor was simple, consisting of a pine bookshelf, an inexpensive TV cabinet, a matching coffee table and a pair of gum-green couches. The curtains were floral and the carpet cream. All in all, the layout had not really changed since she'd first left home to study psychology in Brisbane nineteen years back. They passed through this area, straight to the kitchen and dining where Charlotte's younger sister, Zara, sat eating some toast.

The fifteen-year-old grinned. 'Hey, Mum, off to town again?'

Charlotte tried sending her a meaningful look as she gently removed her mother's handbag from her wrist, but Zara didn't seem to receive the message. Charlotte took her eyes from her sister and guided her mother to a chair. 'What would you like, Mum? Toast or cereal?'

Virginia Templeton glanced from daughter to daughter. She had a blank look in her eyes as though she were coming out of a dream and was trying to find her bearings.

'Tell you what,' Charlotte patted her shoulder, 'I'll get your favourite. Coco Pops.'

Zara immediately frowned. 'That's so unfair.'

Frankly, Charlotte was in no mood to get into an argument. She felt like all she ever did these days was give people boundaries. If it wasn't her family, it was the resort patrons or, more precisely, the workers from the Hay Point Wharf project, situated two minutes up the road.

But for the giant expansion project going on there, Silver Seas would never have had the opportunity to fill all but one of its luxury beachside chalets. In fact, prior to the approach from Barnes Inc, she'd had the resort on the market because they'd been facing bankruptcy. Her contract with the major construction company had saved her parents' business. However, now she didn't know whether their arrival had been manna from heaven or the onset of the plague.

The problem was FIFO workers weren't exactly domestic goddesses. In fact, they weren't domestic anything. They treated her chalets like, well, like dongas. Coal-encrusted footwear was trampled straight into the two-bedroom units, through the white-tiled foyers and down the short, cream-carpeted halls to the bedrooms. Luckily the shoes seemed to come off then. But Charlotte couldn't help but notice that her floors were getting more and more stained. If they kept this up much longer, she would need to replace all the carpets by the time the project was over.

And that wasn't the only bone she had to pick.

There was this one guy the men called 'Fish', and with good reason. His name was his hobby, his diet and his personal life philosophy. Charlotte had nothing against passion. What she did have a problem with were the fish guts he left in the sink every morning after his evenings on the shoreline. Part of the service of Silver Seas resort was housekeeping. She didn't mind cleaning as such. It was something she was prepared to do to keep her parents' legacy alive. But within reason, please! To be greeted every morning by the stench of this man's rotting catches as soon as she threw open his chalet door, and then be expected to clean it up as well, was definitely more than she'd signed up for.

And then there was the level of drinking going on after five. Was it normal for a man to consume half a carton or more every night? Surely there must be some alcoholics among them by now. There had been no damage to property as yet, but Charlotte couldn't see how this good luck could continue. Every night she found the evidence of their consumption littered around her pool chairs and on the outdoor tables. At first she thought she might just put a bin out there. But the large plastic blue hint, even adorned with a sign saying *Place rubbish here*, seemed to have no impact whatsoever upon the revellers who used the space for their booze-ups. Besides the mess, she had a teenage sister to consider. She didn't want Zara getting any ideas. The girl was rebellious enough as it was.

She walked into the kitchen and silently made her mother's breakfast, wondering why the men didn't want to go down and explore the beach like normal tourists. Salonika at twilight was gorgeous. Pristine blue waters, golden sand and usually not a soul in sight. Their little piece of paradise was definitely one of Queensland's best-kept secrets. She instantly got a mental of image of beer cans and bottles making a trail from the surrounding bushland to the water's edge. She shuddered. Maybe it was better that the Barnes Inc workforce stayed as far away from it as possible.

The last thing she could afford to do was offend the project manager. But she was running out of patience. If Mark Crawford would not answer emails, phone messages or even personal confrontational visits, it really was time to bring out the big guns. And in her case that was vanilla and raspberry cupcakes.

She turned around briefly and glanced into the oven to see if they were ready. Not quite yet, but she had time. The aim of the game was to make sure that when Mr Crawford came to visit her that afternoon he stayed for a long and detailed chat about how things could improve. It was important that they moved forward on this matter in a way that was beneficial to them both.

Or what? I'll kick them out? Yeah right.

Without them it would be back to running from the bank. And she already knew how much fun that was. On a sigh, she took the bowl of Coco Pops to her mother and set it in front of her.

Her sister's voice was just as glum as her thoughts. 'I never get to do anything good around here.'

It was clear they'd moved up the complaint ladder from 'breakfast-food choices' to 'everything in general'.

She was tired. 'Zara, please.'

'Well, it's true. Everybody is going to Rosemary's fifteenth birthday next weekend except me.'

'I'm sure not everyone is going.'

'How would *you* know?'

'Call it a hunch. A responsible parent would not let their fifteen-year-old teenager go to an unsupervised beach party at night.'

'Well, you're not my parent, are you?' she pointed out. 'So take a load off.'

Charlotte sighed. 'Zara, you know Mum wouldn't want you to go.'

'Mum doesn't know *what* she wants.' Zara looked at the woman seated listlessly across from her, apparently staring into space. Virginia made no response. 'Mum, can you hear me?' Zara leaned forwards.

Virginia seemed to surface from a very deep pool. Her eyes held nothing of the sparkle that had characterised them only a few minutes earlier. This was sometimes the only indication that she was not having an episode. Her moments of clarity, when she was truly in the present, were getting so rare these days that Charlotte treasured them like polished pink sea shells.

'Yes, dear?' Virginia said slowly.

'Can I go to Rosemary's beach party?'

Virginia licked dry lips. 'I think . . . I think you should ask your sister.' Her voice was breathless, as if she'd been running a marathon or something.

Zara groaned in frustration. 'The Party Police? Great.'

Charlotte clenched her fists behind the counter, wondering how she could explain to a teenager in five words or fewer the potential risks of such a party. In the end, she settled on, 'In this case, I think I know best.'

Oh that's original.

But the cheeky teen wasn't going to let her off easy. 'Give me one good reason why I can't go.'

She wasn't buying into a full-blown argument now. 'You need to get ready for school; you're going to be late. We don't have time to argue about this at the moment.'

'You're not even going to give me a say, are you?' Zara demanded.

'Zara,' Charlotte began, 'it's just –'

'I hate you!' Zara threw at her, pushed her bowl away and walked out of the room.

That went well.

'Don't worry, Lottie.' She felt her mother pat her hand. 'She'll come round.'

'Why do you always make me be the bad guy?' she asked.

Her mother smiled. 'Because you're so good at it.'

She watched as her mother slowly spooned a mouthful of Coco Pops between her lips and felt tears prick her eyes. She knew Virginia was in the present because she was quiet and withdrawn – a stark contrast to her younger self. There were days when her mother thought Charlotte was Zara, others when she thought she was their old receptionist, and days when she didn't recognise her at all. Although Silver Seas was no longer very profitable, it was the safest, most familiar place for her mother to be right now. Virginia and her late husband, Charlotte's father, had bought it just after they had got married. When he had passed, about twenty years ago, it had kept her mother's spirit alive. Now it was Charlotte's duty to keep this place going.

Lowering herself into the chair Zara had just vacated she said, 'I feel like I'm fighting a losing battle here.'

'You were exactly like her at that age, Lottie, and look how great you turned out.'

The corners of her mouth lifted slightly. 'And what about Luke? What was he like?'

'Oh,' her mother's voice seemed wistful, 'you know your brother – he was just like your father and still is. The strong, silent type.'

Charlotte smiled. As far as she was concerned, her younger brother was the one person in the world she could count on completely. Luke lived in Mackay with his wife and kids and came to visit usually once a week for a catch-up. She always looked forward to seeing him. But socialising was the last thing on her mind right then.

She had a zillion things to do. Even with all their units occupied, the business was still struggling. She was using every cent she earned to pay off the debt her mother had amassed. Just yesterday she'd had to let another one of the staff go. Apart from cleaning up the pool area, she had to go pick up some supplies for the restaurant, there was an electrician coming in to fix the air-conditioner at number eight and the website was down again. She was going to have to call the service provider. And this all before ten o'clock. But first and foremost, she had to take those cupcakes out of the oven. They had to be perfect for this afternoon, if they were going to do her any favours.

Mark Crawford darkened her doorway at about twenty past six that evening, though she had been ready since five. Behind the counter she had arranged two chairs facing each other. On the desk, she had set out teacups and a plate of iced vanilla and raspberry cupcakes. In a prominent position in front of the plate were her list and a red pen. She intended to tick off items as they went.

She should have realised that any such intentions were futile when he walked into reception looking like he was about to clear the area for demolition.

'If you'll just hand me the list, Ms Templeton, I'll be on my way.'

He'd obviously come straight from work, as he was still dressed in the Barnes site uniform. One glance at his tall and intimidating frame made Charlotte straighten her own to get some more height. It didn't quite work but it did give her a little more confidence. Especially against those turbulent eyes, a strange wintry grey that sliced through her like cyclone rain.

'Good evening, Mr Crawford. Glad you could come. I hope you had a nice day.'

He frowned. 'It was terrible and it doesn't appear to be getting any better.'

'Right, well, I'm sure you'd like to sit down.'

'No, I came to get the list.'

She straightened her shoulders. 'Right, the list. Actually I was hoping we could talk through it. Can I get you a cup of tea?' She rose out of her seat and half turned towards the kettle plugged in against the back wall.

'No.'

She frowned as she moved the teacups next to the kettle.

Someone needs to teach this guy some manners.

'Well I'm having one.'

She pressed the red button on the kettle to boil. As it bubbled away she pulled out the visitor's chair next to her own behind the counter and politely indicated for him to sit.

His mouth twisted in annoyance. For a moment she thought he was going to refuse again. The man was as prickly as a rose bush. Even if she did find him *mildly* attractive, she was in absolutely no danger of being seduced. After another second of hesitation, he walked around the counter and sat down. She was careful to hide her triumph as he folded his lithe frame into the chair. Not so careful, however, in preventing her gaze from drawing briefly to the way his pants pulled tight around his buttocks and thighs.

Now? Really? She ripped her gaze away, mentally slapping herself.

To her relief the kettle boiled at that moment so she filled the teapot. Cheekily, she poured them each a cup as soon as the aroma of the brew rose. 'Why don't you have one of my delicious cupcakes?' she suggested. 'It'll make the time go quicker.'

As she looked up, she noticed an expression on his face that she had never seen before. It looked like pain. Her professional curiosity was tickled.

'Did I say something wrong?'

He wiped his face, as you would clean a doodle board. 'No.'

The tightness of his response belied the truth. She had learned through experience and study at university that aggressive behaviour was always triggered by something. Abuse in childhood, trauma in adult life, loss, guilt, suffering. But it wasn't her place to ask. Besides, she had no time right now to take on his problems as well as her own.

She put the kettle down and took her seat. Picking up her pen she started at the top of her list. 'Now the first point I wanted to make, definitely the most important, is the booze-ups by the pool –'

'Ms Templeton.' He seemed to be back in full possession of his faculties. 'I do not intend to stay long, so there's no point in –'

She put a cupcake on a plate and pushed it towards him.

He pushed it back towards her.

'You aren't even going to try one?' she asked sweetly, pushing it back towards him.

'No.' He slid the plate back towards her.

'Why not?' she demanded crossly and pushed the plate a little too forcefully back towards him. The cupcake, now charged with momentum, slid off the plate and straight into his lap, icing face down.

'Oh no.' She cringed. 'I'm so sorry.'

He gingerly removed the cupcake from his thigh but it left all its icing behind.

She grabbed a serviette off the counter and quickly reached down to scoop it all off when his hand closed on her wrist like a vice.

'Ms Templeton, I am quite capable of cleaning myself up, thank you very much.'

She looked down at their joined hands and her eyes widened in alarm. *Idiot! I've practically got my hand in his groin.*

Just at that precise moment the door chime rang and in walked her plumber, brandishing a bouquet of pink gerberas. *When it rains, it pours.*

He took in the scene with all the hurt and devastation of a jilted lover. 'So that's why you didn't want to see me tonight.'

Charlotte immediately snatched her hand away, feeling her face colour to match the bunch of flowers. 'Jared, what are you doing here?'

'I came to have a look at your hot-water system.'

'But I wasn't expecting you today.'

He sighed sheepishly. 'I was going to do it for free.'

She glanced at the flowers and he sighed once more as he followed her gaze. 'Guess I shouldn't have bothered with these either.'

'Jared, it's not that I –'

She looked down in annoyance at Mark, who had started drumming his fingers loudly on the counter. 'Do you mind?' she indicated his hand. 'I'm trying to have a conversation here.'

Her words also drew Jared's attention to Mark's drumming hand and the light winked off a thick gold band around Caesar's fourth finger.

Jared's gaze swung to hers crossly. 'Why didn't you tell me you were married?'

Charlotte quickly shook her head and waved both palms in a horizontal slicing motion. 'We're not married.'

'You're having an affair?'

'No, no, no.' Charlotte took a step forwards. 'You don't understand.'

'No, it's all right.' Jared's face was flooding with colour. 'I really don't need to hear your explanation.'

'I wasn't going to give you an explanation.' Charlotte put her hands on her hips. 'There isn't one to make.'

'I think I'll be going now.' Jared jerked his thumb over his shoulder before backing out the door, taking his flowers with him.

As the door swung shut a dry voice beside her said, 'Well, that's five minutes of my life I'll never get back.'

Heat flooded her face, stinging her skin, as she looked down at his derisive expression. In all fairness, she supposed she did owe him an apology. 'I'm sorry about that. I didn't realise he was going to stop by. Or that he was going to mistake you for my husband.'

'What a relief. I should be extremely worried if you did.' He stood up and walked around the desk with the clear intention of leaving even though they hadn't discussed anything yet.

Do something. 'Mr Crawford, please don't go. We haven't finished our business meeting.'

He was now looking across the counter at her. 'Ms Templeton, I was just attacked by a cupcake and accused of being your lover. It's hardly a business meeting.'

Now I've botched it. She scurried around the desk after him. 'Mr Crawford, please stay. I'm sorry. I'm very, very sorry about what happened just now. It was an unprofessional imposition, which won't be repeated. Please sit and discuss these changes that –'

'Ms Templeton.'

'Yes?' she faltered.

He held out his hand. 'The list.'

'Oh.' She reached across the counter and snatched it up. 'Here.'

'Thank you.'

It was obvious he was in no mood to go through it now but desperation made her foolish. She held her palms up. 'I know I put you in an awkward position today, but rest assured it won't happen again. You have my word.'

Mark Crawford opened his mouth to respond when all of a sudden his body lurched forwards.

'What the –?' he rasped, grabbing her upper arms so that just for a millisecond they were nose to nose. He was so close she could see the outline of his irises. Her pulse went through the roof as both horror and arousal pierced her brain. Slowly, they both peered behind him. A hot flush ripped through her body when she saw her mother standing there looking as pleased as punch.

Oh no, did she just pinch his arse?

As if to confirm the awful theory, Mrs Virginia Templeton gave a provocative wink. 'Well, hello there, sweet cheeks. Do you come here often?'

Chapter 4

Mark

Mark dropped Charlotte's arms and turned around to survey the odd creature who had attacked him. He stared in disbelief at the older woman clearly giving him the once over, and tried in vain to formulate a suitable response. He was, however, too stunned to think of anything.

A strangled choke sounded behind him. 'Er, Mr Crawford, this is my mother, Virginia Templeton.'

'Her mother,' Virginia snorted. 'More like her boss. Haven't you got paperwork to do, Sarah?'

Sarah? Who the hell is Sarah?

Virginia turned back to him, face wreathed in a smile. 'I'll attend to the gentleman. He's obviously in need of less clumsy assistance.' She grabbed his hand, pumping it with more gusto than he'd expected judging by her small frame. 'Virginia Templeton, at your service.' She batted her eyes. 'Completely at your service. How may I help you?'

He had to forcibly extract his hand and shake out his fingers to resume blood flow. 'I was just on my way out.'

Virginia was unperturbed, in fact her eyes brightened. 'Really, where to? A bar, a restaurant, a club?' She wiggled her hips. 'You know, I finish in five minutes and I do love a bit of dancing. Do you like to dance, Mr, er . . .?'

He ignored the request for his name. 'No, I don't.'

Virginia pouted. 'Well that's a shame. Not to worry, I'm sure we'll find something to do in town. I assume you're driving?' Her eyebrows waggled as she slipped her arm through his. 'Lead the way, my good man.'

'*Mum!*' Thankfully Charlotte stepped into the fray, trying to pull the grey-haired woman off him. 'Mr Crawford is going home. *Alone.*'

'Not tonight he's not.' Virginia stared lovingly up into his eyes, making him feel like he'd just stepped out of his spaceship and onto the planet Mars.

'You'll have to excuse my mother,' Charlotte said in lowered tones as she managed to disengage Virginia's hand from his arm. 'She has Alzheimer's disease and, well, at the moment she thinks she's about thirty-five years younger.'

Many things at that point began to make sense to Mark:

a. Why Charlotte's mother thought they'd make a good match.
b. Why he never saw Charlotte socialising with his men . . .
c. Why Charlotte seemed so determined to preserve a business that should have seen its demise many, many years ago.

The unfortunate woman was clearly devoting her life to the care of her mentally challenged mother and all her assets – he could imagine she'd try any means necessary to protect this little group of units. They provided a stable if not glossy future. Perhaps that was why she had scorned the attentions of Jared, the plumber. He'd seemed pretty high maintenance and she probably had little time to spare.

He grimaced.

Why he should be sparing even a second thought for this woman's love-life, he had no idea. True, she was very attractive in that girl-next-door kind of way. She had wavy auburn hair and a nose that turned pink whenever she got embarrassed – which unfortunately for her seemed to be every two minutes. He could also see why his men ogled her whenever she walked past. She definitely had a certain something that he couldn't quite put his finger on.

A great rack and legs to die for. He heard Kathryn's musical laugh in his head. *Let's not kid ourselves here.*

An emotion he hadn't felt in a long time scoured at his heart, making him pause for a moment as he tried to figure out what exactly it was.

Aaah, yes, guilt.

It had to be.

He returned his attention impatiently to the conversation unfolding in front of him. Charlotte had her hands resting lightly on slim hips, her chin jutting in annoyance as she tried to persuade her mother to go back to their home. Virginia didn't seem to be keen on taking her advice.

'It's absolutely none of your business where I go after hours.'

'You're not going anywhere. I'm sorry but you're not . . . thinking clearly.'

Virginia's eyes narrowed. 'Sarah, I think it's you who is not thinking clearly. I don't discuss my personal life with my employees.'

A thought seemed suddenly to occur to Charlotte. 'Where's Zara?'

Virginia's face, which only moments before had seemed extremely self-assured, took on a somewhat confused look. 'Who is Zara?'

'Your other daughter. Weren't you two supposed to be doing a puzzle together?'

'But I'm terrible at puzzles.'

'That at least is true.' Charlotte threw Mark a whimsical smile that made his collar suddenly feel a little too tight before she turned back to her mother. 'The doctor said it's good for you to exercise your brain.'

'Doctor?' Virginia's eyes lit up. 'Is he single?'

'So you have a sister too, Ms Templeton?' Mark inquired.

She nodded. 'She's only fifteen, which is why I'm so concerned about the behaviour of your men at my resort.'

Fifteen?

Then there was a huge age gap between them, considering Charlotte looked like she was in her mid-thirties. He wondered why this was the case before realising the information couldn't possibly interest him. Besides, she looked like she was about to try to embark upon her list of complaints again. Best to get out of there as soon as possible.

'I have your list, thank you, Ms Templeton.' He turned to take his leave when he thought of something else. 'You know, while I think of it, I might as well let you know.'

'Let me know what?'

'You might want a word with your chef.'

'Sorry?' Charlotte's eyes sparkled like twin diamonds, making him ponder how much prettier – even prettier – she might be if she didn't exert herself so much at being a pain in the arse. He'd have to put this gently. 'I just thought, with you wanting to pull this dying resort out of its grave to preserve your ragtag family and all . . .'

Her eyes began to get very large so he decided to make his point. 'His scotch fillet is always a little tough. He might want to work on that. You know, for the sake of the business.'

On her gasp of what he hoped was gratitude, he walked out, the bell on the door ringing to punctuate his exit.

Alleluia. Released from hell at last.

The Silver Seas units were quite inviting, even in their rundown, eighties state. For sure, the place could definitely do with a facelift. But all in all Mark had nothing to complain about the level of comfort it provided to a tired man after a hard day's work. He removed his coal-stained boots by the front door. A small tiled foyer turned into a short carpeted hallway that split the unit in two. Bedrooms and bathroom on the right, kitchen and dining on the left. He walked straight to the telephone and picked it up.

After dialling the restaurant, he ordered the salmon. He had room service every day even though the units were equipped with kitchens and it would probably be much cheaper to make his own. Cooking brought back many, *many* memories that only pulled all his dissatisfaction screaming to the surface. Got him fixated on how unfair life was. How brutal. How unkind.

He was angry. He was always angry.

Tonight, however, the memories and the frustration refused to be suppressed by his clever dinner arrangements. Sitting on his dining table in its understated brown packaging was the parcel from his wife. He had brought it in before going over to the Silver Seas reception. He leaned against the wall, arms folded, looking at it for a moment. Trying to work out what its deal was as it sat there, practically burning a hole in the polished pine table.

He certainly hadn't been able to open the thing at work due to prying eyes. At least that was what he'd told himself. Now he had to wonder if he was game enough to open it at all.

Oh to hell with it.

He walked over to the table, put Charlotte Templeton's list down beside the parcel, then picked up the brown tough bag. Ripping off the sides, two things dropped out. A DVD in a white casing, labelled *Watch me first.* And a blue envelope labelled *Read me second.* His hands trembled as he picked up the plastic disc cover first.

Did he dare watch it?

He couldn't afford to go back to that place he'd been two years back. He'd hauled himself out of there by the fingernails, surfacing from the abyss with not much of his soul still left intact. If this was what he thought it was, he didn't know if he could handle it. But what else was he supposed to do? Store it? Watch it in three years? Five years? Destroy it?

No, he could never destroy anything of Kathryn's.

He gritted his teeth. *Damn you, Kathryn! Even now you're still able to get your way.*

Before he lost his nerve he went over to the TV cabinet and opened it. On a shelf below was a DVD player. He supposed he should thank his lucky stars it wasn't a VCR. Taking a breath, he slipped the disk into the player and turned on the TV.

The disc played automatically, nearly flooring him with the sudden image of her smiling on the screen. As though she was really there.

'Hi, Mark.'

Oh God. God help me.

He reached out, blindly grabbing for the arm of the couch as the sound of her voice hit him in the chest like a physical blow.

'Surprised to see me?'

She was wearing a loose T-shirt and a scarf. This must have been just after all her hair had fallen out. Her face was pale but her big blue eyes sparkled with all the love they'd shared on the day they'd first met, back in their early twenties. He sank slowly onto the couch, his gaze never wavering from the screen.

Her eyes grew glassy and her hand immediately went to her cheeks, dashing the wetness away. 'Sorry, this is harder than I thought.'

No shit.

She was sitting on the couch in their apartment, the window open behind her, a gentle breeze billowing the curtains towards her. He never thought he'd see her like that again.

'You're probably wondering how you got this.' She looked down at her hands. 'I, er . . . I'm going to leave it with a solicitor with a delivery date after my death. The fact is, I know,' she glanced up then, 'I know you will need me.'

If only you knew how much.

'I mean, you need me to help you get through this because we both know you're not going to listen to anyone else.'

Tears stung his eyes. It wasn't news to him. He'd do anything for her. All their friends used to comment that she had him wrapped around her little finger.

Used to. He hadn't really spoken to any of them in a while. It reminded him too much of everything he'd lost.

She paused, licking her lips. 'I remember when Simon died and you turned into such a bastard. I nearly divorced your arse. Remember that, Mark?'

How could he not? Losing his twin to a shark attack had been one of the worst moments of his life. The two of them had both been really into water sports, any type, any form. It was their favourite thing to do on the weekend. One innocent day on the beach had cost his brother, Simon, everything. Simon had always been such a strong swimmer and to make matters worse had the fearless attitude of a daredevil. If it occurred to him that a shark might attack him, he certainly wouldn't have expected to die from it. But he did, on the operating table, in Royal Perth Hospital. Shark attacks were frequent on the WA coastline, but Mark had never believed it would happen to either of them. That sort of story belonged on the news, not in his family history.

They hadn't just been brothers but best mates as well. Having that constant struck out of his life was like being pushed out to sea on a brittle raft. He hadn't known what to do at first. But when the shock cleared, he was angry. Splinteringly angry, with a rage that went so deep he had no idea how to fuel it. And so it fed on his life.

He'd retreated into a hole and pushed everyone away, including his wife. It had been months and months before he found his way back to her. He had wanted the world to suffer as he had suffered. How wrong he had been.

'I think you made more enemies that year than you had hot dinners,' the ghost on the TV continued. 'That tongue of yours cuts like a knife, Mark. Doesn't help that you're too smart for your own good. You know exactly where to throw your poisoned darts and you had a lot of them.'

She paused. 'Well, I'm guessing,' she smiled, 'just going on past experience . . . that the same thing has happened again.'

Kathryn, no.

'I mean, we both know that a person doesn't lose the two most important people in his life within five years and then just snap out of it. Especially not you, Mark.'

He closed his eyes. Losing his brother had been like cutting off a limb. But when she had died it had been far, far worse. Like his world had descended into darkness. Everything was black. Nothing was enjoyable because all he could think was that he could have had that moment with her.

As he opened his eyes, he watched her pause, licking her lips and giving him that secret smile that made his heart struggle to beat. His hand closed around the top of his shirt near the collar, fisting the material in his hands. Why did he feel like he couldn't breathe?

Kathryn continued to eyeball him. 'I've got news for you, mister. I'm not letting you drop out of life for me. I'm not letting you burn every friendship you've ever had because I died on you. I'm going to pull you out of this hole you've put yourself in if it kills me.' She laughed, and the achingly familiar sound made an unwanted wetness pool behind his eyes. 'Oh, crap, it already has.'

Cancer.

They'd battled with it for three years. When she was diagnosed with stage-three breast cancer, they had done all the treatments. Surgery, chemotherapy, radiation. He had thought losing his brother was bad but at least that had been quick. Watching the love of your life waste away before your very eyes, helpless to do anything, did something to a person.

And that something wasn't good.

'It's been two years, Mark. It's time to let go.'

Like hell.

He reached for the remote, his fingers trembling over the buttons, his brain malfunctioning so he couldn't figure out which one to push to make her stop talking.

She appeared to be reading his mind. As usual. 'Just hear me out. I've written you a list. It's in the box with this disc. I want you to do all of it. In that order. Promise me, Mark. Promise me now. Don't think I can't hear you, because I can. I know that I –'

His brain finally played ball, his thumb jabbed the stop button and abruptly the TV screen went blank. His breathing was coming short and shallow. Sweat beading on his brow as images of her collided in his head. He shut his eyes against the tears.

I was just starting to get it together. I was fine.

And then you had come along and do this.

What business is it of yours how I grieve anyway? I told you not to worry about me. Why is it that you never listen to anything I say?

He threw the remote across the room and walked out, straight to the bedroom, where he shed his clothes, wrenched at the taps and entered the shower. Hot steam infused the room. The water scalded his skin but he didn't turn the hot down. He wanted to burn her imprint off. How could he recover if she was back in his life interfering? He'd been doing just great – excellent, in fact, recovering beautifully.

Really? Who are you kidding?

He hadn't lived in Perth since her death. When he went home on R and R he stayed in a hotel because he couldn't bear to sleep in the bed they'd once shared. The calls from her family had stopped coming because he'd refused to take them. His friends had given up ages back too, when they realised his anger wasn't going away.

There was not a single person in his life who hadn't been burned by the dark mood that wouldn't release him.

And now here, at Hay Point, the place he thought he'd escape to, his subordinates hated and feared him. At first he'd found it amusing because he liked to be feared. But perhaps being considered cruel and unforgiving wasn't something to be proud of, or at least not something that Kathryn would be proud of.

The fact that he didn't give a damn seemed to pale in comparison.

He twisted the water off, and stepped out of the shower, furiously wrapping a towel around his waist and knotting it. His fingers clenched and unclenched as he started to pace the floor. Finally he stalked out of the bedroom and back to the kitchen; snatching the blue envelope off the dining table, he tore it open. It fluttered to the ground like an autumn leaf as he unfolded the paper that had been inside. The words on the page were handwritten. A lump formed in his throat at the sight of Kathryn's familiar lettering. He could just imagine her writing this, sitting at her desk, chewing on the end of her pen. All at once the note became the most precious thing in his possession. Teeth clenched, he pulled his thoughts together and read:

To Do (in this order):

1. Pay someone a compliment
2. Do someone a favour
3. Get a pet
4. Bake a cake
5. Ask someone you wouldn't normally ask for advice
6. Go diving again: it's been too long
7. Visit an old friend
8. Give all my stuff to the Salvos
9. Buy yourself some new clothes, especially underwear
10. Read a book
11. Go on a date
12. Go on a holiday
13. Talk to someone about me – the good memories

This was the list that was going to change his life? He read it again, turning it over, searching for something more from a message that seemed woefully inadequate.

That's all you're giving me?

His eyes flew back to his 'supposed' first task.

Pay someone a compliment.

'Come on, Kathryn,' he looked up at the ceiling, 'this will change nothing. You can't brow-beat me into being a nice person.'

At first he thought the sudden banging was his wife's wrath being sent down from heaven and he dropped the list on the table with a start. Then reason set in and his gaze swung to the door.

What now?

A muffled voice sounded through the wooden pane. 'Mr Crawford, are you in there?'

For the love of God.

He strode down the short hall and yanked open the front door. Charlotte Templeton practically fell through the threshold as her hand, still in the knocking position, followed the disappearing door. On her other arm she was balancing a tray. His salmon, he presumed. He'd forgotten he'd ordered room service. Funny, the resort manager didn't usually bring his tray around. Was she letting staff go now too?

'Mr Crawford.' She gaped at him and he realised belatedly that he was still semi-wet from his shower and wearing only a towel.

'Your skin –' She shook her head. 'I mean *in*! You're *in*!'

'Of course I'm in,' he growled.

'It's just that I was knocking awhile. Is everything okay?'

'Peachy. What are you doing here? You aren't normally the person who brings my dinner.'

He didn't know why but for some reason he found this sudden and uncharacteristic change of operations unsettling and he hoped that she didn't intend to make a habit of it.

After work he liked to wind down and Ms Templeton always seemed to have the same effect on his nerves as a steel winch. He had no idea why except perhaps that she appeared to be the only one of his subordinates who wasn't afraid of him. It didn't help that her cool green eyes were currently roaming over his now hot skin as though she'd never seen a naked torso before.

Damn the woman!

She blinked, shaking her head again. 'I thought it chest – I mean *best* – to bring you your dinner. After your comments about the steak, I wanted to make sure you knew that I personally oversaw the preparation of your salmon.'

'Really?' His mouth arched.

'I was also feeling a little guilty about what happened earlier and wanted to assure you in person that this meal is cooked to pec . . . pecfection –' She gasped. 'Perfection. I meant *perfection*. I hope you're hunky – I mean *hungry*!'

The woman shut her eyes and breathed deep. 'Can I just put it on the table?'

He stepped back. 'By all means, Ms Templeton.'

As she approached the table, too late he noticed the torn blue envelope on the floor and the brown tough bag sitting on the table. He hurried over just as she was pushing it all aside to lay the tray down. Two bits of paper scuttled to the floor.

He went to pick them up but she was before him. As his nerves twanged like a violin string, she straightened with a smile on her face, holding up her list and Kathryn's. 'I see you've been going over my items. Oh hang on, this one doesn't look like mine –'

He snatched it off her, perhaps a little too sharply. 'No, it's a letter from my wife – a *private letter*.'

Her face turned a deep shade of red. 'Sorry. I didn't mean to intrude.' She looked down, dusting her hands as she backed away from the table. Then she stopped as something seemed to occur to her. His unwinding nerves tautened again.

'What?'

Her eyes darted as though she were trying to figure out a tactful way to open the subject.

'Oh for goodness' sake,' he demanded impatiently, 'just say it; my dinner is getting cold.'

He wanted her out the door and on her way as quickly as possible.

She squared her shoulders, a determined expression on her face. 'I *also* wanted to just make clear that those rumours you heard about this resort being in trouble –'

'I didn't hear any rumours. It was my own conjecture.'

'Oh.' She swallowed hard. 'Well, whatever the case. It's not true.'

'Of course not,' he returned silkily. 'Is that all?'

She tossed him a look of derision before nodding. 'I guess so but –'

'Then thanks for the meal.'

He walked back down the short hall and opened the door, leaving her standing awkwardly by the table, her mouth half agape. She shut it, her eyes sparkling with indignation.

'Well, I'll just get out of your hair then.' She tossed her head.

'Please do.'

Perhaps it was because he was still gripping that wretched list in his hand or because of the sexy way her hips swayed as she moved towards him, he couldn't say, but when she reached the threshold again, God help him, he stalled her.

'Ms Templeton.'

She turned around, standing on his doormat and looking up at him expectantly. 'Yes, Mr Crawford?'

He cleared his throat, one hand gripping the doorknob. 'I don't want you to take this the wrong way.'

'Yes?' she said again.

'You are a very attractive woman.' On these words, he slammed the door in her face and went back to the table.

Grabbing a stray pen next to the tough bag he put a line through item one.

With a grim smile he looked up at the ceiling again. 'Happy, dear?'

Chapter 5

Mark

Mark arrived at work the next morning a man on a mission. A mission to forget the list his wife had sent him the night before, the list he hadn't been able to throw out and which was now burning a hole in his pocket. He glared at his secretary as she handed him his thankfully white coffee and gave him a wide berth. He watched the faces of his men hastily turn away as he moved through the open-plan layout to his office at the back of the room. Hands busied themselves shuffling papers that didn't need to be shuffled. The only person who didn't look away was William Steward. The boy sat there staring at him as if he were a problem that needed to be fixed. He stopped by the twenty-something's computer, returning his gaze over the top of the screen.

'Can I assist you with something, William?' he purred, just daring the little graduate to voice his concern. He could do with a punching bag this morning and a fresh-out-of-uni boy scout who thought he was going to change the world was just the sort of fly he needed to squash.

The boy finally lowered his eyes. 'Nothing that can't wait, sir.'

'Oh be a sport, tell me now.'

'I thought you might like to attend to your morning emails first, sir.'

Was he such a predictable bastard? Time to change that. 'Not today. Today I'm sorting you out first.'

'I'm glad, sir.' William murmured.

His gaze swung to the bowed head, trying to work out whether the boy was making fun of him or not, but there didn't seem to be any hostility in his body language. Boy Scout was always so gracious by nature, though of course it was usually the quiet ones you had to watch out for. He gritted his teeth. 'Tell me your concern.'

'I actually have several.' William lifted his eyes. 'It just seems to me like we need more hands on deck if we're going to have the wharf ready for the shiploader when it gets here.'

'Barking up this tree again, William.'

'I'm not merely barking, sir.' William folded his arms in a restful fashion that for some reason annoyed Mark no end. 'I've actually compiled a list I'd like you –'

This touched a nerve. 'What is it with you people and lists?!'

William blinked at this outburst and Mark felt himself colouring up at his uncharacteristic show of emotion. He reined himself in. 'My apologies, go on.' He waved his hand.

William pulled a conveniently printed document out of the drawer next to his hip. 'I've written a list of things I need to do before the shiploader gets here and it's massive. Clearly the job of two people, not one.' He opened the document to the next page. 'So I sort of split the task into two areas so that two people can progress independently of each other and it works quite well. Considering the fact that we were going to get Lena Todd over here and couldn't, we should still try for someone else. If you'd just look over this list –'

'Put it away. I'm not reading it,' Mark snapped at him. He raised his voice to address the eavesdroppers on his left and right who were not so subtly listening in. 'Nor will I read any other list of items any of you comes up with. I'm done with lists.'

'But, sir –' William began.

'Get your hard hat and vest, William, we're going out.' He inclined his head. 'You can *show* me.'

Surprise and also pleasure lit the boy's face before Mark marched back past Ann's desk, dumping his coffee in front of her. 'I won't be needing this.'

He proceeded to the door where he grabbed a hat and vest off the hooks. Shoving his arms through the fluoro high-visibility garment that did up with Velcro in the front, he was soon joined by William also kitted out in protective gear that included steel-capped boots on their feet.

'Do you want me to drive, sir?'

'No.'

There were only ten utes in the yard. Ann had all the keys on her desk. She was basically the community valet minus good customer service. If management staff needed to go out to the wharf they had to book a car in advance, or hope that one was available when they needed it. Mark was the exception to the rule. He had his own ute, which nobody drove but himself. He wasn't about to change the rules, even if William was the leader of this little expedition.

They both hopped into this vehicle and took off down the roughly hewn road leading away from the white office dongas. Huge stockpiles of jet-black coal against an expanse of deep blue sea provided the backdrop to their ride. Massive bucket-wheel reclaimers like huge metal dinosaurs scooped the black fuel from the mounds and placed it on the conveyor system. Four thousand eight hundred tonnes per hour, all bound for the wharf where the giant cargo ships were waiting to receive it. Nothing was more humbling or more exalting than this sight. The fact that not only could humans move mountains but also that he, Mark Crawford, was instrumental in helping them do it made his chest puff out in satisfaction.

They drove in silence with the windows up to keep the dust out. But once the wheels turned onto the jetty, Mark wound his down, drinking in the salty sea air and the rush of coal as the conveyor hummed next to them.

Funny how this was the only place he was calm.

Free of all the grief in his life, the anger that bubbled in his brain, the pain of living without Kathryn. He forgot that here. Some people listened to classical music; others thought the sound of birds was soothing. Not him. It was the grunt of heavy machinery, the smell of dirt and the buzz of a running conveyor that gave him peace.

'Nice day,' William commented.

He'd also wound down his window and rested an elbow on the sill, wind blowing on his hatless head. He'd taken his hard hat off and was holding it on his lap. Mark looked over at him at first in annoyance.

How dare he speak while I'm thinking?

Then the selfishness of this thought jolted his gaze back to the narrow concrete road, all three and a half kilometres of it jutting out to sea. Begrudgingly he decided to break the silence.

'Is this your first big project, William?' he asked.

The boy, who had to be at least fifteen years younger than him, turned in surprise that was also wary.

I guess I'm not usually prone to small talk. Mark gave a bitter laugh. 'Don't worry. It's not a trap. I'm merely curious.'

'Well, yes, sir. As you know, two years ago I was still in uni. Eight months ago, I was still in Perth. I'm just loving seeing all our hard work on paper come to life.'

'And what do you think of Queensland?'

'Frankly, sir, it's beautiful. I'm glad I came.'

Mark's mouth twisted. Ah, so full of hope and promise – a bit like he was when he first met Kathryn. Like a freshly iced skating rink, before any blades were given the chance to cut their way across it.

'What's your speciality, William?'

'Structural.'

'Mine too.'

'Really, sir?'

'Yes, back in the day, before I was site manager and construction manager and then project manager, I was . . . well . . . I was you.' He wrinkled his nose as though smelling a rather unpleasant aroma. He glanced back at William again. 'Well, a *type* of you. Perhaps a little more competent and a little less . . . what's the word I'm looking for?'

'Diplomatic, sir?'

It was his turn to shoot William a look of surprise. He gave a bark of laughter before acknowledging the hit. 'Exactly.'

The jetty ended. They had reached a T-junction. The top section of the T, more commonly known as the wharf, was over a kilometre in length. It was built to berth and load three massive cargo ships. Two shiploader cranes at least ten storeys in height sat on the wharf and giant booms transferred the coal from the conveyor into the bellies of docked ships.

Barnes Inc was there to build the fourth berth to accommodate yet another ship. This included installing a third giant shiploader crane to load it. Mark drove to the start of the Barnes Inc operation. It was a mess of little cranes and pieces of uninstalled steel sitting on a partially painted concrete deck that was many, many metres above water. There was a very poorly constructed guardrail made out of scaffolding tubing. To fall off the edge and into the water could kill a man. From this height, hitting the water would be like hitting rock.

As if to echo the thought, they put their hats on before they got out of the vehicle.

'So, William, show me what you want to tackle first.' Mark surveyed the lay of the land, trying not to notice as some of his men quickly stopped chatting and focused completely on their jobs as though being nice to one another would incur his censure.

Would it? *Am I such a miserable bastard?*

As they walked past the donga toilets and lattice of scaffolding hanging precariously over the edge, William began to talk about the job ahead. He was actually taking care of two areas, one on land and one on the wharf. On land they were building a new driver tower – basically a multistorey steel and concrete structure that would house the conveyor drive motors for the new section of the wharf. Out at sea, he was constructing an access stairwell. The conveyors climbed to five metres above the deck so there needed to be a way to reach them.

When he began to speak, Mark realised two things:

a. The boy was smart. Extremely smart. Smarter than any other graduate he'd had the pleasure to meet. Probably smarter than he had been when he was the kid's age. He had an eye for detail and a skill for finding the simplest way to work through a problem. This little engineer was going to go far.
b. The kid was right. There was more work here than could feasibly be done by just one engineer. He needed help.

The second point Mark had known all along. He just hadn't wanted to admit it. The thing was, he didn't want another graduate under foot. They generally needed more guidance than the output they provided. He could easily get one of the older guys to lend this kid a hand. That way the work would get done quickly and efficiently and without any of the usual mistakes first-timers make. But, damn it, he found himself liking Will.

Perhaps it was because the boy reminded him of himself or who he used to be before he'd realised that life didn't always hand you second chances – or even that you were likely to need one. He liked the boy's passion and the fact that he had a plan. Not just an engineering plan either . . .

He knew that look. Seen it in the mirror in years long gone.

The boy had it bad.

And so what? Was that such a terrible thing?

It is if she bloody messes up your job. He hasn't thought this through well enough.

He shoved his hands in the pockets of his pants as he gazed out to sea. Involuntarily, his fingers grasped 'the list'. The list he now knew off by heart.

Item 2. Do someone a favour.

'William.'

'S-sorry, sir?' William blinked and Mark realised he'd just interrupted him mid-sentence.

'Never mind about that.' He waved an impatient hand. 'You know that girlfriend of yours? I've changed my mind. Get her over here, will you?'

William's face lit up like a bulb. 'Of course, sir. But, er . . . she's not my girlfriend, sir.'

'Whatever. She's in. It looks like you've got a lot of work to do. You better go sort out the schedule with the supervisor. I trust you'll be able to get a ride back with someone else?'

William nodded eagerly. 'Of course, sir.'

He had been turning away but at this response he spun back. 'And, *William*,' he purred.

'Yes, sir?'

'Stop calling me "sir" in that irritating fashion of yours. Apart from being entirely unnecessary, I'm not your bloody schoolmaster.'

'No, s– Er . . . what should I call you then?'

A ghost of a smile lifted the corners of Mark's mouth as he walked away, throwing casually over his shoulder: 'Why not call me Caesar, like everybody else?'

Chapter 6

Emily

It all seemed like great news, until reality dawned. *I've quit my job. There's no safety net. If this doesn't work out, I'll be left with nothing.*

'Not nothing precisely,' Will told her over the phone. 'You got a free trip to Queensland at the very least.'

'Yes, but doesn't it seem just a little drastic to you?' She chewed on her lower lip. 'I mean, I could quit my job and just stay in Perth to find another one.'

'Where's the fun in that?'

'True,' she acknowledged. 'But it would be a lot less risky.'

'Have a little faith, Em.' Will chuckled. 'You're a good engineer. You just need to give yourself a chance.'

'Easy for you to say, Mr God's Gift to Construction,' she snorted. 'Is there anything I can study, read or memorise to prepare? Perhaps some paper on wharves or piling at sea? What's the name of the geotech professor who wrote that book on deep foundations?'

Will laughed. 'Whoa, Em, relax. You're not going to need that. This will be a learn-as-you-go experience.'

'I was afraid you were going to say that.'

'Don't worry. You've already got one big advantage over everyone else here.'

'What's that?'

'You're not insane.'

Her brow wrinkled. 'Will, don't joke about this.'

'No, I'm serious! I think it's the whole FIFO syndrome. Being stuck in isolation and worked like a dog for long periods of time tends to bring out the crazies.'

'*Oh-kay*,' she drawled. 'That doesn't exactly make me feel a whole lot better.'

'Trust me. It will when you get here. Are you all packed?'

'Mostly.' She paused, her fingers flexing around the cordless. 'I went round to our – I mean Trent's – house yesterday and picked up the last of my things.' She lowered her voice. 'He had a girl there.'

'Why are you whispering?'

'Sorry.' She screwed up her nose as she realised she had been. 'You probably know all this already.' Then she closed her eyes and prayed that he didn't. He soon rewarded her.

'Actually, I had no idea he was seeing someone new.'

'Oh, okay.' Her eyes flew open and she brightened. 'So it's probably not serious then.'

'Do you care?' he asked carefully.

She recognised the sympathetic tone in his voice and hardened her own. 'No.'

Only I do! Very, very much.

She could hardly confide that in Trent's best friend though, even if he was her best friend too. Emily had lost a lot in the last few weeks but luckily the one thing she still had was her pride.

'I mean,' she said with deliberate airiness, 'I wish him all the best. I certainly wouldn't hold back if I met someone new that I took a fancy to.'

She could almost hear Will's grin on the other end of the phone. 'Would you like me to tell him that?'

'Would you?' she whispered.

He laughed. 'Oh for goodness' sake, Em. Forget about Trent and focus on you. The world is your playground.'

That brought a smile to her face and she wondered absent-mindedly how Will always knew exactly what to say to make her feel better. Here she was, standing on the brink of a fantastic opportunity – why did Trent rate a mention?

'Thanks, Will. You're absolutely right. It's time for a change. A big change.'

'Definitely. You were with Trent for five long years and –'

'Long?' she repeated, surprised at his choice of words. 'I didn't think they were long *per se*. I mean, they seemed to go by in a flash for me. One minute we were the next couple picked for marriage, then we were –'

'Long, short, what's the difference?' Will interrupted with a short, self-conscious laugh.

'Actually –'

'*The point is*, it's over now. And you can do whatever you like.'

'Whatever I like . . .' She pronounced the words slowly and succinctly before her voice gave out.

'Exactly.'

That was the other great thing about Will: he loved to give advice but he never tried to tell her what to do. Trent had always been very clear on his position. When she'd been living through it, she had always thought he was being helpful or protective. She had never thought anything of simply following his lead.

Now standing at this fork in the road, with all her freedom back in her pocket, she realised how much of herself she had lost in that relationship. Her head jerked up as clarity hit her like a stream of light.

I really can do anything I like. Anything at all. I'm not tied to anyone or any place.

'You're awfully silent,' said Will.

'Am I?' she muttered. 'I'm thinking.'

'About what?'

'About who I am and what I want out of life.'

For the past five years, she'd been Trent's girlfriend. Every decision she'd made had been based on what he would like her to do and what his plans for the future were, from her bank balance to her wardrobe. She'd turned herself into the perfect lawyer's wife – mild-mannered, well dressed and smart but not too smart. Intelligent enough for him to be proud of her but not so accomplished that she over-shadowed him.

She never complained.

Not about the long hours he did at work.

Or the lack of time they spent together because of it.

She had hated all his friends because they were snobby, judgemental and completely focused on money, but she'd mingled with them more than her own university set because it was good for his career.

'Got an answer yet?' Will asked, breaking her thoughts once more with a joking tone.

'No.' She bit her lip. 'But, damn it, I'm going to find out.'

'Huh?'

'I'm going to try new things, eat new food, buy new clothes,' she said firmly. 'Eat, love, pray, *carpe diem*, the whole nine yards.'

'Sounds like another shopping spree to me,' Will yawned. 'I'm out.'

She ignored his lack of enthusiasm as new plans began to take shape. 'No, this will be fun! "Emily's Year of New Things". New job, new home, new everything. I'm going to reinvent myself and Queensland is the perfect place to do it.'

Will seemed to perk up at that. 'If you want to try something new, we could go sailing. You've never done that before.'

Emily smiled. 'That's exactly what I mean. I'm dying to visit those islands.'

'Of course.'

'I mean,' she rolled her eyes as her confidence grew, 'I'm definitely not going to be sitting around moping about who Trent is taking out.'

'Definitely not.'

'I won't have time for it.'

'No time.'

'I've got better things to do.'

'Better things to do!'

'I mean, I'm going to tropical island central, right? The most romantic place in Australia. I'll probably fall in love myself.'

'Bound to.'

'So do you know any cute guys you can set me up with?'

'Huh?'

She sighed. 'Will, you haven't been listening to what I've been saying again, have you? Are you playing with your Xbox?'

'*No.*' His tone sounded affronted.

'Well then answer the question.'

'I . . . just . . . think,' he dragged the words out one by one, 'that maybe . . . perhaps I'm not the best judge of male cuteness.'

'True,' she assented. 'I'll judge the cuteness. You can tell me if they've got a good personality.'

'Just out of curiosity, what do you think is cute? I mean, on a guy?'

She cocked her head to one side. 'I don't know. Nice face, nice smile, nice eyes.'

'Your key word here seems to be nice. That doesn't really give me much to go on. Arnott's biscuits are nice.'

She sighed in frustration. 'I haven't got a *specific* definition.'

'Okay, for example, do you think I'm cute?'

Um. What? She'd never really thought about that in any great detail. *Do I think Will is cute?*

'Er . . .' She shut her eyes. 'Wii-ill,' it was her turn to drag out the words, 'you're my best friend and –'

'Somehow, I don't like where this is going.'

'Look,' she changed tack, 'don't worry about the whole cuteness thing. I'll know when I see him. I'll get that instant spark of attraction. You know what I'm talking about.'

'Ah yes, the instant spark.' Will sounded glum.

'Am I boring you?'

'No, er . . . yes, maybe just a little. I think I might go shoot some aliens on the Xbox now. All of sudden, I feel like killing something.'

'Oh, okay.' She rubbed her temple and shook her head. 'So I'll see you in a couple of days.'

'All right.'

'Er, Em.'

'Yeah?'

'Just for the record, I think you're cute.'

'Oh . . . thanks.' An uncharacteristic warmth starting in the centre of her chest filled her ribcage and quickly spread up her neck, causing a smile to tickle her mouth.

'Okay, bye,' he said quickly.

'Yeah, see ya.' But the dial tone was already sounding in her ears.

The next thing she did that afternoon was have her hair cut. She'd always worn it long, so it seemed rather appropriate, if a little cliché, to chop it all off. The new style framed her face with gentle waves. Lengthwise, it sat just under her chin, making her look rather fairy-like. She loved it – a great start to her 'Year of New'.

The plane ride from Perth to Mackay was a long and arduous one. She didn't know why but Barnes Inc had not booked her a direct flight. The journey was going to take her all day. First she had to fly from Perth to Sydney, then from Sydney to Brisbane and finally from Brisbane to Mackay. She had to wonder whether this drawn-out, 'hardest way possible' was a taste of things to come.

Will had happened to let slip on the phone a few days before her departure that there were only eight women in the Barnes Inc workforce, which, all up, numbered in the hundreds.

And that the project manager was the devil incarnate.

And the hours were brutal. Seven am to six pm with only one Sunday off every couple of weeks. After four weeks she'd have R and R in Perth. By then, no doubt, she'd be exhausted. She was all for getting ahead in her career, but was losing her leisure time on the side completely necessary?

However, when she got off the plane and breathed in the heavy, slightly sweet-smelling Queensland air she knew she had made the right choice. Seeing the lush greenery and the clear blue skies, and feeling that holidaymakers' ambience about the place, Emily felt her spirits lift as she made her way through Mackay airport.

Next to her baggage carousel was a man in the Barnes Inc uniform and she immediately went up to greet him. He was a swarthy-looking individual with dark hair and a cheeky smile.

He held out his right hand. 'My name's Harold but everyone around here calls me Dipper. Welcome to Mackay.'

She shook it. 'Thanks. I'm Emily.'

'Very pleased to meet you.' It was clear he wasn't lying about this because to her embarrassment he gave her body a rather thorough onceover. 'Not many ladies on site. I'm sure the boys will give you a warm welcome.'

Not too warm, she hoped, but smiled politely.

She got her bag off the carousel and he carried it to the car for her. This turned out to be a white ute that looked like it hadn't seen a car wash for the better part of a year. The Barnes Inc site offices were located just a few kilometres north of Salonika Beach, which was the location of resort she would be staying in. The nearest town was Sarina. Not that she would have any need or time to go there with the size of the operation she was about to join. The coal port's operations stretched over a distance of six kilometres along the coast. On the journey from Mackay to Hay Point, Dipper regaled her with the delights in store.

Diving, sailing, snorkelling, fishing or surfing.

She mentally added them all to her New Adventure wish list.

'Sounds great!'

'What about fruit? Do you like fruit?'

This question seemed out of left field. But she answered it anyway, peeling her eyes away from the stunning scenery whizzing by her car window. So far the landscape had consisted of gentle hills carpeted by a variety of tall grass plants and large grey mangrove trees.

'What kind of fruit?'

'Tropical fruit. Melons?' He licked his lips. 'I love a good melon.'

To her horror, he took his eyes off the road briefly to glance at her chest. As she suppressed the desire to cross both arms over her breasts, he looked away again, saying good-naturedly, 'What about bananas? Do you like bananas?'

'I like all kinds of fruit,' she returned stiffly.

'Noted.' He smiled in way she didn't like. Did he intend to source some for her?

If Dipper thought the path to her bed was laden with melons and bananas he was way off base. He was definitely not her type – too old, and far too forward. She liked her men just a little more subtle. She firmly put the worry over his intentions out of her head. There were other more interesting things to focus on, like her legume diet for instance. Perhaps while she was in Queensland she should substitute beans with mango, lychee, papaya and bananas.

Will would *never* know.

As kilometres disappeared her focus turned to her impending arrival at her new workplace. They arrived on site at about four o'clock that afternoon. Emily felt her nerves tighten the second the coal stockpiles came into view. Eight mini mountains – a testament to how much coal this port moved.

Wow! Now that's engineering.

Dipper ushered her into the first office donga, which was raised on concrete blocks. A gush of stale, dusty air assailed her senses before she saw the desks laid out haphazardly around the room, overflowing with paperwork and people. The buzz of printers and computers made her feel that the best word to describe the room was over-crowded. She craned her neck in search of Will but he wasn't there. Instead, Dipper carted her off to an office in the corner, where a man surrounded by piles of yellow vests and hard hats was seated. He rose to meet her, holding out his hand with a grin.

'Hi, I'm Alan, the HR manager. You'll be wanting a desk and some PPE no doubt.'

By PPE, he meant Personal Protective Equipment, which he certainly had enough of.

'Now what size are you?'

'Um, an eleven.'

Since beginning her legume diet she had dropped half a dress size – a fact she was very proud of.

'An eleven?' He scratched his head, looking worried.

'All right, fine,' she conceded, self-consciously casting her eyes down. 'If you don't do the in-between sizes, I'm a twelve.'

His brow wrinkled. 'We're fresh out of ladies' twelves – actually to tell you the truth, never had any to begin with. But you should fit into an equivalent men's size. Just looking at you, I think you'll take the smallest size we have, which – surprise, surprise – is a small.' He grinned, an expression she didn't return.

Smart aleck.

'Unfortunately, as of yesterday, we're fresh out of both smalls and mediums. So I'm giving you a large.'

A what?

He handed her a vest that she could wear as a dress and a hat that looked like it would swallow her head whole.

'Er . . .'

He ignored her hesitation, rubbing his hands and standing up. 'Now, I'll take you to your desk.'

Clutching her PPE, she followed Alan across the room to a tiny corner by the door. At first she didn't see it. How could she, jammed as it was between a giant photocopier/printer and a tall bookcase overflowing with stationery supplies? The desk was like a fold-out trestle table. It was about half the size of everybody else's desk and she couldn't believe that they'd actually managed to fit a computer onto it.

'I know it's a little crammed,' Alan began apologetically.

A little?!

'But it was all we had. As you can see, we're rather pushed for space at the moment and Caes–, the project manager hasn't seen fit to buy us another donga.' He licked his lips, lowering his tone confidentially. 'We're saving the money to increase Barnes Inc's profit margin.'

How nice.

Emily looked for a place to put down her things but seeing none decided to keep holding them.

'On the bright side,' Alan beamed, 'most of the time, you won't be in the office. You'll be out on the wharf cruising around and making your mark.'

As the girl in the clown suit.

'So, I don't suppose you could introduce me around a little? I'd love to meet the project manager.'

'The project manager never speaks with new recruits,' Alan said firmly. 'You have to have been here at least a couple of weeks before he'll see you.'

Emily stared. 'Why?'

'Because then, "apparently",' he lifted his hands to insert the quotation marks, 'you'll be able to hold a decent conversation with him.' He dropped his hands. 'He doesn't like dealing with people still learning the lay of land. Sorry.'

'That's okay . . . I guess.'

'Would you like a tea or coffee?'

'Sure.'

'Do you have mug?'

She looked down at her full hands helplessly. 'No, I don't.'

'Oh.' He wrinkled his nose. 'Well then you can't. The project manager requires that we supply all our own mugs, coffee powder and tea bags, etc. But maybe tomorrow.' He punctuated the suggestion with an enthusiastic smile and nod.

'Er . . . sure.'

'So if you'll be right, I'll leave you to it.'

'Wait!' She quickly stopped him. 'Leave me to what?'

He blinked. 'I thought you knew.'

'No, I don't.'

'That *is* a shame.' He clasped his hands. 'Well, I'll see if I can find out and get back to you.'

She didn't see head or tail of him for the next hour, or anyone else for that matter.

One guy stopped by the stationery cupboard. Eagerly, she waited for him to say something to her.

He did. 'We're out of pacer leads.' He shook the empty box in her face. 'Put that on order.'

He walked off before she could correct his misunderstanding.

Others stopped to use the photocopier but did not pause for conversation. A kind of panic hung in the air, as if they were all late for some party she hadn't been invited to.

Was she missing something?

At five o'clock, people were starting to switch off their computers and go home. Just as she was wondering what she should do, the office door swung open and Will walked in.

Thank goodness.

Dressed in a hard hat, blue Hard Yakka pants and a fluoro-yellow safety vest, he looked like he had just come off the wharf. He tapped a roll of drawings on his palm as he scanned the room, clearly in search of her. A huge smile broke out on his face when he spotted her.

'You're here!'

She stood up as he reached her. 'Yes I am.'

They didn't embrace, conscious of being in a workplace and not wanting to draw attention to themselves, but his eyes were appreciative as he looked her over.

'You've cut your hair.'

She self-consciously fingered the strands. 'Yeah, do you like it?'

After a moment he nodded. 'I do.' He looked away from her then, as if embarrassed by his own comment. He cleared his throat. 'Is this the desk they've given you?'

'Yeah.' She shrugged. 'I'm hoping it's temporary.'

'Yeah, I'll say. So where's all the rest of your stuff?'

'My suitcase is under the desk.' She kicked it with her foot. 'I packed light, just a few outfits. When's knock-off time?'

'Now.' It was a new voice that interrupted what she had previously thought was a private conversation. It belonged to a tall, lanky man with too confident a swagger for his ageing good looks.

'Hello, hello, hello.' He grinned at her. 'Aren't you going to introduce me, Boy Scout?'

Will sighed. 'This is Nova.'

'Good afternoon and welcome,' he said with a flourish that lacked only a bow. 'I have been dying to meet Will's *special* friend from Perth.'

Will glared at him. 'And now you have,' he said with a finality that was strangely unlike him.

In any case, Nova ignored him and continued to address her. 'Have you been out on the wharf yet?'

'I only arrived today.' Emily found it hard not to smile at his over-the-top manner. 'So no, which is rather disappointing.'

'Of course it is! After travelling all the way from Perth.' He crossed his arms and conveyed mock horror to Will. 'You should take her out.'

'It's knock-off time.' Will frowned. 'All the utes are leaving.'

'Not mine.' Nova jingled some keys. 'I have to stay late tonight. I could lend it to you.'

'And get our arses kicked because she hasn't had her safety induction?' Will shook his head.

'The truth is,' Nova said to Emily, 'we take visitors out all the time without an induction. It's just about being careful and staying with your guide. Last week, I showed around this top manager from Perth who just flew in for the day. It's really no biggie.'

'Really?' Emily brightened. 'It would be nice to see what I've flown all the way here for.'

Especially after the horrendous afternoon she'd just endured. She needed some good news, a little boost in confidence.

'Well, if Will's too chicken, I'll take you,' Nova immediately offered.

'Give me that.' Will snatched the keys off him. 'Come on, Em, let's go before I come to my senses.'

Nova chuckled as he strolled off, like a man who'd just accomplished his master plan – though what that might be, she'd be damned if she knew.

'He seems nice,' she remarked tentatively as she hastily pulled on her vest and rammed on her hat.

'He's a busybody is what he is,' Will said dryly and then sighed. 'But I like him.'

His eyebrows jumped up at the sight of her in the high-vis vest that made her look like she was wearing a tent.

'O-kaay, that's a little sad,' he said. 'Didn't they have anything smaller?'

She put her hands on her hips. 'You think I didn't ask that question?'

He grinned ruefully. 'Okay, let's just go.'

They exited the main office donga like a couple of rebel teenagers looking for a secluded place to smoke. Crossing the car park, Emily received a couple of whistles from some guys chatting by their utes.

'Hey, Boy Scout, who's your friend?'

Will tipped his hat. 'You'll find out tomorrow.'

'Nice vest, honey,' one of the men addressed her directly. 'You could probably fit me in there too.'

She blushed, as he gave her a look that seemed to indicate that all he needed was an invitation. Will unlocked the ute and they both hopped in.

She soon became absorbed in her surroundings as he turned the car out onto the dirt track that led to the top of the jetty. They passed through a foreign city of stockpiles with a maze of conveyor belts and plant machinery connecting them – like a giant game of Snakes and Ladders. Will pointed out the surge bins and the drive tower.

'I'm working on that,' he revealed.

'The driver tower?'

'Yeah.' He nodded and then looked over at her. 'And you'll be helping me with it.'

She sucked in a deep breath. Working on a building that was about six storeys tall as her first project would be pretty bloody exciting. Then the coastline came into view. The ocean, a vast fathomless blue, spread out to infinity. The jetty, though nearly four kilometres in length, was but one small dent in this great expanse. Excitement crept up her bones. It may be one small dent but it was one giant operation for them.

A couple of White-Faced Herons flew out of the way of the ute as they reached the start of the jetty. This consisted of two roads sitting on trestles an average of fifteen metres above the water depending on where the tide was at. Each road provided a pathway, one going out to sea and one coming off. Three conveyors ran parallel to the roads, two through the middle and one on the side going out. As soon as the car boarded this lonely concrete road, walls made of conveyors and metal sheeting rose up around them, blocking out nature. The road was narrow with only a couple of passing bays along the way. She couldn't see the ocean or even hear it among the whir of passing coal. Tonnes and tonnes of it travelling as fast as Will's ute headed out to the ships with unrelenting efficiency. Moving between the two belts was like entering a roofless tunnel made of steel and concrete. Then all of a sudden they came to a T-junction and the view widened.

They were on the wharf now. The concrete deck was much wider and she could see the ocean again as the conveyors moved out both to the left and to the right, heading straight for the shipping berths.

Will turned the car out onto the right arm of the wharf where new construction was taking place. The new conveyor trusses were being installed a couple of storeys above the main deck. She noticed that there wasn't much parking or space. The deck seemed crowded with utes, trucks, small cranes, other machinery and dongas.

'Wow, this is incredible,' she muttered. 'I'm so glad you brought me.'

He looked over at her and smiled. 'Me too.'

They unclipped their belts and got out of the car.

'So what are you working on out here?' she asked enthusiastically.

'The access tower for the conveyors.' He pointed this steel structure out to her.

'Awesome.'

'Do you want the tour?'

'Of course.'

They didn't have to walk very far to see it all because everything was so big you could see it from any vantage point. But they made a leisurely stroll of it anyway. The wharf was mostly deserted, except for the occasional straggler. She felt like she was on a private tour.

He pointed out the two giant shiploader cranes that stood as tall as his drive towers above the deck. The interesting thing about them, though, was that they could move and frequently did, along heavy rails embedded deep in the concrete on the wharf. The shiploaders did exactly as their name suggested. They loaded ships, guiding the coal off the conveyors and into the massive bellies of cargo carriers – like a dinosaur feeding its young.

'And we're installing another one,' Will explained. 'It'll be arriving fully fabricated by ship in four weeks' time. Caesar's beside himself.'

'Caesar?'

'The project manager,' he grinned. 'Everyone around here has nicknames. You'll get used to it.'

'Ah-huh.' She smiled.

He was about to show her the shipping berths and the site of the new one under construction when he suddenly stalled.

'*Oh shit.*'

'What?' She followed his gaze to see a tall, dark stranger talking to some welder near where their ute was parked. 'Who's that?'

'Caesar.'

'So what do we do?' she asked.

'Hide.'

'Hide?' she repeated dubiously as he grabbed her hand and yanked on it. '*Will*,' she whispered hoarsely as he dragged her behind a nearby donga. 'Wouldn't it be better if we just came clean and you introduced me? I mean, he can't be that bad, can he? He'll forgive us.'

He looked at her like she was crazy. 'He's not that sort of person.'

'But –'

He put a finger to her lips. 'Ssshhh.'

Perhaps it was the intimacy of his touch that stalled her rather than the threat of impending discovery. She suddenly realised that she had her hand tucked firmly into his, cradled against his leg. They stood shoulder to shoulder, his finger on her mouth. She could smell the faint scent of his deodorant and hear the gentle rush of his breathing. A sudden overwhelming yearning washed through her like the waves she could hear below the deck. She came up confused and aroused.

This is Will we're talking about here.

Will.

Trent's best mate. Your best friend. You're one step removed from incest, girl. Are the FIFO crazies getting to you already?

'He's coming,' he hissed.

It took all her willpower not to giggle as he pulled her away from the donga and they ran towards a giant plastic portable loo, like a couple of kids playing hide and seek. He opened the door and the pungent waft of urine mixed with some sort of cleaning agent overwhelmed her.

'Get in.'

'Do I have to?' She wrinkled her nose.

With a sigh, he grabbed her by the arm and they both climbed in together. He pulled the door shut behind them, putting his arm around her to stop her from toppling straight into the dunny. There wasn't really enough room for two people to stand in there. Especially if those two people did not want to brush up against the dirty-looking toilet and the grubby-looking sink. So they held onto each other, which was perhaps a little more befuddling than all the rest.

Emily had hugged Will many times in the past, even kissed him on the cheek more times than she could count. But they'd never just stood there in a prolonged embrace – her ear to his heart, his hand at the nape of her neck, his thumb brushing the bare skin there, sending a weird sort of heat creeping over her.

It's just because you're single now. You're seeing every *guy as a potential boyfriend.*

Then there was a loud *rat-a-tat-tat* on the door and they both jumped. A dry, derisive voice pronounced slowly and succinctly: 'William, *what* are you doing?'

Chapter 7

Will

'Er . . . going to the toilet.' Will cleared his throat and closed his eyes, praying for a miracle.

Here he was, a boner in his pants and his boss breathing fire on the other side of a smelly toilet door.

Why do you do this to yourself?

He couldn't help it. As soon as he had Emily in his arms, it was like all his blood had rushed straight to his groin. His brain had triggered the 'Emily Alert' siren, and the cells in his heart had raised the alarm. 'We've got a code red – all hands on deck now!'

So there he was, trying to stand so she wouldn't notice when bloody Caesar steps up to the door.

'Do you take me for a fool, William?' That silky smooth voice oozed like butter through the grooves around the loo door.

'No, sir . . . er, Mark.' He tried to infuse calm into his voice. There had been no discovery yet. He knew nothing.

Didn't he?

'Then I want you back in the office now,' Caesar gave the order briskly. 'You shouldn't be here. It's knock-off time and I've got a stack of technical queries for you to answer. You'll be working late tonight.'

He winced. 'No problem, Mark.'

'Good. I'll see you soon.' They heard Caesar step back from the door but his amused tone was heard briefly before he walked away. 'Oh, and Emily Woods. Good to see that you know you'll be starting your career at rock bottom.'

On this announcement, they heard his footsteps retreat. Will threw open the door and they both burst out choking. Emily looked like she'd been holding her breath and he didn't blame her.

She moved away from him wringing her hands. 'We're in trouble, aren't we? Big trouble.'

He took off his hat briefly and ran his hands through his hair. 'Hard to say, really.'

'Oh.' Her big eyes flew to his; an instant connection ran between them like a hot wire.

'Nah, we're in deep shit. Pardon the pun. But it's difficult to say how much or for how long. Caesar is a little bit of a sadist. You know, he likes to punish people. I mean, I'm already in the doghouse, working late tonight. I never work late. Not after a twelve-hour shift. You need your rest.'

She put a hand to her eyes. 'This is all my fault.'

'How do you figure that?'

'I should never have let you bring me out.'

'It was my choice.' He shrugged and put a hand on her shoulder but she immediately shrugged it off and stepped away. He bit his lip. *Shit.* Had she felt his body reacting to her?

She must be disgusted, given that her relationship with his best mate wasn't even cold in the ground yet. Should he try to explain by saying, 'I was aroused because I've been in love with you for the last seven years'?

Yeah, because then you won't sound like a psycho!

She looked up quickly and he was once more arrested by her eyes. 'We should definitely get you back to the office. I don't want to get us into more trouble than we already are.'

'Good idea.'

They accomplished the drive back in relative silence. She seemed okay. She wasn't saying anything about what had happened in the toilet.

Nothing did happen.

'So it's a real shame we can't hang out tonight,' she sighed as they turned into the office car park.

'I know,' he nodded, taking her disappointment as a good sign. If she was disgusted with him, she would hardly want to spend time with him, would she?

When they got back to the main office donga he said, 'Go grab your suitcase. I'll quickly drop you off at the resort and then come back.'

'You sure you won't get into trouble for coming back even later?'

'It's a one-minute drive.' He shrugged. 'If you didn't have a suitcase you could probably walk it. It'll be no time at all.'

'Okay,' she agreed.

Five minutes later, he was back in the office, looking at a foolscap file that Caesar had put on his desk. The man himself was standing there with arms folded and foot tapping.

'William, William, William.' He shook his head. 'I gave you an inch and you took a yard. Now *I*,' he said succinctly, 'will take a mile.'

He swallowed as Caesar patted the file. 'By morning, thanks.'

With a sigh, Will sat down as the shadow of his nemesis crossed his desk and disappeared.

Caesar was true to his word. Will got about four hours' sleep that night and the following day he had him running errands in Mackay. He did not get to see Emily till after knock-off, which was a shame because he had wanted to start handing over some of his drive tower work to her. Instead, she had sat in the office all day twiddling her thumbs.

'I got so bored,' she told him, 'I got up and reorganised the stationery cupboard. It wasn't a good move.'

'Why?' he asked.

'I got several more demands for pacer leads,' she said.

He did not see Emily in the office the next day either. Alan, the HR manager, said that she was off on her safety induction. He had expected to see her back in the office late afternoon but after a morning full of painful paperwork and meetings that seemed to go in circles, he was called out to the wharf to assist with some issue Fish had.

The problem with lifting something was that once you started, you couldn't leave the job until you'd put the bloody thing down again. And if it refused to slide into place, you could be left standing there for hours. Earlier that afternoon, Fish had lifted the girder off a truck with the crane and when they went to slide it onto the two piles the connector plates didn't quite match up.

As usual the deck engineer had more on his plate than he could handle so the little graduate had been called in to deal with the issue, because obviously he had 'nothing better to do'.

It looked as though he was going to be working late today as well. He pushed himself and Fish's men for the next hour, hoping to get back to the office as soon as possible to see Em.

Just as he was finishing up, his phone rang. Thinking it was one of his suppliers he briskly picked it up. 'Will Steward speaking.'

'What the hell were you thinking?' The voice was easily recognisable.

'Trent?' he said in surprise.

'Of course it's bloody me.'

'How are you doing?' he began tentatively.

'Worse since I found out you've carted Em off to Queensland.'

Will's fingers tightened around the phone. 'I didn't cart her off. She made that decision herself.'

'At your prompting,' Trent threw at him.

Will lowered his voice and walked away from any eavesdroppers that might be near him. 'She was feeling really down. I wanted to help her out.'

'It's not up to you to interfere in *our* relationship.'

At this, Will gritted his teeth. 'You haven't had a relationship since you dumped her, Trent. And thanks for telling me about it, by the way.'

There was a frustrated sigh on the other end of the phone and he knew from experience that his friend was trying to calm himself down. 'Look, I'm sorry,' Trent said at last. 'I'm sorry for everything. I'm sorry for not telling you and I'm sorry for having a go at you just now. I shouldn't have done that.'

Will relaxed a little. 'It's okay. You're going through something. I get it. But why didn't you tell me? According to Em, it's been weeks since you two split.'

'I know, I know.' Trent sounded down and Will couldn't help but feel a little sorry for him. 'I just couldn't. It seemed premature or something. It . . . it still does.'

Uh-oh.

There was an awkward silence on the other end of the phone – a silence he didn't trust.

'I didn't *mean* to break up with her,' Trent said finally.

Will closed his eyes. *This is not what I want to hear.*

'I mean, I love her. You know I love her.'

'Are you sure?' It was hard not to keep the sarcasm out of his voice.

'Of course I do. You know how great she is.' He seemed adamant until he started to explain himself. 'It's just that, well you know, she was getting too clingy and baby-crazy and . . . and I was just feeling really pressured . . . you know . . . about the whole *marriage* thing.'

'Well, you have been together for five years.'

'That's the point. I haven't been in a serious relationship with anyone but Em. She was my first real girlfriend. So how do I know that I'm making the right choice?'

I would know it.

'I can't help you with that, Trent.'

'You're right,' his best mate agreed. 'I have to work it out for myself. But, Will, there is something you could do for me.'

Unease spread up Will's neck. 'Like what?'

'I want you to keep her out of trouble.'

'What do you mean?'

'I don't want her meeting anyone new. All I'm looking for is some time out before I commit myself completely.'

Will frowned. Em had seen a girl at Trent's place when she'd gone to pick up her stuff. 'And by that do you mean time to play the field?'

'Come on, Will. You know what a big deal marriage is,' Trent replied impatiently. 'Can you blame me for just wanting a little time to myself before going into lockdown?'

'I don't know, Trent.'

His friend immediately became defensive. 'After getting her to leave the bloody state, I would think you would at least help me make this right.'

Will took a deep breath. 'I just don't want to see her getting hurt again.'

'I've told you that I love her and do want to marry her . . . eventually. Doesn't that tell you something? I get that you want to be a friend to her too. I've always been glad that you've made an effort with her.'

'I didn't do it for you, Trent,' Will said quietly.

Trent ignored this statement. 'The point is, all I'm really asking you to do is look out for her as you always have. Please, Will, it would mean a lot to me.'

Will paused. Trent had his moments, but overall he wasn't a bad person. Even though they were no longer that close, they had been as kids. When they were teenagers Trent had always been the bigger, stronger one. In school he'd been head boy, captain of the football team, popular and proud of it. Will had always been the nerd – the four-eyed science geek who knew his *Star Trek* minutiae just a little too well. He'd lost count of the number of times Trent had protected him from bullies and threatened to beat up any kid who so much as looked sideways at him. He'd always stuck up for him, given him advice and done all the big-brother stuff that had made up for Will's lack of siblings. They'd had their first beers together, choked on their first cigarettes at the same time.

Fallen in love with the same frickin' girl.

Not that Trent knew it. Will had always been careful to keep his feelings for Em a secret from him. There was one thing best mates should never fight over.

Will took a deep breath. 'Okay, all right. I'll keep an eye on her for you. But that's all.'

'Thank you!' Trent fired at him triumphantly. 'You're the best, Will. I really mean that.'

Damn!

Will clicked the phone off, looking around the wharf but not really seeing anything, as his moral obligations seemed to surround him like the metal bars of a cage.

You don't hit on your best mate's girl. You just don't do it. You don't even think about doing it.

Even though he doesn't deserve her.

'Man overboard!' someone cried out as the siren on the wharf began to wail.

What the?!

Will shoved his phone back in his pocket and looked around. The men beside him were also glancing around for evidence of an emergency. The siren continued to sing. Apparently, it wasn't a drill.

Great!

Time for the climax of his day from hell. The guys next to him began putting down their equipment. His crane driver hopped out of his seat. Dipper grabbed him by the arm.

'Come on, Boy Scout, gotta get to the muster point.'

'I know, I know.' He wrenched his arm free. 'I went to the safety induction too, you know.'

Dipper grinned. 'Did ya? Didn't see ya. But then didn't see anyone go overboard just now either.'

'Neither did I.' Will frowned. 'It's gotta be a false alarm.'

'Well, you can't just ignore it,' Dipper grunted and walked off.

He'd be lying if he said he hadn't considered it. Em was probably in the office by now. He wanted to catch her before the day ended.

He glanced at his watch. It was knock-off. Too late. Emily would be going back to the resort.

Great!

He followed Dipper to the muster point. It was marked with a big red sign located in the right corner where the wharf met the jetty. Wardens in orange hard hats had their lists. You had to get your name ticked off so they could work out who had gone over. It was going to be a time-consuming process given there had to be at least a hundred men there. In the meantime, rescuers were already heading for the tugboat.

With a bit of time on their hands, Dipper began to regale the boys with his adventures from two days earlier.

'Picked her up from the airport in the afternoon. And, *mate*,' he gave them all the look, 'she's a looker!'

Will's ears immediately pricked but he tried to keep his interest out of his face. He hoped Dipper wasn't talking about Emily.

'Hot?' the crane driver inquired.

'Smokin',' said Dipper as the men around him began to close in eagerly.

'Big tits?' asked a rigger.

'Nah,' Dipper shook his head, 'wouldn't say she's got more than a handful but nice legs. Really nice legs.'

'Blonde?' another man asked.

'Brunette,' Dipper informed. 'Big brown eyes. Nice smile.'

Will frowned. They had to be talking about Emily.

Although discussing a good-looking woman was a popular pastime for the guys, he had to admit he wasn't enjoying listening to them discuss Emily's physical attributes like items on a dessert menu. His protective nature was roused even without Trent's request.

'And just so you all know,' Dipper shook his finger at the crowd, 'I saw her first.' They all laughed, but Will couldn't crack a smile. He began to wonder at the wisdom of having invited her to a place where there were so many men. All he'd been thinking about was improving her job situation.

And getting her away from Trent. And maybe finally having a chance with her yourself.

He didn't want to think about his own motives just now. If he'd really brought Emily here to try and hit on her, then he was just as manipulative as Trent, who was busy playing the field back in Perth.

The truth was, it was just one big mess and the person it most concerned didn't even know it. There was also one other issue that he hadn't counted on, which was dawning on him more brightly with each passing second. There were at least four hundred female-starved men on this job, all with their own agenda.

Good one, Will. These guys fought over girls like seagulls over bread scraps. He should have known she was going to be popular.

His thoughts were broken as someone punched him lightly in the arm. 'You're awfully quiet.'

He blushed as everyone looked at him.

'I think the little graduate's considering his chances.'

'Is that so?' Dipper raised his eyebrows in challenge.

'My money's on Boy Scout,' a welder announced.

'I'm backing Dipper. Women like older men,' remarked a crane driver who had to be close to retirement.

A man they called Spooks lifted a long nose to the wind. 'I smell a bet coming!'

'Er, guys,' Will began desperately.

But Spooks, who had always been a bit of a showman, whipped off his hard hat and held it out. Half bowed, he stretched out his other arm, gathering the crowd to him like a circus ringmaster. 'Okay, this is how it's going to work. Place your IOUs now, gentlemen. Dipper or Boy Scout? Choose your horse! Winners will get their money back plus a share in the loser kitty proportional to their bet.'

'Well that's easy.' Dipper laughed, taking out his pocket notepad. In large letters he wrote, *Dipper for $10*, signed it and threw it in the pot.

This unfortunate gesture started a frenzy. To Will's horror several IOUs fluttered into the hard hat and not just ones backing Dipper. He was equally popular.

This is not good.

Spooks turned on him, his eyes twinkling wickedly. 'Not going to back yourself, Boy Scout? Where's your fighting spirit?'

He glared at Spooks. 'You can't do this.'

'Oh, can't I now?'

Just then the warden stepped into the fray to take their names and Spooks smoothly put his hard hat back on head, IOUs and all. The warden was none the wiser.

Five minutes later, they were all told they could go. No man had gone overboard: it was a false alarm triggered by a power failure. The electricity had gone out briefly and when it had resumed one of the alarms had been set off accidently. In frustration, Will turned to confront Spooks and saw him already backing away. The pieces of notepaper were now in his hand and he was shuffling them like a deck of cards. With a wink at Will and a small salute, he turned away. Will wanted to catch him but two other men joined him and Spooks folded the documents and put them in the back pocket of his pants. His gambling operation was now officially under the table.

Damn him!

Will gritted his teeth. Spooks was not going to let this go. The man thrived on drama. He and Dipper had just signed themselves on to Hay Point's own personal reality TV show. Only it was live!

He glanced at his watch. It was nearly six o'clock. By the time he got back to shore, Em would have well and truly left the office. He pulled out his phone, wondering if he should call her.

There was a voicemail message.

'Hi, my safety induction finished at four so I got back to my unit early. If I'm not home when you get here, I've gone to sit by the pool. After all, I should soak up some of this resort magic while I can, right?'

Shit! Could things get any worse?

Her message had been left nearly two hours earlier so he knew it was probably too late to warn her but he sent her an urgent text message anyway.

Don't go to the pool!

Chapter 8

Emily

Behind her unit, indeed behind all the units, was a central courtyard, populated by a few large shady palms, park benches and picnic tables. In the very centre of the community area was a large fenced-off pool with water that sparkled like crystal. Around it were ten white deck chairs, gathered in pairs sharing large blue and white beach umbrellas.

At four-thirty that afternoon it seemed like the perfect spot to relax and think.

Half an hour later she realised that was a misguided assumption. They appeared slowly in twos and threes, a couple carrying Eskies between them. Before long there were at least twenty men standing around the pool. She couldn't help but notice that none of them were wearing bathers and she was feeling decidedly naked in her blue bikini.

She got out of the water and, with as much dignity as she could muster, walked from the pool steps to the deck chair where she had laid her towel. Her legs wobbled as the air thinned and twenty pairs of eyes locked onto her arse like missile-launchers.

She heard the 'pssst' of several cans opening around her as she snatched her towel off the chair and quickly wrapped it around her trembling body. With bare legs and shoulders, she still felt only mildly protected from wandering eyes. The men took a swig and then one of them spoke to her, 'Hey.'

'Er, hi,' she said tentatively, trying to relax under all the attention.

'How about a drink?'

She waved a nervous hand in front of her chest. 'Oh, I don't –'

He pushed an open beer can into her hand anyway. It was all icy wet and slippery. She nearly dropped it.

Nearly.

What did fall was the towel that had been held up under her armpits.

When this covering suddenly pooled at her feet, a few whistles flew round the courtyard. The guy who had slipped her the drink was slapped a couple times on the back.

'Yeah, mate, she likes *you*!'

She hastily picked up her towel, trying to rewrap herself with one hand, sloshing beer everywhere.

'Doesn't hold her drink too well though,' another man laughed. '*Literally*.'

There were guffaws all round. Emily put the beer down and righted herself. The group had now doubled in size. There had to be close to fifty guys in that courtyard – where had they all come from?

'Are you having a party?' she asked the man who had given her the drink.

'Nope.' His eyes twinkled at her. 'Just a small gathering. This happens every night.'

Every night.

'Well, maybe I'll just leave you to it.' She put the beer down on the table next to her and was about to move forward when he barred her path. 'No way. It's not often we get a lady along. Stay awhile. Brighten our evening.'

And so the introductions began. She lost track of the names and the winks that went with them. Emily had nothing against being popular but the men seemed to be as friendly as they were mocking. They switched between talking *to* her to talking *about* her as if she wasn't there at an alarming rate.

She wanted to go but couldn't seem to achieve it, short of being blunt to the point of rudeness and telling them all to leave her alone and get out of her way. Fear and frustration made standing in wet bathers even colder. She was just about to bite the bullet and risk angering them when a friendly female voice surprised her.

'Hey, Emily.' She turned quickly to see the resort owner, Charlotte, walk up to the group. She had met the woman briefly on the evening she'd first arrived. Several men took a step back.

'Take cover!' someone yelled. 'It's the landlady.'

'I suppose it's a waste of my breath to ask you to pack up your booze?' she said to the gathered crowd.

Many laughed uproariously and one guy, who had just finished his drink, threw his can at the bin and missed it by a mile. It was clear many others had been attempting the same target practice and failing dismally.

Charlotte returned her eyes to Emily, ignoring the obvious provocation. 'Just wondering if you're free for me to take a look at your air-conditioning unit now?'

Air-conditioning unit?

'You said it wouldn't switch on.'

'I –' Then she realised what the woman was trying to do for her. She clasped her hands together gratefully. 'That would be perfect. *Thank you.*'

'Great.'

Under a barrage of protests, which they successfully ignored by focusing on each other, Charlotte and Emily took off out of the fence gate and down the brick path to Emily's backyard. They ducked through her sliding door, shut it and drew her blinds.

Phew!

Em's gaze flew to her rescuer. 'Thank you so much, Charlotte.'

Her friend laughed. 'No problem at all but please, call me Lottie.'

'Well, Lottie,' Emily grinned. 'You have no idea how grateful I am that you came along just at that minute.'

Charlotte nodded. 'I saw you through the back window of my house and thought you could use an excuse to leave.'

'Good call.' Emily nodded. 'Can I get you a drink? It's the least I can do.'

'Well . . .' Charlotte glanced at her watch. 'I suppose I've got a little time.'

'Tea, coffee, soft drink, water?'

'A tea would be great.'

As Emily walked into her kitchen, Charlotte sat down at the little dining table in front of her counter. 'So you're from Perth, are you?'

'Born and raised.'

Charlotte smiled. 'There seem to be as many West Australians on this project as there are Queenslanders.'

'I'm just enjoying the opportunity,' Emily responded enthusiastically. 'I think tomorrow, though, I'll check out Salonika Beach in lieu of the pool.'

Charlotte winced. 'Do you have a stinger suit? It's jellyfish season.'

'A stinger suit?'

Charlotte laughed at what must have been the comical expression of dismay on her face. 'Sorry, love, the ocean's teeming with nasties this time of year. Believe me, you wouldn't want to get stung.'

'Oh.'

Can somebody please give me some good news?

'I'm sure you'd be able to pick up a full body suit in town,' Charlotte suggested. 'That is, when you have some time off.'

Emily brought around the tea and sat down. 'Well, that's not happening any time soon. Not that I'm complaining. This is the best job I've ever had, even with all its warts.'

'You're kidding.' Charlotte wrinkled her nose.

Emily's phone, which was sitting in the fruit bowl between them, buzzed. She plucked it out and quickly scanned the message, then laughed. 'My friend Will just warned me not to go to the pool.'

Charlotte also laughed. 'I like Will; he's good value.'

'You know him?' Emily asked casually, surprised at the irrational flood of jealousy and suspicion that suddenly pricked her.

'Not well,' Charlotte acknowledged, 'but he stands out. He's one of the few guys on this job who actually respects my property.'

Emily shot her a sympathetic look. 'Damn, that's no good.'

'Tell me about it,' Charlotte sighed. 'So I take it you met Will when you arrived?'

'No.' Emily shook her head as fond memories resurfaced. 'We go way back – known each other for years. I can't even remember the day we met . . . No, wait, yes, I can.'

She smiled as the memory materialised in her head.

It had been first year, third week of semester one. She was sitting on the steps outside their lecture theatre trying to work out the answer to a tricky assignment problem. He had been leaning against a pillar behind her and, unbeknownst to her, reading over her shoulder. She hadn't even realised he was there till he said, 'It's two hundred and thirteen kilo newtons.'

'It's what?' She glanced up from her calculator and swivelled around to look at him. 'Did you say something?'

'It's two hundred and thirteen kilo newtons.' He smiled in the only way Will could, with enthusiasm and a complete lack of guile.

She pursed her lips. 'And you know this because . . .?'

'I worked it out last night.'

'You could be wrong.'

'I compared my answer to Jake's and Caleb's this morning,' he shrugged. 'It's two hundred and thirteen kilo newtons. Do you want to know the angle as well?'

'No,' she retorted. 'I'll work it out myself.'

'Then I wouldn't put that force vector there.' He bent down and ran his finger on the page against her free body diagram. She remembered a sudden zap of awareness. He was close enough for her to breathe in his scent, which was grass and sunshine. Will had always loved to lie on the lawn between lectures, reading his notes. That or shoot a footy across the oval with a few of his mates.

'Are you always this tenacious?' she demanded.

'Actually not really. My name's Will, by the way.' He'd come down the steps then, folded his tall, lean body and sat down beside her.

'Emily.'

'Nice to meet you.'

She recollected liking his smile immediately and the way his hair flopped into his eyes. The stubble that gave him the just-rolled-out-of-bed look was extremely sexy.

'May I?' He indicated her pen.

'Sure,' she shrugged, 'why not?' She handed it over and he corrected a couple of her formulas.

'There, that's better. You almost had it right.'

'Thanks,' she murmured and retyped the new numbers into her calculator. The answer flashed up on the screen. 'Two hundred and thirteen kilo newtons.'

'What did I tell you?'

'Thanks for your help,' she murmured, meeting his eyes with a shy tilt of her lips.

'Any time.' He stared back, holding her gaze for what felt like just a second too long.

A throat had cleared beside them and they'd both jumped.

'Sasha. Hey!' Will exclaimed, leaping up to greet the pretty, dark-haired girl who had just joined them.

'Hey.' Sasha responded to his peck on the lips but had her eyes trained on Emily. 'Sorry I took so long.'

'That's all right.' Will turned back to her. 'Emily, this is my girlfriend, Sasha. Sasha, this is Emily.'

'Oh hi,' Emily stood up. 'Nice to meet you.'

She remembered swallowing her disappointment with a smile before packing up her bag and hastening away from the couple. It was strange how only now she was recalling that her first reaction to Will had been attraction. Or perhaps not so strange, given the effect he'd had on her in the portable toilet the other day.

Was it poor timing that had kept them only friends for so long? She'd met Trent through Will eighteen months later and the law student had asked her out immediately. By the time Will had broken up with Sasha, she'd been well and truly entrenched in her own relationship.

'What's the matter?' Charlotte asked.

Emily looked up and blushed. She'd zoned out while the other woman was still sitting there. Shame on her.

'Nothing, sorry, just lost in the memory. It's strange how much things change over time.'

'Life does have its twists and turns,' Charlotte agreed, sipping her tea.

Emily's phone buzzed again. 'Sorry. I'll just turn this off.' She picked it up to do so when she noticed the new text message wasn't from Will.

It was from Trent.

'Go ahead and read it.' Charlotte sipped her tea again. 'You look like you want to.'

'It's from my ex.' Emily frowned. 'So I do and I don't. We only broke up about a month ago.'

'Oh,' Charlotte nodded. 'You must have some mixed feelings.'

More like conflicted and dissatisfied.

With sigh of resignation, she clicked the message open.

It was a mere three words.

I miss you.

She groaned. 'Now what am I supposed to do with that?' She showed the message to Charlotte before turning the phone off.

'Does he want to get back together?'

'Who knows? One thing I'm not very good at is playing games. I've always preferred being upfront. So shoot me.'

Charlotte held up her hands. 'No arguments from this end, babe. I think, if you can't be honest, then why are you in the relationship in the first place?'

'Exactly.' Emily put her chin in her palm. If she and Trent got back together, things would have to change, that's for sure. She was only just realising how much of a doormat she'd been in that relationship – letting him call all the shots.

She was having so much fun here, free from his influence. Today she'd gone on a safety induction and learned all about what *not* to do on a construction site. She could see now why Caesar had been so angry with Will for taking her out without proper training. Still, it had been worth it. The wharf was a majestic wonder, the sight of which had given her a confidence boost like no other. Of course, it didn't explain her strange reaction to Will in the loo, where her hormones had taken a giant leap to Planet Crazy.

What was that about?

Pressed up against him, she'd started having all these insane thoughts. Even now just the memory made embarrassment creep up her neck. They'd had a brother/sister relationship for years. He would laugh if he knew what she'd been thinking.

She took a deep breath and plastered a smile on her face. Now was not the time to be mulling over that.

'So,' she focused on Charlotte, 'tell me what I can do here without a stinger suit on. I'm dying to explore Queensland.'

Charlotte grinned. 'Well, lucky for you, it's pretty big.'

They sat there chatting for ages. Before Emily knew it, an hour had flown by, and then another. When they'd exhausted the sights of Queensland, they spoke about the project and then about the men. They swapped stories about some of the funny characters they'd met and the harassment they'd endured.

'You know, if I was a man,' Charlotte complained to her crossly, 'I wouldn't have to put up with all the crap going on out there right now. They'd listen to me when I asked them to clean up their act. They wouldn't dare make a mess of my property like that.'

'If I were a man,' Emily mused, 'my high-visibility vest would fit me.'

Charlotte chuckled.

'I wouldn't be sitting practically under the photocopier *and* I'd have real work by now.'

'We should start a club.' Charlotte grinned. 'We could call it Sisters on Site.'

Emily nodded enthusiastically. 'You can only join if you know how to whinge.'

'Deal!' They giggled as they shook on it. As the moment of agreement ended Charlotte happened to glance out the window and notice how dark it had got.

'Oh no! What time is it?' Her eyes flicked to her watch. 'Zara is going to kill me. I've left her with Mum for two hours!' She hastily pushed out her chair. 'Looks like it's going to be frozen dinners tonight.'

'Does your mum need a lot of care?' Emily asked.

'Yes. She has Alzheimer's disease and her memory is all over the place. Sometimes she's in the present, but most of the time she's living in the past. Her co-ordination is also pretty low. She struggles with simple things like showering and getting dressed. She needs *a lot* of help.'

Emily's brow creased. 'It must be tough on you.'

Charlotte seemed to take her sympathy in stride, dismissing it with a wave of her hand. Emily, however, was sure it was because she didn't want to draw attention to herself. Being a carer like that would be hard and very draining. She looked at her new friend with growing admiration.

'Well,' Charlotte smiled, 'I definitely don't get much time to just hang out like this. Thanks for this afternoon. I really enjoyed chatting with you.'

'Me too,' said Emily and on impulse gave her a hug.

'Oh well, I better go now.' Charlotte pulled away, slightly pink in the face. 'I'll see you round.'

'Definitely.'

As the older woman let herself out, Emily turned back to their two empty mugs sitting on the table and felt the joy of a new friendship spread warmly through her chest. It was just another benefit of this trip away from Perth, her old life and Trent. As her thoughts returned to her ex she frowned.

Why was he texting her?

Wasn't he seeing someone new?

There was knock at the door and she went to answer it. Will stood on her front porch, his worried expression accompanied by the sound of croaking cane toads. There were obviously some hiding in the dark bushes behind him.

'Sorry I couldn't get here sooner.' He seemed to be panting, like he'd come running over. 'Caesar held me up at work again. I was worried when I got your message about the pool.'

His eyes ran over her scantily clad body and she realised for the first time since Charlotte had left that she was still in her bathers with a sarong wrapped around her waist. She was dry now but it didn't stop gooseflesh from breaking out on her skin as Will's eyes travelled over her bikini top, seeming to pause on her chest.

He's not perving on you. He's Will. He doesn't even notice you have breasts. For goodness' sake, stop standing there like a seal with a fish in its mouth and let him in.

She stepped back and croaked, 'Come in.'

'Er . . . sure.' Will scratched his head, averting his eyes from her as he stepped over the threshold.

She reined in her rioting senses. 'I'm fine. Charlotte rescued me and we came back here and had a long cup of tea.'

'Oh, that's great,' he said, turning to face her again, this time keeping his eyes above her neck. 'I'm sorry about today. I meant to go over some stuff about the drive tower with you so you can start doing some real work tomorrow. But Caesar was keeping me so busy. Sometimes I think he's doing it on purpose.'

'Will, don't worry about it,' she assured him. 'I'm in no hurry. I did only just get here.'

As they walked into the main living room again, she saw her phone sitting on the table and said, 'I got a message from Trent today.'

'Did you?' He didn't look up and she wondered briefly if she should tell him about it. After all, Will was Trent's best friend. In this instance, his loyalties were divided. But it was too late now: she'd already opened the topic.

'He said he misses me.'

He still didn't look up. 'Do you miss him?'

'Yes, in a way.' She hesitated. 'But it's not just about that any more. I've been here for two days and I've been focusing on myself and what I want and . . . I was starting to feel like I was moving on and now . . . I'm back to square one.'

'What's square one?' He finally met her gaze.

'Confusion. Worry. Self-doubt. Don't get me wrong, I'm glad Trent misses me. I've been hoping and wishing for weeks that he'd have a change of heart or realise that all we shared couldn't have been for nothing. And now that he has . . . I don't know, it's like an anti-climax. I don't know what to do with it.'

'Well there's no need for you to make any ground-breaking decisions immediately,' Will suggested. 'Just take some time to think, consider your options.'

She smiled. 'You're right, of course.'

'Of course.' He nodded jovially.

'Has Trent . . .' she wrung her hands '. . . has he said anything about me to you?'

Will hesitated. 'Em, I don't think it's fair that I get involved.'

'Of course, I'm sorry.' She bit her lip. 'I shouldn't have asked. Forget I said anything.'

'I'm not mad,' she heard him say above her bowed head. 'I just want you to know that I'd never tell him anything you said about him. And it should be the same vice versa.'

'I know, Will, and I trust you.' She wanted to reach out and touch his arm then but something held her back. Something in the air that made her feel like she'd waded out of the shallow and into the deep. She clenched her fingers tightly into a fist and tried to say lightly, 'So do you want to stay for dinner?'

'Thanks,' he grinned, 'but I'm beat. Just thought I'd make sure you were okay.'

'I'm good.'

'Well, I think I'll head off then.' He pointed at the door. She nodded listlessly as he went off down the hall. She walked back to the living room where her phone lay on the table and picked it up. Opening Trent's message up again, she looked at the words one last time.

I miss you.

With grim determination she typed one word and pushed send.

Why?

Chapter 9

Charlotte

After her long chat with Emily Woods, Charlotte realised there was a lot to be said for having a friend to talk to about your problems. Her brother tried his best, but he tended to avoid touchy-feely subjects like the plague. Her sister Zara was too young and her mother was, let's face it, a space cadet.

Unfortunately, she didn't think she was close enough to Emily to start dumping on her just yet. And Charlotte had a *lot* of things to dump.

Mark Crawford for a start.

Don't take this the wrong way, but you're a very attractive woman.

Charlotte slammed the dishwasher shut and grabbed a sponge to viciously attack the kitchen bench.

What is the wrong way to take that?

As a come on? Not as a come on? The man was married with a recently delivered private letter from his wife.

A *love* letter, obviously.

So she had to ask the question: why come to the door, practically naked, and tell another woman you find her attractive? Why tell her anything at all? She yanked open the pantry doors and began removing items for lunch. Bread, butter, Vegemite.

I mean, it's not like he's a nice person and is in the habit of doling out praise.

Or reading correspondence for that matter.

She was quite sure that he had still not looked over her list. In fact, she was positive about it. There had been zero change. Gathering the plastic bag in her kitchen bin, she tied it in a knot and headed outside.

As if to prove her point there was a Barnes Inc loony sitting in a folding chair out the front of his unit. He was wearing nothing but football shorts and surrounded by a number of squashed beer cans – evidence of his drunken state.

'Hello there, me lovey.'

'Good evening,' she said shortly.

'Why not come and chat to the cane toads with me?' He waved a hand, indicating she should come over. 'They understand you, you know.' His eyes were wild and his tone was hushed. The deep croak of the cane toad echoed in the evening air as though to punctuate his statement. 'They're lonely,' he added. 'They wanna talk to ya.'

Uh-huh. Last time she checked, cane toads were fat, ugly and poisonous. And no matter how lonely and dejected she sometimes felt, she hadn't hit rock bottom quite yet. Until such time she was going to stick to talking to people rather than amphibians. 'No thanks.'

His wicked laugh followed her up the footpath as she walked back to her unit.

Her mother and Zara were seated on the couch in front of the television. Her mother was watching but not actually seeing the pictures moving on screen. Her sister was reading a novel. Charlotte sat down next to her.

'So, how was school today?'

Zara glanced up sullenly. 'Crap. You know, now that I'm a *complete* loser.'

Charlotte looked heavenwards. 'Dare I ask?'

'I had to tell Rosemary that I'm not allowed to go to her beach party,' Zara imparted in the voice of tragedy.

'Very sensible.'

'It was *totally* humiliating. I'm a social outcast.'

'Really?' Charlotte feigned mild interest.

'I might as well go hang out with the nerds and be done with it.' Zara threw her book down.

'Don't knock the nerds.' Charlotte shook her finger. 'One day they'll be rich.'

'Oh yes,' said their mum, who surprised them by showing she'd been listening. 'How very true.'

Zara groaned.

'What's the matter, dear?' her mum asked. 'Do you have a headache?'

'No, Mum,' Zara said through her teeth, frustration seeming to make it difficult for her to speak.

'How was school today?' their mother asked.

Zara ignored the question, addressing Charlotte again. 'Can't you understand that I just *really* want to go?'

'Of course I understand,' Charlotte said softly. 'I was a teenager once myself, Zara. But it's just too dangerous for a girl your age.'

'Nothing's safe with you,' Zara protested. 'I'm not allowed to walk around the resort any more, swim in the pool, eat in the restaurant. You've taken all the fun out of living here. I feel like I'm in jail.'

'Don't over-dramatise, Zara.'

Her sister picked up her book again and returned to her reading. Charlotte decided to let her but her mum broke the silence again after thirty seconds.

'So, Zara, how was school today?'

'Argghhh!' Zara stood up, fists clenched. 'She's like a bloody goldfish.'

Charlotte didn't blame Zara for her frustration but the last thing she wanted to do was upset their mother.

'Zara,' she said quietly, 'don't shout.'

'Don't you hate this place?' Zara asked. Her voice was calmer but seemed all the more deadly for it. Charlotte raised her eyes from rubbing her mother's back.

'Zara –'

'I hate everything about it.'

'You know this is the best place for Mum to be right now.'

'Why?' Zara demanded. 'It's not like she's getting any better. Why don't we leave? Go live in Brisbane. Make a fresh start. Mum can come too. Maybe I can even meet my dad.'

Virginia choked. 'I do not want to live in Brisbane.'

Charlotte quickly passed her a glass of water that was sitting on the coffee table in front of them.

'Zara,' she met her sister's eyes, 'this is not a good time to discuss this.'

'Why not? We're not doing anything else.'

Panic fluttered on Virginia Templeton's face. 'I do not want to live in Brisbane, Lottie.'

'It's okay, Mum,' Charlotte rubbed her back again. 'We're not going anywhere.' She threw a meaningful glare at her sister but Zara ignored her.

'Well, I for one think it would be good for me to meet him. I mean, even if it's just once, for my own curiosity.'

Their mother's glass rattled loudly as she replaced it with trembling hand back on the table.

'You're not meeting him, Zara,' Charlotte said firmly, squeezing their mother's shoulders. 'It's too hard.'

'Much too hard,' her mother muttered weakly. Zara dismissed her and focused on Charlotte.

'It wouldn't be that hard. I mean, jails are like hospitals, aren't they? They have visiting hours, for the family, right?'

No!

'Zara,' Charlotte began slowly and succinctly, 'it's completely impossible.'

Zara was silent and for a couple of seconds Charlotte held out faint hope that she had dropped the subject. Then she lifted her chin and Charlotte saw a calculating sparkle light her eyes. 'Just give it to me straight, Lottie. Does he even know I exist?'

Charlotte glanced sharply at their mother, who had gone a strange shade of green. 'I don't know.'

'Does he, Mum?' Zara demanded.

Virginia Templeton's fists clenched. 'I will not live anywhere near Dennis Mayer.'

'Dennis Mayer?' Zara's eyes brightened. 'Is that his name?'

Charlotte hastily intervened, hoping her mother would not inadvertently tell her anything else. 'Look, Zara, he's just not the type of man who ever wanted children. He won't be pleased to see you.'

'I want to find that out for myself,' Zara returned stubbornly. 'I want to see what he's like. So he stole a few things. Maybe he had a good reason.'

'No, no, no!' Virginia jumped to her feet, startling them both with her outburst. 'I forbid it.'

'Mum.' Charlotte tried to grab her hand but she stepped out of reach.

'Leave me alone.' Virginia stumbled away, babbling incoherently as she left the room.

Charlotte wanted to follow her but knew she had to end this conversation first. Make sure that it never happened again.

'He didn't have a good reason, Zara,' she said quietly. 'He's in there because he's supposed to be in there and he doesn't want to see you.'

'Or maybe you don't want me to see him,' Zara snapped shrewdly.

Charlotte set her face against emotion. 'When you're eighteen you can do whatever you like. I won't stop you. But until then, he is out of our lives and we're going to keep it that way.'

Zara shrugged. 'When the time comes you might not be able to stop me.' On this threat, she stomped out of the room in her mother's wake.

A shudder rippled through Charlotte's body. Her only consolation was that it would be rather difficult for a teenager without a licence to run away from Salonika beach. It wasn't like she could hop on a bus or a train and be out of her sister's reach before she knew it. The only method of escape was walking and there was nowhere to walk to for miles. The bus that came by was the school one and that wasn't going to take her to the airport any time soon.

It didn't stop her worrying for the next couple of days, though.

Zara did not raise the subject of her father again but she didn't speak to Charlotte about anything else either. In the morning, she ate her breakfast in silence. On Tuesday when she got home from school she went straight to her bedroom and closed the door. Charlotte did not see her again till dinner-time. On Wednesday, it was clear she intended to do the same thing. Charlotte was folding laundry in the living room when Zara got home. The girl gave her one mutinous look before taking herself off to her room again. Charlotte sighed as she looked down at her full basket.

I couldn't have been this difficult as a teenager.

This was the downside of being both sister and parent. She wanted to be her friend, not just her drill sergeant, but it seemed they could find no common ground. One of them had to give a little.

What can I do?

A compromise maybe?

She put down her basket and went to knock on Zara's door. There was no answer so she tried the handle and the door swung open. Zara, who had been rapidly texting someone, shoved her phone into her backpack.

'You can't just barge in like that.'

'I didn't.' Charlotte tried to be reasonable. 'I knocked first but you didn't answer.'

Her sister didn't respond. So she took a deep breath and took a couple more steps into the room.

'You know, I was thinking. Why don't you invite Rosemary over one weekend? You could have a sleepover. I can make nachos for dinner and we can eat lots of chocolate.' She grinned. 'I kind of need a bit of comfort food myself.'

Zara rolled her eyes. 'No thanks.'

'Come on, Zara.' Charlotte sat on the bed. 'I'm trying to make an effort here.'

'Well, what are we going to do, Lottie? Sit in this room all day? You won't let me out any more with the Barnes Inc crew roaming around.'

'I told you, it's not safe. There's too much smoking and drinking. I worry about you.' Charlotte tried to take her hand but Zara moved it away petulantly.

'You're always worried. Why can't you just trust me? I'm not stupid, you know.'

Charlotte grabbed her by the face, a palm on each cheek, so she was forced to look into her eyes. Deep blue ones, like her own. 'I don't think you're stupid. I would never think that. I know you're a good kid, Zara. It's not you I don't trust, it's them.' Charlotte released her and put a tired hand to her temple. 'Tell me what it is I can do to make you happy because I am sick of fighting with you.'

Zara bit her lip.

'Tell me.'

'I want to see my father.'

Anything but that. Lottie pursed her lips.

'I know you can help me do it.' Zara raised her eyes bravely. 'We don't have to tell Mum.'

'That's not my call, Zara.'

'You say you trust me. But how can I believe you when you won't even let me see him?'

'You wouldn't want to see him if you knew –' Charlotte broke off.

'Knew what?' Zara demanded, with all the triumph of someone who knew they had stumbled on a secret. 'Tell me.'

'I can't.'

'Tell me or I'll run away and ask him myself.'

'Zara!' Charlotte's mouth dropped open as she was finally faced with the deadliest weapon in Zara's arsenal.

'Tell her.'

Both their gazes flew to the door.

'Mum,' Charlotte exclaimed, rising to her feet. 'How long have you been standing there?'

'Tell her, Lottie,' Their mother leaned heavily against the frame. 'Tell her.'

Sweat broke out on Charlotte's upper lip. She hadn't thought this hateful task would come so soon or that it would fall to her.

'Are you sure?'

Her mother shut her eyes briefly. 'No. Wait.'

'Wait for what?' Zara asked as their mother left the room. 'She's babbling again, Lottie. She doesn't know where she is.'

Charlotte bit her lip. 'We don't know that.' It seemed like just for a second her mother had been herself again, back in the present, where that haunted look marked her face, her shoulders drooped and her soul stepped back from her eyes. In a way, having Alzheimer's had provided her with a means of escape and that was at least one aspect of the disease to be grateful for.

Charlotte watched the door waiting for her to return.

'Is she going to come back?' Zara demanded, completely oblivious to everything but her own need. 'Or is this just a joke?'

Charlotte's fingers dug painfully into the palm of her hand as she wondered frantically whether her mother really meant for her to tell Zara, and if she should. She'd read the studies done on this. Zara was old enough to know. She just needed some time to plan this, get Luke over, and make some bloody tea.

As if that's going to help.

Zara stood up. 'I'm going after her.'

Charlotte got up as well and followed her to their mother's room. It took them about two seconds to discover that Virginia Templeton had passed out on her bed and was snoring gently.

With a heavy sigh, Charlotte put the heel of her palm to her forehead. 'She must have had an episode and forgotten what she was doing.' She dropped her hand. 'Just as well, I suppose.'

At least this way she had more time. She could even contact that therapist in Mackay. After all, there was no telling whether Zara would be comfortable talking to her about it.

'What's this?' Zara said, twitching what looked to be a newspaper clipping out of her mother's hand.

Charlotte's head snapped up, but it was too late. Zara was already scanning the article. A gut-wrenching gasp ripped from her throat. And fear, like a shaft of ice, cut straight through Charlotte's heart.

Oh crap.

The clipping fell from Zara's fingers, fluttered to the ground like a stray piece of ash from a bonfire that had just ignited. Charlotte snatched it up, her eyes whipping across the headline.

Serial Rapist Finally Jailed.

The photograph beneath the damning words was a black-and-white picture of a forty-something man with frizzy hair, worn too long over the ears. Instinctively, she knew this was Zara's father even though her mother had never shown the article to her before. She looked just like him. There were many things her mother hadn't told her. Many secrets she felt still stood between them . . . not that she wanted to know everything. But seeing him, this man, who had ruined her mother's life and hacked away at some of her own, was a shock.

Her throat dried, her temperature fluctuated wildly between hot and cold. Putting a face to a name for the very first time was like reopening the wound.

His hands were cuffed. His dead eyes, the colour of which she couldn't discern, stared back at her emotionlessly. He neither smiled nor frowned at the camera but his expression of contented conceit made her lunch boil in her guts. She threw the article away from her, taking in shallow wheezy breaths. She couldn't bring herself to read the entire thing. She was so lost in her own painful memories of that time that she had forgotten her sister. Her eyes flew across the room and she found her at the foot of their mother's bed in the foetal position, rocking on her backside.

'Zara,' she cried, immediately sitting down beside her.

Her sister was weeping uncontrollably.

'Zara, talk to me.' She tried to put her arms around her sister but Zara flailed violently and then stood up.

'Don't.'

'Zara –'

Her sister's eyes, red and raw, flicked to their mother, her hand flinging out hysterically.

'She said he was a thief!'

'I'm sorry, Zara.' Charlotte made haste to explain. 'She had to lie to protect you.'

'No! You're lying now!' Zara clutched her belly and for a moment Charlotte was sure she was going to be sick. But the moment passed.

'Zara, you need to sit down. Here,' she grabbed a box of tissues from her mother's bedside table, 'let me wipe your face.'

'You're trying to trick me.' Zara pushed the words out between her teeth. 'This can't be right.'

Charlotte felt tears on her own face now. 'I wish it wasn't the truth, but it is. Mum was going to tell you when you were older.'

'I don't believe you. You're just trying to keep me away from him.'

'Zara, look at me,' Charlotte choked, holding out her hand though not daring to touch her. Zara raised her chin, defiance in the line of her jaw. 'Do you really think we'd be that cruel?'

Zara heaved a sob so big, her whole body convulsed before she turned around and stumbled out of there.

'Zara!' Charlotte called. 'Wait!'

But her sister had already broken into a wild run, fuelled by adrenaline and grief. This time she did not run to her bedroom though. She ran out the back door and onto the road. Charlotte ran after her, calling out. Zara did not stop. Instead she doubled her pace, running down the street, passed the widely spaced residential housing and then onto a lonely stretch of road leading to the jetty. It was only quarter to four in the afternoon, so the air was thick with tropical heat. Insects chirped and the smell of baked green leaves assailed her senses. Charlotte followed at least a few metres behind.

She began to sweat, her skin slick with moisture, but didn't break pace. She panted and heaved. Each breath became more difficult to inhale as her muscles began to burn from the exertion. A stitch threatened in her side but she ignored it.

She had to catch up.

Ahead, she could see that Zara was losing momentum and fight. Her body was swaying and she had wandered into the centre of the road.

A ute came around the corner at speed.

There was no energy left to scream.

Chapter 10

Mark

The figure was a blur on the road, which he saw mere seconds before he swerved to avoid it. His wheels hit the gravel of the shoulder in a cloud of dust as the car jerked to a halt.

'What the fuck?!' said Fish from the back seat, the papers he was holding flying up out of his hands and scattering on the floor. 'Aw shiiiiiitttt.'

Ignoring him, Mark threw open his door and got out in time to see the girl in the centre of the road collapse in shock. She moaned as her legs buckled under her and connected with road. It had been a very hot day and he knew it was probably burning through her jeans. In a few strides, he was by her side, lifting her off the scorching tar.

He carried her to the side of the road and placed her on the weedy but softer ground in front of the car. Another car door slammed. 'Well, I'll be bloody damned,' said Fish.

'Is she all right, Mark?' It was Will, who had also been in the car.

'Bring me some water,' he barked.

The girl slowly opened her eyes as the other two men walked over to them. They were the same miraculous blue as the ones belonging to the woman he was beginning to regard as his nemesis.

For a second, the girl's expression was blank, before fear crowded in.

'Here.' He placed the bottle of water that Will had brought over near her lips.

'Let go of me,' she croaked, struggling to sit up.

'I would by all means,' Mark purred, 'if I believed I wouldn't have to scrape you off the road again. If there's one thing I hate, it's having to do the same thing twice.'

'I'm not going to faint,' she rasped.

'Try to drink some more water,' Will suggested.

Running feet sounded on the road and they all turned around to see a curvaceous figure in tight jeans and a black singlet.

Of course, who else would it be? 'Ah, Ms Templeton. Your timing is impeccable.'

She was breathless and sweaty, strands of her auburn hair stuck to her forehead, her breasts heaving in gentle rhythm as she came to a stop, dropping immediately to her knees.

'Thank God,' she muttered.

'As much as I like to be thanked,' his lips curled, 'prayer is quite unnecessary.'

'Oh, just give her to me,' Charlotte snapped rather impatiently at his quip.

He transferred the girl into her arms, noticing with interest the way she closed her eyes and squeezed her tight, like she was the most precious thing in the world. It had been so long since he had held anyone like that, or been held like that. Love was so far removed from his life that looking at it now, naked before him, made him physically ache.

'Oh, Zara,' Charlotte whispered hoarsely into her girl's hair, 'they could have killed you.'

'I'm fine,' the girl responded.

'I was worried sick. Please don't do that again.'

'I . . . I'm sorry,' Zara said. 'I just lost it.'

'I know. I'm sorry too.' As they continued to hold each other, Mark cleared his throat and Charlotte finally opened her eyes again. 'Er, thank you,' she said. 'I can take it from here.'

There was obviously more going on than she was letting on but it was none of his business. Hell, the last thing he wanted to be involved in was Ms Templeton's personal affairs. Talk about nightmare.

He nodded curtly and was about to stand up when Zara gasped.

'What is it?' he asked. But she seemed too overcome to speak. Was she more hurt than he realised?

'It's the bird, Mark,' Will explained. 'I think we killed it.'

With relief, he followed the direction of Zara's gaze back to the front wheel of his car. There, lying beside it, certainly as if it were dead, was a scrub turkey, a black-feathered native bird with a fan-like tail, a bare red head and yellow wattle. It must have been roaming in the bush by the side of the road when the car swerved onto the shoulder. It was quite impressive when standing but this one lay limp on its side.

'Zara –' Charlotte began but the girl ignored her.

She put out her hand to stroke it. The bird shuddered and then to all their surprise tried to stand up. Unfortunately one of its rubbery legs didn't want to function. The limb was bent at an odd angle. It squawked in pain, the lame leg trembling as it tried to draw it up. It failed and collapsed on its side again.

Zara put the bottle of water down and scooped the bird into her arms. 'This turkey is hurt,' she announced quite unnecessarily.

'Not as hurt as you could have been,' Mark returned drily. 'What were you doing running in the middle of the road?'

'I wasn't thinking,' she muttered as she carefully felt the bird's wings.

'Why is it,' Mark mused to no one in particular, 'that people always give me that excuse? It's not even an excuse; it is an insult to their own character.'

His words made no impression on the girl. She was examining the turkey's wings. They didn't appear to be broken. She didn't look up, drawing the bird into her arms, a grim expression marking her young face. It pecked at her hand, its red head swaying about in panic. She tried to hold it close.

'I'm so sorry.'

All these apologies. Whatever were they for? And, more importantly, why were none of them directed at him?

'Wouldn't do that if I were you.' Fish looked derisively at the girl. 'That thing's dirty as hell. Full of germs, might catch something.'

Zara glared at his engineer. Not that Mark blamed her. He could have said the same thing about Fish. He was by far the most unkempt human being he had ever seen.

'What?' Fish raised bushy brows.

Will's mouth twisted as though he were trying hard not to laugh. He put a hand on his colleague's arm. 'Let it go, Fish.'

'You guys don't have to stick around,' Charlotte said again. 'I'm with my sister now. I'll make sure she's okay.'

'Yes, I thought she must be your sister,' Mark murmured. 'She looks like you.'

His casual remark seemed to have an entirely uncasual effect on the person it was directed at. Charlotte's wide eyes flew straight to her sister, who immediately looked up from the injured turkey, a kind of dead expression on her face.

'Really? You think I look like her?' Pain of some kind made Zara lose a little colour. 'I always thought I must look most like my father. And I do. I've seen his photograph.' She gulped in air but it didn't seem to help as she practically choked on the words. 'I . . . I look just like him.'

'Listen,' Charlotte interrupted her monologue to reclaim his attention, 'you were obviously headed somewhere. We don't want to make you late.'

'We have a meeting with a contractor in Sarina,' Mark told her, now wanting to stay just because he knew she wanted him to go. 'But it doesn't matter if we're late. Perhaps, Ms Templeton, you would like me to drive you and your sister back to the resort?'

'Here.' Will kneeled down beside Zara. 'I'll help you.'

He tried to take the turkey from Zara but she swung her body away.

'I'm not leaving it. Can't you see its leg is broken? It'll die of starvation or worse without treatment.'

Fish clucked his tongue. 'Come on, girlie, it's just a bush turkey. They're a dime a dozen. Like rats, really.'

'So you just want to abandon it?' Her voice shook.

'Well,' Fish shrugged, 'I suppose we can break its neck, if you think that would be more humane.'

Zara gasped in shock and choked back tears. 'Yes, that's what most people would do, wouldn't they? Kill it. Because it's not worth saving.'

Her eyes grew glassy and Charlotte immediately went to her side.

Mark frowned. 'Surely this turkey can't mean that much to you?'

'If he wants to kill it, he'll have to go through me.' Zara glanced up fiercely at Fish then turned to her sister. 'Lottie, we need to take this turkey to the vet.'

Ms Templeton, he noticed, was looking decidedly uncomfortable as she gazed down at the feathered victim no longer struggling in her sister's arms. 'Zara, I'm not really in a position to be footing heavy medical bills . . . or surgery for a turkey right now.'

Zara's mouth set into a mutinous line. 'We can't abandon it. It can't take care of itself.'

'Well,' Fish rubbed his chin thoughtfully, 'she doesn't want to break its neck but if you guys are keen maybe we could tie a brick to its foot and I could chuck it off the back of my boat tonight. It'll put me out a bit but,' he glanced at his watch, 'I'm willing to do it if I can get to this meeting on time.'

Mark watched Zara mentally throw a brick in his face and laid a hand on her shoulder. 'It's not your turn yet, my dear. In line, *please*.'

Charlotte, who had been examining the bird quietly, said, 'Honey, by the looks of him, even if we did take him to a vet, they would probably just advise us to put him down.'

'No.' Zara shook her head. 'We'll insist on treatment.'

Her sister winced. 'Zara, it'll be very expensive.'

'I'll pay for it.'

'Sweetie,' Charlotte pulled a face, 'you're not really in a position to pay for it either. Apart from the fact that we'll have to take care of the bird as it recovers. Give it medicine, buy it a cage or something. It's just not practical, Zara.'

'I won't let you or anyone kill it. I'll take care of it.'

'You say that now.'

'I know.' Fish raised his right hand as though the question had just been asked. 'Why don't we just back up the car and run over it again? Bound to kill it properly the second time.'

'Fish,' Will said warningly, 'if I were you I'd quit while I was ahead.'

Zara's eyes brightened as they rested upon the young man. Mark found himself feeling slightly piqued that she didn't consider him as the saviour in the bunch. After all, he had picked her up off the road.

'You would never drop it off the side of a boat, would you?' Zara said to Will sweetly.

'Er, no I wouldn't,' Will agreed.

'He doesn't have a boat!' Fish snorted scornfully. 'So how could he?'

'The man does have a point,' Mark mused.

Zara ignored him. 'Will you take him?'

'*What?*' Will started.

'Well, obviously we can't let him die. You just said you wouldn't kill him.'

'What I meant was –'

'Go on, William,' Mark murmured. 'What did you mean?'

'If all you intend to do is stand around mocking people, Mr Crawford,' Charlotte interrupted crossly, 'then I would appreciate it if you just stayed quiet.'

Mark pulled the sunglasses on his head down over his eyes. 'My apologies, Ms Templeton. But you'll find it very difficult to foist a half-dead turkey on any man even if he were of a sensitive spirit, as is young William.'

'He just called you a pussy,' Fish jeered.

Will glared at him.

Charlotte, however, was still focused on Mark. 'Thank you for that brilliant illumination, Mr Crawford,' she said scathingly. 'I don't suppose you have any further advice for us?'

'As a matter of fact I do, Ms Templeton. Give the bird to me.'

'What?' Zara looked up as he began to roll up his sleeves. 'Why?'

Mark's lip curled self-mockingly. 'As it happens, I'm in the market for a pet.'

'A pet?' Charlotte repeated scornfully. '*Please*.'

'You wound me, Ms Templeton.'

'He's going to secretly slaughter it.' Zara clutched Charlotte's hand in terror. 'I won't give it to him.'

'Then get in the car,' Mark gestured to the door, 'you can take it to the vet yourself. I'll just watch.'

'What about our meeting?' Fish demanded.

Mark glanced at his watch. 'We'll never make it now. Will, cancel it.'

'All right,' Will slowly agreed. 'Did you, er . . . want us to come to the vet as well?'

'No. You two will return to the office.'

'All right.' Fish seemed annoyed but resigned. 'Let's get back in the car.'

'No, there's no room now.' Mark shook his head. 'You'll have to walk.'

Fish gasped in outrage.

'And you've just been bumped for a turkey,' Will whispered smugly.

Fish growled.

'You mean it. You honestly mean it?' Zara was watching the proceedings in disbelief.

Mark inclined his head. 'I never say anything I don't mean.'

But Charlotte wasn't buying it. 'If you're playing some sort of game, Mr Crawford, this is not the time for it.'

Mark raised his eyebrows. 'Then perhaps you would like to accompany us as well, Ms Templeton, just to make sure I'm not taking the bird down some dark alley in order to put an end to its charmed life.'

He walked towards the car as though there were no question that they would follow. By now, Fish was bristling with anger and Will was looking down with a hand firmly over his mouth. Zara, on the other hand, was completely sold on the idea. She picked up the turkey, walked towards the car and slid straight into the backseat behind him.

'Come on, Lottie,' she called out. 'What are you waiting for?'

Charlotte glanced from her to Mark and then back again. 'I wish I knew.'

By the time Mark got back to the office it was past six o'clock. He still had a stack of work to do due to having wasted the balance of the afternoon on a turkey he was sorely beginning to regret adopting. Firstly, there was that God-awful trip to the vet in a car that was now fumigated with the smell of buttermilk and raspberries. Honestly, you could probably use *that woman's* shampoo as a topping for scones. And then there was the interminable wait in the vet's reception, in which he was sure she must have lost all blood circulation in her legs. How could you not, in jeans that tight?!

The turkey, a truly ungrateful creature, squawked at incessant intervals, reminding them all that it was in pain. As if he weren't experiencing some himself, listening to a fifteen-year-old go on and on about how soft its feathers were, how cute its clawed little feet and how intelligent its beady little eyes.

Yeah right.

More like how lucky its feathered little arse was to be alive.

He said as much in frustration and earned a pointed glare from *that woman*.

'If you don't like the bird why on earth are you adopting it?'

His throat had tightened because it was exactly the sort of question he didn't want to answer. 'A whim,' he said at last.

'Right,' she snorted.

Fortunately, the vet managed to fit them in before he shut up shop for the day and was very efficient in resetting the bone and fastening a split to the leg. He also put a plastic collar on the turkey so that it couldn't peck at it. A wise move, as the turkey had already proven itself to be remarkably stupid. Fortunately, the turkey did not need surgery but it would need to be brought back in a week for a check-up.

'A task that will no doubt fall to me,' he said as they were waiting in front of the reception counter to pay the bill, glancing intermittently at his watch.

'You need to get back to the office, don't you?' Charlotte said, watching this movement shrewdly.

'I'll have to stay back late tonight,' he sighed. 'I didn't expect this to take as long as it did.'

'Well, don't blame me,' she sniffed. 'It was all your idea.'

'Thank you for the reminder.'

'No problem.' She tossed her head. 'And just so you know, I'm not having that bird sleeping inside my unit.'

'I'll buy it a cage and it can sleep outside.'

'And when do you propose to buy this cage?' she asked, hands on hips. 'You just said you have to go back to work after this.'

'Well, maybe,' he glared at her, 'you'll just have to buy it for me and I'll sort it out with you when I get home.'

'I knew this was going to happen.' She glanced at her watch. 'I'm going to have to hurry if I want to get there before they close.'

'Er . . . excuse me.' The receptionist knocked on the desktop to get her attention. 'Will you or your husband be paying for today?'

Zara covered her mouth.

'We're not married,' Charlotte choked, going that cute but annoying shade of pink.

He clenched his teeth against an answering shade spreading up his chest and slapped his credit card down on the counter before snarling at the startled receptionist, 'I'll be paying.'

He finished work at eight o'clock that night, leaving the office when it was dark and making the short trip back to the resort bone-weary.

He was in no mood for a battle of wits with Charlotte Templeton, a circumstance that seemed to characterise all their meetings, but he had a feeling she would be very put out if he didn't show up to collect his turkey.

He walked into reception and rang the bell. She appeared a few minutes later not looking nearly as fresh as she usually did. Was it his imagination or did her eyes seem red-rimmed and her nose a little pink? She put the cage with the turkey in it on the floor in front of him.

'Good luck,' she said darkly as though hoping his new pet would punish him rather than really wishing him well.

She turned to go and something made him say, 'Ms Templeton, wait.'

Looking back she said somewhat impatiently, 'Yes, Mr Crawford?'

The words, *Are you okay?* hovered on his lips unasked. How was it any of his business? Why did he even care that she looked like she'd been crying? Or that her delectable lower lip was swollen as though she'd been chewing on it while nutting out a problem.

'Well, Mr Crawford?' She folded her arms.

'What should I call it?' he finally asked, lamely.

A twinkle lit her eye and he was glad to see that at least he had improved her mood. 'How about a family name, like Augustus?'

Refusing to acknowledge her jibe at his nickname, he merely nodded. Besides, he rather liked the calling; it had an intelligent ring to it. Picking up the cage by the handle, he said, 'Please tell your sister she may visit Augustus whenever she likes.'

'Trying to palm off responsibility, Mr Crawford?'

'Not at all,' he murmured. 'I just thought it might help.'

She drew in a sharp breath. 'Help with what?'

Realising that he was once more involving himself in her personal life, he hastily ignored the question. 'Good night, Ms Templeton.'

'Call me Charlotte,' she called after him.

He ignored that too.

The turkey proved to be rather easy to look after. He put it outside next to his bedroom window and it made not a peep all night long. In fact, he put its wellbeing completely out of his mind until the following morning while eating his breakfast. At this point, he realised that he hadn't given the bird anything to eat.

After yesterday's debacle he was already behind on his workload, so he decided that this was definitely a task he needed to delegate. He took Augustus into work with him.

'Ann, I need you in my office. *Now.*'

Momentarily stunned by the sight of him and his new pet, it took Ann a couple of seconds to grab a pen, a notepad, his morning coffee and follow him into his office, thus breaking for the second time in a fortnight his hour of silence. He hoped this wasn't the beginning of a string of more inconveniences.

He put the cage down on the desk and turned around. She handed him his coffee.

'Thank you.' He took a sip and then gestured to the cage. 'Ann, do you observe my turkey?'

She looked at it, licked her lips and inclined her head. 'Yes, sir, I do observe your turkey.'

The bird looked at her, cocking its head, its wattle trembling on its rubbery neck.

'Excellent. His name is Augustus. I would like a steel pen built behind this donga for him. Nothing fancy, you understand. I'm sure there's plenty of mesh and old steel members lying about. Have Dipper and a few of his men knock something up.'

She did allow herself a momentary pause before writing this down. 'All right, sir, I will notify him.'

'And I would also like you to buy some food for Augustus.'

'Food, sir?'

'Yes, food.' He raised his eyebrows. 'Turkeys eat, you know.'

She swallowed. 'Yes, I do know that, sir. But what do they eat?'

'How am I supposed to know?' Mark retorted crossly. 'Do I look like a turkey expert to you? Honestly, Ann, sometimes you can be incredibly tedious. Call someone. Find out.'

'All right, sir. And once I have the food, where should I put it?'

Mark rolled his eyes. 'In its mouth, of course. You will need to feed the turkey. He is quite sick and with that bucket on his head will probably need assistance.'

'From me, sir?'

Mark looked heavenwards for patience. 'Is there anyone else in the room?'

She squared her shoulders. 'I'm sorry, sir, but I have no experience taking care of turkeys.'

'Please don't apologise,' he sighed. 'I find forgiving people incredibly exhausting. If that's all your questions, I think you can go now, Ann.'

'But,' Ann blinked as though realising for the first time that she wasn't going to get out of this, 'but . . . I –'

She opened her mouth and then shut it again. As she began to walk out of the room, he stalled her. 'Er . . . Ann,' he murmured, 'aren't you forgetting something?'

She slowly spun back to observe that he was holding the cage out to her. The bird inside gobbled, though it did not move.

With a trembling hand she reached out and took the cage.

He dusted his hands. At least that was one task done for the day.

Charlotte must have told her sister about his offer because Zara turned up after school that day. Out the window of his office, he saw her talking to the bird while a couple of his men built a large pen for it under a grey mangrove tree. She was talking to Augustus with such animation that after a moment he had to go outside and listen to what she was saying.

'Anyway, that's why Taylor Swift is way cooler than Miley Cyrus.'

'Who are Taylor Swift and Miley Cyrus?' Mark inquired.

Zara jumped and then looked over her shoulder at him, her lip curling in a superior little smile. 'Friends of mine,' she quipped in a way that made him certain she was mocking him. Surprisingly, he found this intriguing rather than offensive and the next day when he saw her sitting outside with Augustus he deliberately went out again.

Unlike his men, she had no regard for his position or his power.

She chatted to him about her life like he must be interested in it so he feigned that he was, only to discover halfway through their conversation that he was actually enjoying the naive perspective of a fifteen-year-old. For the next four days, he went out and spoke to her when she came to visit. Whether it was for a break from work or the masochistic need to spend some time with this pet, he did not know. But it was almost a routine now.

'Anyway,' she told him on Monday afternoon, 'so I didn't go to the party and now everyone at school is talking about it. I feel so left out.'

'So talk about something that they didn't do.' He shrugged.

'I'm not that cool.'

'Coolness is all relative. Look at me.'

'You're not that cool either,' she grinned.

He chuckled. 'Tell them you snatched a turkey from the jaws of death and are now nursing it back to health.'

Her brow wrinkled. 'That's not cool, just stupid.'

'You're lucky: most teenagers with the exception of yourself aren't that bright.'

'Geez, Mark,' she laughed, using his first name with ease now, just as though she wasn't one of two people in town who did so. 'You never pull any punches, do you?' She got up off the ground next to Augustus, dusting her jeans. 'I better get back home before my sister flips out.'

He looked at her. 'Doesn't she like you coming here?'

'She doesn't like me going anywhere. But it's worse lately.' Zara hunched a shoulder. 'We aren't really speaking to each other.'

'Why is that?' He couldn't understand why he had asked the question and even as the words were leaving his mouth he regretted it. Now he would have to listen to the answer and being embroiled in Zara's problems was the last thing he wanted.

She hesitated, however, and for a moment he thought he was in the clear until she said without looking at him, 'To be honest, it's more me than her. I'd rather keep my distance.'

The way she wriggled uncomfortably made him sigh. 'What have you done?'

Her face snapped to his. 'What makes you think I've done something?'

'You look guilty as hell.'

She grimaced. 'It's not as bad as you think. I'm probably freakin' out over nothing . . .' She looked almost scared as her words dried up.

He groaned inwardly as he realised he was about to do the unthinkable and give her advice. 'I think you need to make a full confession to your sister.'

Zara chewed on her lower lip. 'I . . . I find it difficult to talk to Charlotte sometimes. She's never said anything but I know I've already cost her a lot. She had to give up her career in Brisbane to help raise me.'

He considered this thoughtfully. Unbidden, Charlotte's beautiful yet forthright expression appeared in front of his mind's eye. His landlady may look like an angel but there was nothing remotely soft about her. He knew instinctively, even without the benefit of Zara's insight, that she'd been through the wars and come out swinging.

He saw the scene in the Silver Seas reception again. That earnest way she'd lobbied him for the sake of the family business. Charlotte Templeton clearly had a huge sense of responsibility. She had continued to press him even to the point of embarrassment. He saw her pert pink nose, her wide irises and her mouth formed in that mortified 'o'. As annoying as she was, she was a generous soul and sacrifice came as naturally to her as milk to a cow.

'Earth to Mark! Earth to Mark!'

He looked down. Zara was tapping her feet impatiently with hands on hips.

'You're not even listening to me any more, are you?'

'Yes, you are quite right.'

She rolled her eyes and then gave a dismissive flick with her hand. 'It doesn't matter. You wouldn't understand what I'm going through anyway.'

How trite of her. He was sure he would very much understand if she gave him half a chance. But he wasn't going to push it. It was none of his business what went on between her and the woman who kept disrupting his life . . . and now his thoughts as well.

Chapter 11

Charlotte

That blasted turkey.

What's that about?

A pet, be damned. The man was up to something. And it was up to her to find out what.

Why? Can't you just leave well enough alone? Don't you have enough problems?

Immediately, the image of Zara's tear- and dust-streaked face as she sat on the edge of the road holding the injured bird rose in her mind's eye. She wished she knew what was going on in her sister's head right now.

Her mother had slept the entire time they were at the vet. She had rung a member of the resort staff and asked them to keep an eye on her while they were out. When they returned she clearly didn't remember anything of what had been going on earlier that day. She was in a very cheerful mood, chatting about the shocking news report she'd just witnessed on the television. Zara went straight to her room and when Charlotte tried to talk to her she found the door locked.

Not the silent treatment again!

Her mother had certainly left her with one colossal mess to clean up. How many years had they spoken about the day they would tell her? How they would do it properly, sit her down and let her ask questions. Maybe have Luke there too. Zara was never meant to find out by accident. In fact, at one stage that had been her mother's worst fear.

Charlotte angrily opened the Vegemite. The jar scraped loudly on the countertop before she dipped in her knife and then proceeded to mascara her slice of bread.

'Lottie, is everything all right?'

'Fine,' Charlotte snapped, looking up to see Virginia watching her. Her mother's eyes were round and bright, indicating she probably wasn't in the present.

'I hope that sandwich is not for me.'

She looked down at what now looked more like a piece of dough. 'No, this is mine. What would you like?'

'I want to know what's bothering you.'

'Nothing.'

She doubted her mother was thinking about the same thing she was. And if she didn't remember what had happened with Zara the week before, she wasn't going to burden her with it. The doctor had been very clear about not putting her under any sort of stress, as it could lead to aggressive behaviour.

She couldn't help but wish that they'd concocted a better story to cover Zara's father's absence . . . like he was in Africa on safari – an environmentalist with a passion for the Earth. It had been her mother's wish to embellish as little as possible so when the time came it would be easier. But at least a well-thought-out lie would have invited fewer questions . . . and less heartache.

Now her sister seemed even more unreachable than ever. She had barely spoken to her in days. She had no idea what she was thinking or feeling, except for the fact that she was bloody obsessed with Mark Crawford's turkey, visiting it every afternoon after school and on the weekend at the Barnes Inc work site. She would make the trek up the road and stay there till it was almost dark.

She talks to that turkey more than she talks to you. This can't go on.

She felt a hand on her shoulder and looked up to find her mother's watery eyes gazing at her with some concern.

'It's about the baby, isn't it? You don't want me to have it?'

Charlotte swallowed. A yucky feeling slipped down her spine like pond slime on rock. They were back in the past again, only this time it was not far enough.

'Do you think I don't feel dirty? Like my own body has betrayed me?'

Charlotte chewed desperately on her lower lips. 'Mum, please.'

'I know it's hard for you to understand. I'm forty-five. I never thought I would fall pregnant either and now it's too late.' Her eyes looked sad. 'I've seen the ultrasound, Lottie. I heard its little heart beating.'

'Mum,' she choked up, 'there's no need to explain.' *Not again*.

'Then what is it, Lottie? Are you worried about your brother?' She shut her eyes. 'I am too.'

Wow. How much did she *not* want to have this conversation again? Slowly, she put the bread back in the cupboard. 'Mum, perhaps we can talk about about this later?'

'I will tell him.' Her mother looked away, determination and anxiety marking her face. 'I'm just scared of what he'll do.'

Well, she'd been right to be scared. Her brother had disappeared for days when he'd found out. They were worried that he'd gone on a manhunt because their dad's rifle had been missing from his gun cabinet as well. Then one night, two weeks later, he'd returned home and passed out drunk on the front doorstep.

'Actually, I'm afraid of everything.' Her mother's voice was small and childlike. 'I'm terrified of the questions people will ask when they see I'm pregnant and I'm ashamed to answer them.'

Her mother had really retreated into herself after Zara was born. For ages she hadn't been able to go into a supermarket even without feeling paranoid. It was why Charlotte had quit her job in Brisbane and come home to help raise Zara and run the business. As a young woman she had thought it would be a temporary thing. It was now fifteen years later and she was still here.

'What do you think, Lottie?' Her mother grasped her hand almost desperately. 'Tell me what you are thinking?'

'I think . . .' she swallowed and blinked hard. 'I think your favourite show on television is just starting.'

'Is it?'

She led Virginia around the kitchen counter to the couch, gently pushing her onto the cushions. Grabbing the remote, she turned on the television. *Judge Judy*. It was indeed her mother's favourite show. Thankfully, after a moment, Virginia was completely absorbed. Charlotte turned away, pressing the wetness in the corner of her eyes with thumb and forefinger.

She had crawled her way through that part of her life by her fingernails. As for Luke, he eventually calmed down and turned into a rock for them both. She didn't know how they would have got through it without him.

It was Luke who had found their mother a therapist in Mackay when she wouldn't talk to Charlotte about it. He who had taken Zara into his arms the day she was born and uttered the one thing they all needed to hear.

'She's beautiful, Mum. I love her already.'

He was a quiet pillar of strength and, but for him, she knew her mother would have lost all faith in men.

She'd always meant to return to Brisbane eventually – to go back to her career in psychology. But when the business started going downhill from neglect and then her mother developed Alzheimer's eight years later, a good time never seemed to come. And now she had to wonder whether her career was over before it had really begun.

Her mind spun to the present as the door swung open and Zara walked in. She was home from school, lugging a big blue backpack, which she unceremoniously dumped on the floor.

'Hi, love,' Charlotte began tentatively. 'How was your day?'

'Fine.'

'Learn anything interesting?'

'Nup.'

'Any gossip to share?'

Silence.

'Zara?'

Her sister looked up, a kind of spacey expression on her face. 'I'm getting changed,' she announced. 'I'm going to see Augustus.'

No surprises there.

As her sister left the room, she glanced at the couch. Her mother was still fully absorbed. She decided to put the kettle on: perhaps a cup of tea would wash off all this angst.

Just as it finished boiling, the back door opened again and Luke walked in. She'd never been happier to see anyone.

'Luke!' she cried, coming out of the kitchen to throw her arms around him.

'Thought I'd better check on you,' he said gruffly and gave her a peck on the cheek. 'How are you holding up, Lottie?'

'I've been better, that's for sure.'

'I should come around more often.'

'It's all right.' She shook her head. 'I don't want to disrupt your family.'

'You guys are my family too. How is Zara coping? Is she okay?'

She had told him over the phone what had happened with Zara the day Mark Crawford had adopted the turkey. She threw up her hands helplessly. 'I have no idea. She won't talk to me about it.'

He released her, running a hand through his dark messy hair. 'Where is she now?'

'Getting changed. She's off to see that turkey again.'

'And Mum?'

She indicated the couch. 'Watching *Judge Judy*.'

He was silent for a moment, taking on that thoughtful look he always had when making a decision. 'I'll stay with Mum, Lottie. You go with Zara.'

'To visit the turkey?'

'It might help to open her up.'

'Couldn't hurt, I guess.'

Just then Zara came flouncing back into the room. 'Luke?'

'Hey, Freckle-face.' He hugged her.

'What are you doing here?' Her tone was suspicious.

'I came to see Mum.' He turned away from her.

'Oh.' She was silent for a moment and then headed for the back door. 'Okay, well, I'm off to visit my turkey. I might see you later.'

Charlotte followed her to the door. 'I'll come too.'

Zara spun to her. 'No, I don't need you.'

'Okay.' Charlotte tried not to let the hurt creep into her voice. 'But I want to see how Augustus is healing up.'

'Why?'

'Aren't I allowed to care?'

Finally, Zara shrugged and walked out the door. Charlotte glanced at Luke.

'Good luck,' he mouthed.

She nodded and went out.

At first, they walked in silence. They crossed the car park, passing several dirty white utes, before hitting the main road. They turned out onto the gravel verge and headed towards the Barnes Inc work site. For a moment, all Charlotte could hear was the scrape of their sneakers on stones. Thoughts bounced around in her head as she searched for an icebreaker. Surely, there was some innocuous way she could start the conversation.

And then Zara sucked in a shaky breath. 'Did he . . .?' Her voiced cracked. 'Did he rape Mum?'

A muscle twitched in Charlotte's jawline. For a moment she couldn't answer her. The shock of hearing the question on Zara's lips was far worse than imagining it. 'Yes,' she whispered. 'He did.'

'Is that how she got pregnant with me?'

'Yes,' she said again. She wanted to say more, but there was a tightness in her throat that squeezed her voice box into silence and made her body seize up.

Zara burst into tears, both hands immediately covering her face. 'No, no,' she moaned. 'I didn't want you to say that.'

Charlotte felt wetness on her face and realised she was crying too. She put an arm across her sister's shoulders, pulling her in tight. 'I didn't want to say it.'

Zara tried to shrug her arm off. 'You must hate me. *I look like him.*'

Resolutely she held on tight to Zara, chewing heavily on her lower lip. 'You do. And it was hard for Mum at first but she had therapy to deal with triggers that may remind her of the rape.'

'Great,' Zara hiccupped, 'that just makes me feel sick.'

A fist squeezed Charlotte's heart. 'I'm sorry.' She laid her head against her sister's as they continued to walk. 'But if you think looking at you makes me feel anything but love you're wrong.'

'How is that possible?'

'Because you're you. You're Zara. You're my sister. You're Mum's daughter. That's how *she* feels.'

'What if I'm like him? What if I turn out like him? Did she consider that?'

'Listen to me.' Charlotte stopped walking to grab her by the shoulders. 'You are nothing like him. You've always been such a special person. Even when you were a toddler you were warm, kind and giving. You couldn't even let that stupid scrub turkey die! You inherited nothing from him but nose shape and hair texture.'

'I'm scared, Lottie. I feel dirty and terrible for Mum. Just terrible.'

Before she'd succumbed to Alzheimer's, her mother had said almost exactly the same thing to her once, except with reference to Zara. It only seemed to prove how much they loved each other.

'Zara, you need to remember, none of this is your fault.'

An echidna stirred in the undergrowth; they momentarily took their eyes off each other to watch it roll in the dirt. Its elongated, slender snout brushed through patchy bits of grass hunting for food.

She took her sister's hand. 'Come on, let's go.'

'I want to know how it happened,' Zara whispered.

Charlotte hadn't spoken about the rape in years. She didn't like to think about it and hadn't asked her mother for a lot of detail. Even now she felt a lump forming in her throat.

'Lottie?'

Sweat broke out on her upper lip. 'I was in Brisbane at the time. She was at a pub in Mackay celebrating her birthday with friends. He was there, a friend of a friend so to speak. He bought her a drink. She was really flattered because he was a younger man and she hadn't had any male attention since Dad died. They chatted for ages and most of her friends went home. They were sitting by the bar and she decided to have just one more drink before finishing up for the night and then . . . I don't know. She says it's all a blur. Her next coherent memory is waking up in a hotel room the following morning. He wasn't there. She was naked from the waist down. She doesn't remember anything. That's the worst part.'

Her sister considered all this. And, bless her, was silent for a moment, seeming to act with a maturity beyond her years. 'So she was drugged,' she finally said.

'We assume so,' Charlotte responded. 'Back then she didn't have Alzheimer's and she'd never lost her memory from alcohol like that before. But she didn't get tested or anything.'

'What do you mean?'

'When she woke up she just got dressed and went home.'

'Why would she do that?' Zara demanded. 'Wasn't she angry? Didn't she want him to be caught?'

'Actually she was ashamed.' Charlotte grimaced.

'But it wasn't her fault.'

'Unfortunately, that's not how she felt. She didn't want to go to the police and be examined and questioned. She just wanted to forget that she'd ever been so stupid. It is actually how a lot of rape victims feel. They partially blame themselves.'

'I don't get it,' Zara said stubbornly.

Charlotte patted her arm. 'I know it's hard to see from where you're standing. But try to put yourself in her shoes for a second.'

After her mother told her what had happened she'd gone back over some of her uni notes and read everything she could about rape victims. She had wanted to be across it all, to help her see why her mother's spirit was deteriorating before her very eyes. Her mother had always been such a strong woman. When her father had died, she had run the resort on her own for nearly three years before this happened. Charlotte just hadn't been able to understand how such a strong will could lose its way so fast.

'Did she eventually report him?' Zara asked at last.

'Yes. But not for at least a couple of weeks. They didn't catch him based on her statement and description. He'd paid for the hotel room with cash and there weren't any CCT cameras in the pub she was at. He was a professional. He'd thought of everything. That newspaper clipping you saw came out a couple of years later when he resurfaced in Melbourne. Mum actually had nothing to do with him being put away. It was some other victims who brought him to justice.'

Just then the Barnes Inc office dongas came into view and they turned onto the dirt track that led to the ute car park.

'Zara.' She squeezed her sister's hand. She had to say this. 'I love you. Mum loves you. Luke loves you. You're part of our family. You always have been from the moment you were born. Mum couldn't let you go.'

Zara looked up at that. 'But she was going to, right? I wouldn't blame her.'

'She was going to give you up for adoption. In fact, she was pretty adamant about it – and then you were born and we all held you in our arms for the first time.' Charlotte paused as a gentle smile curved her mouth. 'I saw that you had her eyes and her hands. And you squeezed my thumb so tightly in your little fist with so much trust.' Her voice dropped to whisper. 'It was a done deal.'

'Thanks, Lottie.'

'Any time.'

They fell silent as they crossed the car park and walked around the main office dongas. Unfortunately, when Augustus's pen came into view someone was already standing in front of it. Charlotte's ribcage constricted at the sight of him. *Why today of all days?*

'Mr Crawford,' she said tightly in greeting.

'Ms Templeton,' he responded equally frosty. 'Zara.'

'Hi, Mark.'

Charlotte turned startled eyes on her sister, who immediately bent over to pat the feathers on Augustus's back. Since when were they on first-name terms? And was he waiting for her? No. Couldn't be.

The turkey preened at Zara's caress.

'I must say,' Charlotte had to admit, 'he does look much better, doesn't he?'

'Yeah,' said Zara. 'I've been teaching him to do tricks.'

'Tricks?'

'Uh-huh.' Zara turned to the turkey. 'Augustus, have you had a nice day?'

The turkey bobbed its head up and down once as though it were nodding.

'See,' Zara gestured at him. 'Augustus,' she turned back to the turkey, 'did you eat all your lunch today?'

It bobbed its head again.

'Saying yes to everything is not a trick,' Mark stated. 'It's actually a lack of discipline. Observe. Augustus?'

The turkey looked up.

'Are you dumb?'

The turkey nodded.

'I rest my case.'

Zara laughed. 'We'll work on that.'

Charlotte cleared her throat, not quite knowing how to take their friendly banter. 'So how are you finding your new pet?' she asked Mark politely.

'Satisfactory.'

Only he would describe a new bond of friendship in this way. As he turned away she allowed her eyes to run over him curiously. What was it about him that unsettled her? He was handsome, that was for sure. But arrogant and rude too. Even in the Barnes site uniform: he wore it like he was above it. His shirt was well ironed, unlike the wrinkly ones worn straight from the drier by his employees. His hatless hair was unruffled. Parted and neat. She longed to shove her fingers in there and mess it all up.

She bit her lip when she realised where her thoughts had wandered and reminded herself he was married.

'What does your wife think of your adoption? Have you told her?'

'It was her idea to get a pet,' he bit out. Was it her imagination or did his shoulders sag ever so slightly? 'She wanted me to get a pet.'

'Oh.'

Why did she see pain in his eyes? It didn't make any sense. She would have explored the thought further if another woman hadn't interrupted them. She was dressed in plain clothes and carrying a notebook. Charlotte could only assume she didn't work at Barnes Inc. The second she opened her mouth, she confirmed it.

'Hi, I'm Casey Williams from the *Mackay Times*. Are you Mark Crawford?'

His eyes narrowed on her. 'Yes.'

'I was just wondering how you felt about the fact that your project is disrupting turtle mating season.'

His expression turned completely blank. Charlotte wished she had the talent to do that the way he did. 'You'll have to make an appointment with my receptionist,' he said smoothly.

Casey ignored the suggestion. 'I mean, you obviously have an affinity with animals. Rumours say you've adopted an injured turkey. Is this the one?'

'*We've* adopted an injured turkey.' Zara jutted her chin. 'We did it together.'

Casey turned on her and then Charlotte with interest. 'So it's a family project, is it?' Her eyes sparkled as they rested on Charlotte. 'Tell me, does your husband normally do this sort of thing? And if so, why is he turning a cold shoulder on our turtles?'

'He's *not* my husband,' Charlotte snapped.

'She's not my wife,' Mark Crawford growled, his blank expression now perfectly ruined.

Casey waved her hand nervously. 'An easy mistake to make.'

'Really?' This time it was Charlotte who put her hands on her hips and took an intimidating step forwards. ''Cause I don't see it.'

Zara giggled. Augustus bobbed his head excitedly.

Casey bit her lip, her eyes darting from one to the other. She jerked her thumb over her shoulder and whispered, 'Maybe I'll just go inside and make that appointment.'

'You do that,' Charlotte responded as she backed away slowly. Crazy, tactless woman. What was she thinking?

'That was pretty funny.' Zara chuckled again. 'Isn't that like the second time you two have been mistaken for marrieds?'

It was actually the third time if you counted the incident at the vet plus the one in Silver Seas reception. But she wasn't going to correct Zara and embarrass herself even further. Mark didn't look pleased either. He was glaring at her like it was her fault. Like she'd orchestrated these misunderstandings to annoy him.

Was it really that bad that people mistook her for his wife? Was he above her too?

Pride pricked her. And also a pinch of mischief. This guy needed to be taught a lesson and maybe now was the right time to do it. She tossed her head. 'Well, Zara, you can stay a little longer but I really think I should get back to Mum.'

'A very good idea.' Mark's eager nod only consolidated her thirst for revenge.

'Before I go,' she said demurely, casting her lashes down over her eyes, 'I just wanted say, Mr Crawford, and please don't take this too seriously.'

His eyes narrowed. 'Yes, Ms Templeton?'

'You're a very handsome man.'

She watched him blink in shock, his skin pinkening, his lips moving but no sound emerging. She turned away smugly.

That'll teach you to call me attractive.

And on this 'satisfactory' thought, she walked away.

Charlotte kept busy for the rest of the week, her spirits slightly brighter with hope. The barrier between herself and her sister had been broken. She knew Zara still had more questions to work through, but they had made the first step: they were talking about it.

'It's hard knowing,' Zara said to her one day at dinner with head bowed. 'But at the same time, I'm so grateful to Mum.'

Charlotte put out her hand and squeezed it tight.

'I mean, she could have chosen not to have me.' Zara swallowed hard.

Charlotte squeezed tighter. 'I was wondering . . . would you like to see a friend of mine? A psychologist in Mackay. Sometimes, it's easier to talk about things with a third party or someone who wasn't involved.'

She had expected Zara to say no immediately but her sister surprised her. After a moment's pause she said, 'Maybe just once or twice.'

'It's all thanks to that stupid turkey,' she told Luke over the phone a couple of days later.

He coughed. 'Not entirely. You have a stronger bond with her than you realise, Lottie.'

'Thanks.'

'Now it's time for you to start taking better care of yourself.'

'What do you mean?'

'I think when you accepted all Mum's burdens, you didn't allow any room for your own goals and dreams.'

She'd heard this song before and was happy to cut him off. 'When things settle down –'

'Lottie, things are never going to settle down. Don't you get that? There's never going to be a good time and then you'll be dead.'

She gasped. 'Thanks a lot.'

'Just giving it to you straight. You should do something for yourself. Get a sport or hobby. Join a club. Something just for you. I'll come over and look after Mum. Just say the word – you know I'll be there.'

'I know,' she responded defensively, feeling the pressure already building. 'I'll think about it.'

As she hung up the phone she supposed it wasn't *bad* advice. His question put her in mind of the long chat she'd had with Emily Woods the other night. That had been fun and relaxing. Perhaps she should try catching up with her again.

So on Wednesday evening she decided to pop in, just to see

how her young friend was doing. She left her mum with Zara at around five o'clock and knocked on Emily's door.

Emily greeted her with a big bright smile. She was the embodiment of all that was good in life. Young, fresh-faced and ready to take on the world. If only she knew it. 'Hey, Lottie, I was just thinking of you. Come in.'

Thank goodness Emily was pleased to see her. After knocking on the door, she suddenly had an attack of paranoia about showing up announced. 'I hope I'm not intruding,' she said as she stepped over the threshold. 'I hadn't seen you around and was wondering how you were getting on.'

'Much better, thanks.' Emily smiled. 'Will's finally got around to briefing me on some of the work I'll be doing for the drive tower.'

'That's great.' Charlotte followed the girl into the kitchen, where she was buttering hot-dog rolls.

'I mean, I'm going to have to do some research first, so I know what I'm doing,' Emily went on. 'But overall I'm really pleased. What about you? How are things?'

My sister is seeing a therapist. My mother has started wetting her bed. And I find Mark Crawford very attractive. 'I'm good.'

Emily laughed. 'Why do you sound like you need convincing?'

Charlotte sighed. 'Probably because I do. Tell me, what's your family like?'

'My family?' Emily pressed her hand to her chest. 'Well, my parents live in the suburbs. Mum's retired, Dad's on the verge and my sister, Megan, is a schoolteacher – married, two kids.'

Charlotte leaned against the counter. 'Sounds delightfully uncomplicated.'

Emily regarded her sympathetically. 'Hard week?'

'No, just tiring.'

'Well, looking after your mum and raising your little sister as well can't be easy. Where does your dad fit into all this?'

'He passed away when I was in my early twenties,' Charlotte sighed. 'I miss him so much.'

'That would have been hard,' Emily nodded and then her brow furrowed. 'Wait, does that mean Zara has a different father?'

Charlotte tensed. 'Er, yeah. But I shouldn't be dampening your day with my worries. Would you like some help buttering those rolls?'

'Don't be silly. And I'm done.' Emily put down her knife and dusted her hands. 'But it does sound like you need a hobby other than taking care of your family.'

'Have you been talking to my brother?' Charlotte demanded, but didn't wait for her response. 'The truth is, I do have interests apart from the family business.'

'Really? What?'

'Before I got roped into taking care of Zara, I lived in Brisbane and I worked as a social worker.' A wave of nostalgia washed over her. All her big bright plans flashed before eyes. Those days of carefree adventure were long gone.

Emily started chopping some onions. 'You studied psychology?'

'Yep, got a degree and everything. Really enjoyed it too. But when I moved back home to help out with the resort and Zara, I couldn't really continue with it so I used writing as an outlet.'

'Writing?' Emily's nose wrinkled. 'How is that linked to psychology?'

'I wrote self-help books,' Charlotte said proudly. 'Three of them even got published.'

'That's not a hobby,' Emily accused. 'Sounds suspiciously like work to me.'

Charlotte sighed, thinking fondly of the three slim handbooks she had produced. 'Well, it wasn't. It was almost therapeutic really. I used to write about issues I'd had to deal with myself. So it all came rather naturally.'

Emily nodded. 'Are you staying for dinner? I've got stacks here.'

'I'm not sure,' Charlotte replied. 'I don't like leaving Mum with Zara for too long.'

'At least stay for a little while,' Emily urged and continued chopping. 'So are you writing a book now?'

'Sadly, no,' Charlotte shook her head. 'When my mum was diagnosed with Alzheimer's my focus had to switch to her.'

'Well, if you're not doing it now, then you can't call it a hobby.' Emily shook her finger. 'What else are you interested in?'

Charlotte stopped to think. 'You know what? I have absolutely no idea.'

'Spoken like a true workaholic,' Emily grinned, holding up a bottle. 'Wine?'

'I thought you'd never ask.'

'Do you think you'll ever go back to being a social worker? Even part-time?' Emily asked as they retired to the couch with a couple of glasses.

'I don't know. I'd love to. Part-time work is very difficult to come by though.' She sank gratefully back onto the cushions. 'Enough about me, what else has been happening with you? Has your ex texted you again?'

Emily groaned. 'A few times, actually, and I've responded. But we seem to be talking in circles. He won't give me anything definitive.'

'That must be frustrating.' She wished she had something more illuminating to say, but relationships, even failed ones, weren't her forte. She had never allowed herself to get close enough to a man to want him as a permanent fixture in her life. And marriage . . . it was a concept that scared her more than anything else.

'Well, it's not helpful,' Emily confirmed. 'Sometimes I wonder why he's bothering to text me at all.'

There was a knock at the door, making them both look up.

'Oh, that must be Will.' Emily stood up. 'We're going to watch a movie and eat hot dogs for dinner. You really should join us.'

Charlotte immediately felt bad again for showing up without calling first. 'Oh no . . . I wouldn't want to be a third wheel.'

'Third wheel?' Emily blushed. 'Whatever gave you that idea?'

She got up so quickly to answer the door that Charlotte had to wonder if she had offended her. But she came back into the room a second later all smiles.

'Hey, Charlotte!' Will called from the kitchen. He was carrying a plate of sausages and a bag full of DVDs. 'How are you?'

'Fine,' she said, smiling. 'And call me Lottie.'

'So what are we talking about?' Will asked as he put a saucepan on the stove and turned on the heat.

'Oh, you know,' Emily said with a wink at Charlotte, 'just girl stuff.'

Will grimaced as he separated the sausages. 'So I guess we're watching a romantic comedy tonight? Should I slit my wrists now or after dinner?'

Charlotte laughed and then, much to Will's embarrassment, Emily regaled her with an account of all his failed relationships. She watched the two of them in wonder, finishing each other's sentences, teasing each other like two kids in a playground. Did they honestly not see themselves?

'You never did tell me what went wrong between you and Sasha,' Emily said light-heartedly as she poured a glass of wine for Will. Charlotte couldn't help but notice how he took it but looked away.

'Didn't I?'

'No, you didn't,' Emily took a swig of her own. 'Why *did* you break up with her?'

'*She*,' Will went back to the fry pan to check on the sausages, 'broke up with me.'

Emily lowered her glass. 'Yes, but *why*?'

'She said she didn't trust me.' Will glanced up, his eyes strangely intense. 'Accused me of being in love with somebody else.'

Emily let loose a peal of laughter. 'Well, that was pretty dumb of her, wasn't it?' She turned to Charlotte and said informatively, '*Will* is physically incapable of being dishonest. He couldn't tell a lie to save his life.'

'Good to know,' said Will dryly.

'So I take it you're both single at the moment?' Charlotte asked nonchalantly.

'Yeah,' Emily nodded.

'No one's caught your eye?' She looked carefully at Emily.

'Well, I'm pretty fussy,' Emily sighed. 'After Trent, I want to be really careful.'

She walked out of the kitchen to sit down with Charlotte on the couch again, happy apparently to let Will take over all the cooking.

'So what are you looking for?' Charlotte asked quietly.

Emily tilted her head in thought. 'I want someone who isn't going to stuff me around. They have to be in touch with their emotions and know for sure how they feel.'

'Ow! That's hot.' Will dropped the sausage he'd been trying to put into a hot-dog bun.

'I want someone who cares about my opinions, who asks me what I need.'

'Em, do you want onions in yours?'

'I want him to be hot, don't get me wrong. But it can't all be physical. He's got to be content to just talk to me sometimes.'

'Earth to Emily. Earth to Emily!' came an irritated voice from the kitchen. 'I'm speaking to you!'

She rolled her eyes and threw over her shoulder, 'Yeah, yeah, onions.' She turned back to Charlotte. 'Do you hear what I'm saying?'

Charlotte's gaze passed from Emily to Will, who was piling five hot dogs on a plate, and threw the question back at her. 'Do *you* hear what you're saying?'

'Huh?'

Just then Will sat down on the couch next to them, putting the plate of hot dogs on the coffee table. 'Personally, I think we should watch *Zombie Land*,' he said from left field. 'It's definitely the pick of the bunch.' He finally noticed the silence that had fallen between Emily and Charlotte. 'What?'

'You know, I might leave you guys to it.' Charlotte got up under a chorus of protest. 'No, I really should go. I should get back to Mum. Have fun, you two.'

They said goodbye and she smiled to herself as she shut the front door behind her. *Some people have the best problems.*

Chapter 12

Mark

It had been a very difficult fortnight to say the least. First, the painting subcontractor's team was playing up. They were working far too slow and putting everyone else's schedules behind. A couple of the workers were refusing to come in. Something about poor amenities for their use or some such rubbish. What did they expect? A five-star lunch room, complete with chef and hot dinner towels before your meal? Honestly, he wasn't even going to credit their complaints with a comment. Then Will's girlfriend had rocked up, immediately decreasing the level of concentration in his office by half. He couldn't conceive how he had ever agreed to that one. The girl was eager enough but that only served to make her all the more attractive and he wasn't running a Miss Australia pageant.

Now it was Thursday and he found himself in his office, not answering technical queries, not planning his four-day look ahead, not scheduling progress meetings but glancing at the clock.

In one hour he had to take Augustus for his check up.

There was an annoying knock on his office door. *What now?* 'Come in.' The door opened and a head poked around. It was the planning manager. 'What do you want?'

'Um . . .' His eyes darted. 'We have a three o'clock meeting, don't we?'

Mark frowned. He'd forgotten about that.

The planner swallowed. 'I can come back.'

'Come in,' Mark gestured sourly.

The planning manager complied, bringing with him a couple of large bar charts, which Mark eyed suspiciously. This distrust was not unfounded. The figures were in fact worse than his own mental projections. They were behind in all areas of the project. *All areas.* Not a single team was running on schedule. What was wrong with his staff?

At the end of the meeting, Mark left his desk and went to the kitchen to get himself a coffee. From this vantage point, he was able to observe with disgust the following occurrence. His new graduate, who, much to his great fortune, he had not yet had the pleasure of meeting face to face, wasn't sitting at her own desk. Where her desk was, he had no idea. That wasn't the point. The point was, she just appeared to be flittering about his office. Taking this drawing from that file. Going to this bookcase and then to that one. Photocopying God only knows what. No doubt, something important in *her* mind.

The point being, as absorbed as she was in her task, no one else was absorbed in theirs.

His piling engineer observed her walk from the bookcase to the photocopier.

His procurement officer watched her stroll from the layout table to the pin-up board.

And his quality manager craned his neck to watch her bend over to pick up a highlighter she'd dropped.

No wonder they were so behind. Enough was enough.

Why had he ever agreed to let this girl in? Oh yes, another one of Kathryn's bright ideas. Well, maybe he could kill two birds with one stone: increase his men's concentration and increase the productivity of his painting team.

He walked over to the girl and stood in front of the layout table until she noticed him. She looked up, her big eyes rounding even further.

'Er . . . hi.'

'You must be my new graduate.'

'Yes, Emily Woods. I'm very happy to be here. Thank you for taking me on. I've been really enjoying –'

'Yes, yes, we'll dispense with the pleasantries. What are you doing?'

'Well,' she began shyly, 'we have ten pre-fabricated trusses arriving next week and I'm trying to organise –'

'Yes, that is next week. This week, the painters have fallen behind as they have the week before and the week before that.'

'The painters?' she faltered.

'I have ten deck beams in the yard that are just sitting there doing nothing. I can't use them because the painters haven't got around to spark testing them yet. I need you in the field.'

Her face lit like a bulb. 'You want me supervise the installation of these beams? Sir, I can't tell you –'

'No,' he cut her off. 'I want you to spark test them.'

'I don't understand.'

'I want you to make sure that they've all been properly painted and then release them to be used.'

'But I'm not a painter –'

'Ben will show you how.'

Ben, the quality manager, who had been rather ineffectually pretending not to eavesdrop, stood up. 'Beg your pardon, sir?'

'Show her how, will you? I'm going out. Oh,' he thought of something, turned back and held out his hand to the girl, 'welcome to the Hay Point Wharf Expansion, Emily. I'm Mark Crawford.'

In a sort of daze, she lifted her hand and gave him what could only be described as a wet-fish handshake. He disengaged himself and made for the exit.

It was time to get Augustus. As he put his cage into the ute, he hoped that both his luck and his project progress improved next week. It would be a colossal embarrassment if they were not ready in time for the shiploader.

As he fished his keys out of his pocket, his fingers brushed Kathryn's ever-present list. Unable to resist the pull, he took it out to read it again, as he often did. His wife's last instructions were too hard to throw away. To make matters worse, he found himself involuntarily following them. Even now, he was scanning the list to see what he was up to.

Number four. Bake a cake.

Kathryn had been a chef. As far he was concerned she remained the most talented cook he'd ever met. Ever since they had married, food had infused his life, blanketing it with delightful smells and tastes and textures. He missed watching her experiment at weekends. He missed coming home to a house filled with the juicy aroma of roast beef. He knew exactly which cake she wanted him to bake.

Comfort food had been Kathryn's answer to everything. (How his wife hadn't been the size of house he'd never know.) When she was excited about something, she'd make chocolate tarts. When she was feeling down, she'd make stew. 'Something hearty to warm the soul.' When she was angry, seafood seemed to be the dish of the day. How many times had she given him prawns with severed heads when she was pissed off, or crab cooked whole?

But cake . . . cake was reserved for those moments when she just needed to stop and think.

Whenever she was faced with a difficult dilemma, a ticklish predicament, an interesting but irreconcilable problem, she would head straight to the kitchen to bake. There was nothing that helped Kathryn nut out a problem better than mixing flour, butter and eggs. And if it were a particularly stubborn problem the cake would be chocolate. A decadent mud variety. It got to the point where he wished they had more issues in their lives.

I can't do it.

Even if he could cook, which he couldn't, doing something like this would release memories he couldn't face again. He grunted. Maybe that had been her plan.

He started the engine and drove to Mackay.

The appointment was shorter than expected. Augustus's splint did not need adjustment and they were back in the car again within an hour. Mark put the turkey on the front seat. Unable to stand for too long, it sat there rather listlessly, the small plastic bucket still encasing its head.

'I suppose you think you've got it tough,' Mark remarked.

Augustus ignored him.

'You do realise that I'm your benefactor?' he said, as he restarted the engine. 'The only reason you're alive is because of me.'

The bird finally raised its head and gave him a beady stare.

'Fine, it was me who ran you over in the first place, but you have to admit, that wasn't my fault.'

The turkey averted its head.

'You know, insolence doesn't look good on you.'

The turkey closed his eyes.

As the scenery flew by the windows Mark dared to say what was on his mind. 'I just wanted to ask you . . . you know, just in case, when you were lying there under my car tyre heading towards the light . . . Did you happen to see my wife?'

Augustus did not stir.

'I guess not. It was a long shot, I know, as technically you didn't die, but it's just that I wish I knew what was in her head when she gave me this damn list to complete. So,' he tried conversationally, 'feel like baking tonight?'

The turkey finally opened both eyes and put his head up in what could only be described as the bird version of horror.

'Relax!' Mark shot at him. 'I wasn't talking about putting you in the oven. I'm thinking of baking a cake.'

The turkey's expression did not change.

After swinging by a supermarket to pick up the ingredients, Mark was home an hour later. He ordered his dinner – chicken and vegetables – set the turkey cage on the dining table (Charlotte Templeton would never know) and then put his two bags of groceries on the counter. He stood in the kitchen, rubbing his hands together. The turkey, which was clearly visible over the bench, squawked.

'What's your problem?' he asked. 'I know *exactly* what I'm doing.'

He was pleased to note that his voice sounded very convincing. The truth was, he had no idea of Kathryn's precise cake recipe. But surely with a cake precision wasn't crucial. He had seen her make her decadent chocolate mud a million times and did recall what went in it, just not exactly how much. And of course he knew what it tasted like. So those two items of knowledge combined should allow him to guess his way through it. It couldn't be that hard surely – certainly a lot easier that getting the correct mix of cement and aggregate to achieve the specified compressive strength.

'Right,' he rubbed his hands together as Augustus rubbed the rim of his bucket headpiece along the bars of his cage, 'I'm pretty sure the first thing she did was melt a lot of chocolate with other stuff.'

He took out a saucepan and popped in a block of chocolate, sugar, butter and a little bit of water. Then he turned the stove on high and put the pan on.

'Now I guess we just wait till that's all melted and runny,' he told Augustus, who gobbled agreeably.

Mark went to the couch and sat down. Drawing a computer magazine from the coffee table, he began to flick through it.

As the smell of chocolate infused the room he started to feel very relaxed.

It was a relief. He was sure this would have been too hard – too close to the bone. But maybe enough time had passed to enjoy this again. Sitting here, flicking through his magazine with the heavy aroma of chocolate swirling around him was almost like getting a hug from his dead wife. It was very therapeutic and surprisingly easy.

The turkey squawked.

'I'm sorry.' He looked up imperiously. 'Are you bored? You can't possibly expect me to entertain you. I'm very busy at the moment, baking a cake.'

Augustus gobbled and banged his head piece against the cage with such force that Mark was sure he must have been very close to knocking himself out.

'It amazes me sometimes how incredibly stupid you are,' he sighed. 'I suppose that's what turkeys are in general, aren't they? That's why they're called turkeys.'

He lifted his nose to the air. 'Hmmm, that doesn't smell quite right.'

He got up and went over to the stove. The butter appeared to be boiling, which was good because it was definitely melted. The chocolate also looked soft . . . ish. He got a spoon and began to stir it. But the chocolate just wouldn't liquefy. In fact, it rather had the consistency of Play-Doh. The sugar grains stuck in it like pimples.

'I think this chocolate is off,' he told Augustus. 'We're going to have to start again. It's a good thing I bought three blocks.'

He took the saucepan off the stove, shoved it in the sink and got out a new pot. Again, he added chocolate, butter, sugar and water and put the pot on the stove. He went back to the couch. Augustus banged his head again.

'Stop that,' said Mark. 'You are going to hurt yourself and I'm not letting you out.'

The turkey dropped its arse and hit the paper-littered floor of its cage with a gentle *whoosh*.

'Much better.'

Five minutes later Mark returned to the stove to discover that the same thing had happened. 'I suppose the question we're all asking then is, should I try again or cut my losses and move on?'

He laced his fingers together and flexed them. 'I mean, let's use the knowledge we know to be true. Most cakes are fairly crumbly. With mud cake you want it really hard and firm. I know Kathryn's were always that way.'

Augustus squawked.

'Just give me a second here. Why don't we just break up the chocolate rather than melt it, so that it's more like aggregate? That way we have some nice chunky bits to improve strength.'

He got out a large mixing bowl and did just this. Then he melted the butter with the sugar in a plastic bowl in the microwave because he couldn't bear to use the stove again. He added this to the mixing bowl and then tried to recall the rest of the recipe.

'Well, there's definitely water in there, and eggs, cocoa and self-raising flour. I'm just not sure how much of each.'

Augustus put his head down.

'You're right . . . for once. Let's think about this. With concrete we look at the water-to-cement ratio. For something nice and strong we might go sixty per cent cement. If we think about the self-raising flour like the cement, I think that's our proportions.'

Augustus bent over and put his bum in the air, his tail feathers flexing.

Mark frowned. 'You know, you've really got to stop doing that. It's incredibly rude.'

Augustus shat.

Mark closed his eyes in pain. 'I've got to get a cover for

your cage. I think it would be better for both of us if we each had some privacy.'

He put all the ingredients in a bowl, greased a cake tin and shoved it in the oven. 'Done.'

Suddenly, there was a knock at the door. His dinner had arrived. Perfect timing.

He collected his dinner from one of Charlotte's kitchen staff. Then after putting Augustus's cage outside he sat down to have his meal in front of the television. By the time he was finished, forty minutes had easily spun by. It was time to check on his cake. He tested it with a knife in the way he had seen Kathryn do many times before. Surprisingly, it didn't seem to be ready. He thought about cleaning up the kitchen but couldn't face all those pots and pans just yet.

'I'm going to have a shower,' he told Augustus and left the room.

When he was dressed he returned to the kitchen to test his cake again. It smelled like it was burning and it was, on the outside. But when he stuck the knife in again it was still gooey in the centre.

'Why isn't it setting?'

Suddenly there was another knock at the door. No doubt the woman from the kitchen was back to collect his dirty plates. He wondered if he'd be able to persuade her to take all the dirty chocolate dishes he'd created in the kitchen as well.

He flung open the door, his most formidable expression firmly in place. After all, one needed to be adamant if one was to explain to anyone what was in their best interest to do. But instead of the fifty-year-old woman who usually worked in the Silver Seas kitchen, his visitor was Charlotte Templeton.

'What are you doing here?'

She wrinkled nose. 'What is that smell?'

He set his mouth stubbornly. 'I asked you first.'

'We need to talk,' she said briskly and brushed past him into the room. Her floral scent infused his nostrils briefly as her body wafted the air around him.

'About what?'

'It's been over two weeks and your men are still having pool parties and –' She stopped talking abruptly, her nose wrinkling. 'What on earth have you been doing?'

'Baking.'

She choked. '*Baking?*'

'Yes.' He stared stonily back, daring her to challenge him.

Unfortunately, as usual she wasn't intimidated by this haughty demeanour and spoke again, much like she was talking to a toddler standing next to a play kitchen. 'And what have you been baking?'

Before he could stop her, she had marched over to the oven and opened it.

'Crap, that looks bloody awful. What is it?'

His lips were so tight they almost refused to move. 'It's a decadent chocolate mud cake.'

Her eyes danced as she looked back at him. 'Oh, it's decadent all right.'

He lifted his chin. 'It's still soft in the middle.'

'Honey, I think it's done.' She turned off the oven.

He felt the hairs on the back of his neck fly to points as the endearment tripped off her tongue without any concern for his feelings at all. He knew instinctively that she meant nothing by it, except maybe to patronise him a little. But he still couldn't help an uncomfortably tight feeling from taking hold in his chest. Really, the woman was way too familiar for her own good. He didn't like her bustling about his kitchen either, getting another mixing bowl out of the cupboard. A dangerous scowl curled his mouth.

'I think you ought to go, Ms Templeton.'

'Mr Crawford, have you read my list?'

'What list?'

She shut her eyes for what seemed to be a moment in prayer before saying, 'Figures.'

She went to his cupboard and removed a measuring cup.

'What are you doing?'

She tipped three-quarters of a cup of self-raising flour into a bowl. 'I'm going to make you a new cake.'

'Ms Templeton –'

'And I'm going to continue baking until you listen to what I have to say.'

He folded his arms, a muscle in his cheek twitching while she placed three tablespoons of cocoa powder into the bowl.

'Fine.'

She cracked two eggs. 'Mr Crawford, I find your complete lack of interest in the well-being of your men concerning.'

'I thought we were talking about your list.'

'We are. Why do you think your men are such alcoholic, vandalising, disrespectful louts?'

He watched maddeningly as she scooped some butter into a container and went to the microwave. 'Continue.'

'Your men are living away from home, away from their families, working twelve-hour shifts, with very little time off. They have virtually no contact with the outside world except through phones and television. Their loved ones are too far away for them to have an influence on their lives.'

'And you know this how?'

'Observation, conversation, deduction,' she said a little too succinctly for his taste. That was his forte, not hers. He pursed his lips.

'So what's your point?'

She gaped at him but after a moment shut her mouth, opened the microwave and removed the melted butter. 'They are depressed and lonely. They feel powerless being so far away from their families, wanting to help but unable to return home because by the same token they need to earn a living. Are you aware of the statistics regarding suicide among FIFO workers?'

She poured in half a cup of caster sugar and gave the bowl a vigorous stir. He noticed that she cooked completely differently from Kathryn. Kathryn carefully measured her ingredients, savoured the smells, tasted the dough by dipping in her pinkie finger. Even sang to herself sometimes as she lovingly beat her mixture. Charlotte, on the other hand, attacked the ingredients, slapped them together, briskly whipped them into shape, like a drill sergeant shouting orders to his men. He noticed she hadn't melted any chocolate either. Her focus was functionality. Her pace was efficient and her movements were almost second nature, as though she was used to doing three different things at once.

'Mr Crawford, do you hear what I'm saying to you?'

'Of course,' he snapped, turning away. 'That's the nature of the industry we work in. The men knew what they were getting themselves into when they signed up for these roles. Furthermore, I don't see how this has anything to do with you.'

'It's the drinking, mainly,' Charlotte told him as she bent over and took his cake from the oven with mitts. Her perfectly proportioned rear might as well have had its own neon arrow. It drew the eye like a lighthouse. He took a stunned step back as his loins stirred, pulling on the collar of his shirt, which again appeared to be choking him.

'I need a glass of water.'

She filled one and passed it to him.

'Thank you.'

'No problem.' Then to his utter indignity she tipped his chocolate mud pat straight into the bin.

'Hey!'

She shook her finger. 'You weren't going to eat that, trust me. I saved you a tummy ache. Now . . .' she clasped her hands '. . . let me cut straight to the chase.'

'Are you sure you wouldn't like to bake another cake?'

She ignored his sarcasm, punching her fist into her palm. 'The drinking is the catalyst and everything flows from that.

The late-night parties around my pool, the litter, the vandalism, the defacing of property, the fighting, the complete lack of respect for me and for each other.' As she washed and dried his cake tin she looked over her shoulder at him. 'It has to stop.'

His mouth pulled into a hard line. 'Easier said than done, Ms Templeton.'

Really, the woman was being unrealistic. His men hated him. Imagine how far morale would drop if he suddenly demanded that there was to be no drinking after work. The shit would hit the fan then! If she thought things were bad now, imposing any sort of strictures on the men in their spare time would be tantamount to creating a riot. So far he'd ruled with fear. Anarchy was something he was not prepared to deal with.

She eyed him with misgiving. 'I didn't say it was going to be easy.'

'Why don't you make a list of damage to property instead and I will endeavour to compensate you.'

'I'm not fixing anything until I know it's not going to be damaged again.' She poured her mixture into the cake tin and placed it in the oven, frowning the whole time.

'I'll send out a memo about it.'

'How big of you. Tell me, Mr Crawford, do you miss your wife?'

He started. 'I beg your pardon?'

'It's a simple enough question.'

He was ashamed to hear his voice waver slightly. 'Of course I miss her, with every fibre of my being I miss her. So much sometimes it hurts.' He hadn't meant to say all this, but his heart seemed to take control of his voice box. The passion in his voice had clearly startled her because she was watching him with a sudden stillness about her, as though seeing him for the first time. The real him.

He didn't like it.

He didn't like it one bit.

'Then I don't get it,' she cried. 'I don't get how you can be so insensitive to these men. You are so hard on them when the situation they are in is hard enough.'

He kept his face as expressionless as he could. His only power in these situations was his mask. 'As I said before, Ms Templeton, if it's monetary compensation you want –'

'It's not all I want,' she shot at him. 'I just wish you realised that being project manager isn't just about giving orders.' She gestured at his oven. 'It'll be ready in forty minutes, damn you!'

On these words, she headed back to his foyer, swiping his dinner tray off the table as she went. The slam of the front door left him bereft. She was like a mini-cyclone. Whirring in, uncovering his soul and then leaving it naked and vulnerable surrounded by the debris of his shattered life. He looked down, realising his fingers were trembling. He slowly flexed his hands and headed outside. Augustus was sleeping. He decided to bring the cage inside anyway. He'd never admit it but he found the sight of the turkey strangely comforting. Perhaps he saw in the creature proof of his own humanity. If he were really that heartless wouldn't he have let it die? He placed the cage on the counter and turned on the television. He began watching the news but not really listening. The smell of that cooking cake was filling his lungs and making his eyes water, burning a hole right through his heart.

It didn't smell exactly like Kathryn's. It was different. Not as heavy. But nice. And when he pulled it out of the oven it sprang back immediately to his touch. He tipped it out onto a plate to allow it to cool. Kathryn had always used a rack but unfortunately the units weren't equipped with them. By this time, Augustus was stirring. The bird raised its head curiously to see what was going on.

'Do you think I should ice it?' he mused. Even he could whip up some icing, surely? There were instructions for a simple glaze written on the back of the icing sugar packet. When he was done, he stood back to admire his creation. It looked nothing like Kathryn's rich and perfect creations. For starters the glaze was a translucent white. It dripped down the sides of a cake that was rather rough and crumbling around the edges. It wasn't the work of a chef but it looked nice, homely . . . comforting.

And yet, he couldn't eat it.

The walls of the unit seemed to loom menacingly around him.

Alone, in this dimly lit room, he realised why he had feared baking so much. Not because of the process but because of this moment when he discovered there was no one to share it with. He stood looking at the cake for a long time, wondering what to do with it.

Augustus squawked.

'What do you reckon?' he looked inquiringly at the bird.

Augustus gobbled. His head moving up and down.

He sighed. 'I think you might be right.'

Chapter 13

Emily

Life seemed to have taken a nosedive – personally and professionally. At some point, her glorious new Queensland adventure had lost its honeymoon glow.

First there were the confusing but non-committal phone calls and text messages with her ex. Initially, she had thought, it was nice to catch up and good to hear how their dog was doing because she had been missing him a lot too. But essentially nothing had changed. Trent was needy but not apologetic. In fact, he was more demanding than anything else. Twice he asked her, 'Why did you leave before we had a chance to work through this?'

The query was baffling. After all, it had seemed pretty cut and dried to her when he'd asked her to move out. She said as much and he got defensive.

'I needed some space to think, you know that.'

If that wasn't a cop out, she didn't know what was. All the same, she had to ask herself the question: if he wanted to get back together would she say yes? To be honest, at that point, the decision was no longer clear. They had a lot of history and her heart still ached at the loss of the future she'd thought they would have together. But she couldn't decide what she missed more, him or the plans they'd made.

Unfortunately, in this instance, Will was not very helpful, though not through any fault of his own. She just didn't feel she could talk to him about it. She had no desire to set him up as piggy in the middle, besides the fact that talking about her feelings with Will seemed to be getting harder and harder. She had no idea why. She'd always been able to tell him anything without feeling embarrassed.

The problem was that she needed advice. Bottling up her feelings wasn't helping. So she turned to Charlotte, whose friendship was really starting to mean something to her. The resort manager often took her mother for a walk on the beach in the evening and on Thursday night Emily had joined them.

The red sun on the ocean at twilight was a wonderful backdrop to self-reflection. They walked very slowly and not very far because Mrs Templeton got tired easily.

'So, let me get this straight,' Charlotte said, picking up a seashell and passing it to her mother. 'Trent is Will's best mate.'

'Yes,' Emily nodded. 'They've known each other since primary school. Will actually introduced us.'

'Well, isn't that a pretty pickle?'

'Why?'

Charlotte laughed. 'Honey, if you don't know, I can't tell you.'

'Here.' Virginia distracted her from Charlotte's cryptic words by placing the seashell Charlotte had just given her into Emily's hand. 'For your collection.'

'Thank you,' Emily responded uncertainly.

'You spend too much time at home.' Virginia closed her fingers over the shell. 'When I was your age, I met your father. You should go out, have some fun.'

Emily bit her lip, not knowing what to say. She looked over at Charlotte, who smiled sadly. It was clear Virginia thought she was Charlotte, at least a younger version of Charlotte.

'What about that boy I see you with?' Virginia pressed her hand eagerly. 'He seems to like you.'

'Er . . .'

'Look,' Charlotte pointed at the sky, 'a sea eagle.'

Virginia looked up and they stopped walking to watch the majestic creature fly overhead. Emily stood back with Charlotte as Virginia walked forward to pick up more shells on the water's edge.

'Sorry about that,' Charlotte whispered.

'Don't be silly. I understand.'

Charlotte took a deep breath. 'So tell me, what is it that you like about Trent?'

'Well, he's handsome.' Em shrugged. 'And successful. Very successful. He's really good at what he does. I mean, his boss reckons he practises like someone with twice his level of experience. I'm in awe at the way he handles himself as a lawyer.'

Charlotte's mouth turned up wryly. 'Key word here *lawyer*, not *boyfriend*.'

'True.' Emily bit her lip and fell into a thoughtful silence.

'You know what I think?' Charlotte broke it a few seconds later.

'No, what?'

'I think it's a good thing you came to Queensland. Forget about Trent. Especially when you seem to be doing just fine without him. Do what you came here to do. Have a good time and invite me along.'

Emily laughed. 'No problem. Have you come up with that hobby yet?'

Charlotte groaned. 'I've been kind of distracted lately.'

'Well, you *are* raising a teenager and caring for an invalid. You have an excuse. I really admire you for that, you know.'

Charlotte blushed. 'Thanks, but it's really not that big a deal.'

'Of course it's a big deal. Does Zara's father ever help out?'

'Nope. Never.' Charlotte's lips pulled into a hard line. 'Not that I would want to him to.'

Emily eyed her carefully. 'You don't like him?'

'That's an understatement. But anyway,' Charlotte gave a breathy sigh as she shifted the conversation away from the touchy subject, 'about that hobby. I'm thinking something outdoorsy.'

'Oh, I'm definitely in then.' Emily nodded decisively. 'But what?'

'How about diving? I've always wanted to go, though I've been too scared to try it.'

Emily pressed her hand. 'Let's go this weekend. We have Sunday off. I'll get Will to come too. We can go out to the reef, book a tour or something. Do some snorkelling.'

Charlotte's face immediately brightened. 'That's a magnificent idea.'

It was certainly the only star on Em's horizon.

At work that week, Caesar had decided to begin his own punishment regime for her and she had been exiled to the yard. She was aware that as far as engineers went, she wasn't anywhere in Will's league. But even she knew that engineers weren't supposed to be standing outside spark-testing beams all day. That was a painter's job.

Basically, all the steel beams were painted with a hardwearing coating specifically designed to have protective properties for a marine environment. The paint was grey, the same colour as the steel, so it was actually difficult to tell with the naked eye if a spot had been missed. It was important that the beams were painted thoroughly to stop the onset of rust. Prevention was better than cure.

What she had to do was run a brush hooked up to an electric battery over a recently painted beam. If there was a spark, it indicated that this area on the beam had not been coated. To be honest, she'd quite enjoyed doing the first beam and learning about the science behind the spark test from the quality manager. But thirty-six hours later, she was ready to rip her hair out.

She had lost count of the number of beams she had brushed. At first, she had thought the most sensible thing for her to do was just get through the job so that she could get back to her real work. After all, she couldn't expect her new job to be all roses and peaches immediately. There were going to be bad days.

However, the painting team was down two guys and even with her help they weren't catching up any time soon. She could be stuck with them for days, which didn't bode well for her mental health – and, let's face it, that was already on the back foot because of Trent.

The worst thing about the job was that all the steel was laid out in a yard that was nowhere near the office dongas. It was in an area beyond the coal hills at least a five-minute drive by ute away from the main office. There were other men working in this area, a few assembling steel trusses to be driven out to the wharf and a couple of carpenters cutting up formwork. There was one toilet for them all to use. A male toilet – very dirty and equipped with one urinal and one cubicle. At first, she thought she might just bite the bullet and use this, but it was rather embarrassing having to knock on the door and ask loudly if anyone was in there first. The men within earshot would laugh loudly and yell, 'Quick, Roger, pop your dick away. She's coming in!'

They'd say this or something similar whether 'Roger' was in there or not.

When she started driving back to the main office to go to the toilet, just for a bit of privacy, the painters scoffed at that too.

'Too good for the loo, are you? But it's all right for Tanya and Jill.' Their sarcasm was potent.

The truth was finally out. Tanya and Jill were the two *female* painters who never showed up to work. Apparently, they had demanded their own toilet and their request had fallen on deaf ears. Specifically, on Caesar's deaf ears.

In all honesty, she couldn't blame them and thought it was just like Caesar not to take note of what was the heart of the problem but just give orders and expect them to be followed without question. She began to realise that if she wanted to do some real engineering she was going to have to get Tanya and Jill back at work. And to do that she needed a toilet.

Of all the things she hoped to achieve on this job, she never thought this would be one of them.

After nutting through her options, she decided to beg and plead with Caesar on their behalf. In fact, she had decided to do it that morning after Caesar's first hour of silence. Unexpectedly, an earlier opportunity presented itself. He did something rather unusual. Instead of going straight to his office that morning, he went to the kitchen.

She happened to be already standing there placing twelve bananas on the counter top with a Post-it note beside them: 'Please take one.'

They had been another present from Dipper. The loony had been leaving fruit on her desk every morning. Lost in her own annoyance at Dipper and thoughts on how to get him to stop leaving her fruit, she turned around and walked straight into Caesar.

'Oh,' she started, momentarily taken aback. 'Good morning.'

'We'll see,' he growled.

As she tried to think up a neutral reply to this remark he jumped in again.

'Would you like a slice of cake?'

She blinked. 'A slice of what?'

'A slice of cake,' he repeated, the kindness wholly belied by the impatient tone in which it was uttered. 'I've brought some in for the team. Homemade too, iced it myself.'

Her eyes widened. 'Is it your birthday, sir?'

'No. I don't celebrate birthdays.'

She could quite understand that. In fact, she was sure that he didn't celebrate Christmas, Easter, Valentine's Day or any other occasion that involved giving and smiling. The cake was an anomaly. She looked around nervously at the rest of the office. Many of her co-workers, who had stopped to gape at them, quickly and noisily turned back to their computers and resumed working at what seemed like an unnaturally efficient pace. Ann, who had been staring at them from across the room in shock, holding Caesar's morning coffee in readiness for when he passed her desk, quickly set it down and bustled over. Her face was set and her hands were wringing as she moved straight into crisis management mode.

'Can I help you with something there, Mr Crawford?'

She threw a glare in Emily's direction as though she had been responsible for this uncharacteristic turn of events.

'Ah, Ann,' Caesar actually looked rather pleased to see his secretary, 'take this.'

He shoved the large plastic container he'd been holding into her hands. 'I've brought in a cake for the office staff. See that everyone gets a piece, won't you?'

'Yes, sir, I will. If I may ask, sir . . . are you all right?'

'All right?' he repeated with raised brows. 'Of course I'm all right. Why shouldn't I be all right?'

Ann cleared her throat. 'No reason at all. In fact, might I inquire if today is a special occasion, sir?'

'No,' he snapped. 'Why does there have to be an occasion? Can't a man just feel like baking without being pestered about it?'

She visibly shrank. 'My apologies, sir. I just wanted to check to make sure you didn't want me to assemble the team so you could make a speech or something.'

'Definitely not.' He shook his head. 'It's very simple, Ann. Just cut and serve it.'

'Would you like me to bring in a piece with your coffee, sir?'

'No.' He baulked. 'That wouldn't be a good idea.' He glanced at the counter. 'But I might have one of those bananas.'

As Ann walked off, he turned to detach one from the bunch and it suddenly occurred to Emily to seize the moment. Before she lost her nerve, she quickly said to his back, which was far less scary than his front, 'Sir, might I have a word?'

'A word, a second,' he mused. 'People always underestimate how much time of mine they intend to waste.'

As he resumed facing her, his brows twitched together and she swallowed hard. Yes, he was definitely scarier face to face.

'Er . . .'

He sighed. 'And the sad thing is, I already know what you are going to say.'

'You do?'

'Of course,' he nodded dispassionately. 'You wish to complain about being made to spark test beams.'

She smiled, grateful for his ready understanding. *See, this isn't so bad.* 'Well yes, as a matter of fact I –'

'I understand but I can't help you.' His interruption was so brusque that it took her a couple of seconds to register it was over.

'But –'

'We're two men down in the painting team, we're behind and there is no one else to do it. It's nothing against you personally, it's just a matter of need. I have a need of you there. And might I say,' he offered almost kindly (*almost* kindly), 'since I've had you helping out the painters, their productivity has improved and our schedules are looking much better.'

'But we could get the real painters back if we improved the amenities.'

'Couches in the lunch room, I suppose,' he scoffed. 'No, I think not. If it's good enough for us, it should be good enough for them.'

'That's not –'

'Your contribution is putting us back on track.' He folded his arms, regarding her thoughtfully. 'I don't say this often but well done.'

'But I don't like spark testing,' she blurted angrily. 'I think we should try and get the other painters back.'

He nodded with anything but understanding. 'Listen to me, Emily, and let me make it clear that I am making a huge concession by telling you this because frankly I don't normally exert myself as much for my employees. I prefer in general to let them navigate their way through their careers on their own merit. But in this case,' he nodded again ever so graciously, 'I am willing to now give you a sage piece of advice that will open your mind. Advice that was given to me by a site supervisor when I was your age. He said to me and I quote, "Never be good at a shit job." There, now you know everything.' He smiled. 'Best get back to work. And don't worry, eventually all those beams will be spark tested and you can return to your previous tasks. I'll keep you posted.' Clearly the subject was closed because he was walking away. She glanced down at her sweaty palms, then rubbed them down her hips.

That went well.

Here she was, back again in the same place she had been when she'd left Perth. A doormat. Why was it that every man she met, including Trent, thought she would just accept her fate and do as she was told?

Because that's what you do. That's what you've always been. The yes girl.

You count cracks. You spark test. What next? Making sure every bolt on the job had a nut.

She shook her head so fiercely that she nearly did her neck. Perhaps it was time to break the mould. She would get that toilet donga for the painters without Caesar's help. Of course, the decision was easier made than enacted. She put on her hard hat and massive yellow vest and went out back to the yard. While spark testing, she continued to stew about her predicament. The dilemma was a bit of a challenge. How did one acquire a toilet donga on a site like this, if one had no money, no permission and no experience?

One didn't.

If she couldn't buy one or rent one without funds then the only other option was to borrow one from somewhere else. Her thoughts immediately flew to all the portable loos she had seen on the wharf thanks to Will's game of hide and seek. There had been many of them. Surely they could spare one.

At lunchtime, she returned to the office hoping to catch Will and bounce a few ideas off him. She went inside to her desk to retrieve her lunch box, which was in her backpack, and her eyes alighted on two mangoes that had been left next to her keyboard.

What the . . .?

She sighed as she picked up the Post-it note attached to it. *Love from Dipper.*

Twice in one day? How was this possible? Yesterday she'd asked Will to pass on a message to Dipper on the wharf saying she didn't want any more fruit. He said he'd passed it on so why had the fruit doubled in quantity?

She picked up the mangoes and went outside. There was a man leaning on the side of the office smoking a cigarette.

'I need to talk to Dipper. Do you know where he is?'

He grinned. 'Oh ho ho ho, but that's good news for the riggers.'

'Why?'

He tipped his hard hat to her. 'Maybe you should ask Spooks.'

Spooks? Who the hell was Spooks?

She noticed that all the men had nicknames. It seemed to be a site tradition, and there was always some sort of reasoning behind the name. For example, the men called the safety manager Wally. His name was actually Paul. The man was constantly wandering around telling people off for not doing the safe thing. For example, getting into a tug without a life jacket, not wearing your PPE, ignoring signs, etc. He was very over the top with his nit-picking but apparently his stealth was just as incredible. He would creep up on you when you least expected it. Pounce on your crime like a cat out of a box with an 'Ah-hah!' so smug it was almost comical. So whenever someone seemed to be doing something dodgy the men would call out, 'Where's Wally, where's Wally?' Like the cartoon character from the children's books – the face hidden in the crowd that suddenly leaps out.

She didn't have a nickname yet but was sure it couldn't be long before she did. She hoped they would go easy on her.

'Where is Spooks?'

'Right over there.' He pointed to where a tall, skinny man was seated at a white trestle table. The table was located with many others in a courtyard framed on three sides by office dongas, a shade cloth over the top. Emily often ate her sandwiches there, sometimes with Will if he wasn't on the wharf but most of the time with any random who decided that today was the day he was going to tell her his life story.

And there were a lot of 'randoms'. Men who just had to get it 'off their chest'. From fights at home with the wife because he was working away too much to worries about becoming a father for the first time when he was on the other side of the country. She listened to men talk about their kids, their dogs, their parents, their illnesses, their shortcomings, their hopes, their dreams and even their aspirations.

Basically, all the things men couldn't or rather *wouldn't* talk about with other men. She supposed because she was female it seemed to be okay to let a more sensitive, more human side of themselves show and some of them were simply desperate for it.

Mangoes in hand, she crossed the courtyard and sat down next to Spooks. 'Hello.'

He looked up in surprise, first at her, then at her mangoes.

'Do you like fruit?' she asked sweetly.

'Yes.'

'Then please take them. And in return I want you to take me out onto the wharf to see Dipper.'

And Will.

Maybe she could get his ideas about the toilet business as well.

'Now hold on a minute there.' Spooks pushed the mangoes away. 'I'm not risking my neck for no second-hand fruit.'

Her eyes narrowed on him. 'So you know I got these mangoes from Dipper.'

'Of course I do. Everybody does.' He grinned. 'We've all been watching his courtship of you with great interest.'

'His courtship?' Emily repeated, wrinkling her brow. 'But he's much too old for me.'

'Really?' Spooks inquired. 'Perhaps you'd like someone a little younger . . . like Boy Scout?'

'Will?' Emily's eyes widened before she shook her head. 'Oh, I don't think of him like that.'

'At all?'

She felt herself flush as she thought guiltily of that moment back in the portable loo. An incident that seemed to play on her mind a lot these days. Could it be that her feelings for Will weren't as innocent as she was trying to persuade herself? Charlotte had hinted at it. Now Spooks was too.

She pushed the thought aside and averted her face. In any case, Spooks was being a little too intrusive for someone she'd only just met. 'Will you take me out to the wharf or not?' she said between her teeth.

Spooks considered the matter for a second, licking his lips. 'All right.'

She observed his crafty expression for a moment. There weren't many men who would cross Caesar willingly. She had the feeling, however, that Spooks wasn't doing it for her but for his own enjoyment. She could see that he was the kind of man who thrived on drama. Still, what other option did she have? Neither Will nor Dipper seemed to be coming in for lunch and as far as she was concerned, her need to see each of them was urgent.

So after a few minutes, they headed over to his vehicle.

It was a gorgeous day. The sun glistened brightly on the ocean, giving her hope. Activity buzzed and whirred around her – both of man and machinery.

Spooks turned the car out onto the right arm of the wharf where most of the men were working on installing the new conveyor trusses. The piling barge was setting up beside the jetty a little further down. It had floated into position and was now in the process of dropping its giant steel legs. Men in vests bustled about carrying rope and shackles. It seemed like everyone was in the process of lifting something.

'We need a clean out and some order around here,' Spooks commented as he gingerly navigated around a cluster of dongas. 'I really think we could do with more working space and less dongas. They just encourage the men to loiter.'

Emily looked at the dongas thoughtfully. Getting a lunch room as well would definitely be a plus. 'I wonder . . . do you have spare one?'

He squeezed the car into a tight bay behind another ute. 'I wouldn't be surprised. Why do you ask?'

'Just thinking out loud.'

She wasn't going to explain herself to Spooks until she had a fully formed plan in her head. For now, she'd stick with finding Dipper.

And she did find him. Only he was in a man cage being hoisted ten metres above the deck by a five-tonne crane so that he could perform some welding on the new conveyor trusses. She was left standing at the base of the crane, bending her neck while shielding her eyes from the sun to look at him. It didn't look like he was coming down any time soon.

Damn!

She had really hoped to make this quick.

Many of the men commented on her position there.

'Lucky man,' they said, 'to have such a dedicated woman.'

The observation irritated her. Given Spooks' earlier comments about Dipper's 'courtship' she had to wonder if he really did have the hots for her.

Her peripheral vision caught a third person and she spun eagerly to see Will walking towards her. To her surprise, her heart immediately picked up pace as she took in his familiar scruffy facial hair, the quiet confidence of his walk and that lopsided smile.

Oh damn!

The shocking confirmation hit her. *I* do *have feelings for Will.* She wasn't sure how deep they ran, but they were definitely there. A white-bellied sea eagle flew overhead, the shadow of its body passing across her own, almost making her feel like she'd transitioned from one dimension to another. She shivered.

'Hey, Em.'

'Er . . . Hi, Will.'

'Why are you staring at me like that?' He took off his headgear. 'Do I have bird shit on my hard hat again?'

'No,' she choked. *Pull it together.* 'I, er . . .' Why was she there again? She straightened her shoulders. 'Your message didn't work. I got another two more mangoes today.'

'Oh.' He didn't seem surprised. 'He thought I was lying.'

'Why would you lie?'

He examined a graze on his left hand. 'Look, there's something you should know . . . about Dipper.'

'Don't worry,' she made haste to reassure him, 'I already know.'

He seemed relieved. 'You do?'

'Yes.'

'You're not mad?'

'No, why should I be?' She shrugged. 'I mean, he's not my type, but that's not his fault.'

'No, I guess not.'

'*Although*,' she drawled, keeping her eyes on a crack in the pavement she was kicking with the toe of her boot, 'I've been thinking lately that I should be more open to dating people I wouldn't normally date.'

Will cleared his throat cautiously. 'Really?'

'Well, yeah.' She kept her gaze firmly on the ground. 'Have you ever thought about going out with someone you would never normally go for?'

'Seems like a bit of a waste of time to me.' He shook his head. 'If there's no attraction there's no attraction. Weren't you the one who was talking up the instant spark two weeks ago?'

She bit her lip. 'Yeah, but –'

'Em, you're not seriously thinking about going out with Dipper, are you?'

'No.' She shook her head. 'But what about other people?'

'What other people?'

'I don't know. *Other people*.'

He frowned.

'Look, forget I said anything.' She broke off, kicking herself for even raising the topic. 'I asked Spooks to bring me out because I wanted to ask your advice on something.'

'*Spooks*.' He glanced around, saying the name as though it were the source of all the evil in the world. His eyes alighted on the man himself who was standing only a few metres away. Spooks lifted his hand for a cheeky wave and Will's expression darkened. He moved closer, grabbing her by the arm and pulling her out of earshot. A ripple shot through her body at his sudden closeness.

'You can't trust Spooks,' he hissed. 'All he wants is gossip and a good show. You really need to watch yourself around him.'

'Why do they call him Spooks?'

'He –'

'Hey, Boy Scout!' a voice called out. 'Stop trying to steal her. She's come to see me. Play fair, mate! Play fair!'

They both turned around in time to see Dipper's man cage touch ground again. 'Hello, lovely,' he grinned at her as he unclipped his harness from the cage and jumped out. 'How wonderful to see you.'

Will gave a long-suffering sigh, causing Dipper's gaze to touch him briefly. 'If you'll excuse us, Boy Scout,' he snorted, 'we'd like a bit of *privacy.*'

Will didn't immediately follow the order, but looked askance at her instead. 'Perhaps we'll talk about that thing you wanted to ask me later?'

She nodded.

He hesitated, with another glance at Dipper, and then shaking his head walked away.

'So how did you enjoy those bananas?' Dipper zapped her concentration back as she realised she was watching Will walk away.

'To be honest, I gave most of them to other people.'

'And the pineapple?'

'That too.'

His face fell. 'Perhaps I shouldn't ask about the papaya and the mangoes then.'

'The truth is, Dipper, I just can't eat that much fruit and I would really appreciate it if you would stop leaving it on my desk.'

He scratched his head and looked at the ground in embarrassment. 'I was just trying to get your attention.'

'Why?' she asked.

He looked up in hope. 'I thought maybe you'd like to go out with me sometime.'

So it was true. She shouldn't have asked. She should have just backed away quietly when she had the chance.

'I was thinking I could show you some of the sights of Queensland. Perhaps we could go sailing.' He looked at her sincerely. 'You told me how eager you were to try new things.'

'Er . . .' She searched for an excuse that wouldn't hurt his feelings. It was very difficult to find one. 'The thing is, Dipper . . .'

Interpreting her reluctance he tried something different. 'What about the beach? I could take you to Airlie Beach for a sunbake. You'd love it.'

'I don't really do sunbaking, Dipper. I burn easily.'

'There must be something I can do for you, something you want to see.'

She was about to reiterate there was nothing, when a thought occurred to her. The passion in Dipper's voice was just the sort of drive she needed behind one very big 'ask'.

The fact was, she knew what she needed and Dipper could easily provide the manpower. She was an engineer – technically, higher in the command chain. So why not use her clout? What there was of it, anyway.

'Actually there is something . . .'

He stood tall and brave. 'Name it.'

She winced. 'Are you sure? Because it's kind of unusual and not exactly in your schedule this week.'

His expression darkened determinedly. 'Just tell me what it is.'

'I want a toilet.'

His brows drew together over the bridge of his nose. '*A what*?'

'You heard me.'

'Geez, women have really changed from flowers and chocolates!'

Emily dismissed this. 'I'm asking you as an engineer, not as a potential girlfriend,' she said calmly. 'I need a portable loo in the painting yard and a lunch room, too. Spooks reckons you guys would probably have a vacant office donga. Maybe,' she suggested slowly, 'you could get a few of the guys together, a flatbed and a crane and move those things out there for me?'

'Does Caesar know about this?'

She squared her shoulders and lifted her chin. 'No.'

Was he going to wimp out on her now? She wouldn't blame him – job on the line and all. Maybe she shouldn't have asked. He paused, the fingers of his right hand rubbing the bristles on the base of his chin.

'I tell you what,' the hand dropped as a decision seemed to be made, 'I'll do that for you *if* you let me take you out to dinner in Mackay tomorrow night.'

Was she really going to use a date to get ahead? Her gut reaction to the suggestion was abhorrence. But as she looked at his face, she realised something. He was doing her a favour. A big favour. She owed him something.

'Can't I just give you a carton?' she asked.

'Will you drink it with me?'

'No.'

'Then it has to be dinner.'

'Fine.' They shook on it. 'But just as a friend, mind you. I'm . . . not really interested in you like that.'

'Of course.' He winked at her.

She felt heat travel up her neck as he walked off whistling.

That toilet better bloody well get the painters back on site.

She turned around to find Spooks looking at her.

'So . . .' His nose seemed to twitch. 'You've got a date with Dipper.'

'Not yet.' She tossed her head. Dipper still had to make good on his promise.

He clicked his tongue. 'So you want to go chat up Boy Scout next?'

'No.' She glared at him. 'Will you drive me back now?'

He smirked. 'Suppose.'

The truth was, she had no idea what she was going to do about Will or the revelation that had occurred on the wharf that afternoon. It was going to be a struggle just to act normal. When she met up with him after work that night, she didn't tell him about her deal with Dipper. She tried to tell herself it was because of Trent – that she didn't want Trent finding out about her dinner date. But it was just another self delusion because when her ex texted her just before bed with:

So any big plans this weekend?

She wrote back immediately:

Yeah, I got a date.

Trent didn't respond to that and she was glad. She didn't want to think about him or about Will. All she wanted was some 'quiet time' in her head.

The next morning at around ten-thirty, a truck arrived in the yard. She didn't know how, but Dipper had come through for her and in record time too. He hopped off the back of the beeping truck as the driver reversed it into place.

'One portable toilet, one lunch room,' he announced, jerking his thumb over his shoulder with a grin. 'I even got you a table and fridge.'

It was true. While small, the vacant office had a power point in it. They could connect the fridge Dipper had sourced. The grubby old trestle table wasn't luxurious but it was functional. Pity there was no sink. But she supposed she didn't really have time to be digging leach drains to accommodate that anyway.

'Wow.' She felt a rush of warmth towards her admirer as she examined the treasures he had brought her. 'Thank you, Dipper. It's all perfect.'

'So are you.' He smiled right back. 'I'm looking forward to tonight.'

She wanted to curl up as his eyes eagerly appraised her from head to toe before he turned away. 'I'll pick you up at seven, okay?'

She couldn't go back on her word now. Not after accepting the donga he'd gone to great lengths to procure.

'Sure.' She tried to infuse enthusiasm into her voice. It was just a meal. She could use the time to let him down gently.

Explain to him that she'd just come out of long-term relationship and that as a couple they would never work out.

Dipper and a couple of men with him used the crane in the yard to take the donga off the truck. They set it on some stray concrete blocks that weren't really meant for it. Emily knew that probably wasn't the best thing to do and if they were doing this right she should have had some proper concrete footings poured. But who had the time to wait for them to cure? She wanted those painters back at work as soon as possible. By the end of the day her wish was granted. When the men from Queensland Coats saw what she had done they called their female teammates and let them know. Both girls would be back at work Monday. She couldn't believe it. She was off the hook. In two days she'd be in the office doing what she'd come here to do.

As soon as she'd notified Caesar, of course . . .

Inwardly, she quaked. *Shit! What have I done?*

She came in from the yard to have lunch in the courtyard. She was so lost in her own thoughts about the upcoming confrontation that when Will pounced on her as she got out of her car she nearly jumped out of her skin.

'What the hell is going on?' he rasped.

She put a hand to her chest and concentrated on slowing her breathing. 'Will, you scared the life out of me.'

He ignored her reprimand. 'I thought we were going to the reef this weekend.'

'We are.' Her brow wrinkled in confusion.

'Then why do you have a date?'

'It's tonight.'

'Who with?'

'Dipper.'

'Dipper! You said you weren't going to go there.'

'Wait a minute. Who did you hear this from?'

From his wording and ignorance as to who it was, she gathered that he hadn't heard the rumour on site. Hurt and distrust arced through her body like a whip. 'Trent told you, didn't he? You two have been chatting about me, haven't you?'

His skin stained red but he neither confirmed nor denied it.

'I thought you said you don't talk to him about me! That you didn't want to get involved.'

'He texted me,' Will protested. 'He wanted to know what was going on.'

She wasn't listening to his excuses though. 'Talk about a double standard.'

'You've got it all wrong.'

But she'd already shut shop. 'Just leave me alone, Will. I don't owe you or Trent any explanations.'

'Em –'

'I can see whoever I want.' She flicked her pointer finger around the car park and several interested construction workers stopped to grin and watch. 'It's nothing to do with either of you.'

On this cutting remark she stalked off. He didn't join her for lunch. She ate on her own and felt miserable through every bite. She hated fighting with Will. She hated these new feelings she had for him. And she hated that he was more concerned about Trent than the fact that she was going on a date with someone new.

Emily came in from the yard early that day, about half an hour before knock-off. She wanted to square things away with Caesar so she wouldn't be worrying about it on her day off. She was also hoping to see Will around. Try to patch things up or something. Were they still going to the reef the next day? She didn't want to stay mad at him forever.

Unfortunately, he was nowhere in sight.

With no best friend to stall her, she found herself standing outside Caesar's office, feeling all her daredevilry melting away. Yesterday, her bold move had seemed smart and worth it. Today she felt like she was about to confess an act of terrorism to the US president.

She knocked.

There was a lengthy sigh from within.

Great! A good omen, just for a change.

'Come in.'

When she walked in, Mark was standing by the window. He was gazing unseeingly out at Augustus's pen, holding a piece of paper that looked like it had been opened and folded many times over. As if to prove the theory, he refolded it now – twice in half – before placing it in his shirt pocket.

'So,' he said, voice deadpan, 'turns out you're a rather resourceful young lady. I take it you've come to tell me that you're no longer needed in the yard.'

She swallowed hard. 'Yes.'

His mouth twitched. 'When I wouldn't listen to you, you sorted things out for yourself.'

She waited with baited breath. Was there actually an apology coming? Wow! She hadn't dared to even hope –

'Don't do it again,' he barked.

'No, sir.' She shook her head most vigorously. 'Of course not.'

'Rest assured, however, I will be paying much more attention to you in future. Obviously, it seems, you have an opinion worth sharing.' He turned back to the window, gazing out at the same scene he had been studying earlier, though she had a feeling it was not Augustus's pen that he was watching so closely. 'I wonder,' he mused, 'if you might have some advice for me.'

'Me, sir?'

'Yes, I know, funny I should ask you, isn't it? The new kid on the block, who can't follow orders and comes with a very lacklustre resume?'

Gee thanks.

'But, believe me, I wouldn't be asking you unless I'd been strongly advised to do so.' He paused, looking up at the ceiling momentarily as if expecting his speech to be punctuated by some divine bolt of lightning. Nothing happened.

Confused, she also looked up at the ceiling but the plasterboard was an uncomforting, unmarked and undamaged white.

'Emily,' his soft voice recalled her attention.

'Sorry, sir.' Her gaze quickly flew back to his. He was amused, like a cat playing with his food. 'I'm concerned,' he began levelly, 'about the level of drinking and depression on this job. I've seen you talking to many of the men at lunchtimes. Your ear is probably closer to the ground than mine is. Do any of the men confide in you?'

Her lips tilted wryly at that. 'You could say so, sir.'

'What is it they need? What do they want? What can I give them?'

'Oh that's easy, sir.' She smiled. 'What they need is therapy. And lots of it.'

'Really?'

'No, sir, I'm joking. I just meant that many of them, not all of course, seem to keep things bottled up. If they had someone to talk to about it, it might ease some of the tension around here.' She rolled her eyes. 'It would certainly free up my lunch breaks.'

'Is that so?'

'It was just a thought, sir.' She looked at his reflective expression with some surprise. She hadn't seriously considered that he would listen to anything she had to say – least of all some over-the-top suggestion that some of his men needed counselling. She might as well say he was running a loony bin and hand in her resignation now.

Seriously, Emily, do you think through anything you say?

'But I can see your point.' He nodded as he turned things over in his mind.

You can?

'They need an unbiased third party to complain to. More improvements could lead from there.' He looked approvingly at her. 'I wouldn't be the first project manager to hire a social worker to counsel his FIFO workers on a part-time basis. The problem is,' he ran a frustrated hand through his dark hair, 'it's more work than I have time for right now. I'll have to get head office involved to find some likely candidates. Then there's the interview process. It'll be minimum a month before anyone gets here.'

'Really?' Emily blinked and then a startlingly brilliant idea happened to tap on the side of her brain. 'Actually, I happen to know someone who lives locally, is fully qualified and would love part-time social work.'

He turned on her with undeniable interest. 'Is he any good though?'

'It's a she,' Emily went on eagerly. 'And of course she's good. So good that she writes self-help books too. I've heard they're excellent and based on some of her own life experiences, so very moving and inspirational.'

'Really? Do you have her contact details?'

Emily took a deep breath, pleased to be so much help this morning. She smiled widely. 'It's Charlotte Templeton.'

Caesar's gaze returned to that mysterious patch of ceiling. 'That'd be right, wouldn't it?' he said quietly.

Chapter 14

Will

They were both mad at him – Em *and* his best mate. He'd completely stuffed up everything. In hindsight, there was a lot to be said for minding one's own business. But when Trent had told him angrily that Em had a date this weekend and why hadn't he mentioned it, the blood had shot straight to his temples. And not because he was angry for Trent's sake. No, that emotion would at least have been rational.

Instead, he was up and off like a crazy person demanding answers and explanations like he had a right to be jealous. Which he didn't.

Trent had been very clear about his intentions this time. 'It's made me realise the truth, mate. I need her. She's my rock. I should never have let her go. Is there any chance you could convince her to come back to Perth?'

'I think it's a bit late for that now,' he'd said in response. 'She loves it here.'

Besides, he didn't believe it was in Em's best interests to give up the best job she'd ever had. Trent had seemed keen to argue about it at that point but he just wanted to get off the phone and find out what the whole 'date' thing was about.

As though that had helped his cause.

She'd told him to get lost in short order. And in all seriousness, he needed a reality check. Trent wanted them to get back together. And Em probably wasn't over him yet either. Otherwise, she wouldn't be doing crazy stuff like dating Dipper. That had *rebound* written all over it.

He had to give these two some time. Allow the dust to settle before he made any moves. The last thing he wanted was for Trent to think he betrayed him or for Emily to use him to get over his best mate.

So there he was, sitting in the office, resigning himself to his new friend *patience*.

His stomach was gurgling because he hadn't eaten lunch and the guys on site were annoying the hell out of him. He was designing some temporary platforms for them to stand on while they worked on the drive tower. The problem was they needed the design yesterday. He had men coming in every hour asking, 'Are you done yet? Are you done yet?' Which not only stressed the hell out of him but made him want to punch them in the face, and a couple of times he nearly did.

It didn't help that his concentration was shot to pieces over Emily's dinner plans. Of all the crazy things he thought she'd do next, that was definitely not one of them. Over the years, he'd got used to accepting the fact that she was dating Trent. That she was off limits and forever more would be. But this!

This was different. There was no way in hell she was falling for Dipper of all people. But how could he stop her?

'So I, er, heard about the bet.'

He looked up angrily to see who was addressing him and Nova immediately held up both palms in surrender.

'Whoa! Did I say something wrong?'

'What do you want, Nova? And before you ask, no I haven't finished designing the platform and no you can't have member sizes yet.'

'Rest easy,' he drawled. 'I'm not after member sizes. I just want to know the latest instalment of this wharf's hot new drama.'

'I'm not in the mood, Nova.'

Nova ignored him. 'I heard Dipper's winning the competition. Gotta date with the little princess tonight. Impressed the hell out of her with some fancy new toilet.'

'A toilet?' Will's eyes widened.

'You don't know anything, do you?' Nova chuckled. 'Apparently, she got Dipper to move a toilet and lunch room off the wharf to get the painters back in the yard. Worked a treat too.'

'Why didn't she ask me for help?' he accidentally asked out loud.

Nova laughed. 'So your nose *is* out of joint. I knew it!'

Will turned back to his computer screen petulantly and stared at his design model in annoyance.

'You know what your problem is?' Nova began knowledgably.

'I know you're dying to tell me,' Will sighed.

Ignoring his lack of enthusiasm, Nova rolled across the room on his chair from his desk to Will's. 'You've put your relationship in a box labelled friendship and it's been there so long you just don't know how to get out. Make that leap, jump that moat.'

How true. And how misplaced.

Will turned back. 'Nova, I don't care what you think you've heard about this bet, but you've got it all wrong. I'm not going after Em.'

'Why the hell not? Every man and his bolt cutter can see you're more than half in love with her.'

'Don't be ridiculous, she's my friend.'

'Exactly,' Nova agreed. 'And in order to get out of the friendship zone, you need her to see you in a new and different light. You need to show her *sexy* Will.'

'*What?*' Will shut his eyes and prayed for patience.

'Do you know how to flirt, Will?' Nova asked thoughtfully. 'I'm not talking about paying women compliments 'cause any dickhead can do that. AKA Dipper. I'm talking about getting under a woman's skin.'

'Okay, you need to stop now.' Will lowered his voice to a whisper. 'Because now you're just embarrassing yourself.'

Unfortunately, Nova did not agree. 'I'm trying to help you. I think if you –'

'She's my best mate's girl, all right!' Will blurted. 'They might be *technically* broken up right now but they're going to get back together. I can't go there.'

There he'd said it. The truth was out. That, at least, ought to shut him up.

It didn't.

'Why?'

Will remained silent.

'Would he keep his distance if the roles were reversed?'

Will glared at him. 'I don't know. Probably.'

'If he's such a good mate, why don't you ever talk about him?'

Because I'm too busy feeling guilty about wanting to screw him over. He shook the thought from his head and said tightly, 'He's in Perth. My focus is the project at the moment. That's where it should be.'

Nova rolled his eyes. 'Let me get this straight. He's not really her boyfriend and he's in another town but instead of seizing the opportunity you're being a Boy Scout – all noble and shit. For crying out loud, Will. One of these days, you're going to have to take some prisoners.'

'Not today.' Will pushed a drawing he had marked up in red across the desk towards him. 'Here are the final member sizes for the platform. Can you knock that drawing out in an hour? I'm pretty sure that's when Spooks will come back in nagging for it.'

He stood up, gathering another wad of drawings from another file.

'Where are you going?' Nova demanded.

'To inspect the concrete slab for the pour tomorrow.'

The truth was, he'd already checked all the reinforcing in the drive tower first-floor slab that morning. But he couldn't stand being in the office a second longer, especially if Nova was going to persist in giving him unwanted advice. Before his friend could protest he grabbed his hat off the filing cabinet and walked out. Breathing in the sweet tropical air, his heart rate began to slow, his blood pressure dropped and he stopped sweating.

He should never have invited her to Queensland. He'd learned to live without hope and bringing it back into his life had been a colossal mistake. If he had to live through losing her again, it was going to be worse. Much worse.

He marched on, trying not to grind his teeth. *Just get through tonight.*

Perhaps he could go on a long run. Burn off all this jealousy making his body toxic. Then have a shower, dinner and get on his Xbox. He could kill aliens till his brain went dead. When he could no longer think, then he'd go to bed and hopefully smother any further frustration in sleep.

Satisfied with this plan, he put part one into action as soon as he got back to the resort that night. Changing into shorts, T-shirt and sneakers, he took off down the road and straight towards the beach. His feet hit Salonika's white coastline and he began to run right along the water. His thighs burned as the sand made it that much harder to keep pace. But he loved it. Running along the beach was his favourite thing to do around here. Where else could you get a more picturesque workout?

The surrounding bushland was alive with the sound of cane toads and birds. Occasionally a white-faced heron or crow would squawk at him as he ran past. He ran till it was dark and his whole body ached.

Physically, he felt great until he saw Emily getting into a vehicle with Dipper when he walked across the Silver Seas car park. A muscle cramped in his neck as he clenched his jaw too quickly. Their eyes met across the car park but she neither smiled nor waved. Clearly she was still angry with him.

She was dressed in a pair of jeans and a white top with no sleeves – nothing particularly spectacular but he thought she looked beautiful. Those jeans were as snug as a glove, showing off her shapely hips and long legs. And the top looked soft and silky to touch. The neckline skated the top of her breasts in an inviting fashion that made him yearn. So much so that his voice came out on a croak.

'Hi, Em.'

No response.

'Have a good night, Boy Scout,' Dipper called out to him, as he opened the door for Emily. 'We certainly intend to.'

As they drove away, he realised that whatever benefit he had gained from the run was gone. He was now back to square one. He walked into his unit, had a quick shower and ordered dinner. When he caught himself pacing the floor at one point, he sat down on the couch and turned on the television. The pictures moved past his unseeing eyes in abstract flashes. And then there was a knock at the door.

Dinner had arrived.

He got up to answer it and found he was wrong.

It was Nova with a large bottle of tequila and a bucket of fresh prawns.

'I've cancelled your dinner. We're having prawns and getting pissed.'

'What?'

As he was still processing what was happening, Nova pushed past him and went straight into his kitchen. 'You got a pot in here?' He began opening cupboards.

'Nova, I don't think I'm in the mood for this.'

His friend snorted. 'What are you talking about? You're in the perfect fuckin' mood. Depressed, lonely and bored. Consider me your saviour.' He took a bow and then went back to opening cupboards.

For a moment, Will stood there in indecision, his hand still resting on the doorknob. The image of Emily getting into Dipper's car once more flashed before his eyes. Her smile so uncertain and yet so kissable.

He shut the door. 'Did you bring any lemons?'

Nova dropped a bag on the counter. 'Now you're talking!'

Will awoke to a sharp tapping on the side of his head – like someone was trying to carve him a second nose. He swatted his hand clumsily in the vicinity of the pecking and it momentarily stopped. But he was awake now. Or at least awake enough to register that his mouth tasted like he had fungi growing between his teeth. He opened one eyelid a crack only to be blinded by the light blazing through his sliding door. He shut it again and moaned. The sound of his own whimpering hurt his ears.

Wait? Sliding door?

He opened one eyelid briefly again before squeezing it shut.

Yes, he was in his living room. On the floor. The reason why his back hurt so much suddenly became clear. He must have been here all night. Something pecked his shoulder. This time, when he put his hand out to brush it away, his fingers felt feathers. And he heard gobbling.

Great. He groaned. *There's a turkey in here.*

No doubt the flyscreen on his sliding door was open. As the bird continued to peck at him, he sat up. The room spun for a moment and he cradled his head in his hands while it took its time to right itself.

What happened? And why does that thing keep pecking me?

They weren't usually this forward or aggressive. Then he realised it wasn't trying to attack him, it was actually trying to pick something off him.

Is that hair?

It did, indeed, seem to be human hair cuttings. All over his shirtless chest and all around him on the floor. *Wait a minute.*

If the hair was on the floor then what was left on his head? He reached up desperately to feel his face. His chin was as smooth as a boiled egg. *I've been shaved!*

His fingers roved upwards into his hair. Thankfully, he wasn't bald. But huge tufts had been cut in random places all over his head. On the coffee table, just at his eye level, was a selection of empty bottles and lemon skins and a saltshaker.

Two tequila.

One bourbon.

And some dodgy-looking Mexican stuff, no doubt bought on special at the local pub.

'You had quite a night, didn't you?'

He nearly jumped out of his skin as a crackly voice penetrated his senses. His gaze swung to the couch where seated quite primly was a rather frail-looking woman in an old-fashioned pink nightgown. She smiled indulgently at him, her eyes travelling down his naked torso with some interest. 'I hear celebrities like you like to trash hotels all the time.'

'Who are you?' he demanded.

'I'm Virginia Templeton.' She held out her hand, which he took gingerly. 'Thank you for staying in my resort. It's not often we get a member of the Brisbane Lions with us.'

'I beg your pardon?'

'It's great you're back in the team for another season. They must really like you.'

'Right.' He winced because it hurt to talk.

This woman had to be Charlotte's mother – the woman with Alzheimer's. Had anyone or anything else wandered in last night while he wasn't looking?

He felt around on the floor for his glasses so he could get a better look at her. Luckily they were on the rug, near where his head had lain previously. He put them on and swore. Someone had removed the lenses from the frame. It was like wearing a useless piece of wire.

'Are you all right, dear?' Virginia asked.

'No so much,' he croaked and, standing up, stepped over a smelly plate of prawn shells and then over an empty bag of chips. Where the hell was Nova? That guy had a lot to answer for. He went to the phone on the wall and dialled reception.

A rather breathless-sounding Charlotte picked up.

'Hi, Lottie, it's Will,' he said. 'Are you looking for your mum? Because she's at my place.'

'Oh thank God!' she said, sounding relieved. 'I'll be right over.'

With effort he hung up the phone and turned around. 'Okay,' he pointed at Virginia, 'you stay right there. I'm just going to go put a shirt on.'

'Don't do anything on my account,' Virginia called after him.

Rubbing his temple, he made the small but painful trek to his bedroom and stopped in the doorway.

What the . . .?

There was screwed up white paper all over the floor. He must have emptied at least a ream last night. Where he'd got it all from, he had no idea.

He had very few clothes in addition to his site uniform, so he didn't bother to hang them in the wardrobe but just lived out of his suitcase. Paper crunching beneath his feet, he walked over to the brown case sitting under the window and flipped the lid.

It was empty.

Where the hell are my clothes?

He went into his walk-in robe and was relieved to see a couple of uniforms still hanging there from when he'd washed them last.

Stumped, he walked back out again and looked at the floor. He picked up one of the bits of paper and unravelled it. Holding the crumply paper a couple of inches away from his face, he squinted at the page and just managed to discern his own handwriting.

Dear Emily, I don't know how to tell you this but

That's where it stopped. He dropped it and picked up another.

Dear Emily, Do you remember when we first met? Well

That one broke off too. He looked around the room at the rest of them and then shut his eyes.

'Aw shit!'

The doorbell rang and he glanced down at his boxers.

Oh stuff it!

It was only Charlotte come to collect her mother anyway. He'd just hurry her along and then sort this mess out later. He threw open the door.

'Emily!'

'Will!' Her mouth dropped open. 'What's happened to you?'

Oh crap.

'What are you doing here?'

She wrung her hands. 'After we left things yesterday, I wasn't sure if we were still going to the reef today.'

The reef!

Oh crap.

'I mean, I'm still mad at you,' she said sternly. 'But I'm willing to talk about it if you are.'

'Of course I'm willing to talk about it.'

Just not right now!

'Can I come in?'

Just then, Charlotte strolled up, repeating quite unnecessarily, 'Shit, Will! What happened to you? That's the worst haircut I've ever seen.'

Geez! Can't a guy catch a break?

'Thanks,' he muttered.

'Where's my mum?' She stepped round him and went into the unit; her voice sounded again a second later as she entered the main living space. 'Damn it, Will! I thought you were different from the rest of the louts paying me to destroy my rooms.'

'I'll clean it up!' he yelled over his shoulder. 'Promise!'

And when I get my hands on Nova, I'll strangle him.

He turned back to Emily, whose eyes he noticed were running down his bare chest with some interest as though she were noticing some strange birthmark on his skin that hadn't been there before.

He cleared his throat. 'Er, do you want to come in?'

'Yeah.'

She stepped inside.

He shut the door. 'Look, Em, I'm sorry about Trent.'

Her eyes lifted from his chest as she crossed her arms. 'It's okay. I think I probably over-reacted anyway. I just got really angry thinking about the two of you gossiping about me.'

'It wasn't like that. I haven't told him anything you've told me in confidence,' he assured her. 'He was angry about you dating someone new and he texted me to find out what was going on. It just sort of threw me when I received his message because I didn't already know about it. I was really surprised because normally you tell me everything. And it just seemed really weird, especially when you assured me you weren't going to go out with Dipper.'

Her chin lifted and she looked rather satisfied. 'Really? He was angry about Dipper?'

That's what you took from what I just said. He sighed. 'Yes.'

She smiled delightedly. 'Good. It's about time he had a taste of his own medicine. I hope he was stewing all night.'

'Yeah,' he said weakly.

'So if I went out with Dipper again . . .'

'I wouldn't.'

'Why not?'

'A man can only take one night of pain before he cracks.'

'But –'

'Trust me.' He shuddered. 'Trust me.'

Just then, Charlotte and Virginia rejoined them in the hallway. 'So,' Charlotte drawled, 'are we still going to the reef?'

Will glanced at Emily. 'I'm still game if you are.'

She groaned. 'Fine. I can never stay mad at you for long, can I?'

And then she hugged him, which would have been fine if he'd had a shirt on and her bare cheek hadn't been pressed against his chest, giving him an instant flash of lazing in bed the morning after.

Virginia snorted. 'Some people will do anything to sleep with a celebrity.'

Charlotte cleared her throat uncomfortably and Emily quickly pulled away, blushing like a red traffic sign.

'I'll just take Mum back and get her sorted,' Charlotte said hastily. 'My brother's coming by in an hour to look after her while we go out.'

'Er, Charlotte, I don't suppose your brother's got any clothes I can borrow?' Will asked desperately. 'All of my casual gear has been stolen.'

Emily wrinkled her nose. 'No offence, Will, but I don't think anyone's interested in your old-man cardigans and those dorky T-shirts that should have been replaced ten years ago.' He glared at her and she rolled her eyes. 'Who could possibly have taken them?'

'Nova!'

'Nova?' She shook her head. 'I doubt it.'

'I'll give Luke a call and see what he can rustle up before he comes over,' Charlotte promised. 'In the meantime, you might want to try and do something about your hair.'

He touched his head. 'It is rather uneven, isn't it?'

Emily giggled.

'Any chance I can get your autograph before I go?' Virginia called as Charlotte pulled her out the door.

'Come on, Mum.'

As the two of them left, Emily reached up and touched his damaged locks. The gesture was so intimate his heart rate doubled.

'Do you want me to neaten that up for you?' she smiled roguishly. 'To tell you the truth, I've always wanted to take to your hair with a pair of scissors.'

'Thanks.' He shook his head and stepped out of her reach, which was becoming more and more dangerous by the minute.

Chapter 15

Emily

It was strange how much a haircut and a lack of glasses could make everything clearer. Will looked fantastic. Once he was dressed in surf wear he obviously didn't own, it was almost like she was meeting someone new. Emily could appreciate for the first time how bloody good-looking he was. He was lean, but muscular, like he did a lot of physical activity. It wasn't until this point that she'd thought about how much. She knew he loved running and did so on a regular basis. There were other hobbies too that she hadn't until now taken much notice of. She remembered all through university he'd been a big fan of Aikido because it was a martial art that used swords. She had to wonder if he was still into it.

The other thing was . . . now she could see his face . . .

It seemed like a silly point to make but it was true.

When he was hidden behind that scruffy beard of his, she hadn't realised how startling his eyes were, how easily he blushed and how strong and prominent his jawline. She'd seen a muscle clench in his cheek when she brushed her fingers through his hair earlier, which was so soft to touch and not nearly as coarse as it looked.

She'd seen his cheeks stain pink when she saw all the paper on the floor in his room. In fact, she'd never seen him so embarrassed but then she supposed Will was a bit of a neat freak.

'What have you been doing in here?'

'Leave it!' He quickly stalled her from bending over. 'I'll sort it out later. You don't want to be cleaning up my mess.'

They pulled a dining chair into his bathroom and he positioned himself in front of the mirror for his haircut. Sitting in that tiny bathroom, her fingers wading into his hair – the whole act seemed way too familiar. Almost forbidden.

A new awareness moved through her body as she worked, deeper and more potent than anything she'd known before. It brought to the forefront so many things that she knew but had always taken for granted or never looked at too closely.

The way their eyes could connect across a room because they got the same joke.

The way they talked for hours about the most inconsequential subjects.

Or when they sat in silence, it didn't really matter.

The way they ate like pigs and reprimanded each other for being gross.

The way they both sang loudly in the car when a song they liked came on the radio.

When she was in trouble, he was always there for her.

When she needed someone to talk to, he was always there for her.

He knows everything there is to know about me.

Every dirty little secret.

Every embarrassing moment.

Every fault.

Every failing.

And yet . . . he was still here.

She'd been sitting with Dipper at dinner last night in Mackay. They'd gone to Victoria Street, Mackay's restaurant hot spot. There had been plenty to choose from. Spicy Asian cuisine, Italian and, of course, plenty of Aussie favourites. Dipper had chosen a pub, which was definitely really nice. Good atmosphere. Great food. Yet all she had thought about was how much she'd love to come back to that area with Will.

'Except maybe we'll go to that Asian place on the corner,' she told Dipper. 'He loves spicy food.'

Dipper sighed.

'What?'

'You've mentioned Boy Scout three times since we got here.'

She bit her lip. 'Sorry. It's just that we are such good friends, it's kind of hard not to.'

Dipper dejectedly moved his pasta around in his bowl without actually eating any. She could appreciate that he'd gone to an effort over this dinner. His hair for a start was wet and combed. She'd never seen Dipper with a parting before. He was wearing a collared shirt, a sure sign of an occasion, and the faint smell of his cheap aftershave wafted across the table towards her whenever he moved. He looked up. 'I suppose that's your way of telling me I've lost.'

'Lost what?'

'The competition.'

'What competition?'

'You don't know?'

'Don't know what?'

Dipper began to turn a strange shade of purple. His fat lips formed a wide 'Oh' and he looked down into his bowl, confining his gaze there and refusing to look up. 'Aw shit.'

Her lips pulled into a taut line. 'Dipper, what's going on? You better tell me right now.'

'I thought you knew,' he protested. 'I mean, there's so much money changing hands over this. And, you know, the bets on me went up this afternoon thanks to our date. Even

I put in an extra fifty bucks on myself because I was feeling confident.'

'*What?*'

'I meant no disrespect.' He waved one beefy hand, his eyes wide with honesty. 'Just thought, you know, why not? Everyone else is doing it. And if I get the girl, why not make a fortune too? I would have shared half with you.'

'Half of what?'

'My winnings!' he said as though she was daft.

'Let me get this straight. There's a bet going on at the moment, that you're going to what – sleep with me?'

'No, no,' he assured her. 'It's a completely respectful competition between two guys for a meaningful relationship.'

'Yeah, it's respectful all right,' she snapped. 'Who's the other guy?'

'Will.'

This took her aback.

'Wait, does he know about this?'

Dipper snorted. 'Of course he knows!'

A flower began to unfurl its petals inside her stomach.

Why hadn't he told her? Did he think about her that way and was too embarrassed to say so? She felt ill with both excitement and trepidation.

Rationally, she should have been fuming. He hadn't told her about the bet. It was just another dishonesty on top of him discussing her private text messages with Trent. But she couldn't seem to muster up the anger, at least not above mildly annoyed. The thing was, she was too taken by the frightening but tantalisingly new possibility that suddenly occurred to her. Will wanted more than friendship. Perhaps this new tension between them wasn't all in her head. Could he feel it too?

Her teeth clamped down on her lower lip as it began to stretch into an excited smile. It was too early to get all hopeful.

She made a plan to sound him out about everything that morning. But many things had thrown her off kilter. His extreme makeover for one and Charlotte's presence in the car for another. It would be ages before she caught a private moment with him in order to grill him about Trent, the bet or his own feelings.

Fortunately, the time went fairly quickly. The drive to Shute Harbour was a gorgeous one, straight through the cane fields, over lush green hills. The air around them was saccharine and heavy. Emily felt her mind open up as the sweet breeze of freedom wafted across her face and hair through the window of the car.

They passed through a gorgeous coastal town known as Airlie Beach. It was small but buzzing with activity. Because the ocean in the area was teeming with stingers, the local council had built a swimming lagoon on the foreshore, which was free for anyone to use.

Emily looked longingly at it as their car sped past.

'Maybe we should just spend the day here and have fish and chips for lunch.' She pressed her nose to the window. 'It looks so relaxing.'

'I thought you were trying new things this year.' Will laughed. 'You've definitely lazed on the beach and eaten fish and chips before.'

Emily sighed. 'That's how I know it's so good. What do you think, Lottie?'

'If I don't want to risk my brother calling me a chicken, I think I'm going to have to learn how to dive.'

Five minutes later their ute turned into the car park at Shute Harbour, the main boarding point for ferries to the Whitsunday Islands and the Great Barrier Reef. The plan was to catch a ferry out to a giant floating pontoon that sat on a particular section of the reef called the Hardy Reef. The ferry they boarded was an enormous catamaran with two decks. They sat on the top one, which was open-air, and Emily enjoyed taking in the breathtaking panoramic views as the ferry churned smoothly through ocean, white foam in its wake. The voyage was seamless. Giant lush green mounds rose out of aqua-blue water. There were many islands about. Some inhabited, others untouched. Some too small to be more than a couple of rocks sticking out of the ocean.

'It's so beautiful out here,' she exclaimed. 'Like paradise.'

When they finally reached the pontoon, Emily was stunned at how big it was. It was three storeys, two above water and one under, so that, if you didn't want to get wet, you could still view the reef from the underwater viewing platform.

'I don't think I need to learn how to dive,' Emily told Charlotte. 'I'd just be happy to snorkel. Never done that before and there seems to be plenty to see on the surface.'

'Well, I think I'd still like to try learning,' said Charlotte. 'I'll book a lesson for myself and meet you guys later for lunch.'

'Good idea,' Emily agreed.

Emily was glad to finally have some time alone with Will. There was a lot on her mind that she needed to get straight. And yet suddenly there they were standing on the wooden deck and he took off his shirt again. All her questions dried up, as he stood there half naked handing her a snorkel. He really was beautifully built. Not bulgy like a weight lifter but more like a Greek nude – just a hint of definition in all the right places. His physique had a discreet strength that in many ways matched his personality.

He tilted his head. 'Are you all right?'

No. She licked dry lips. 'Should we be wearing stinger suits?'

Will shrugged. 'We can rent some if you like.'

'I think that would be a good idea.' And not just for the jellyfish protection. Since when had Will's bare chest been anything more than skin to her? *Greek gods and weight lifters? Where's your head at, girl?*

They rented some suits and then returned to the side of the pontoon. Emily fitted the snorkel and mask over her face while she worked up the courage to ask him the question that had been sitting on the tip of her tongue all morning, and was getting harder and harder to ask by the second.

'Er . . . Will . . .'

Splash! He was in the water, having stepped off the edge of the pontoon without so much as a toe dip. 'Come on, Em, it's gorgeous.'

His head disappeared under the sparkling blue and she sighed. 'All *right.*'

Instead of jumping straight off the edge she made for a small steel staircase that descended slowly off the side of the pontoon. He was actually pretty spot on about the water. It was warm, crystal clear and calm. Only gentle waves lapped at her waist as she once more made sure her mask was firmly fitted. She could see shadows of colour under the water but nothing too spectacular to behold. She popped the end of the snorkel in her mouth and then pushed out horizontally into the water so that liquid enveloped her body in one gentle glide.

WOW!

Diving in was like being transported to another world. A magical world. *It's just like* Finding Nemo *down here.* She had always thought that the Disney cartoon must exaggerate the vibrancy of the reef. But now, she realised, it didn't do it justice.

The colours that had seemed dull above water now jumped out at her so vibrantly it was hard not to be humbled by the beauty of it. Everything was alive.

Everything.

As an engineer she found that fascinating. This structure, so enormous in size you could not see where it started and ended, was fully organic. Coral of all different shapes and varieties clung together, flat and plate like, thick and spikey, leafy or like bare branches. It didn't matter. It pulsed with life she had never seen the like of before.

And the fish . . .

The fish were just spectacular. Tiny fish, fish the size of her head, fish that were bigger than her. They swam around her arms, through her legs. They pecked on her mask, kissed her lips and cheeks. And they were so pretty. It was like being enveloped by a swarm of butterflies. Reds, greens, blues, yellows, hot pink! Fluoro colours were certainly very fashionable down there. This one fish the size of her hand was mad at her for some reason and kept charging her. Perhaps she was swimming directly above his family's home. He'd back himself up and then charge at her snorkel mask. Just before he hit her face he would dart away and then do it again.

She felt a hand slip into hers and turned in the water to see Will now floating beside her. He smiled and tugged. She nodded and floated with him across the surface of the coral. There were giant clams below about half the size of her body, which would snap shut without warning when she glided over the top. They gave her a fright at first but then she got rather used to them. Their lips didn't completely seal, so you couldn't lose an arm or a leg or anything. It was just funny. She saw turtles and morays and even a reef shark.

The reef went on forever. Everywhere she went there was something new to look at. It was like a giant magical underwater forest lit by the sun. In some areas the reef stopped and went vertical, as though she'd reached a cliff face. She imagined this was where it would be great if she had diving gear on. But she wasn't disappointed. There was so much to see with snorkel and mask alone. Also, at least on the surface, everything was so well lit. She figured the deeper you went the less you would see without artificial light.

She didn't know how long they frolicked for. An hour, probably two. But the time seemed to go so fast in that underwater city that Emily hardly noticed it. She and Will couldn't talk but they still managed to communicate, pointing at things and dragging each other through the water. Silence had never been an issue for them and nor was it now as they played like children. Occasionally, they surfaced to chat about what they had seen but Emily didn't ever feel it was the right time to ask him the question. So she waited until he asked her if she'd like to go to lunch.

They swam towards the sunken stairway attached to the pontoon and a crazy desire shot through Emily's heart. Will took her hand again to help her up the stairs and this time, instead of leaving it innocently held for balance, she shifted her fingers and threaded them through his. She knew exactly what she was doing. But she didn't care. She wanted to know what it would be like to make that shift away from friendship to something more. Something so much deeper and more profound that she could feel the power of it aching in her bones as they ascended the stairs. His hand tightened around her own, making her feel like just for a second he understood, like he knew what she wanted to know. She pushed her mask off her eyes, enjoying the fresh air on her face. He halted at the top of the stairs and she stopped walking a second later so that her body pressed into this. He didn't move to make more room for her on the top step. Instead he pushed back his own mask and looked down at her for a second.

An expression, a strange mix of hope, pain and regret, crossed his features. And disappeared. She had never seen him so guarded.

'Em . . .'

'Yeah?' she breathed.

He disengaged his hand and walked on. 'We should go get lunch.'

'Oh . . . yeah okay.' She followed him to the change rooms in silence, feeling she'd done something wrong.

Before she could query it, however, he said, 'I'll meet you in the dining room, okay? After we get changed.'

'Okay.'

She removed the stinger suit and towelled herself dry but didn't take off her bikini. They might want to go snorkelling again after lunch. So she wrapped a sarong around her waist as a temporary measure before leaving to go to the buffet deck.

He met her there about five minutes later. She took in the dry cargo pants and T-shirt in surprise. 'Aren't you going back in the water after lunch?' she demanded.

He didn't look at her. 'No, I think I might read on the sun deck.'

'Read?' Emily squeaked. 'But we're sitting on the Great Barrier Reef!'

'It'll still be here next week.'

'Will,' she took a deep breath, 'there's something I need to ask you.'

He looked pained. 'Em, don't.'

'Don't what?'

He seemed to struggle within himself as he first looked at the buffet then at his hands, then out the window before back at her. 'Fine, ask me.'

'Are you . . .' She decided to go with the easier question first. 'Are you part of some bet with Dipper over who can score with me first?'

Will seemed to freeze for a second before his eyes closed in something akin to relief. 'Yes.'

'Why would you do that?'

'Do what?' he inquired, his eyes meeting hers and not wavering. 'Being part of the bet? Or trying to score with you?'

'Both,' she said quickly, knowing which answer she wanted to hear more.

'For starters, I'm not trying to score with you.' His mouth twisted. 'I *never* have.'

Rationally, she had already known this. But actually hearing the words was like a kick in the shin. How could she have been so silly as to suppose differently? He was right. He had never shown any signs of being that way inclined.

At her deafening silence, he threw back his head and gave a self-mocking laugh. 'I mean, Trent's my best friend, for freak's sake. I couldn't do that to him.'

'He doesn't own me and we're not together any more,'

Em protested numbly, crossing her arms protectively over her chest.

He ignored her and continued. 'As for the bet, I didn't enter into it on purpose. I was innocently standing by and got roped in. I thought I'd be in it to protect you.'

'Protect me? Protect me how?'

'From some other fruit loop who might want to compete with Dipper over you.'

'Because only a fruit loop could possibly be into me, is that what you're saying?'

'*No.*' He immediately baulked.

'Don't you find me attractive?'

He blinked. 'Am I supposed to find you attractive? Is that what you want?'

'Not if I have to talk you into it,' Emily retorted. 'Why didn't you tell me about the bet? Don't you think I'd like to know about it?'

'I thought you *did* know about it. You said you knew what Dipper's game was.'

'I knew he had the hots for me, I didn't know about the bet. He only just told me the full story at dinner last night. You should have been more specific with me.'

'I didn't want to upset you.'

'That's a cop out, Will, and you know it. I'm a big girl. I can handle being a little upset. What I can't handle is being lied to and you seem to be doing a lot of that lately.'

'I'm sorry.'

She studied him irritably. Secretly, she'd been hoping that he'd been personally invested in the bet and had been too embarrassed to tell her. It had seemed at the time like the only reasonable explanation. But Will didn't have feelings for her. He'd just told her so.

It was dumb of her to have even considered it when Trent was his best friend. Of course, in his mind, he couldn't go there.

There was also the fact that they had been friends for nearly seven years. A person didn't just suddenly change their mind about you. It didn't make sense.

Then how do I explain my own feelings?

She wasn't sure how they'd got out of Pandora's box. All she knew was that at this particular moment, she wished she had a way of putting them back in.

'Em, listen to me.' Will's rational, reasoning tone was more infuriating than all the rest. 'There are heaps of guys on this site. And I don't know if you've noticed, but you're very popular. I was just trying to keep you safe. I mean, you've just broken up with Trent. What if the two of you want to get back together later on or something . . .?'

Her mouth dropped open. 'What the hell?!' Realisation dawned on her. 'He put you up to this, didn't he? That's why you didn't tell me about the bet.'

'What?' His brow furrowed. 'What are you talking about?'

'This isn't about us.'

'Us?' He was startled.

'This is about Trent. This is about keeping me away from other guys. That's why he was angry about Dipper. He asked you to keep an eye on me, didn't he? I should have guessed.'

'You gotta understand, Em, he's my best friend too.'

'Don't worry.' She held up her hand. 'I get it. I completely get it.'

I've just been utterly delusional – living in fantasy land.

He was about to say something more when Charlotte walked up. 'Hey, guys, why aren't you eating?'

Emily didn't know whether to be relieved or annoyed at this timely interruption. If they argued about this any more she might say something that she would regret. Or worse, reveal something she didn't want him to know! She looked across at the fully laid out buffet. A veritable feast of shellfish and salad had been brought in while they were fighting.

Will closed his open mouth and turned with a smile to Charlotte.

'Hey, Lottie. How was your dive?'

'Rather eventful.'

For the first time they took in Charlotte's rather pale and wan-looking face.

'Hey, are you okay?' Emily asked, momentarily forgetting her own pathetic woes.

Charlotte jerked a thumb over her shoulder and Emily and Will looked towards the entrance.

A tall, insolent-looking figure strode into the room, his casual clothing belying the destructive forces simmering beneath his skin.

'Caesar's here!'

Chapter 16

Charlotte

She had been looking forward to this day ever since she and Emily had planned it. It was her chance to get out and do her own thing. Spend time with her friends. Be inspired. Get a new hobby. Why not? She deserved it. Didn't she work hard enough?

Finally, there she was sitting on the sun deck at the muster area for diving lessons among some other first-time hopefuls when Hell's angel swooped in from the sky.

Literally from the sky.

Mark Crawford arrived via helicopter. He and a few other passengers, too rich or too late to catch the ferry from Shute Harbour, had taken advantage of a helicopter tour of the reef before landing on it. A roof sheltering half the sun deck was actually the platform for a helicopter pad. When Charlotte first saw Mark's rigid figure descending the steel stairs she was sure she was hallucinating. But no, it was definitely him. Dark hair, dark features, that ever-prominent scowl on his ever-dissatisfied face. Dressed casually for a change, he looked so out of his depth that she almost laughed.

What does he intend to do here? Have fun? Relax? Does Mark Crawford even know what those words mean?

No sooner had she thought it than he looked up and noticed her before she could wipe the smirk off her face. It was obvious from his expression that he wasn't exactly pleased to see her either. His step slowed and a scowl formed.

Who cares? she thought. *I'm sure he can stay out of my way and I'll stay out of his. It's a big pontoon.*

Apparently, not big enough.

'Ms Templeton.'

His shadow crossed her body as she sat on the bench and she shaded her eyes to look up at him. 'Mr Crawford.' She nodded, hoping this was a good enough acknowledgement for him to walk on.

But he stayed put. 'What are you doing here?' He asked the question as though she had better have a bloody good explanation for intruding upon his space. As much as the suggestion exasperated her, he *was* still a valuable client, so she decided to return his obnoxious tone with pleasantness. 'I'm here for a diving lesson, Mr Crawford. Why are you here?'

He growled. 'For the same reason.'

She couldn't help it: this time she did laugh. 'You've got to be kidding me.'

'You may have noticed, Ms Templeton, that I don't, in general, make jokes.'

She grinned wickedly. 'Yes, of course. I forgot you don't laugh.' She tapped her chin. 'So it begs the question, why on earth do you want to go diving? You do realise it's not work-related and you might accidently have a good time.'

His face didn't even slightly crack at her teasing tone. 'True as that is, Ms Templeton, I've decided . . . that I, er . . . I need to broaden my horizons.'

He made this announcement as though he'd been coerced and prodded into the decision by an authority higher than himself.

'Really?' She tilted her head. 'Just like you decided you needed a new turkey?'

His lip curled. 'Something like that.'

'Curious. Has your wife been making suggestions again?' As far as she was concerned, the elusive Mrs Crawford was the only possible candidate who could fall into the higher power category.

'You could say that.' He shoved his fists into the loose pockets of his board shorts rather roughly. 'Ms Templeton –'

'Call me Charlotte,' she purred, more because she knew it would annoy him than really wanting him to call her that.

'*Ms Templeton*, what's more curious is what you are doing here. Don't you have a resort to run?'

Charlotte lifted her chin. 'My brother is looking after the show today. He thought I could do with a break. In fact, he suggested that I learn something new . . . like diving.'

'I see.'

Just then one of the diving instructors, wearing an orange Adventure Pontoon hat, joined the group in the muster area. She began taking reservations, equipment hire and payment for the next class, which was in ten minutes.

'Hello, you two.' She smiled all bright and happy, clearly not picking up the mood between them. 'Let me guess, honeymooners?'

Charlotte turned on her with round eyes. *If this happens one more time* . . . 'We,' she said slowly and succinctly, indicating herself and Mark with a flick of her wrist, 'are. Not. Married. Never were. Never will be.'

The diving instructor took a step back. 'Sorry. I just thought I'd ask because we're doing a two-for-one special for newlyweds.'

'Oh.' She blushed.

'I didn't mean to cause any offence,' the instructor huffed. 'Guess you'll both be paying full price then. Here are your forms.' She tossed them in their laps. 'Fill them out and then head downstairs to the teaching room.'

'Sure,' Charlotte responded, nearly crumpling in embarrassment.

'Well handled.' There was no disguising the smirk on Mark's face.

'Just fill in your form,' she snapped. They completed their paperwork, indemnifying Adventure Pontoon from all liability should they drown, get the bends, lose a leg to a shark or be stung by something poisonous and become permanently or partially disabled.

Nice.

They also agreed to pay quite a bit of money for the privilege. By the time she had finished reading the disclaimer she had to wonder whether this was really the right hobby for her.

'Cold feet, Ms Templeton?'

She quickly signed her name on the dotted line. 'Not a chance. What about you?'

'I've already signed my name, see.' He held up his form to show her and then a rather strange thing happened. He smiled.

She nearly fell off the bench, her balance momentarily disappearing as she took in the devastating warmth that suddenly appeared on his face. It transformed it so completely that all she could do was stare. He had crow's feet around his eyes and a dimple, *a dimple*, in his right cheek. Where the hell had that come from? And what business did it have on his face?

He ignored her fixation and stood up. 'Are you coming?'

Collecting her wits, she scrambled to stride along beside him. 'Yes.'

They moved along the wet timber that formed a walkway around the perimeter of the pontoon. Beyond the steel hand railing there was nothing but big blue ocean and the sound of waves. She breathed in the clean salty air and sighed. Her mood, however, was unable to transition completely into relaxation mode because Mark spoke again.

'Actually, Ms Templeton, I've been meaning to call you.'

She cleared her throat. 'You have?'

'Emily Woods mentioned you used to be a psychologist.'

'Yes, yes, I was. I am.'

He nodded. 'How would you feel about taking on a part-time role with Barnes Inc, as our counsellor? You'd only work a few hours a week.'

Excitement, hope and fear collided in her chest. 'Are you serious?'

He sighed. 'Didn't I just mention that I don't, in general –'

'Make jokes,' she finished for him. 'Yes, yes. Got it. What I meant was, why do you need a counsellor?'

'I'm concerned about my men. I think they need an unbiased third party to talk to. You're right about the alcoholism. I think it's on the high side.'

She couldn't believe it. Was he finally going to do something about the problem she'd been raising for weeks? She nearly jumped for joy but didn't. They had just reached the top of some stairs and leaping definitely wouldn't be a good idea.

'I would need to check with my brother,' she said, slowly descending. 'If I'm at Barnes Inc I'll need him to help look after Mum. I don't think Zara will be very reliable even if I only worked afterschool hours.'

'Oh, I don't know about that.'

The fact that he even had an opinion on the subject momentarily took her aback. Her brow furrowed. 'Zara's a teenage girl. Her social life always comes first.'

'If you haven't noticed, she's also a very sensitive young woman.'

She bit her lip, stung by his words. It wasn't that she hadn't noticed . . . Okay, she *hadn't* noticed. But even before the revelation about Zara's father, they had been far too busy fighting to have any meaningful conversations.

'I'm sure,' he continued smoothly, 'she would be willing to help out if you explained your emotional situation to her.'

This jarred her out of reflection. 'My *emotional* situation?' She coughed so indignantly that she nearly skipped a step and tumbled down the stairs.

'Your deteriorated self-worth after having had to give up your career to look after her.'

Her mind boggled. 'How dare you? You know nothing about me or how I may or may not feel about *anything*.'

'On the contrary, Ms Templeton, I know a great deal. I know how hard you work, how worried you are about your mother and how protective you are of your sister. You don't have any friends because you don't have any spare time. You can't help your sister with her problems because you're too close to them. You hold onto everything so tightly, which is why, Ms Templeton, your brother has told you to get a hobby.'

'Wow.' Her throat was as dry as her tone. 'Ten points to you. And what possible proof do you have to back all this up?'

'Zara told me.'

Great.

So there was probably no use denying it then. By this stage they had arrived on the lower deck and were being told to pick out their wetsuit sizes, flippers, masks and tanks from the racks and bins around them. She used the opportunity to move away from him, so she wouldn't have to talk any more – especially about herself. Of all the people Zara had to get chummy with, why him?

She prayed to God she hadn't told him anything about her biological father. She really didn't want a man like Mark Crawford knowing something that intimate about their family.

The job at Barnes Inc, however, was another story. She wanted that. As reluctant as she was to admit it, over the years she *had* felt she'd lost a lot in giving up her profession to raise Zara and look after their mother. She couldn't say that she didn't often feel short-changed. This was her ticket back to her career. And it would just be part time – a few hours a week.

Perfect.

She chose her wetsuit and a pair of yellow flippers in her size and got changed. She had her bathers on under her clothes, so it was easy enough to slip off her dress and pull on the suit. As she zipped up over her chest, she caught him watching her with a peculiar intensity and thought it a good time to walk back over. He already had his suit on too.

'I accept your job offer,' she said formally. 'When do you want me to start?'

'As soon as you can.'

She wanted to say more but the diving instructor, now also in a wet suit, was calling the attention of the group.

'Before we even enter the water, we'd like to give you a short twenty-minute demonstration on equipment use and safety techniques. Then we'll do some practice above water. We're also going to teach you a few hand signals because, as you know, speaking underwater is impossible. Please be aware that after doing this course you are not a professional diver. We aren't going down too far today so this presentation is designed just to help tourists see the reef.'

Charlotte pulled her mind back to the task at hand. She couldn't afford not to be concentrating right now. After signing that indemnity form she was under no illusions as to the possible dangers she faced under the water. The diving instructor went on to explain the gear. In particular, the vest that controlled their buoyancy or BCD while diving. It was operated by a simple push-button mechanism.

'You dump all the air to get to the bottom,' he said, 'then adjust air in your BCD while at the bottom to obtain neutral buoyancy during your dive. When it's time to surface, you dump all the air in your BCD and swim to the surface in a controlled manner.'

When Charlotte first tried the breathing apparatus she was very nervous and didn't realise that she was taking in short sharp breaths.

The instructor laughed. 'Just breathe normally or you'll use up all your air.'

Yikes!

Consciously, she slowed her breathing down and started to get used to having the mask over her eyes and nose and something in her mouth. On the diving deck there was a giant hole in the floor so that the class could all sit in the water and practise near the surface. They did a short test of the equipment to make sure everyone had the hang of breathing underwater. They also learned how to empty their masks, should they accidently fill with water while they were swimming.

Mark sat calmly beside her. It was funny watching him taking instructions instead of barking them. His submissiveness intrigued her. It also made her cross. How was it fair that he knew so much about her and she barely knew a thing about him? He was a constant mystery to her. While he apparently found her utterly predictable, she had no idea what he would do next or why. There was no pattern to his behaviour at all. At first glance, one would say he was a rude, arrogant bastard. But he had saved that scrub turkey's life and made friends with her sister when no else had been able to reach her. Not even Charlotte herself.

Now here he was offering her a job because he claimed to 'care' about his men and going diving because he needed to 'broaden his horizons'. Or perhaps his wife thought he did. Her mind turned suddenly to Mrs Crawford. Who was this woman? What was she like? And how had she ever agreed to shack up with such an inflexible, immovable man?

There had to be another side to Mark Crawford that she didn't know about. She remembered that brief glorious smile he'd given her on the sun deck and a shudder rippled through her body. Yes, she had a feeling there was a lot more to Mark Crawford than she knew.

'Ms Templeton.' She quickly glanced up as the subject of her thoughts claimed her attention. 'It's your turn to go in.'

Heat infused her face.

Damn it!

She hadn't been listening again and now it was do or die time.

'Ready to go in?' One of the instructors held out his hand to her. Pride made her nod and pull her mask down over her eyes. 'Remember to hold onto the rope,' he said before pulling her into the water.

Oh shit! What rope?

She really should have been listening instead of speculating about Mark's personality – a mystery that in her case would probably never be solved. To her relief, she saw immediately what he was referring to and was able to fill in the blanks in her own head. There was a rope attached to the pontoon that seemed to go down into the ocean alongside the coral reef. She could not see the end of it but there were other amateur divers in front of her holding onto it. It was clear the rope was the path of the tour and as long as they stuck near to it they would be fine.

She took the rope and followed the person in front of her.

Cured of her panic, she was finally able to take in the new world around her.

It was magic.

The coral was so full of life and colour. The fish surrounded and engulfed her. Bubbles from their fins burst against her mask until the scene before her cleared again. Her body began to relax. The weightlessness of being in the water started to feel less alien and more enjoyable. It was so peaceful down there with the main sounds the inhale and exhale of her own breath. The coral was beautiful. A bed of flowers in the spring wouldn't be as glorious.

Slow, steady and gaining confidence, she continued to hold onto the rope and moved forwards. There was a point beside the reef where it stopped. It was attached to some sort of mooring buoy that was anchored to the ocean bed. Here divers were encouraged by the instructors to leave the rope and move in closer to the reef for a better look.

One instructor came up to her and lifted his hand to signal, 'Are you okay?'

She returned it with a nod and he swam on.

It was easy to get lost in the enchanted world around her. To watch as a manta ray swam beneath her feet and tiny fish danced across the knuckles of one hand. For ten wonderful minutes, she was enthralled and then she turned around and realised she was alone. The tour group had moved on.

What! Surely not?

In panic, she swam back from the reef so that she could see further around it in both directions. It only took her a few seconds to respot her group. They were all swimming towards the rope and were heading up to the surface again. The tour was over.

Her relief, however, was short-lived. She tried to swim back to her group but couldn't. The current was against her and seemed to be pulling her out in a completely different direction. She kicked desperately towards the group but barely moved. After a few minutes her arms and legs ached from the exertion of trying to break free of the current. The worst part was she couldn't scream or call out to the others that she was being dragged off by some sort of underwater rip. Her eyes boggled from their sockets as she grew tired.

What do I do? What do I do?

Pain shot up her leg. She had a cramp and treading water was now near impossible. As she began to float away, she saw one of the divers detach from the group and swim towards her. She didn't know whether to be grateful or flabbergasted. If the person came for her, he or she would be caught in this current too. Swimming with the flow, he reached her easily.

It was Mark. Even masked, she'd know him anywhere.

He took her hand and held tight. He wasn't trying to swim or anything. They were simply riding the stream. He showed her his thumb indicating they should surface. She supposed it wasn't a bad plan. They couldn't ride this current indefinitely. Their tanks certainly weren't limitless.

So instead of trying to swim back they swam up, pausing briefly halfway to equalise. She used her BCD to help her gain more buoyancy and lift out of the rip. They made it to the surface at least a hundred metres from the pontoon, erupting from the water with a splash.

Mark pushed his mask off his face and spat out his mouthpiece.

'Are you out of your fuckin' mind?'

'I couldn't help it. I got caught by a current.'

'Of course you did! That's exactly what they said would happen if you moved too far away from the reef or the rope in precisely that direction.' He had been holding tightly to her wrist but at these words he tossed it away from him in disgust.

'Yeah, well –'

'Weren't you listening when the instructor was telling us the tour pathway?'

Wasn't that when I was daydreaming? 'Of course!' She lifted her chin defiantly.

'Then why didn't you get back on the rope? Have you got a death wish? Do you want to drown?'

Now she was beginning to get cross. It was rather sweet and a little strange that he cared about her safety but it didn't give him the right to give her a lecture. She wasn't one of his engineers. 'Now just hang on a minute there –'

'Of all the irresponsible, reckless, thoughtless, dumb –' He broke off as words failed him.

'Look, I'm sorry –'

'You're *sorry*.' He spat the word like it was the height of inadequacy and for a second she glimpsed his pain. It streaked across his face like a splash of red paint. And in that moment she realised there was more going on here than her brush with a runaway stream of water. 'Don't you think I've had enough loss in my life?' He flung the words at her before turning and swimming towards the pontoon. Just as he was leaving, another diver surfaced beside her. It was one of the instructors, who pushed his mask off his face and grinned at her.

'You two catching a quick romantic getaway or something?'

She wanted to scream but took a deep breath before saying, 'No, I got caught in the current.'

He nodded. 'Yeah, I saw. Your partner was quicker than me and very good. If I didn't know any better, I'd say he's been diving before.'

She turned her head and watched Mark cut through the waves back to the pontoon and for once was too distracted to tell the instructor he was not her partner. Yes, there was a lot about Mark Crawford she didn't know.

She also swam to the pontoon and hauled herself up onto the deck beside the instructor. They removed their flippers and carried them to the diving instruction room. They found Mark already there, peeling off his wetsuit.

'I need to return to the group to help everyone else surface,' the diving instructor said. 'So I'll leave you two to get changed.'

'Sure.' Mark said flippantly and threw his mask into a bin that was labelled for them.

Charlotte also put her mask in the bin but a little more gently.

The instructor nodded and then walked over to the far side of the room and re-entered the water through the hole in the floor.

'You want to tell me what's going on?' She moved closer to Mark, trying not to notice the way his chest heaved and fell with each shuddering breath.

'Not particularly, Ms Templeton. I think you've done enough to aggravate me for one day.'

'Aggravate you?' she repeated, also unzipping her wetsuit and peeling it off. 'I'm trying to help you. It's clear you're really upset about something.'

His eyes blazed a trail across her body and she was suddenly conscious of the fact that she had a lot of skin on display.

'I'm upset about a lot of things, Ms Templeton,' he hissed. 'Most of all, I'm upset that you're standing there in nothing but a green string bikini minding my business!'

A flush rolled through her body but she didn't move away; instead she tried to stand a little more confidently. 'I can't change what I'm wearing, Mr Crawford, but I'm listening if you need someone to talk to. You said earlier that you were worried about your men. But maybe they aren't the only ones who need to get something off their chest.'

He sat down on a wooden bench behind him and put his head in his hands.

Her heart clenched at the sight of him in this pose. She walked over and sat down beside him. Using the hint the instructor had given her, she decided to take a risk. 'Mr Crawford, this isn't the first time you've been diving, is it? You're not an amateur, are you?'

He didn't look up. Didn't say anything for a moment and she thought she'd lost him until he said quietly, 'I had a twin brother who was attacked by a shark. He died in hospital from his wounds.'

She swallowed hard. 'Was he diving?'

'No, surfing. We both were.'

She examined his hung head, wanting to touch him more than ever but not daring to. Her instincts told her what happened next. 'You haven't been near the water since losing him, have you?'

'No.'

She bit her lip at his return to silence, cursing herself for her own stupidity. For bringing back all these memories for him. This pain. This loss. No wonder he had been so angry at her.

The fingers of one hand curled into a fist against her bare thigh. And as for his wife . . . what the devil was she thinking sending her husband off diving? And alone too. Couldn't she have at least come with him?

'What is her problem?' she accidently said out loud, making him turn his head to look at her. His dark eyes were more tumultuous than the sea outside but he seemed to have got some of his old arrogant self back. That chest of his was so close, it practically beckoned for her hands, so she balled them both up this time.

'Who are you referring to?' he demanded.

Crap! Now she was in it.

With a toss of her head she said defiantly, 'Your wife. She seems completely insensitive.'

A ghost of a smile tickled his mouth. But it wasn't anything like the smile that she had seen on his face earlier. She didn't like this expression at all.

'Actually, Ms Templeton, you're quite right. My wife does have a problem.'

'She does?'

'Yes,' he said briskly. 'She's dead.' He stood up and crossed the room.

'W-what?'

Confusion roared like a train through her head and then all she wanted to do was curl up and cringe. Of all the *faux pas* you could make, this was up there at the top. She moved her dry mouth searching desperately for something to say.

'I'm sorry –'

'Don't be.'

The blunt way he cut off her words, as though he couldn't bear to hear them, showed far more than he realised. Here was a man trapped in his own tragic past. He still wore his ring, he still spoke about his wife as though she were alive. His anger, so strong and so cruel, was a deep reflection of his agony.

'Oh, Mark . . .' She began standing up.

'Don't pity me,' he said. 'It's a waste of your time.' He held up his palm as she tried to step closer.

'Honey, you can't go on like this.'

He shut his eyes and said through his teeth, 'Don't call me honey.'

'Look, speaking as a psychologist –'

'I'm not one of your patients!'

She bit her lip. 'Okay, as your, um, friend then. The way you've been acting is not healthy. You need to let go.'

'Don't you think I want to?' he threw at her. 'When Kathryn was diagnosed with cancer we'd only been married a year. We decked out the nursery because she was pregnant.'

She gasped. 'Where, where is . . .?'

'Where do you think?!' he bit out. This time she did move towards him, reaching for his hand. But he moved out of her reach and headed back to the bench, sitting down again.

He drew in a shuddering breath. 'She took three years to die. Not that I grudge that time. But it took every drop of tolerance I had left in me.'

She sat down beside him again and he looked at her this time. Eye to eye. Nose to nose. Like she was the vessel into which he was pouring all his suffering. The air was sucked from her lungs. Charlotte had never felt so bereft, so enveloped deep in a chasm of grief. No wonder he was the way he was. He'd lost the two most important people in his life and his unborn child as well. How could she blame him for looking at the world he had left with contempt?

Like the Tin Man in *The Wizard of Oz*, beneath his hard metal exterior he was so empty, so sad and in so desperate need of a heart.

She stretched out her hand and laid her palm against his face, brushing her thumb across his cheekbone. He froze and the air around them thickened like caramel. With all the gentleness she could muster, she leaned in and kissed him.

It wasn't meant to be sexual. It was a kiss of comfort. Of compassion. Of deep empathy.

Despite the rigidness of his body, his lips melted against hers like butter. Soft and sublime, the brush of their noses made a lump form in her throat. Her fingers moved into his hair, playing with small locks behind his ears. He lifted his own hand and cradled her cheek in his palm. And for a few fragile seconds, they remained in this calm, safe world of gentle understanding.

Then everything changed.

His mouth slanted over hers in a manner that was entirely unchaste. She felt engulfed – like a boat out at sea, hit by a wave. Nothing prepared her for the rush of desire or the shock of longing.

She laid a hand on his chest, bracing herself against these sudden and unstoppable feelings. But instead of slowing down, he took it as an invitation, scooping her onto his lap as effortlessly as if he were picking up a child.

Charlotte gasped as he crushed her to him. His hands on her thigh and behind her neck demanded a response, which she gave wholeheartedly.

A splash broke them apart almost as if they'd been doused with water themselves. It was the rest of the group returning from the diving lesson. Grimly, Mark stood up, taking her with him, before setting her firmly on her feet.

'Mark –' she began.

But he shot her a look so formidable she broke off.

'This time, Ms Templeton, you've gone too far.'

She gazed at him incredulously. '*I've* gone too far?!' *He* was the one who'd pulled *her* onto his lap.

But Mark wasn't staying to listen to her protests. He grabbed his T-shirt from the bench and walked out, leaving her standing there seething. Of all the . . .

She walked over to her dress, which was hanging on the wall, trying to ignore the knowing looks she was getting from the other divers emerging from the water. Grabbing it off the hook, she quickly threw it over her head.

She just wanted to shake the man. This wasn't all her! *No way.*

Maybe it was now impossible to ignore the fact that she had the hots for the most unapproachable, unaccommodating man in the state. Yes, shame on her! But it wasn't entirely a one-sided affliction either. She knew instinctively that he was just as drawn to her. Couldn't he take responsibility for his own actions?

It was still a while before lunch so she went back up to the sun deck to stew about it.

For a long time now, she had fought her attraction to Barnes Inc's most intimidating project manager. Firstly for the business, secondly because he was married and thirdly because the thought of entering into a serious relationship with anyone (let alone a man as arrogant as Mark Crawford) was as scary as entering a lion's cage with a piece of meat strapped to her chest.

The first and second reasons no longer held much sway but the last one certainly did. She may be attracted to the man but she didn't like him. He was very complicated. Too complicated for someone like her, whose life was already filled with psychologically damaged people.

Besides, after that earth-shattering kiss he'd more or less told her to get lost. She gritted her teeth. Her luck with men certainly hadn't improved over the years, that was for sure.

She stood there gazing out at the ocean and made the decision to hold onto her dignity and stay out of his way. The decision only strengthened when she went to meet Emily and Will for lunch and saw him enter the buffet dining room.

'Oh crap,' said Will. 'Do you think we should ask him to join us? He doesn't appear to be with anyone.'

'Really?' Emily wrung her hands. 'What on earth are we going to talk about with him?'

Charlotte purposely turned her back as his gaze met hers across the room and made haste to reassure her friends. 'I don't see how we're under any obligation to say anything to him.'

'Are you sure?' Emily wrinkled her brow. 'The last thing we want to do is cause offence.' She shot a glance at Will.

'Remember what happened to us at work last time? I got spark testing and you got a thousand and one TQs.'

'He's very good at punishing people.' Will nodded grimly.

Charlotte was beginning to get a little desperate; if these two cowards invited him over, she'd be stuck with him and his attitude for the rest of the afternoon. 'Well, I don't see how he has any right in this case. After all, you're not at work, are you? It's your day off. It's *my day off*.' She lifted her chin defiantly as Emily tried to cut her off. 'No, I gotta be honest here. The very last person I want to have lunch with is Mark Crawford.'

'Good to know, Ms Templeton.'

Oh shit.

She spun around, trying to control the wince on her face as she found him standing right behind her. Despite all previous resolutions her heart immediately knocked itself out against her ribcage at his close proximity.

A man like him didn't deserve to be so good-looking. Even so, he did appear a little pale.

As though to echo her thoughts, Will spoke up. 'Are you okay, Mark? You don't look too well.'

'To be honest, I think I'm a little seasick.'

'I've heard they have ginger tablets in the first-aid office on the lower deck,' Emily suggested helpfully. 'Perhaps you could go ask for some. Might make you feel a bit better.'

'Or perhaps you'd like to sit outside?' Will recommended. 'The fresh air might settle down the nausea.'

Mark turned to Charlotte, his all-seeing gaze seeming to scorch her face. 'And what about you, Ms Templeton? Don't you have any suggestions that might help get rid of me?'

She raised her eyebrows and then said tightly, 'I wouldn't want to *go too far* again.'

His face closed, his mouth hardened. 'I see.' He turned back to her companions. 'To be honest, I find I'm not in the least bit hungry. Rest easy, I will not be burdening any of you with my company.'

On these clipped words, he turned and left them. His dignified exit almost made her retract her biting remark and call him back. He'd been through so much and lost a great deal. Was it really his fault that he didn't know how to handle human compassion when it was aimed in his direction?

But the words dried on her lips. How was it her responsibility to be balm to his wounds? Especially when he had nothing but contempt for her efforts.

'Wow.' Emily raised her eyebrows. 'I can't work out whether we dodged a bullet or took one in the throat.'

Will had his eyes on her, however, and she blushed under his steady gaze. She coughed into a fist. 'Who knows? Who cares? Let's eat.'

Charlotte made a beeline for the buffet and filled her plate but wasted most of it. The food, so succulent and fresh, only tasted like dust in her mouth. She was too distracted thinking about Mark sitting all alone on the sun deck sucking a ginger pill.

Why do I feel guilty? This is not my fault!

'Do you think we should check on him?' Emily asked when lunch was over. 'I mean, what if he really is sick?'

This time she didn't protest and they went up to the sun deck to discover that Mark and a number of others had already left the pontoon via helicopter. Just as well. She didn't know if she could deal with another shot of emotional adrenaline.

Their own ferry wasn't leaving for another hour, so they killed the time sitting on the side of the pontoon on the lower deck, chatting and snorkelling intermittently. If she didn't know any better she would have to say Emily and Will seemed relieved to be back in her company. She had to wonder whether something had occurred between them while she was gone. But after the lesson she had learned on her dive that afternoon, she wasn't going to start prying into their personal affairs. She kept conversation topics neutral, although she did tell them about Mark's job offer and her acceptance.

'I just hope I haven't lost it all by my comment at lunchtime,' she added sourly. *Not to mention the kiss beforehand!*

Will grinned. 'I wouldn't worry. If you don't join our team how can he punish you slowly? It's in his best interests.'

Fabulous.

As it turned out, Will wasn't far wrong. When she got home that evening, Luke handed her an A4 envelope.

'Some guy from Barnes Inc dropped this off this afternoon.'

With furrowed brow, she ripped it open and looked at the document in surprise. It was an employment contract with a note attached.

I'll see you tomorrow around 4pm.

'What is it, Lottie?' Luke asked.

She looked up uncertainly. 'I've been offered a job as a counsellor.'

'What?'

She quickly explained Mark's job offer and, as she had known he would, Luke jumped on board with all the enthusiasm of a proud brother. 'You have to take this!'

'But what about Mum?'

'We'll work something out, between you, me and Zara.'

Zara walked in half an hour later after visiting Augustus. She also turned out to be surprisingly agreeable to the idea. 'I think you should definitely do it. I can help look after Mum.'

'You can't flake out whenever you feel like it.'

Zara rolled her eyes. 'I know! I'll do a really good job. Promise.' She headed off to her bedroom after that, not really interested in chatting more about it.

Charlotte frowned. Despite having broken some boundaries with their talk five days ago, they hadn't really spoken much since then. Zara seemed to have withdrawn into herself and she didn't know whether that was a good thing or a bad thing. Just then, she had a momentarily flash of Mark and heard his words again: 'In case you haven't noticed, she's also a very sensitive young woman.'

Damn the man!

She followed her sister and hovered in her bedroom doorway. 'So how are things with you, Zara?'

Her sister, who was sitting cross-legged on her bed, looked down at her hands. 'Fine.'

'I know you've been finding things difficult lately and I just wanted to reiterate that I'm here for you. Anything you need. Anything you want to talk about.'

Zara was silent, which was actually a good sign. Usually she kicked Charlotte out of her bedroom at the first sign of unwanted probing. So Charlotte came over to the bed and sat down at the edge of it.

'How's school?'

'Fine.'

She searched for another topic. 'How's Augustus?'

'He's good. Getting better.'

'I saw Mr Crawford today,' Charlotte went on. 'He mentioned you. I notice you're getting rather chummy with him these days.'

'Yes, I am.' Zara tossed her head rather defiantly in a way Charlotte had been doing herself a lot lately. She almost laughed at the similar way they both dealt with being challenged.

Zara shrugged. 'I like him.'

Charlotte had to ask, '*Why?*'

'He's not fake, like a lot of people are. He tells it how it is. And you may not notice, but he's kind too. He's given me a lot of good advice.'

Something between jealousy and chagrin bit her. 'Zara, you haven't told him about . . .?' She couldn't say it but, by her sister's horrified expression, she seemed to guess what she was referring to anyway.

'No, of course not! I just . . .' She didn't finish.

'What?' Charlotte squeezed her hand. 'You can tell me.'

Zara bit her lip and looked down. 'I'm scared, Charlotte.'

'Oh honey.' Charlotte immediately threw her arms around her and pulled her close. 'I know you are. But there's no need to be. Luke and I will protect you and love you, like we always have.'

'No,' Zara pushed back, 'you don't understand. I've done something really stupid and you're not going to like it.'

Charlotte pulled away, dread raising goosebumps on her skin. 'What? What have you done?'

Zara sucked in a breath. 'When you said I couldn't go to Rosemary's party, I was so angry. I wrote to him, to my father, explaining who I was and telling him that I wanted to see him. Mum accidently mentioned his name that night. You know, Dennis Mayer. So I put that name on the front and posted copies of the letter to all the prisons in Queensland. I didn't know then . . . what he'd done. I was just hurt and angry and I wanted to do something.'

Charlotte bit down hard on her lower lip and tasted blood. Pain shot straight to her temple. She shut her eyes and threw back her head. *No*. The mere thought of her sister having any sort of contact with that man was horrifying. Unthinkable. Her fingers trembled as she clasped them tightly together.

'You're angry,' Zara stated.

What was the point in being angry when the damage was done? Panic on the other hand was perfectly reasonable. Her chest tightened as she struggled for breath. 'Did he write back? Have you received a reply?'

'No, nothing.'

She shuddered. 'Well, that at least is something.'

Zara began to cry. 'What do you think is going to happen now?'

'I don't know.' Charlotte reached for her again and squeezed tight. 'But I'm not going to be a sitting duck when it does.'

Chapter 17

Mark

After dropping off Charlotte Templeton's employment contract to show that their little trip to Inappropriate Park had not fazed him, Mark Crawford went home in a mood that would have sent the devil ducking for cover.

To date, Charlotte Templeton had been a thorn in his side or an annoying fly that he couldn't seem to swat away. She had been irritating but he could deal with it.

Today was different.

Today she'd cut too deep. When she'd been swept off by that current, every drop of the grief and terror he had felt when he lost his brother had returned full force.

He knew he shouldn't have gone diving. Number six on that damned list! He was a fool to continue following the wishes of his dead wife, who due to the fact that she was dead no longer had any real perspective. Water sports were something he had shared with his twin and only with his twin. When that shark had taken Simon, he'd let it all go.

Forever.

Or so he thought. Even his love of diving, which back in the day had been his favourite pastime, had not tempted him to return. Naively, when he saw Kathryn's stipulation on the list, he thought he'd ease in slowly. Take a lesson or two. After all, it had been at least six years since he'd been underwater. He figured he'd get away from site for the day to a place where nobody knew him. Think about something else other than the project.

He didn't realise that the something else was going to be Charlotte Templeton.

Lips as soft as cream, with a taste just as delectable.

He wanted to groan in agony at the memory.

Kissing her had been a paradox, a kind of orgasmic pain within which a sandstorm of feelings had welled. Even now the grains had still not settled.

Longing, need, desire, frustration . . . guilt.

Guilt.

That was the main one.

He didn't understand how his respect for Kathryn could be so completely compromised. He knew that he would always love his late wife. She had brought so much to his life, and when she had died a part of him had gone with her. So how could he think about another woman in this way? It seemed unfathomable and yet such a relief.

What do I do?

What do I do?

For the first time in his life, he had absolutely no idea. He took out the list from his pocket. The folded bit of paper he now regarded as his link to Kathryn was rather worn looking. The creases were so etched it was impossible to fold it back another way. He had read the damn thing so many times that he already knew what the next item was. But he wanted to see the words in Kathryn's handwriting. Savour them. Worry about them.

Visit an old friend.

The prospect of contacting people from his past, none of whom he'd spoken to for over two years, was scary. Who was he kidding? It was terrifying. He had retreated too far into himself. Closed every door. Locked every window and ignored the knocking, which in any case had stopped ages back. In fact, he'd pushed people away so firmly that he was not sure they would be want to be welcomed back into his life. They would probably enjoy shunning him as he had shunned them when they'd tried to reach out.

All the same, making contact with his past actually seemed less dangerous than trying to sort out his feelings for Charlotte. And if he were truly honest, there was one friend he had left in Perth who he often thought about.

Kathryn's brother, Bill.

Their friendship pre-dated Mark even knowing Kathryn. They had met because they worked for the same company. They had liked each other due to their similar senses of humour. Until Kathryn had died, of course. Then Mark had grown more darkly cynical about everything.

Bill had been the first person he'd cut after Kathryn died. He hadn't been able to look the man in the face without seeing his wife – they had similar features. Now, when he thought of Bill, a sadness welled in his heart. At the very least, he would like an opportunity to apologise.

Perhaps a trip to Perth was in order. It wasn't like he didn't have a copious quantity of R and R saved up. Besides, he needed to get away – pull himself together after what had happened on the pontoon.

Ann booked his flight for ten the next morning. He went into the office early to sort out management while he was gone. He chose Fish to run the show in his stead. He may not be the cleanest or most sweetly spoken individual but he had more experience on open sea wharves than anyone on the job, even Mark himself. He had known the man a long time and seen him in action on several jobs, which was why he'd accepted him on his own project even after he heard he'd been fired from the last one. All Fish needed was a clear pathway. It was choice that led him into trouble. With this in mind, Mark gave him a very detailed list of instructions. He also left Ann and Zara with a note about care for Augustus. They could sort out a bird sitting roster between them when he was gone.

Having sorted out management, Mark then drove to Mackay to catch his plane. Forty minutes in the car, alone with his thoughts, it was very hard not to think about the fact that Charlotte would be starting work that day and he would not be there to receive her.

Never mind.

He'd left that job to Will. Boy Scout was sure to make her feel welcome. The two of them seemed to get on really well. His brow crinkled. Though not too well he hoped. William was a nice enough young man, too nice on most occasions, but Mark had not previously considered him any sort of distraction to his female staff. Unfortunately, the boy seemed to have cleaned up his appearance recently. He'd seen the way Ann had stumbled over her feet when he'd walked in that morning and the way little Ms Emily had glared at her as though she was eating out of her plate. He sincerely hoped Charlotte wasn't going to be affected by a messy haircut, crude shave and a lack of glasses.

As he realised where his mind was wandering he reined it back in but it didn't behave for long. The simple truth was, he was going to have to do something about Charlotte Templeton. And he had better decide soon, if not immediately, what that was.

He whiled away the flight to Perth watching movies and dreading his return home. Walking through the front door was going to be the hardest thing he'd done in a while. It had been months since he'd checked on the place.

Surprisingly this time, his arrival was different.

Yes, when he first stood on the threshold gazing across what had been their main living area, that familiar overwhelming sadness rolled through him. But then as his eyes adjusted more fully to the room, a new sense of purpose began to form. Her favourite throw blanket was still strewn across the back of the couch, her magazines on his coffee table, her favourite photo of them on the wall. The wall they'd painted together. He could see a thick film of dust on all the wooden surfaces. The place no longer smelled of her. It smelled musty and unkempt. For the first time in the years since Kathryn's death, he thought, *I need to clean this place up*.

Before he lost the urge, he dropped his suitcase at the door and went to the laundry to fill a bucket with cleaning products. For the next three hours, he dusted, he vacuumed, he wiped, he mopped. And it felt great.

He got a box and collected all Kathryn's things. Her blanket, her magazines, the winter slippers that were still strewn under her side of the bed, almost completely grey with dust. There were even some old tablets and other medical paraphernalia lying about, which he threw roughly into a bin bag. He took her books off the shelf and her handbag from the hall table. He tried not to look at anything too closely so that memories wouldn't have a chance to crowd in. Soon there was a giant pile of her stuff by the door and he collapsed on the couch feeling partially sated.

He looked around at the place. It looked sparse but much less depressing. Certainly a place he could relax rather than stew in. After a long hot shower he fell onto his freshly made bed, straight into a deep sleep, unfettered by dreams.

The following morning he rose feeling much rejuvenated but at the same time unsettled. He lay in bed staring at Kathryn's list trying to work out how to approach her task.

Should he call first or just show up on Bill's doorstep?

The problem with calling was that he might be told not to come. After all, he couldn't blame the guy for not wanting to see him after he'd ignored him for two years. But now that he'd made the decision, he simply could not, not go. Even if he was rejected.

In procrastination, his eyes flicked to the next few items on Kathryn's list.

8. Give my stuff to the Salvos.
9. Buy some new clothes, especially underwear.
10. Read a book.

Perhaps while he formulated a plan he could tick a few other items off. He'd already half started on number eight. With renewed energy, he jumped out of bed and went into the wardrobe. This time her smell did hit him like a slap in the face and he felt tears smart in his eyes. But he grabbed the clothes, hangers and all, and threw them on the bed. When the wardrobe had been cleaned out he transferred the pile into garbage bags, not bothering to sort too carefully. He didn't want to look at the dress he'd met her in. Or the chef uniforms she'd worn to work. Or, God forbid, her wedding dress.

He stuffed it out of sight and put it next to the door with the rest of her stuff.

There were some things he did keep, like her jewellery and photo albums. But he found a large box for these too and put them right at the back of the wardrobe to look at later. Much later.

After a quick shower, he loaded up his car and drove to the nearest Salvos store. A few minutes later the deed was done and he felt no pang. In fact, he noted en route to a department store, he felt nothing at all, except a strange stoic emptiness.

Shopping seemed like a good way to fill the void, though he barely registered what he purchased. A few shirts, a few pants and a stack of underwear. Yes, Kathryn had been right in her forward thinking. Shopping was so tedious and his tolerance for it so low that his current stash was full of holes.

Last stop was the library to find a book. This proved more difficult than he had first supposed. He had once enjoyed reading and read widely all different types of fiction and non-fiction. He barely had time for it these days, though. He worked such long hours that by the time he got home, had a meal and watched an hour of television, he just wanted to sleep and often did. Now faced with such variety he had no idea what he felt like. He ended up borrowing about six books with still no clear plan of which one he was going to attempt first.

As he returned to his car, books in hand, he realised that there was nothing left to do but make the visit he'd been dreading. All the same, he waited until after five. Bill could still be at work. It was a Tuesday after all.

At six o'clock, he was standing uncertainly on his brother-in-law's doorstep. Before he lost his nerve he knocked. The door swung open and an extremely large man with Kathryn's big brown eyes stared at him, dumbstruck. Eventually the man managed to croak, 'Mark! What the hell?'

He was equally affected. This man looked nothing like the one whose phone messages he'd stopped returning two years earlier. Bill had always been a large man but now he was the size of a house and there were streaks of grey in his hair. He'd aged prematurely.

'Bill! What happened to you?'

'What happened to me?' Bill repeated. 'What happened to you?'

He supposed this was a valid question and scratched his head looking for the right words. As his brother-in-law watched him with raised eyebrows, he knew there wasn't any point in beating around the bush so he went with the truth. 'I'm sorry. I just needed to be alone.'

'For two years?' Bill snorted. 'Pretty long time to sulk, if you ask me. I'm sorry you were having a hard time, Mark, but so was everyone else.'

'I know, Bill, but –'

'They call me Chub now,' said his brother-in-law.

Chub? He could see why. He was twice the size of the man he'd known. He couldn't help but repeat his earlier question. 'What happened?' Was this how Bill had dealt with Kathryn's death? Comfort food?

Bill looked at him slyly. 'Do I look different to you?'

Mark cleared his throat. 'Yes.'

Bill snorted. 'I had a hair cut.'

He then turned away from the open door and walked into the house. 'I guess you might as well come in.'

Uncertainly, Mark stepped over the threshold. Bill, or Chub, had already disappeared down the hall connecting to the kitchen. When Mark entered this space, it was to be met with a very welcome array of smells. A round table near the door was laden with a variety of platters. Scones, cupcakes, freshly baked biscuits, mini quiches, sausage rolls and slices both sweet and savoury.

'Are you expecting company, Bill?'

His friend looked up innocently. 'No, why do you ask?'

Mark cleared his throat as he searched for a point of reference.

Bill chuckled and his whole body seemed to wobble in amusement. 'Just *kidding*, Mark. And call me Chub, by the way. It's been too long since anyone called me Bill. I'm not used to it any more.'

'All right, Chub.' Mark straightened, determined to make an effort.

Chub grinned. 'Still take yourself way too seriously, I see. Have a scone, it'll make you feel better.'

Mark frowned. 'Does it make you feel better?'

'It's a bit too late to worry about me, Mark.' Chub's jovial expression disappeared. Just for a second he did look incredibly sad. 'I will admit, food does give me comfort. And, you know, Kath. Food was her thing. Every time I ate something delicious for one incredible bite I had her back. It was wonderful. But,' he dusted his hands, 'now I don't eat for grief but for pleasure.' He grabbed his belly like it was a trophy. 'You're actually very lucky to have caught me. A week ago I still would have been in Cape Lambert. Barnes Inc just moved me back to Perth.'

Mark nodded. 'Is the project over?'

'It's getting there.' Chub grinned. 'You know how these things drag on. They're definitely not hiring though, so a resident HR manager isn't really warranted.'

'I see.'

Just then a gorgeous-looking brunette entered the room. She was the embodiment of painted, polished and pampered. Dressed in a tight white top and floral skirt, her hair was a mass of coiffured curls piled on top of her head.

'This is my girlfriend, Annabel,' Chub offered by way of introduction and clearly enjoyed the way Mark did a double-take. 'Annabel, my brother-in-law, Mark.'

She pouted, as only a woman of her physical appearance could. 'Oh, I thought one of my girlfriends had got here early.' She regarded Mark with a frown. 'You can't possibly be here for the Tupperware party.'

'No,' said Mark. 'I won't be staying long.'

Chub grabbed him by the arm and steered him towards the door again. 'We'll just go chat in the living room, sweetie,' he said to Annabel, shoving Mark before him. Rather suspiciously, he also grabbed a plate of jam and cream scones just before he crossed the threshold.

'Chub, we need that for the party,' she called out after him.

'Yes, I know. I'm just putting it on the coffee table,' he threw over his shoulder.

'Perhaps this is not a good time.' Mark frowned as Chub waved him forward and then into another room halfway back down the hall. 'Maybe I should go.'

Chub set the plate on the coffee table and shut the door. 'And leave me entertaining ten giggling women? Not this week. Have a scone and tell me what the problem is.'

Mark sat down on the couch with a sigh, rubbing his hands uncomfortably across his lap to his knees. 'What makes you think there's a problem?'

'I don't see you for two years and then all of sudden you turn up on my doorstep without warning,' he grunted. 'There's a problem.'

'There's no problem,' Mark retorted. 'I just wanted to reconnect.'

Chub let loose a bark of laughter and picked up a scone. 'Denial is the first sign.' He took a large bite and chewed happily.

Mark folded his arms and buttoned his lip. Bill/Chub had changed so much. Too much for his taste.

'Oh, for Pete's sake, it's a woman, isn't it?' Chub sighed. 'Are you riddled with guilt because of Kath?'

His words cut so succinctly to the truth that for a moment Mark simply looked at him in shock.

Chub picked up a scone and passed it to him. 'Eat.'

Mark hesitated and then took the scone from him and bit into it. It was light, crumbly and buttery. The strawberry jam was a perfect foil for the cream, which was cool and refreshing. He closed his eyes as the sensation took him immediately into the past. Evoking all sorts of memories that made him want to cry like a child.

Kathryn.

Guilt lashed him like the flick of a whip as he realised how far he'd stepped away from her these last few weeks.

'They're very nice,' he said with effort, more to fill the awkward silence than because he really wanted to pass on compliments.

'Yes,' Chub agreed simply. 'Better than beer. Though I have some if you want it.'

Mark shook his head. 'No thanks.'

'So what's her name?'

'I don't know what you're talking about,' Mark snapped crossly.

'Oh well,' Chub chuckled, 'we've got a whole plate of scones to get through before you need tell me.' He rubbed his hands and took another. 'I'm in no hurry.'

The thought of eating that many scones did not appeal to Mark at all. So he said, rather tight-lipped, 'Her name's Charlotte.'

'And you like her.'

'No,' Mark barked, 'I definitely do not like her.'

'Oh,' Chub's eyes widened as he nodded, 'that bad, is it?'

'You're not making any sense.'

Chub held up a hand. 'Bear with me.' He took another scone and bit into it before saying, 'I'm actually rather good at this. I've already been responsible for one couple getting together . . . well . . . sort of. The point is –'

'The point is,' Mark interrupted, 'we're not getting together.'

Chub looked at him and said gently, 'Why not?'

'Because –' Mark opened his mouth and then it shut again, putting his half-eaten scone down on the table, the crumbs in his mouth turning to dust.

'Kath is dead, Mark,' Chub said bluntly. 'She's been dead for two years and she's not coming back. It's sad but it's reality.'

He flinched at the unfeeling way Chub announced it but his companion continued unheeded. 'The world has moved on without you. You need to catch up. She would want that. I know she would. All she ever wanted was your happiness.'

It was true. He reached into his pocket and clutched the list she had written for him. He even had it in black and white. So what was holding him back? Why couldn't he leave this limbo? Why couldn't he move on?

'All that's standing in your way now is fear,' said Chub as though Mark had asked these questions out loud.

Fear.

Yes. He was *afraid*. Afraid of putting this heart on the chopping block again and waiting for that knife to fall . . . as it always did. Nothing good in his life ever endured for long.

He swallowed hard, seeming to stare into the deep dark chasm of his own demise.

'You know,' Chub picked up another scone, 'when we were friends, back when I spoke to you and you used to speak back –'

Mark winced.

'– you gave me a lot of interesting advice. Much of it was about risk taking. I guess 'cause you're a project manager, everything was always about the big picture. The finish line, you used to call it. Without your advice I never would have gone to Cape Lambert. Never.' He took another scone and grimaced. 'They don't sell donuts there. *But* my life was stagnating and I just had nothing to look forward to in the city any more. I remembered what you used to say about the big jobs so I took a leap of faith.' His tone grew low and serious. 'It was the best thing I ever did for myself. And that's what you need to do.'

'I beg your pardon?' Mark responded, once more retreating behind his haughty mask.

'Okay, to summarise,' Chub ticked off his fingers. 'I'll say it again: big picture, finish line, leap of faith. That's what you need right now. And maybe a donut or two.'

Just then Annabel walked in carrying two other platters to set on the coffee table – one of cupcakes, the other of mini quiches.

'*Chub*! Half the scones are gone.'

Chub stood up and kissed his girlfriend. 'Sorry, honey. I couldn't stop him.' Then he looked sternly back at Mark, who stood up.

This was probably a good time to leave, so instead of calling Chub's bluff he said, 'On that note, I should go.' As he turned to head for the front door, his brother-in-law stalled him.

'Don't let years go by before I see you again. But next time call first.'

He gave a reluctant smile in response. 'All right. And thank you.'

Mark spent the next couple of days in Perth trying to read those books he'd borrowed from the library without much success. He'd start one, get bored and then start another until that one lost his interest as well. He was just too distracted to focus.

He'd actually booked himself the entire week off work. But ever since he'd spoken to Chub, he was just itching to get back to the job. Or, if he was truthful . . . back to Charlotte.

He felt as if Chub had released his shackles and he wanted to test this new emotional freedom. He wanted to see how she was doing in her new role. He wanted to enjoy her company without feeling guilty about it.

The more he thought about it, the more he just wanted to head back to Hay Point. Finally, he quit merely pondering and brought his flight forward a few days. Then he returned the unhelpful library books and, in one last attempt to get a good read, went to a bookstore in Perth city and browsed the shelves.

Something had to catch his fancy so he could cross another item from Kathryn's list. Before his mind knew what his feet were doing he was standing in the Self Help section.

He might have known he'd end up there.

Even miles from Charlotte, subconsciously he still wanted to make a connection. Reading one of her books seemed like a good way to do it, given Emily had said she tended to write about her own experiences. It was almost like discovering a hidden window into her life.

He found her name on the shelf easily enough and there was a small selection of titles there. None of the books were very thick. But he figured this was just her style. He could easily picture her writing intelligent, concise little handbooks on coping with life. He ran his fingers casually over the slim spines, reading the titles one by one.

Dealing with the Loss of a Loved One.

Tips for the Single Parent.

Life after Rape.

He nearly broke his finger on the last one.

What the?!

He snatched the book off the shelf, a pain throbbing in his temple as he flicked through the pages. Chapter headings jumping out at him like sharp spikes.

The Psychological Effects.

Self Blame.

Rape Trauma Syndrome (RTS).

The Reorganisation Phase.

Distrust of Men.

Flashbacks.

Depression.

Guilt.

Panic Attacks.

He slammed the book shut and went to the counter to pay for it. Adrenaline was pumping so fast through his veins he almost felt sick with it. Emily had said Charlotte wrote about her own experiences . . . Now he had to see her.

Urgently.

Chapter 18

Charlotte

The morning after Zara confessed to sending a letter to Dennis Mayer, Charlotte got on the phone to Woodford Correctional Centre. At least she had the benefit of actually knowing which maximum-security prison Dennis had been sent to. The other letters Zara had sent didn't matter. They had probably been binned or returned to the post office. Zara said she had put no return address on the envelopes for fear that Charlotte would receive mail that bounced back. The most important thing was to discover what had happened to the one letter that had gone to the right place. It was a long shot phoning them but she knew she had to try.

The woman who answered the phone sounded surprisingly normal. Charlotte had no idea what she'd been expecting. Just not the cheerful unconcern of the person on the other end of the line. For some reason she thought people who worked in prisons must be quiet and subdued so as not to provoke the inmates.

You're just being silly. She's probably not anywhere near any of the prisoners.

'Er, hi,' she began cautiously to the woman's chirpy offer of assistance. 'I was just wondering . . . this is going to sound like a really stupid question, but do your prisoners often receive mail?'

'All the time,' the operator responded. 'Did you wish to send something through?'

'No, actually, I already have. I just wanted to know if he got it.' She paused. 'Would you know if Dennis Mayer has received any mail within the last two weeks?'

The woman laughed. 'We have over a thousand inmates here. I wouldn't know who received what. I'd have to ask his prison guard to find out for you.'

Charlotte chewed on her lower lip. 'You see, I don't want him to mention to Mr Mayer that anyone's asking.'

This time the woman sounded stern. 'I see.'

'No, you don't understand. The letter never should have been sent in the first place.'

She heard the clicking of a tongue on the other end of the phone. 'Actually, I've logged into our system and looked up Dennis Mayer. Apparently he's been released.'

'What?' Charlotte nearly dropped the phone. 'When?'

'Two years ago,' the woman informed her. 'So he wouldn't have received your letter, unless someone forwarded it.'

She was still trying to grasp the woman's first sentence. 'Two years ago? He's been out of prison for two years?' This was more shocking than all the rest.

'Yes. I have a forwarding address here, if you'd like it. It's for an apartment block in Brisbane. Our mail clerk might have taken the trouble to forward the letter.'

Oh shit!

Her head was spinning but she said quickly, 'Er, yes, yes. I'll take that down.' The woman narrated it to her as she scribbled with pen and paper. She put the phone down and stared at the address as goose bumps puckered all over her body.

All this time.

He'd been out and they'd been none the wiser. How irresponsible of them not to check! And how naïve of her to assume that because he'd been convicted for three counts of rape he'd be jailed for life. She snorted as she mentally calculated the time he'd actually spent in prison.

Twelve years.

What was the world coming to?

On the other hand, in those two years he'd been free, they had heard nothing about him. Not from those friends of their mother who had known him. No one in the surrounding community had warned them that he'd been in town again. This meant that, unless Zara's letter had reached him, he wasn't interested in coming back to Sarina. Not that she thought anyone would welcome him. Few people knew he was Zara's father, other than some of her mother's closest friends, who had guessed at the time. But everyone knew he was a rapist. When he was convicted, the friends he had stayed with in Mackay had been shocked and had told everyone how betrayed *they'd* felt, as though harbouring him for that short period had been their own personal horror story. If Dennis had been back to Sarina she would have heard about it. So it was clear he wasn't interested in their mother any more. He must have made a new life for himself in Brisbane, where he had come from originally. With trembling fingers, she turned back to her computer and typed in the name of the apartment block to get a number for the strata manager.

Three seconds later she was on the phone again.

'Hi, would you be able to tell me if Dennis Mayer is still one of your tenants? He was in number 305.'

She heard the flutter of paperwork and then to her relief good news came back.

'No, he is no longer here.'

'Do you have a forwarding address?'

'No.'

Good!

With any luck, if the letter had been forwarded here, it had also been lost. She put down the phone still shaking but with relief. Hopefully, it was languishing in a bin somewhere at the post office. It seemed horribly unfair that Dennis Mayer had slotted right back into society as easy as a hook through a fish's mouth. She clicked off her computer, stood up and walked out of reception and back into her house. Her mother was seated in front of the television sipping a cup of tea, her face wan and unreadable.

If she could remember anything, anything at all, what would she say now?

It didn't matter. She certainly had no intention of asking her. Why bring back the horror when it would all blow over soon enough? In the meantime, she had other things to worry about . . . like starting her new job that day. Mark Crawford certainly hadn't given her much time to prepare herself. At the very least she would have liked to brush up on what she knew about alcoholism. But her professional capacity was the least of her problems.

What of the kiss they had shared? The confidences he'd trusted her with? The horrible words he'd overheard her say to Will?

She felt terrible after the way they'd left things.

Too much had passed between them to just ignore it. They needed to talk about it all. Should she bring it up at the office? Wait till after work? It would be awkward being around him with all that hanging over her head. Inwardly, she groaned. If she hadn't been so distracted by Zara's revelations last night she might have called him this morning.

She needn't have worried, however, because when she turned up at four pm at Barnes Inc he wasn't there. The receptionist Ann took her to see Will, who apparently had been briefed on what to do with her.

'Hey!' His greeting was friendly enough and much less confrontational than anything from Mark would have been. It was unfathomable that she should feel pique instead of relief.

'How's it going?' he asked.

'Er . . . good.' She must have been frowning because he grinned knowingly.

'Wondering why Caesar isn't here to greet you?'

Is it that obvious?

'The truth is,' Will broke her thoughts, 'he doesn't talk to new recruits for a few weeks.'

Of course.

'Let me guess,' she demanded, 'because he doesn't want to answer silly questions.'

'Sort of.'

She couldn't stop the rebellious retort. 'What if I demand to see him?'

'You can't.' Will sighed. 'He's out of town. Won't be back for a week.'

She stared in amazement. 'What? When did he leave?'

'This morning.'

Wow. That was a slap in the face if ever there was one. After everything they'd been through together yesterday, gone without so much as a goodbye. Was she making too much of it? Or did she just get snubbed?

'He did leave strict instructions on how you were to be received, though,' Will informed her.

'How kind of him.'

Turned out they *were* rather strict instructions. Her office was located in a different donga from the main office. It was open plan but at one end there was an enclosed meeting room. Apparently, this was to be her working space. Here, she would be able to have some privacy if she was in a meeting with one of the men. They had given her a computer and a filing cabinet. Will told her that the HR manager would come to see her shortly about PPE and an induction.

'You probably won't need to go onto the wharf. But we thought we'd give you one just in case,' Will explained.

Caesar wanted her to work Mondays, Tuesdays and Wednesdays from four to six o'clock. And for most of that she'd be just talking to the men. In fact, he wanted her to screen everyone on the job as a first pass. All employees had been instructed to book an appointment with her. She was going to have a rather busy couple of months building a file for everyone in the office. None of this was disagreeable to her. It just might have been nice if he'd told her all this himself.

She went home that evening feeling strangely bereft.

Why do I even care? It's not like we're friends. It's not like he's ever used common courtesy with me before. Why should it be different just because we've kissed?

In the days that followed she began to worry less about him and more about the men in her care. She had seen only three of them so far but there was a lot there when you dug deep. Alcohol abuse for a lot of these workers was only a symptom that hid so much more.

One man felt so helpless being away from his family. He had a son with autism and it was killing him not being able to be there to help his wife on a daily basis. Another man had a teenage daughter who he felt had gone off the rails. Apparently, she was doing drugs and he blamed his own absence for that.

There was a lot she could do here and she even began to feel some gratitude towards Mark for having given her the job. In fact, the more she thought about her absent boss, the more she thought of him as 'Caesar'. They had a business relationship and she shouldn't have built it up to be something more. She should just stick to being his landlady and his employee rather than trying to get emotionally involved. Especially when she should be focusing more on her sister right now.

Zara's confession about the letter had really rocked the ground under her feet. For the first time, she realised how little she knew about what actually went on in her sister's head. She really should be paying more attention to her.

Emily caught her reflecting guiltily on it when she dropped by her office close to knock-off time on Wednesday.

'Hey, you, everything all right?'

'Sure.' Charlotte sat up straight, ironing out the creases on her face. Emily wasn't fooled.

'You've been rather quiet lately.'

'Have I?'

'Guess it kind of sucks when the only counsellor in town is yourself,' Emily remarked shrewdly.

'Very funny,' Charlotte threw at her. 'If you must know, I'm just worried about Zara.'

'Still mad about the party?'

Charlotte sighed. 'If only.' That particular issue seemed light years in the past. 'A little more serious than that, actually. She's recently made contact with her biological father.'

'The guy you don't like.'

'To honest, I've never met him,' she admitted. 'But I just don't want him in our lives. He's a criminal.'

'Oh.' Emily frowned. 'I see.'

'Don't let me drop your mood.' Charlotte waved a hand at her to take a seat. 'Tell me some good news.'

Emily sat down, but her expression didn't lift. 'I wish I had some. I actually came to see you because I need some advice.'

'Ask away.'

'Well,' Emily wrung her hands, 'you see, I think I might be falling for this guy on site.'

'Go on.'

'And it's *really* awkward.'

'Why?'

'Long story. Let's just say there's a history there. Anyway, so I've tried to get rid of these feelings but I've been seeing so much of him of late that –'

‘Oh, for goodness’ sake, Em,’ Charlotte rolled her eyes, ‘just tell Will, already.’

Emily blushed a deep shade of red. ‘I *never* said it was *Will*.’

‘I’m sorry but it’s a little obvious.’

‘Does *he* know?’ she asked in a small voice.

Charlotte sighed. ‘Unfortunately not.’

‘And you think I should tell him?’

‘What do you stand to lose?’

‘Our friendship for a start,’ Emily protested, ‘and the fact that I’ve just come out of a long-term relationship with his best friend. He’s practically programmed to give me a wide berth in that regard. *And* on top of *all* that we work together.’ She screwed up her face. ‘How could I bring this up with him? He’d probably run a mile.’

‘You can’t be sure of that,’ Charlotte said softly. ‘Keeping quiet might just be stalling the best thing you ever had.’

‘I guess,’ said Emily, content for a moment to just stare out the window, deep in her own thoughts.

It was easy to see the younger girl’s dilemma. If *she* met a man, a completely inappropriate man, who she knew she couldn’t have due to her own history and his as well, would she tell him? Or would she hide the feelings that could only lead to heartache?

Oh crap, no. She closed her eyes as Mark’s face suddenly filled her mind. *I’d keep my bloody mouth shut too.*

Chapter 19

Will

Nova was singularly unapologetic for his behaviour on Saturday night. In fact, he was positively gloating on Monday afternoon.

'Tell me,' he rubbed his hands together, 'did she get a kick out of *sexy* Will?'

'I have no idea what you're talking about.' Will glared at him.

'I did you a massive favour.' Nova seemed surprised at his lack of understanding and shook his pointer finger. 'Don't think that what happened on Saturday was all a coincidence. It was all part of my master plan.'

'Believe me,' Will said as one goaded, 'I'm under no illusions. What the hell did you do with my clothes?'

'You don't remember?' Nova blinked. 'We took them outside and lit them on fire.'

'We didn't!' Will was horrified.

'Okay, we didn't.' Nova seemed disappointed by the admission. 'That's what I wanted to do but you were against it. Thought it would wake the neighbours.'

'Well, where are they?'

'The neighbours?'

'No, you idiot, my clothes!'

'I think we just binned them.'

Will put his head in his hands. 'So I'm going to have to go through the rubbish tonight.'

'Wouldn't bother. Just buy new ones when you go on R and R. You can borrow some of mine in the meantime.'

The last non-Barnes Inc shirt Will had seen Nova in had a picture of two leatherback turtles having sex on the front, with the caption *Slow Poke*.

'Er, I don't think so,' he said rubbing his eyes and then cursing. He hated wearing contact lenses: that's why he'd stopped. Now he had no choice but to revert. He still had his prescription for disposable lenses so it had been easy to pick up a box in Mackay before coming to work that morning. It would take at least a few weeks before the new glasses he had ordered would come in and frankly, he wanted to be able to see the shiploader when it arrived in nine days. That was going to be one big event.

'*So* . . .' Nova was still hell-bent on annoying him. 'What did she think?'

'She didn't think anything,' Will responded irritably. 'Or at least if she did, she didn't say anything about it.'

Of course, there was that one incident where she pressed herself against him at the top of the stairs.

It was probably an accident. You were in the way.

And the way she'd laced her fingers through his with all the intimacy of a long-term lover.

She was trying to get a better grip. The stairs were slippery!

He clenched his jaw, resisting the urge to grind his teeth. There was nothing there. It was all in his over-eager head. They'd had a big fight in the buffet lounge, which he was sure they still hadn't come back from despite the fact that apologies and even a hug had been exchanged when he dropped her home that evening.

In fact, if he was to be fully honest with himself, things had been rather strained between them since the Great Barrier Reef incident.

She was so jumpy.

Every time he greeted her she would turn around, start and cough, like he'd caught her doing something she shouldn't be. Nor would she look at him for prolonged periods when they spoke. She talked to the wall or the ceiling or the floor and occasionally at his hands or chest. But never directly to his face for more than a few seconds.

When you took eye contact out of their relationship, he discovered, it was actually a rather large minus. It was like she had erected a big electric fence around herself and every time he tried to breach it, he got zapped.

On Wednesday afternoon, he had to ask the question. 'Em, are you still mad at me about the whole bet/Trent thing?'

'No, I thought we sorted that out.' Again she was looking at her clipboard rather than at him. 'He's your best friend too and I can understand that you wanted to take his side.'

'I didn't take his side,' he said crossly.

'No, no.' She shook her head, still not looking at him. 'That's right. You wanted to protect me as a *friend*.' She ground the word between her teeth with a sigh before taking off to talk to one of the cement-truck divers.

They were doing a concrete pour that day and only one of the trucks had arrived. It was very important that they had enough concrete and that it was all the right mix. They had to pour the slab in one go. If they ran out of concrete halfway through the pour, what was there would dry before they could fill the rest and a cold joint would form along the area they had poured to.

Dipper and a couple of his men were on stand by to help out. The older man had been rather subdued with Will of late, neither heckling him nor boasting to him. He had to wonder what had changed.

What had Emily said to him when he'd told her about the bet?

Emily walked back, throwing him the swiftest of smiles before averting her eyes again. 'We should be right. The other trucks are only ten minutes away. He just called both drivers. I say we start.'

With a determined sigh, Will nodded. 'Em.' He stalled her as she moved to walk away and notify the driver.

'Yeah.'

'I never asked you about your date with Dipper.' *Too afraid of what I'd hear.* He swallowed. 'How was it?'

She shrugged. 'Good. He's a nice guy.'

'He didn't say anything else about the bet?'

She looked up at that. A strange, eager expression on her face. 'Was there anything else to say?'

'No, it's just that –' He decided to bite the bullet. 'It's just that you've been acting a little weird lately.'

'Weird?' she squeaked. 'Really? Me?'

'Yeah,' he stepped towards her, 'is everything okay?' His hand reached out to touch her shoulder.

'Sure, of course, why wouldn't it be?' She stumbled back away from his hand so quickly that she tripped on her own feet and landed on her arse. 'Umph!'

He put his hands under her armpits and hauled her up. 'I'm sorry. I didn't mean to –'

'Why are you sorry?' she snapped at him. 'You didn't do anything wrong. Let go of me.'

'I just –' He allowed his hands to drop as she roughly extracted herself from his hold.

'I think I need to take a break.' She handed him the clipboard. 'I might see if Charlotte's free to see me this afternoon. I think I'd like to get my appointment out of the way, if you know what I mean.'

He had no idea what she meant.

*

That night he did not see her. She was 'tired'. And the following morning he had no time to catch up with her as two things occurred simultaneously: Caesar returned to site and the bogies showed up.

Neither of these parties had been expected for at least a couple more days.

He wished he could say Caesar was the more unwelcome entity but the fact was, seeing those bogies or wheels lying on the back of two semi-trailers – one hundred and twenty tonnes each – put the fear of God into every worker on the job. 'God' being Caesar, of course.

You see, those wheels were supposed to be attached to the shiploader. Not arriving there on their own.

'Are those bogies I'm seeing in the yard?' Caesar demanded of Will when he walked unannounced into the office at ten that morning, sending papers flying and everyone around Will scrabbling for their desks.

Ann, who had been chatting in the kitchen to the planner, squeaked, 'Sir!' and hastily ran over.

'Answer me!' Caesar's eyes burned into his face and for a second Will struggled to remember the question. Ah, yes, the bogies.

'Er . . . yes, that would be them,' Will replied, knowing instinctively that this was the wrong answer but not able to hit upon a way to immediately conceal the truth believably.

'Who cut them off the shiploader without my permission?'

'I assume someone in Brisbane before it left port.'

'Don't get smart with me, Boy Scout, or I'll have you personally welding them back on.'

'Sorry, Mark.'

'Where is Fish?'

'In the yard, with the bogies.'

'Then I better go rip his throat out,' Caesar said bleakly.

'Is there anything I can get you, sir?' Ann clasped her hands together.

'A cup of coffee, two biscuits, our progress chart and the phone number of the man who cut those damned wheels off,' Caesar snapped before starting to walk on but then stopped.

He looked back at Will, his expression seeming to grow even more harried than before – if that were possible.

'Did Ms Templeton start work on Monday?'

'Yes, Mark.'

'How did she find it?'

'Fine.'

'*Fine*,' Caesar growled. 'I have always found the word to be grossly undescriptive, irritatingly unspecific and too commonly employed. Why use it at all?' He stalked off, leaving Will feeling like he'd just been hit in the face with a brick.

Nova chuckled delightedly.

Turned out, the reason the bogies had been cut off in Brisbane was because it was found that the shiploader was too heavy to lift onto the ship with the cranes they had organised. So they'd cut them off to reduce the weight. The balance of the shiploader had been put on another ship and was even now en route to Hay Point.

Normally when the shiploader arrived it would be lifted from the ship and set on the rails that ran up and down the wharf. Now, however, they would have to set the wheels or bogies up on the rails, then land the legs of the shiploader onto the wheels. This was going to make the lift that much harder.

It was no wonder Caesar was in such a mood.

The next couple of days became all about those wheels. The shiploader in all its glory was sailing in on Tuesday and every man and his dog was going to be there. The local media, the national media, the wharf owners and most of their staff and every cringing fool at Barnes Inc (who all had their fingers crossed behind their back).

In the lead-up to D-Day, Will allowed his stress to take over and tried to focus less on what he might be doing wrong with

Emily and more on what he could do right with regard to having his section of the wharf clear and cleaned up.

Trent didn't make things easier by calling him all the time. He was the very last person he wanted to speak to right then. So at first he just let the calls go to voicemail when he saw his friend's name on his phone screen. But then Trent managed to get his work number and was put through to Nova by mistake.

'So you're the famous best mate?' he heard the cheeky drafter say. 'I thought Boy Scout had made you up.'

Will's head snapped up so quickly he almost broke his neck. He pushed out his chair and snatched the phone off Nova, nearly pulling it off the desk.

'Why are you calling this number?'

'You never called me back before.'

'I'll call you back now.'

With a glare at Nova, he hung up and then walked outside, mobile in hand. A few seconds later he had Trent on the line again, though this time next to Augustus's pen. The turkey eavesdropped with interest.

'You haven't been returning my calls,' Trent explained, 'and I was beginning to wonder whether your phone was stuffed.'

'No, no.' Will sighed. 'I've been busy at work. Real busy. The shiploader is arriving in a matter of days.'

'Wow. You must be getting excited. I know that's the reason you took on this job.'

'Not so much excited as stressed,' Will replied.

'Still, it's good that you've got a chance to do something that gives you so much satisfaction.'

Stop being nice to me. I don't deserve it. 'Er, thanks,' Will said. 'How's your work going?'

'Badly: I can't stop thinking about Em,' Trent groaned. 'How is she?'

'She's good,' Will began cautiously.

'How was her date with that Dipper fellow?'

'She says it was good.'

Trent swore. 'So she likes him.'

'I wouldn't say that.'

'But you wouldn't rule it out.'

'Trent,' Will closed his eyes as he forced himself to say the words, 'if you want Emily, you have to do something. You can't just wait around in Perth hoping she'll come back. Because I'm telling you,' he swallowed hard, 'there're a lot of guys in Queensland who would love to make a move on her and are going to.'

Myself included.

'Thanks for the advice, Will,' Trent replied grimly. 'I'll keep that in mind.'

After a few more pleasantries they rang off, leaving Will feeling rather empty inside. At least he'd given Trent fair warning, if not complete honesty. Not that he had time to think about where he himself stood with Em, of course.

The shiploader was due to arrive the next day. As it stood, he had Caesar up his arse and a number of other blokes relying on him to get his part done before evening. He worked late that night and as a result overslept.

It was his mobile that jolted him awake at seven-thirty the next morning. Nova was on the line.

'Where the hell are you? The shiploader is here! And it's fuckin' amazing.'

Will threw his covers off but his legs were tangled in them so he followed them off the bed onto the floor. 'Omph,' he groaned as he hit the ground. 'Okay, okay. Be right there.'

In a mad rush, he showered, dressed and exited his unit but was immediately frustrated by the fact that he was going to have to walk to site – there were no utes in the car park. Everyone had already left.

'Hey, excuse me? Where is everyone?'

Will turned around and saw a man in his late fifties standing by the entrance to reception. He had short, fizzy hair that was both thinning and going grey on the top of his head. He indicated the windows with a flick of his hand. The blinds were drawn and there was a sign on the door that said *Closed*.

'Isn't this supposed to be a motel?' the stranger asked again. 'How do I rent a room?'

'You won't today,' Will said with a chuckle. 'The shiploader has arrived at the wharf.'

The older man didn't look too impressed with this. He scratched his head. 'What's a shiploader?'

'A giant piece of machinery that loads ships. Do you want to come watch us instal it?'

'No, I need to see Virginia Templeton. Is she on the wharf?'

Will smiled. 'No. I think she's staying with her son for the next few days.'

'Where's that?'

'I have no idea. But her daughters Charlotte or Zara will know.'

The man nodded, seemingly thoughtful. 'Where can I find Charlotte?'

'She'll be on the wharf.'

'Where is that?'

An idea struck Will. 'Would you like to go there now? Cause I could do with a lift?'

The man's mouth stretched into a smile. 'Perfect.'

They hopped into his too-clean green Mazda and Will gazed down at the spotless car mats.

'Are you from out of town?'

'Brisbane,' the man said as he started up the engine.

'I'm Will Steward.' Will held out his hand.

The man shook it cordially. 'Dennis Mayer. Good to meet you.'

Chapter 20

Emily

The office was a flurry of activity. There were people everywhere. Some of them didn't even work there. Ann was handling a couple of reporters and their camera guys who had just finished watching a twenty-minute induction DVD in one of the meeting rooms. Due to the bad press about the turtles, Caesar had gone into overdrive with PR. He'd even roped in Charlotte to work a few extra hours on the big day. There was going to be a media viewing area on the wharf and Charlotte was put in charge of it.

Emily was glad it was their nightmare, not hers. Looking after reporters was like walking a bunch of dogs that had been locked up for hours. They were too eager, had no sense of danger and didn't want to stay on their leashes. But she was sure the forthright resort owner would be able to rein them in. As if to echo her thoughts, Charlotte walked into the main office donga carrying hard hats and vests for the guests waiting by Ann's desk.

'Now have you all completed your forms and got your visitor identification cards?'

The media personnel nodded, holding up their white necklaces, which consisted of a shoelace-style cord and laminated visitor's card.

'If you'll come with me,' Charlotte smiled at the group, 'I've got a ute waiting out the front to take us to the wharf.'

They all nodded excitedly and left with her.

This is crazy, Em thought, I need to get out to the wharf where the real action is.

Having given up her guests to Charlotte, Ann walked over and echoed her thoughts. 'I would have thought you'd be out looking at the shiploader by now.'

'I thought I'd wait for Will. Where is he?'

Nova sidled up as though he hadn't been eavesdropping on their conversation. 'Just called him. He's on his way.'

'Well, he better get here soon,' Emily grumbled, 'or he'll miss it.'

Nova laughed. 'They don't lift it that fast, sweetheart. Speed of snail is about right. It's going to take four or five hours minimum. But,' he acknowledged, 'there're currently only two utes left in the yard. I'll take you and him out together if you like.'

'That'll be great.'

All their eyes swung to the door as three more people walked in. Will, and two other men she didn't recognise. He lifted a hand and waved apologetically at her.

'He's turned into a rather tasty morsel, hasn't he?' Ann said in her ear. 'I mean, with the new haircut and all. What do you think my chances are?'

Emily looked at her in horror. 'I beg your pardon?'

Unfortunately, before Ann could respond, Will and his two companions had reached them.

'Hi, guys, this is Dennis and Aaron. They both need to see Charlotte. Aaron is one of the camera operators.'

'Sorry I'm late.' Aaron wrung his hands. 'Are the others from Channel 7 here yet?'

Ann rolled her eyes. 'They've already left for the wharf with Charlotte.'

'Is she coming back to the office soon?' Dennis asked.

'No.' Ann shook her head. 'She can't leave those reporters on their own. They're like children. No offence.'

Dennis shrugged. 'None taken.' His features looked rather familiar and Emily tried to pick out where she'd seen them before but couldn't quite place it.

Aaron glared at him and stepped forwards. 'Well, I need to get out there or I'm going to get fired.'

'Aren't we all?' Nova murmured.

'So.' Aaron ignored him. 'What do I need to do?'

'Well, first you need to have a short induction, get some PPE together and then Nova can drive you both out.'

'Hang on a second there.' Nova shook his head. 'I'm not waiting for half an hour.' He patted the rolled-up documents under his arm. 'I've got drawings to give to Fish.'

Ann immediately turned to Will, eyelashes batting and placed a hand on his arm. 'Can you do it, Will? There's one ute left in the yard after Nova takes his.'

Will frowned. 'I wasn't planning on hanging around either.'

Emily glanced smugly at Ann. *Damn straight!* Why would he want to hang around waiting on media personnel, when a mammoth shiploader was being lifted by two kick-arse cranes?

'Can't you take them?' she demanded of Ann.

'Then who will look after reception?' Caesar's assistant demanded with some of her boss's pomp. 'It can't be left unmanned on a day like today. Please, Will.' She put her hand on Will's arm again and Emily groaned inwardly. This was torture to watch.

But as usual, Will, the Boy Scout, who always came to the rescue of any woman who ever asked, stepped up to the mark. 'All right.' His moan echoed Emily's internal one. Why did he have to be such a nice guy?

He looked at Emily. 'Are you going out now?'

'I was going to wait for you.'

'Nah.' He waved her off. 'Go with Nova. You'll want to see it all from the beginning.'

Nova was already heading for the door. 'Come on, Toots.'

Great! She glared briefly at Nova before looking back at Will. 'Are you sure?'

'Positive.'

She threw him a grateful if frustrated smile before grabbing her hard hat. 'Okay, I'll meet you out there.'

She'd been looking forward to sharing this experience with him. It was a shame that it had to be ruined by Can't-keep-her-hands-to-herself Ann.

Emily frowned as she followed Nova to the car park, her mind harking back to the conversation she'd had with Charlotte the day before. As much as she didn't want to go there, her friend was right. She had to reveal her feelings for Will and, by the looks of Ann, sooner rather than later. She got into the ute and barely registered Nova driving out of the car park and onto the dirt track that led to the top of the jetty.

The creases on her brow deepened as she visualised Ann with her hand on Will's arm, batting her eyelashes at him like she was so helpless. *Come on.* The week before the assistant barely gave him the time of day. She was in lust. *Not in love.*

The thought yanked Ann out of her head and threw her off the side of the jetty.

Oh shit, am I in love with Will?

After asking the question, she didn't really need more than a second to answer it. *Of course I am.* How could she not be? He was the perfect guy for her. Perfect in every way. And had been for years. *You're such an idiot.*

'Penny for your thoughts,' said Nova, making her nearly jump right out of her skin. 'You look pretty intense over there.'

She chuckled nervously, running sweaty palms down her Hard Yakka pants. 'Just worried about the shiploader.'

'Not your problem really,' Nova said reassuringly. 'It's Caesar's arse on the line today. Can't say he's been taking it too well either.'

Yes, Caesar had been in an awful mood that morning. And she didn't blame him. But even dropping a million-dollar structure that weighed more than a thousand cars into the ocean didn't seem as important to her as the fact that all the smoke in her head was clearing.

I'm in love with Will. I love Will Steward. What the hell am I going to do about that?

As Charlotte had been only too quick to point out yesterday, there really was only one option and that was to reveal her feelings. She had to tell him or kiss him.

As the latter thought shot madly through her head, it brought all her screaming nerves to a shattering halt. She repeated the words again. Savouring the idea. Letting it roll around in her head until it reformed into a goal. *I'll kiss Will. Tonight.*

And then doubt returned. She couldn't say that her skills in seduction were that much more sophisticated than Ann's. But what was the harm in just going with tried and true? Invite him over for dinner, make sure the wine was flowing freely and then make a move on him.

Eeek! If Nova hadn't been sitting in the car next to her, she would have put her face in her hands. *I can't!*

Will would just at laugh at her if she attempted to flirt with him. She really only had two signature moves. The 'I'm cold' move, which involved faking freezing and climbing into a man's lap. Or the 'I'm tired' move, which involved pretty much the same thing. Will was familiar with both those moves as they'd often joked about the time she tried them on –

His best friend!

This time she did put her head in her hands. Luckily by this stage Nova had stopped the ute and in this moment turned to open his door. She quickly followed suit and stepped out onto the concrete deck to take in the scene around her.

Her thoughts dissolved at the sight of the shiploader. Taller than a ten-storey building, the lattice of steel trusses rose up from the deck of the ship docked at berth two. The structure was shaped like a crane, and its function was similar too. The shiploader was supposed to sit on the wharf next to the conveyor so that coal could move up its structure and down its giant boom into the tanks of the ships.

The massive concrete counterweight hung off the back and the control room for the driver sat in the front. The boom of the shiploader, or long steel arm that was usually responsible for loading ships, was currently detached from the main tower and lying beside it on the deck of the transporting ship. They would need to be connected later, once they had placed the new shiploader back onto its wheels, which were currently in position on the rail. The tension in the air was so thick, Emily could have put a skewer through it.

A gentle breeze rustled her fringe.

Nova lifted his nose to the sky as he felt it too. 'Hmmm, that's no good. They'll want it absolutely still.'

'It's barely there,' Emily tried to assure him. Her eyes went to the red flags that fenced off some equipment out of use. 'See – the flags aren't even moving.'

'Just as well,' Nova nodded. 'Caesar won't want that thing waiting in the wind. I better find Fish.'

As he went off to find the second in charge, she was at liberty to scan the deck. Surprisingly, it was not the pandemonium she had been expecting. Instead, there was a rather reverent silence. Many of the Barnes Inc workers were simply clustered in twos and threes craning their necks at the giant structure currently floating beside the wharf.

She had no problems understanding their noiseless fear. They were about to lift one thousand and fifteen tonnes off the deck of that ship and the entire state would probably be watching the highlights on television that evening. Heavier than two hundred African elephants in their prime, the shiploader was going to be lifted by two giant cranes capable of holding six hundred tonnes each. They would perform the job in co-ordination.

'Co-ordination' being the key word.

Every second guy on deck had a radio. All ears would be tuned into every centimetre the shiploader moved. She saw Fish talking to one of the media personnel in Charlotte's group. Even he looked freaked out. She could tell because he was dressed in brand-new jeans, a brand-new blue shirt and a brand-new safety vest. She knew they were brand new because they still had their factory creases; he'd clearly pulled them direct from their plastic packets and dressed up for the cameras. There were three of them currently pointing at him. Caesar wasn't there and she searched the deck for him, finally finding him standing by the rail. He was looking out to sea, lost in his own thoughts, his hands deep in the pockets of his pants. Two men, like sentries, stood nearby as though guarding his solitude. She wouldn't be surprised if he'd asked them to keep the media off his back.

There's a man who didn't sleep last night.

Everyone was just watching, waiting. She had one of the company cameras with her, so she took it out and snapped a couple of photos of the shiploader. She was sure the staff would want to remember this moment in years to come. Her nerves buzzed as she put the camera back in its bag and looked around again. Activity on the radios seemed to have gone up a notch and Caesar had moved from his position by the railing to talk to his men.

Emily went over to Charlotte, as the resort owner was, like herself, pretty much a spectator in all this.

'How's it going?' she asked with a flick of her eyes at the media personnel behind them.

Charlotte grinned. 'They're excited, but who wouldn't be?'

Now there were several men clustered around Caesar. Decked out in hats and high-visibility vests, they looked almost military in their movements. Charlotte had a radio on and they could hear them talking status on the airways. The cranes that would lift the shiploader were actually seated on the ship itself rather than on the wharf. Once they had the shiploader in the air and then more particularly over the side of the ship, the hull took in water to counter-balance so that the boat stayed stable the whole time.

Just then Caesar nodded and she heard, 'We're all hooked up and good to go, over,' on the airways.

One man detached from Caesar's group and gave the hand signal to the men driving the cranes. With bowed head, he simply raised one finger to the sky and the lift began. The shiploader creaked and moaned as it left its bearings.

They lifted it a mere twenty centimetres before stopping to check everything. Men standing on the ship scurried around it. One of them said over the airways after a few nods from the others, 'Okay, guys, she's airborne and looking good. Over.'

Emily realised she'd been holding her breath and hastily exhaled. A cheer rose up around the watching crowd. A few claps too as they looked at the structure dangling there for the first time in mid-air.

Wow!

'I somehow expected it to be faster,' Charlotte mused.

Emily shook her head with a smile. 'A few centimetres in the wrong direction can cost us an hour in correction. Everything has to be just perfect.'

Charlotte smiled. 'Okay.'

They both continued to watch the shiploader inch its way higher into the air, and Emily felt an overwhelming sense of satisfaction claim her. All the crap she'd been through when she'd first arrived on site seemed worth it now. And to think, she never would have had this opportunity without Will.

Will, the man I love.

He always knew what she needed without her even having to verbalise it. Whatever doubts she'd harboured previously about where she wanted to take their relationship fell away. Will was a very special guy and she had to fight for him. Yes, she'd already made a lot of mistakes. Wasted five years on his best friend for a start – an error in judgement that was going to be a very difficult hurdle to overcome. Especially for Will. But she had to try.

Trent was a smart and decent man. But even if he'd been in love with her, he didn't love her the way she wanted to be loved. He was selfish. He hadn't been interested in her as a complete, separate human, but as an extra bit of himself. She wasn't her best self with him, either. She had been timid and even, in a way, lazy. And apart from all of that they weren't soulmates the way she and Will were and always had been.

'Are you okay?' Charlotte asked.

'I've just realised what an idiot I've been.'

Charlotte looked confused. 'About the shiploader?'

'No, about Will.' Emily sighed. 'I'm in love with him. There's no use denying it any longer, as much as I would like to.'

Charlotte grimaced. 'We can't choose who we fall in love with. It could be our best friend or . . .' Her gaze travelled across the deck to where Caesar, Fish and the guy in charge of the cranes were examining a drawing together. '. . . Or our worst enemy.'

Emily paid very little attention to that. 'Well, I'm going to do something about this tonight.' It felt good to voice her decision out loud. Suddenly she laughed as a thought occurred to her. 'But first I think I need a little confidence-booster.'

Shielding her gaze against the sun, she scanned the deck before her eyes alighted on Spooks, who was standing by the bogies surrounded by his usual group of cronies. They were chatting away nonchalantly, like the crane guys weren't about to swing a thousand tonnes over their heads.

'Hey, Spooks,' she hailed him.

He looked up in surprise. 'What can I do for ya?' He grinned toothily at her.

'It's about the bet,' Emily began, and watched smugly as all eyes immediately turned to her.

Chapter 21

Mark

His return to site was not the homecoming he'd expected. On top of the stuff-ups they'd made with the shiploader, Charlotte wasn't talking to him.

No, scratch that, she *was* talking to him. Just not in the usual, bossy, teasing manner he was used to. *And*, if he was man enough to admit, had actually grown to enjoy. Charlotte was the only person who challenged him – questioned everything he said and did. He enjoyed the cut and thrust of their sparring and her opinionated perspective on the little nuances of his life. But ever since she'd joined his team, it was Yes, Mr Crawford; no, Mr Crawford; and will that be all, Mr Crawford? with no additional commentary.

He wanted the old Charlotte back.

In an attempt to draw her out he'd even gone so far as to apologise. Yes! Apologise for not having been present when she first started at the job. But she'd merely blinked and said, 'Oh, that's all right. Will took care of me just fine,' before walking off.

Then he'd tried giving her more work.

He told her he needed her to babysit reporters when the shiploader arrived because everyone else would be too busy. This wasn't entirely true and it wasn't in her job description, besides the fact that her brother would have to take the day off from his own work to look after their mother while she was on site. He was sure that would raise a protest. But all she said was, 'Sure. I'll work something out.'

Huh?

He couldn't decide why she was being so submissive. Was it because he was now her boss as well as her client? Was she worried that he held too hefty a piece of her livelihood in his undeserving hands? *Or* was it because she was still upset about the way he'd treated her after that kiss they'd shared?

A kiss she hadn't mentioned at all but that he couldn't get out of his head.

Her taste, her touch. The way her body moulded to his to make the other half of their whole.

He'd read her book, *Life after Rape*, cover to cover in a few hours and then read it again. It had been written rather factually and in no way with a personal flavour. It was definitely an advice-style book that addressed the reader rather than spoke of the author. The only personal reference was a very brief dedication at the front.

For Mum. Your courage in the face of adversity is an inspiration to me.

It was a slim window into Charlotte's soul and told him nothing he didn't already know. She loved her family. She would do anything for them and had. Still, at every chapter heading he found himself asking questions.

Did this happen to you? How do you know all this?

A rage so deep it nearly curdled his blood grew in the pit of his stomach, making his skin feel toxic and his thoughts run rampant at times. He couldn't stand the thought of anyone hurting Charlotte. Least of all in a way so abhorrent it made him want to do violence. He wanted to talk to her about it but didn't dare. Instead, he skirted around the edges of it with Zara when she came to visit Augustus.

'So does your sister date much?'

Zara, who had been sitting cross-legged on the ground next to Augustus's cage, choked on the biscuit she'd been eating. 'Why do *you* want to know?'

He frowned. 'Just making conversation.'

Zara smirked and then gave him a sharp look that unfortunately saw more than he wanted it to. Her astuteness was starting to become bloody annoying. He couldn't understand how Charlotte was unaware of it. He remained determinedly silent, waiting for her to speak again.

'She has had a few boyfriends. Or so I'm told. I've never met any of them.'

'Why?' He tried not to sound too interested.

'I don't know. She just likes to keep that part of her life separate from us.'

'Why?' he pounced.

'I don't know,' Zara responded stiffly. 'Perhaps she just wanted to be certain they wouldn't interfere with our family. Mum has always needed a lot of help even before she got Alzheimer's.'

It was clear there was more to the story than she was letting on. Mark had to clench his fists to stop his anger from bubbling over. 'Doesn't your sister ever get a break? Where was your father in all this?'

'My father?' Zara looked away, barely muttering the words.

'Yes, your father.'

'His name is Dennis Mayer.' She lifted her chin. 'I would never call him my father.' From the finality in her tone, he knew the conversation was over. As if to confirm his thoughts, she stood up, dusting her jeans. 'I think I'll head off now. I've got homework to do.'

Since when had Zara ever been interested in homework?

She waved a hand over her shoulder but didn't look back as she walked off.

Damn!

He hadn't meant to offend her. He should have known there would be no love lost between her and the man who had refused to be a part of her life. He couldn't understand how some men could just abandon their children. Even if they were selfish with no sense of responsibility or love for their child, would not curiosity at least bring them back for visits? Augustus squawked, seemingly annoyed by his unusual lack of attention, particularly after being away for several days.

'You know, you seem to be almost recovered now,' he remarked. 'Maybe it's time we set you free again.'

Augustus immediately put his head down.

The threat gave him little satisfaction and he reflected with a grunt that perhaps he was getting soft. Or perhaps his reign of tyranny was no longer an outlet for his pain. It just left him emptier than ever. His thoughts immediately turned to Charlotte and that kiss . . .

Closing his eyes, he went back inside, cursing his own weakness.

Now standing on the wharf a few days later watching them lift the enormous shiploader painstakingly over the main road, he marvelled at how hollow this achievement was to him. Even in these final hours of glory, with the media marvelling as he proved that a man could move mountains if he dared, he felt nothing.

Sure, he had another huge piece of plant installation to add to his already overflowing resumé. So what? He'd been doing this for years and, while it had given him fleeting pleasure, it couldn't even attempt to fill the void in his heart. The only person who had given him pure joy was Kathryn and now she was gone. He thought back to his visit to his brother-in-law and knew that he couldn't stay in hiding forever. As Chub had said, he needed to consider the bigger picture and take a leap of faith. His hand went automatically to his pocket, where Kathryn's list safely resided. He didn't need to look at it to know what was next on his agenda. *Go on a date.*

Such a simple order poleaxed him. Kathryn couldn't have realised what she was asking. Should he really take this leap of faith or would it be his own undoing?

'I need a break,' he told Fish, whose chin was still tilted as far back as it could go, both his eyes on the shiploader dangling above them like an oversized mobile in a baby's cradle. 'I'm going to get a coffee,' he announced. 'Call me if you need me.'

He doubted they would. At this stage, there was little he could do but watch and cringe. His job had been preparation. Now it was up to those crane drivers to finish it off. He could stand there and hold his breath all day or he could go and get a little sustenance. So he went into the smoko donga and began to make himself a hot drink.

A few minutes later, the door to the empty donga swung open and his heart clenched as a familiar face appeared.

'Oh sorry,' Charlotte murmured. 'I didn't realise you were in here.'

She turned as though about to walk right back out, pulling on the rim of her hard hat.

'Ms Templeton,' he said quickly, unable to bear her just leaving like that. The very last thing he wanted from her was space. But how did he convey that? 'This is not a private lunch room. Come in.'

She hesitated with her hand on the doorknob. 'I didn't want to disturb you if you were collecting your thoughts.'

He frowned at her meekness. 'I realise you don't like my company but I hope it would not make you ignore your own thirst.'

'Your company . . .' She blushed. 'I think I owe you an apology for what you overheard me saying to Will on the Adventure Pontoon.'

He remembered.

'A lot of things happened that day,' she went on, 'and I wasn't in my right frame of mind. So I'm sorry, and on that note,' she gave him a weak smile, 'I should leave you in peace.'

Leave him in peace?

He put down his teaspoon with a snap. 'I do not know what I have done to warrant this behaviour from you, Ms Templeton, but I hope you will cease and desist it.'

She blinked. 'Behaviour. What behaviour?'

'This.' He flicked his hand out as though the gesture explained everything. 'Since when have you ever cared about my peace?'

She let go of the doorknob and came towards the kitchen counter. 'Don't you believe in respect in the workplace, Mr Crawford?'

Finally!

'Of course I do,' he snapped back. 'Just not from you.'

'Wow.' Her eyes widened. 'What a high opinion you have of me.'

Belatedly realising that he wasn't enjoying this particular spat quite as much as he usually did, he decided to turn the tables a bit. Fancying himself rather clever, he said, 'As a matter of fact, I do have a rather high opinion of you. Despite my better judgement, I actually appreciate your brashness, lack of respect for authority and pushy nature.'

'*Pushy!*'

'Should I have said assertive?' he inquired. 'Yes, perhaps that is a much better word.'

'I suppose you think I should take that as a compliment?'

'Definitely,' he nodded, pleased at last with her understanding. 'Because as ill-thought-out as this might be, I am about to ask you on a date.'

'*W-why?*' she demanded, like he was some sort of idiot.

He straightened his shoulders and stood taller. 'Didn't I just say?'

'There's got to be a better reason other than the fact that I'm pushy.'

'Assertive,' he corrected her. 'I changed that to assertive.'

She took her hat off her head and put it on the trestle table closest to her, threading her fingers into her hair and scrunching with all the frustration of Einstein at the brink of the Theory of Relativity. 'Do you even hear yourself?'

'Quite clearly.'

'Then you must realise,' she threw at him, 'that I'm not going to go anywhere with a man who has just insulted the hell out of me.'

His expression hardened. 'And nor should you,' he said firmly. '*Ever*. Perhaps I should have been a little more sensitive in that regard.'

'A little more sensitive.' She laughed mockingly up at the ceiling. 'A frickin' axe through a window would be more sensitive than you, Mr Crawford.'

A muscle twitched in his cheek. 'I apologise. It was not my intention to insult you and I will try to express myself more succinctly.'

'What a relief.'

'There's actually a number of reasons I wish to go out with you, Ms Templeton. Most of them are irrational and a result of a certain weakness I have with regard to your physical attributes.'

Her eyes widened and he hastened to continue, 'But the most pressing reason that springs to mind, is, well . . .' He sought for concise way to sum up his emotional limbo, his visit to Chub and dead wife's master plan. 'It's on my To Do list.'

'I see. Your To Do list,' she said through her teeth. 'That's so flattering.'

He studied her sarcastic expression gravely, wishing he'd approached this now from an entirely different angle. How could he have so easily forgotten everything she had been through in the past? 'I'm sorry if my admiration is making you uncomfortable. A woman of your history probably finds this situation rather difficult.'

She blinked. 'A woman of my history? What the hell are you talking about now?'

He licked dry lips. He really should have planned this rather than being spontaneous. He was now locked in a place he certainly did not want to be. And as he didn't have that much experience dealing with nerves – he barely felt anything but apathy these days – he was afraid that he wasn't handling it very well.

'Don't hold back now.' Charlotte's hands went to her hips. 'Not when you've come this far, Mr Crawford.'

He took a deep breath. 'I read your book, *Life After Rape*. In it, you did discuss the difficulties associated with future relationships after the trauma occurred. After everything you've been through . . .' He trailed off as the subject seemed beyond expression even for him.

'Wait,' her pointer finger flicked from herself to him, 'you think that I . . .' She swallowed hard. '. . . That I was raped.'

He reached for her.

'Don't you *dare* touch me!' She took a giant step back and his hands immediately dropped to his sides.

He was now fully aware that things had gone completely and horribly wrong.

'Not,' she squinted at him in a way that made him wish the floor would open up and swallow him, 'that it's any of your business, but no, I was not the one who was raped. And if I had been, I would not be sharing the details with you. I get that you're a little confused right now because we had that kiss on the reef, which,' she held up a finger as he started to open his mouth, 'was, I admit, very nice and did make me contemplate for the briefest of milliseconds that maybe you and I could be good together. But anything I felt for you that day has been completely and utterly squashed by your squalid assessment of my character and this illuminating display of your own.'

'Ms Templeton –'

'I am *not finished*! It is not your place to speculate about my family's history, judge me or bring up subjects you clearly know nothing about. And I certainly would not date a man just because it's on his To Do list!' She turned and headed for the door.

'Ms Templeton –'

'No, *Mark*,' she snapped. 'You need help! But not from me.'

She slammed the donga door behind her, leaving him gasping for breath. His heart pounded painfully in his chest as if he'd just run a marathon. He tipped his undrunk coffee down the sink. Well, he'd screwed that up royally! His leap of faith had landed him right in the centre of the road where a semi-trailer had taken him out. He allowed ten minutes to pass while he just stared into space, searching for a way to recover.

The door opened and he looked up expectantly, hoping she'd come back to talk it through again, but it was only Will.

'Mark, we've just started descent alongside the conveyor. We thought you might want to be there for that.'

This was the trickiest part of the lift. The conveyor was very close to the rail and you didn't want to accidently knock it with a million-dollar structure. It could be a rather costly error.

'I'll come out,' Mark growled and put on his hat.

He walked out of the donga after Will, his eyes automatically looking towards the area that had been roped off for the media. He couldn't see her. 'Where's Ms Templeton?'

Will frowned. 'Wasn't feeling well, so she left Em in charge of the troops and took a ute back. Shame, 'cause I have a guy here who came out specifically to see her. But Dipper will give him a ride back later when we're through this stage of the lift.'

Mark dismissed his words as the view of the shiploader met his eyes. While he couldn't do anything but watch for the moment, he had to be present at this precarious stage.

As much as he wanted to just jump in a ute and follow her, he needed to stay to witness the momentous milestone.

An hour later they had passed the danger point and were getting ready to set the shiploader back on its wheels – a procedure that was just as hairy but for completely different reasons. Spooks's welding team moved into readiness as the shiploader slowly descended.

Will came up to him again as he watched the team assembling its equipment.

'Sir, just wondering if I can borrow your ute.'

He turned on the boy in annoyance. 'Why?'

'It's the only one left on the wharf. One of the welders has ripped his insulated gloves. Just want to duck back to the office and get a spare pair. I won't be long.'

'Where's your ute?'

'Dipper took Dennis Mayer back to see Charlotte.'

Dennis Mayer?

Where had he heard that name before?

It seemed so bloody familiar.

'Who is Dennis Mayer?'

Will frowned. 'Come to think of it, I'm not exactly sure.'

And then the memory of Zara sitting by Augustus's cage, telling him about her father resurfaced.

Or rather . . . not telling him.

The conversation had died the second this guy's name had been mentioned. He'd never seen such a look of hurt in her eyes. A look that matched Charlotte's when she had yelled at him that she hadn't been raped. No: her exact words were, *I was not the one who had been raped.* Someone she knew, then? The book had felt so personal.

Like flash of blinding light, horror struck him right between the eyes. First he heard Zara's adamant words. *I would never call him my father.*

And then Charlotte's loving dedication. *For Mum. Your courage in the face of adversity is an inspiration to me.*

And in the next second, he put it all together.

'Sir, you still haven't answered my question.' Will chattered annoyingly at his elbow.

'You can't have my ute. I'm taking it!' He spun on his heel. 'I need to get back to the office now!'

Will gasped. 'But we're about to put the shiploader down.'

'Fish will supervise.'

'But –'

'Tell him for me, will you?' He was already walking away. 'I'll send some gloves back when I get to the office.'

'But, sir,' Will called after him, 'it's the shiploader! We can't . . . You can't – just *leave*.'

'Watch me.'

Chapter 22

Charlotte

Charlotte was so angry. Her skin literally tingled with it. She knew it was irresponsible of her to walk off the job. But *really*. She wasn't even supposed to be there. She was the part-time counsellor, for goodness sake. He'd put her there to annoy her. The truth was she knew none of the answers to the questions the media were asking her. So when Em had offered to take over so that she could run back and get a Panadol for her 'headache' she'd jumped at the chance.

She just needed some space. Never in all her life had she met a man who infuriated her more. And yet . . .

Why did she feel so sad? As if she'd just shot herself in the foot for turning him away. Was it wrong of her to want more from a potential mate than insults and jibes?

A date with Caesar? The thought was laughable.

And yet strangely . . . erotic.

She arrived back at the Barnes Inc office in a frenzy of emotion and actually did need that Panadol, which she gulped down with a glass of water as she sat at her desk. With the door shut, the office was quiet. Everyone was on the wharf. She began to relax. With a secret smile curling her mouth, she mused how long she could stay holed up in there. Would anyone miss her?

Caesar might, a small voice muttered in her head, which she vehemently ignored. A few days earlier, when he had been on leave, his absence had literally filled her head. How many times had she wavered between confronting him and not confronting him about that kiss they had shared?

But as soon as he returned, unchanged and unmoved, so did her senses. He didn't mention the kiss once, so she thought her feelings were unreciprocated. That is, until today when he'd asked her on a date almost as though the request had been torn from him under the lash of a whip.

His manner, his behaviour, his attitude towards her were twisted to say the least. And to make matters worse, she felt like his dead wife's ghost loomed over them, judging every mistake she made. Was this the kind of relationship she wanted to enter into?

Suddenly there was a knock at the door and her eyes automatically flicked to her desk calendar. It was blank. Belatedly, she remembered that of course she didn't have an appointment that day. The shiploader was being installed.

'Er, come in,' she called out croakily.

And then as though in slow motion the door opened and a figure appeared. A figure so nondescript, so ordinary and so *recognisable*. All her senses came crashing to a halt as her heart jumped into her mouth, causing her head to throb.

She stared at the man she had only seen in photos, mouth agape, frozen in the moment.

He smiled at her.

She had never thought she would find a smile so grotesque.

'Hi, I'm Dennis Mayer.'

'I know who you are.' She was surprised to hear her own voice as the rest of her body couldn't move. If he was here to rape her, which surely he wasn't, given his MO was crowded bars and drug-induced stupors, her physical defences against him were shot to pieces. 'What are you doing here?'

He didn't immediately answer the question but simply came into the room, shutting the door behind him. This time she did stand up, scooting around her chair and holding it in front of her like a barrier between them. Again he smiled. He was in no hurry as he clasped his hands in front of him. 'Are you Charlotte Templeton?'

'I am.'

'I'm here to see your mother. I hear you manage her affairs.'

'My mother has no wish to see you,' she spat.

'Your mother has no choice, given the crime she has committed against me.'

'*What did you say?*' This was too much. 'You raped my mother, you fuckin' bastard. Get out of my office and my workplace.'

'I'm afraid I can't do that.' That horrible smile just wouldn't leave his flakey face and she could feel fear beginning to seep up her legs from the vinyl floors. 'Not until justice has been served.'

'Then go back to jail!'

'I've served my time,' he folded his arms, 'though I've always maintained my innocence and will continue to do so to my deathbed.'

She wanted to vomit.

'And should your mother wish to accuse me falsely of rape, that's her prerogative. Though with her mental incapacity, I wouldn't advise it.'

He took another step forwards and she stepped back, dragging the chair with her.

He laughed, a horrible sound that grated on her ears like a garden rake on the back of a steel shed. 'Why are you afraid of me?'

'I'm not *afraid* of you.'

He spread his hands. 'I am an upstanding moral citizen and

have been for the last two years. I'm not here to hurt you. I just want a little understanding.'

Yeah right! 'What sort of understanding?'

His face hardened slightly. 'Understanding for a father who has already lost fifteen years of his child's life.'

Her hands went to her throat as it closed to suffocate her. 'Leave Zara out of this.'

'How can I leave her out of this, when she is precisely why I am here?' he mused at her complete lack of comprehension.

She couldn't speak; she couldn't think. She could barely hear what he was saying.

'Your mother's concealment of the truth left me unaware that I had a daughter until now. I was unable to know her, be a father to her. But now all that's going to change.'

'Like hell,' Charlotte choked. 'You stay away from her. You stay away from all of us. We don't want you here.'

'I was hoping we could work this out amicably between us, like civilised human beings,' he said grimly.

'You can't force me to let you see Zara.' Despite her conviction she heard her voice shake.

He shook his head sadly. 'But I can, you see.'

She did not see at all and her shoulders straightened as her confidence buoyed. 'I'll get a restraining order, I'll double our home security, I'll –'

'You can do what you must, of course.' He nodded. 'But I'm no criminal and if you think I'm here to resort to violence you're wrong.'

He opened his jacket and pulled forth a folded document from the inside pocket. 'I'm suing for custody. Virginia is no longer fit to care for our child and I have been robbed of time with Zara from the beginning.' He held out the document, which she refused to take.

'Very well.' He put the envelope on her desk. 'Look at it later. But consider yourself served, Charlotte. You and your lying mother.'

The horror was more than she could bear. It was a nightmare so vile that it hadn't even dawned on her consciousness that such a thing *could* occur till now. A rapist demanding custody of the child birthed from his crime? It was unconscionable. How did he even have rights?

'You can't do this,' she whispered, her face numb with the absence of blood. 'You're a criminal: they will never grant you custody.'

His face hardened further. 'I suffered through the system that punished me for crimes I did not commit. But that blight on my life is over. I am a new man now. I own my own business. I'm married with a stepchild already. Financially, I'm much better able to provide for Zara than you ever could. So don't call me a *criminal*.' He leaned forwards, both hands on her desk. 'According to my lawyer, my case is very solid when compared, for instance, to yours. How many mortgages do you have on that dump you call a resort now, Charlotte?'

When she remained silent, he seemed to calm down somewhat and straightened, smiling again. 'See you in court.'

And as he walked out, she wished that he had tried to attack her physically instead. At least then, killing him in self-defence might have been an option.

Chapter 23

Emily

With Caesar having walked off the job, it was left to her to appease the media with reasons she literally plucked from the air at random. The truth was, no one knew why the project manager had left at such a crucial moment. All they could do was push through and hope that all the careful planning they had done beforehand paid off.

Luckily, it did.

The lift points they had chosen on the shiploader allowed them to bring the large structure down without it tipping slightly in the wrong direction and thus putting lopsided pressure on the bogies. If this happened it would bend them out of shape, which would be a colossal disaster.

The weather wasn't an issue either, even though Spooks reported that the breeze was starting to pick up.

Unexpectedly, Fish calmed everyone down with his surprisingly good leadership skills. Perhaps the man just worked well under pressure. After a few nail-biting attempts they landed the shiploader back on its wheels and in good time too. The welding crew moved in to make the new position permanent.

It was a massive relief but also the point where the media lost interest. Fortunately, Dipper had returned with Will's ute and Em was able to drive them back to the office in groups. Here, she noticed that neither Charlotte nor Caesar were anywhere to be found. Both their offices were empty. Not that this bothered her. There was only an hour left of the day and she was probably going to spend most of it thinking about how to orchestrate her master plan.

She went on the internet and Googled 'flirting', to get a few ideas to expand her dismal repertoire. Better to have a full arsenal if she was to do this properly. There were quite a number of good suggestions online that she hadn't thought of already.

Apparently, emulating body language was a form of flattery. So was laughing hard at all his jokes. Listening attentively. Batting eyes. Innuendo.

And laying hands on him any chance she got.

Reading these naughty little instructions made her feel like a fourteen-year-old tossed in puberty. She wanted to giggle self-consciously at her own daring. But was any of this really going to lead to a kiss or should she just hand him a bottle of vodka and tell him to drink? It didn't matter. She was going to try anyway.

Just before knock-off, she left a note on his desk. *Dinner, my place. 7pm. I'm cooking. See you there.*

She spent a minimal amount of time on the meal. As far as she was concerned the actual food they ate wasn't really that important. So her signature penne chicken pasta seemed like a good idea. She left it in a pot on the stove and then ordered a couple of bottles of wine from the Silver Seas resort bar. They brought them around while she was choosing something to wear.

Of all the preparation she was making that evening she figured this was definitely her priority. Normally when she spent a night in with Will, she chose loose-fitting, lounge-about-the-house wear. Today she put on the only dress she'd brought with her from Perth. It was short and sleeveless with a low-scooped neckline. She'd packed it for its versatility. It was her little black dress, though it wasn't black but dark green.

In all honesty, it was probably a little over the top for pasta at home but she knew she'd definitely have a better chance in it than in trackpants that sported knee holes. Combined with make up and half an hour spent on her hair, she was very pleased with the end result.

Will certainly did a double take when she opened the door. His eyes dilated and made an interesting crawl from her feet to her lips and she wondered how she hadn't wanted to revel in this sort of attention from him earlier.

'Er, are we going out?'

'No.' She smiled.

''Cause I can change.' He jerked his thumb over his shoulder. Personally, she thought he looked delicious just the way he was in jeans and a T-shirt, smelling fresh from the shower. She still couldn't get over how much his lack of facial hair really revealed how masculine his features were. At her lack of response, he nodded more decisively. 'Yes, we should go out. Probably safer. I'll go get changed.'

She laughed. 'You're not going anywhere.' She grabbed him by the wrist, pulling him inside so that their bodies bumped. (Another great tip from the internet.) 'I just felt like dressing up tonight, that's all.' She nudged him in the ribs. 'I never get any wear out of this dress.'

His Adam's apple jerked. 'Right.' He turned and marched determinedly into the kitchen. 'What's for dinner?' He lifted the lid of the pot and seemed relieved to note its ordinary contents.

'Just pasta,' she said.

'Great. I'm famished.'

Use some innuendo here. She licked her lips, sidled up beside him and then looked up like he was a big warrior just in from battle. '*Hungry*, are you?'

'Y-yeah.' He drew out the word slowly and uncertainly. 'Didn't I just say that?'

'I guess so,' she muttered, feeling dumb. Her eyes darted away and caught the bottles of wine resting on the counter beside the stove. Best to get the mood juice flowing. She grabbed one by its stem. 'Wine?'

'No thanks.'

What? Her head snapped up sharply. 'Are you sure?'

'Yep.'

'Because I've heard this one's pretty good.' She hoped her tone didn't sound too desperate. She glanced at the bottle and plucked an attribute at random. 'It's made at Mount Tamborine.'

'Really? Where's that?'

She had no idea. 'Er, somewhere.'

He laughed. 'I'll pass. I'm happy just to skip to the main course. Love your pasta.'

Damn it! She should have served baked beans.

'Okay.' She put the wine down and tried to emulate the way he was standing, which was kind of half leaning on the kitchen counter with one foot crossed in front of the other.

'Um . . .' He looked at her strangely. 'Are we waiting for someone else?'

'No,' she said quickly and, in her haste to move on, turned around and stuck her hand out behind her. 'Come on, let's set the table.' She had meant him to take her offered palm. Instead, he walked straight into it and she grabbed a fistful of –

'Eeek!' She snatched her hand away, spinning full circle and backing up till she hit the opposite bench. 'Sorry! I didn't mean to do that.'

'That's all right –'

'It was a complete accident.'

'Em, it's okay,' he said, even though his face was a rather alarming shade of red. She didn't think she was faring too well either in terms of colour. She might be trying to seduce him, but she wasn't *that* forward.

'I was reaching for your hand,' she tried to explain.

That gave him pause. 'But you never take my hand.'

'I did on the Adventure Pontoon last weekend,' she said softly.

For a moment he just looked at her in stunned silence before reaching across the stove and picking up the bottle he had rejected only seconds earlier. 'I've changed my mind about the wine. Do you have glasses?'

Awesome.

'Sure.' She strolled across the kitchen to open a drawer. 'I also know there's a bottle opener in here somewhere.'

'Right,' he said, all business. 'While you're finding it, I'll fill two bowls with our dinner.'

They each completed their separate tasks. She found two glasses and filled them. As he was still dishing out pasta, she quickly gulped down some of her wine and then refilled her glass again. She could do with some Dutch courage. The fruity elixir from Mount Tamborine certainly went straight to her head, giving her a much-needed sense of lightness. By that time, Will had walked around the counter to the other side where her small round dining table for four was located. He placed the bowls there and she brought over the wine.

He sat down and determinedly attacked his meal with eyes downcast.

She cleared her throat but he didn't look up.

'So,' she drawled, trying to slide sexily into her chair, 'what did you think of the shiploader installation today?' As she was speaking a thread of her dress caught on some cane that must have been sticking out of the woven seat. The chair rocked slightly. She caught the edge of the table with both hands and managed to steady herself before the chair completely went over.

'I thought it was awesome.' He finally looked up, catching her frozen in this position after the near miss. 'You okay?'

'Fine,' she choked, praying she hadn't ripped her dress. *Okay, regroup. Regroup!* She pulled her bowl towards her, took a fortifying sip of wine and then copied the way Will had one arm lying beside it. The conversation dipped into their usual companionable silence broken only by the sound of their cutlery and the clinking of their glasses after they were lifted and set back down on the table again.

'Do you know why Caesar ran off at the end?' she asked some minutes later. 'It seemed really odd of him.'

Will's brow wrinkled in a way that she hadn't realised until now she found endearing. 'Something to do with Lottie, I think. We were talking about her when he suddenly decided to go.'

Impulsively, she reached across the table and laid her hand over his. 'I love how you're so intuitive with people.'

It was the truth, but she got the impression that she'd said too much. He looked at her like she'd just sprouted antennae and dragged his hand slowly back across the table from underneath hers.

'Er, thanks.'

She glanced at her abandoned palm stretched too far across the table into his space and hastily pulled it back. *Strike three! Am I out?*

She gnawed on her lower lip like it was cheap squid. How could she have imagined that this would be easy? Or that he would even go along with it? Will was her best friend. This was going to be the hardest and scariest thing she'd ever attempted. She shoved her hand in her lap. *Don't make any more sudden moves.*

They ate in silence for a few minutes and she concentrated on her breathing, which was irrationally shallow. *Calm down.*

'So you want seconds?'

She looked up in surprise to see that he had already finished everything in his bowl. The question seemed moot given her bowl was still full. 'Um, no thanks.'

He got up to get himself some more pasta from the kitchen, leaving her stewing at the table by herself. It was very hard to know where to go from here.

Will sat down at the table again, shovelling in another mouthful of pasta.

'Okay,' she began firmly, 'I'd like to talk about kissing.'

Chapter 24

Will

Will choked on his penne, grabbed the glass of wine sitting near his bowl and chugged furiously. 'I beg your pardon?'

What was going on with her tonight?

And why wasn't this alcohol dulling his senses like it was supposed to? He was on fire and had to curb every impulse to cross his legs.

Em in her scruffy tracky dacks looked scrumptious to him. But dealing with her in this get-up was an exercise in self-control. She looked amazing. The way her hair brushed her dimple when she smiled made him literally ache. She cupped her chin and leaned forwards on the table in an intimate way.

'I am *single* now.' She put great emphasis on the word, making his ears tingle like a cymbal that had just been smashed. '*And* about start dating again.'

'Uh-huh.' He hoped he sounded tuned out rather than turned on.

She didn't pause for breath. 'After being in a relationship for five years I can't help but feel a little rusty on the protocols.'

'There are protocols?' he squeaked.

'Aren't there?' She tilted her head to one side, exposing the long kissable line from ear lobe to collarbone. 'You're a guy –'

'Nice of you to notice,' he croaked.

'It would be great to get a few free pointers on the male perspective.'

Rule number 1. You don't consider dating your best mate's girlfriend.

Rule number 2. Even if they're on a break.

Rule number 3. Even if she's the love of your life.

Rule number 4. Even if she's your soulmate.

Satisfied that this comprehensive list of rules should (in theory) keep him in check, he took another fortifying sip of white wine.

'Like, for example,' her mouth twisted, 'what sort of kiss do you think is appropriate for the first date? On the cheek,' she tapped that area of her face, 'or on the lips?' She pressed her finger there too.

What was rule number 1 again?

He looked at his empty glass. 'I think I need more wine.'

'Me too,' she said and stood up just a smidgen faster than he did. 'I'll get it. I'm closer.'

She turned around and walked back towards the kitchen. His eyes narrowed on her delectable rear end, but with more reason than its obvious allure. There appeared to be a tear in the back of her dress just under the zipper.

He was privileged with a peek at a pair of pink polka-dot knickers. It was the straw that broke the camel's back. His overloaded senses were now completely fried. He had to get out of there before he did something he'd regret. He stood up as she was bringing the bottle back.

'What's wrong?'

'I'm leaving.'

'But we haven't finished dinner yet.'

He glanced at his bowl. 'Well, I have, and it's going to be an early start tomorrow so . . .'

She put the bottle down, with a frown. 'Will, the shiploader is in. No one's going to care if you even show up. What's the matter?'

'Nothing.'

She put her hands on her hips. 'Yes there is. Tell me what's going on.'

'Well, for a start, I can see your knickers,' he blurted.

'*W-what?*' Both her hands whipped around to her bum. She must have felt the tear because she threw back her head with a provocative moan and her eyes closed. 'It needed only that.'

He glanced away from her exposed throat. 'What do you mean?'

A chuckle gurgled up her windpipe that turned into full-blown laugh. Only it wasn't a reassuring sound. It was the cackle of a crazy person, one part futility, the other part hysteria.

'Em, are you okay?' He reached for her arms just as she straightened and his fingers brushed the sides of her breasts. 'Oh shit, I'm *so* sorry.' He yelped like he'd stuck his hand in a fire. 'I didn't mean to – I was just trying to – I –'

His broken apology only made her laugh all the harder. 'No, that's all right,' she cried. 'It's not like I didn't grab your penis first.'

'*Em!*'

'Well, it's the truth, isn't it?' she hiccupped. 'Along with all the other mistakes I've made tonight. I can't win with you, can I, Will?'

'I don't know what you're talking about,' he muttered, running his hands through his hair.

'That's the problem exactly,' she said sadly. 'You have no idea.'

'Then you might as well lay it on me,' he said.

For some reason her shoulders shook again. 'I thought you'd never ask.'

Her lips trembling with mirth, she grabbed his face between her palms and, standing on tiptoe, pressed her mouth to his.

He'd daydreamed of this moment for so long that now that it was actually happening it seemed kind of surreal and his body stiffened in shock.

'Sorry, sorry,' she muttered in stricken tones. 'I've ruined everything, haven't I?' She would have pulled away if he hadn't grabbed her face before she moved more than an inch.

'No,' he rasped. And they stood there for a moment holding each other's faces, their mouths mere centimetres apart, their eyes unable to break connection. He let forth a deep breathy sigh. He didn't care any more about anything except her and this particular moment that he'd thought would never come. 'The first kiss was bound to be awkward,' he whispered.

'Really?' she whispered back.

He nodded, curling her hair behind one ear. 'After all, we've known each other for such a long time and we've never done this before.'

'True.' Her eyelids fluttered.

'No matter how much I've wanted to,' he added for good measure.

Her eyes were so close he literally saw her pupils dilate. 'You have?'

'You bet.'

She licked her lips. 'Then I have a question. What's the second kiss bound to be like?'

He didn't quite know who closed the gap between them first. Their mouths simply came together as one.

He tried to be respectful. After all, this was Em. He had no idea where this was going. *If* it was going anywhere. He had their friendship to consider. At least that was what his brain was saying while his hands left her face and curved under her bottom, bringing her right in close against him.

He'd always known she'd taste good. Not just intoxicating to his senses but mind-blowing. In general he was not the sort of man who 'ravished' women. In his previous dating life, he'd always been conscious of being 'tender' and 'gentle'. But in this case, it was as though someone had flicked a switch in his brain, making it literally impossible to hold back.

Kissing Em didn't feel like kissing any other woman.

This wasn't just some random encounter but rather a turning point in his life after which nothing would be the same again. Now that this door had been opened, there was no closing it against the flood of emotion that came whooshing through. And when Emily flung her arms around his neck and pressed her soft breasts into his chest, something in his brain exploded. He just wanted to rip her dress off.

It was only then that he realised that she was tugging at his shirt. Actually, more like yanking. So he graciously pulled it over his head. 'Better?'

'Much.' She slid her hands over his shoulders. 'I think you're beautiful.'

He laughed at her words. 'Have you seen yourself recently?'

'I've got a giant hole in my dress.'

'You're right.' He nodded seriously. 'We should take it off.'

'You think?' She gave him a secret smile that made his toes curl.

'Definitely.' His hands reached for her zipper. The dress pooled at her feet.

When he saw her in her pink polka dot underwear, he chuckled again.

She pushed him backwards into the living room. 'Why do you keep laughing?'

'I just can't believe this is happening,' he said as he felt the back of his knees hit the arm of the couch.

'It's happening,' she murmured and then squealed as he grabbed her around the waist before falling back on the cushions, her soft body splayed on top of his.

They kissed and they kissed, unable to get enough of each other. He cupped her breasts and she moaned. He tried to roll on top of her and they both toppled from the couch onto the floor, laughing against each other's mouths. It was delicious madness until there was a rap at the door.

Both their heads jerked up. There was another loud knock.

'Who could that be?' Emily muttered.

They both looked at the door again and a specific voice brought reality crashing into the room like a tsunami. 'Em? Are you in there? I can see the light on.'

'Trent,' she whispered and then scrambled up. 'Trent!' she said louder, panic tingeing her voice.

'Yeah, it's me, honey,' came his dulcet tones. 'Can you open the door?'

She looked at Will, who was starting to feel rather sick. Her eyes were wide and her hands wrung as she mouthed, 'What should I do?'

'You have to let him in,' he said calmly. This was the part of their story he was already very familiar with. Still, he had to rein in his feelings to brace for impact. He moved around her and picked up her dress. 'Here.'

She quickly put it back on and he zipped her up from behind. He grabbed his shirt off the floor, flinging it on and rapidly doing up the buttons.

'Em!' Trent called out again.

'Coming,' she cried and glanced back at him for support.

'It's okay. Invite him in.' He gave her a gentle shove.

He heard rather than saw her walk to the front door and open it.

'Trent, what are you doing here?' He was pleased to hear her voice sound rather exasperated. Good. He had no idea what they were going to say to his mate when he came in but he knew that keeping his own feelings bottled up now was an impossibility.

Trent had never treated his relationship with Emily seriously enough. For years, he'd watched Em fawn over him, expecting more and never getting enough. Now his friend had let her go, even moved on with other women. If he wasn't prepared to give Emily what she wanted, did he really deserve her? He squared his shoulders and turned to look at them.

There was Trent, standing precise to a pin in a black suit and tie, almost like the undertaker come to take away the happiest moment in his life. A light travel bag rested on the mat by his feet while he grinned sheepishly at her. He didn't seem to have noticed his best friend watching tensely from the lounge area.

'I thought I'd surprise you.'

'Well,' her hand went to her hip, 'you've certainly succeeded there.'

He grinned. 'We need to talk.'

'No kidding.'

'There's something I need say, that I should have said months ago.' He sucked in a deep breath. 'Em, I've been a fool.'

'Trent –'

'No, let me finish. I've come to ask you something. Something that will change our lives.'

And then to Will's horror Trent got down on one knee. 'Will you marry me?'

Chapter 25

Mark

When he arrived back at the office, she was nowhere to be found and his first instinct was to panic. He spied Ann sitting unconcerned at her desk and marched over.

'Where's Charlotte?'

His secretary looked up in surprise. 'She went home.'

'Are you sure?' he demanded. How did she know she wasn't dragged out by Dennis Mayer to some ditch somewhere? Her hesitation nearly made him burst a vein. '*Answer me*.'

'Okay, okay.' Ann fidgeted in her seat. 'Yes, I'm sure she left. I saw her myself about fifteen minutes ago. She said she had a migraine, but I didn't believe her.'

'Why didn't you believe her?'

Ann shrugged. 'It just seemed more than that. She was very pale and spacey. I think that man who was here must have said something to her. '

He swore inside his head. 'Was he with her when she left?'

'No, he left ten minutes earlier. Would you like me to get her on the line, sir?'

'No.' He shook his head. 'I'm going back to the resort to check everything's all right.'

'Oh . . . okay, sir,' she responded even though he was already a few metres away from her desk, shrugging out of his vest and tossing his hat on the lay table.

'Ann,' he called from the door, 'send some welding gloves to the wharf, will you?'

'Who to?'

But he had already crossed the threshold and didn't stop to answer.

His ute tore up the dirt as he sped out of the site car park and back down the road to the resort. Thoughts of what might have taken place while he was still on the wharf were making him crazy. He had to see for himself she was okay.

When he pulled into the car park, reception was still dark, deserted and locked. Undeterred, he went round the side to the back door of her home and knocked on the flyscreen.

No answer.

Without hesitation, he tried the door handle and was both pleased and displeased to note it was unlocked. He let himself in and then locked it behind him. With purpose, he entered the main living area of the house. His arrival was punctuated by a gasp.

He glanced immediately to the left and saw her seated there across the room on the couch. Her eyes were red and rubbed raw. It was clear she'd been sobbing.

'Oh.' She sagged. 'It's only you.'

'But it could have been anybody.' His voice was rough. 'You should not leave your doors unlocked, Ms Templeton. It's not safe.'

'Ah.' She nodded, with a complete lack of her usual gumption. 'Have you come to lecture me, Mr Crawford?'

'No, I have come to see if you're all right.'

'As you can see, I'm absolutely fine.'

'Rubbish.' He advanced into the room and sat down on the coffee table opposite her. Close enough to see every nuance on her face, not close enough that they were touching.

Something seemed to occur to her and her eyes widened for a moment. 'The shiploader! What's happened? Why aren't you on the wharf?'

'They can drop it in the ocean for all I care. Did he come to see you?'

'Who?' she asked.

'Don't play coy with me. Dennis Mayer, of course.'

Her lower lip trembled and she looked down at her hands where he saw for the first time that she was clutching a document. 'So you know.'

'Of course I know.'

She gave a mirthless laugh. 'Because you know everything, don't you, Mr Crawford?'

'Yes,' he said briskly. 'Now tell me what he said to you.'

'Or you'll do what?' Some of her spark returned and he didn't know whether to feel relieved or thwarted.

'Or I'll fire you.'

She sat up straighter. 'On what grounds?'

'Walking off the job without permission.'

'But you just walked off the job as well,' she pointed out.

'That's different. I don't need permission.'

'Never in all my life have I met such an insensitive man,' she said, standing up crossly and would have walked away from him if he had not grabbed her by the wrist.

'Please, Charlotte,' his quiet tone came out strained, '*let me help you*. At least give me that.'

If she refused to let him into her confidence, he didn't know what he'd do.

She stopped. Perhaps it was the desperation in his voice, perhaps it was the sound of her first name on his lips, but for a moment she just stood there, allowing him to hold her hand, as she struggled with her own decision. Finally she turned to him, her eyes wet with tears. 'Even if you want to, I don't think you can help me.'

'No one is beyond help. What did he do?' He ground his teeth. 'Did he touch you?'

'No.' She sat down again. 'It was nothing like that.'

'What do you mean?'

She hesitated and then handed him the document in her hands. 'Here, you might as well see it.' She sat back on the couch again. 'He gave it to me.'

It took him about five seconds to take in the horror that was its contents. 'Zara,' he whispered, and realised for the first time how much he had grown to care for the young girl. 'He can't take her.'

'And I'm going to do everything in my power to prevent him.' She sounded so fierce that for moment he was taken by the determination in her voice, but it evaporated as quickly as it had come. She wrung her hands. 'If only I knew what that was. The court date is for seven days' time in Brisbane and I have to prepare for that. I have no idea if his case is as solid as he says it is.'

'Surely a rapist has no rights.'

'You would think. He was never convicted of raping Mum, though. She filed her police report too late for it to be used as evidence. He could spin it that they had a one-night stand. Especially if she's not mentally healthy enough to explain herself.'

He shook his head. 'You will win this, Charlotte. You just need a good lawyer.'

'Apart from the fact that I have no idea how to discern whether a lawyer is good or not, it's going to be very expensive. I've just let another of the staff go to help pay our second mortgage on this place. Of course, if it's a choice between bankruptcy and Zara's safety, I know which one I'm going to choose.' Her fingers trembled. 'It's just that this is Mum's home. She might only have a couple more years. Her disease will only cause her to deteriorate more and more. I just –' She choked back a sob. 'I just can't believe this is happening. How could we not have seen it coming?'

Just then the back door slammed and Zara walked in, home from school. She started when she saw him seated on their coffee table. 'Mark! What are you doing here?'

He glanced at Charlotte and she gave the most infinitesimal shake of her head. So he folded the subpoena and said rather blandly, 'Staying for dinner.'

Charlotte stepped on his foot but he ignored the pain. 'Your sister has kindly invited me over to discuss . . .' He searched for a believable topic. '. . . A mutual project.'

Zara raised her eyebrows. 'Really? How'd the shiploader installation go?'

Mark shrugged. 'No idea.' And Charlotte stepped on his foot again. 'I mean, fine, I think.'

'O-kay,' Zara said in the voice of one who didn't want to over-excite the sensibilities of a madman. 'Well, I'll just go visit Augustus.'

'No!' they both said at the same time. If Dennis Mayer was in town, subpoena or not, he might try to see his daughter without their permission.

Mark cleared his throat. 'I mean, I'll come with you.'

'Great!' Zara said. 'I'll just get changed.'

As she hurried off, Charlotte folded her arms. 'What do you think you're doing?'

'I will make sure Zara is okay, and then I'll come back to help you. We need to get a strategy going. When is your brother bringing your mother home?'

'Tomorrow morning.'

'Good. We have tonight to sort through this.'

'I still have a hotel to run,' Charlotte swallowed. 'The dinner rush is the worst time for calls.'

'Then I will help you with that too. And don't worry about the expense: I'll pay for the lawyer.'

She gasped. 'I can't let you do that.'

'Then I'll give you a raise.'

'Mark, please be serious.'

'You know I never joke.'

Her lips curled reluctantly. 'So you are always telling me.'

'Zara is my friend. If you think I'll let some defiler of women take possession of her life like she's some goods he can use to cause pain you have another think coming. I trust you will not stand in my way, Ms Templeton.'

She shook her head. 'I will pay you back when I'm able.' She laid a hand on his arm, thus stalling the protest that had hovered on his lips. 'I preferred it when you were calling me Charlotte.'

'Very well, then,' he agreed (for the first time). 'Charlotte.'

Chapter 26

Emily

For so long, she had wanted to hear those words on Trent's lips and now, as she looked at him on bended knee, she felt nothing but impatience.

'Oh, for goodness' sake, Trent, get up.'

'But you haven't given me an answer.'

All she could think about was Will and wondering if he was hearing this and how it would affect him. Trent's declaration would no doubt make him feel as guilty as hell. The last thing she wanted was what they'd shared to be tainted in any way.

'I'm not giving you an answer till you come inside.' She turned around and walked back into her unit, expecting Trent to follow but neither knowing nor caring if he did. When she returned to the living room, one thing was very apparent. Will was gone.

The curtain billowed about the open sliding door where he had clearly let himself out.

Great.

She spun around to see Trent entering the room. He put his bag on the chair next to Will's empty bowl. 'I'm sorry to turn up like this but I just knew I had to come,' he said. 'I've been such an idiot, Em.'

You're only just figuring this out? 'Trent, I can't marry you.'

His brow wrinkled. 'But I know that's what you want. What I couldn't give you before.'

'When I wanted it,' she corrected him. 'Past tense. A lot has changed since then.'

He frowned. 'Surely not. It's only been a couple of months since we broke up. Has Queensland been that big an influence on you?'

'As a matter of fact –'

'Okay.' He held up his hands. 'I've been talking to Will about the project and I know it's a big deal. I realise how much you've enjoyed it and maybe that's the sort of thing you want to get into now. Well,' he smiled at her like he was handing her a thousand dollars no strings attached, 'I support you.'

'That's great, Trent, but it's not just about my career.' She paused, not really wanting to hurt him just after he'd proposed to her. After all, that was a show of commitment and couldn't have been easy – especially for a man like Trent. 'I just don't think it's a good idea.'

'Why?'

'Because . . .' She hesitated, then went on. 'I think I'm in love with someone else.'

For a moment there was dead silence and a muscle twitched in his jaw. 'I see. And can this Dipper person offer you as much as I can?'

She choked. 'It's not *Dipper*.'

'Then who is it?'

Oh crap! How do I tell him? An icky feeling welled in her stomach. Shouldn't Will be here when he found out? Trent might not be the man for her but he deserved some honesty.

He and Will had been friends since primary school. Shouldn't he hear it from both of them?

'Do we have to talk about it right now?' she stalled.

Trent looked down at the items on the table. Two wine glasses. Two bowls and dirty cutlery. 'He was just here, wasn't he?'

'Yes.'

A hurt expression entered his eyes.

'Come on, Trent,' she said a little impatiently. 'It's not like you haven't been seeing other women.'

'I saw one other woman for a couple of dates. And I can't say I fell in love with her,' he said tightly. 'She's out of my life now, though she taught me a valuable lesson.'

'And what's that?'

'How wonderful you are,' he exclaimed. 'Think about it, Em. We had five great years together.'

Actually it's more like three great years and two crap ones.

'We have a house together and a dog,' he continued enthusiastically. 'My mother loves you! Do you really want to throw all that away on a fling?'

'It's not a fling. I've had feelings for him for a long time. I just didn't realise it. I didn't get it,' she said desperately.

He was silent for a moment, his gaze returning to the bowls. 'Look, after everything we've been through as a couple, can I just ask you for one thing?'

'What?'

'That you'll at least sleep on it. I have to stay for tonight anyway.'

She supposed he was right. After all the years they'd spent together, perhaps he did deserve more than a knee-jerk decision. 'Okay.'

'Can I stay here?' he asked. 'Or would you like me to go stay at Will's instead?'

The thought of him putting all this to Will tonight did not appeal to her in the slightest. 'No, just stay here. You can have the couch. I'll ring for some bedding.'

She went to the phone and spoke briefly to Charlotte. Her friend didn't quite sound herself either but she was too distracted by the man in the living room to enquire too deeply.

A few awkward minutes later, there was a knock at the door and she went to answer it.

'Sir!' she exclaimed.

There, in all his glory, stood Caesar – shocking to behold in jeans and a T-shirt. To her amazement in his arms he was holding a pillow, a set of sheets and a blanket. 'Good evening, Emily.'

'Er . . . Good evening, sir.'

Under her stunned gaze, he stepped straight over the threshold and into her unit, much like it was his domain rather than hers.

He put the bedding down on the couch and she pulled herself out of her stupor. There must be some sort of explanation as to why he was here instead of a member of the Silver Seas staff.

'Is Charlotte okay?' she asked.

'Absolutely fine.' His eyes ran over Trent, less than impressed. 'And I suppose this must be your guest.' He sighed. 'Shame.'

Em choked on this last word.

'Did I say that out loud?' he mused. 'I beg your pardon.'

Trent, who was bristling under this bald assessment, said, 'And who are you?'

'Your girlfriend's boss,' Caesar informed him. 'And I suppose you went to uni with her as well.'

'No, what makes you think that?' Trent demanded.

'No reason, a lapse in judgement on my part.' Caesar looked like he was growing rather bored with the conversation and he turned once more towards the door.

'I'm not an engineer,' Trent returned as though the calling were beneath him. 'I'm a lawyer.'

This made Caesar pause and he spun back to study Trent as if seeing him for the first time. '*Really*? Now that does interest me. What sort of lawyer?'

'Family law mainly,' said Trent rather proudly.

Caesar's eyes flicked over him thoughtfully. 'Still, you don't look like you've been out for very long.'

Trent raised his chin. 'I've been practising for over three years and I'm very good.'

Caesar raised his eyebrows sceptically. 'Really?'

'Of course.'

Caesar turned to Emily, who was watching the unfolding of this strange scene with growing trepidation, and demanded, '*Is* he any good?'

She nodded. 'Actually, yes. I've attended quite a few of his work functions and he's got a very good reputation among his peers.'

'Then I have a job for you, if you'd like it,' Caesar once again addressed Trent, 'or rather, the owner of this resort does, Charlotte Templeton. It's a custody battle.'

Trent smirked. 'I'm sorry but I'm on holiday right now.'

Caesar sighed. 'Believe me, as much as I'd like to hire a different lawyer, perhaps one with a little more experience and a little less ego, I just don't have the time to find one. You'll have to be it.'

Trent's lips thinned. 'I don't just take on any client who walks in off the street. I like to take on cases I'm sure I can win.'

'With the fire I'm about to light under your arse, you'll be sure you can win,' Caesar returned glacially. 'The matter is urgent.'

Trent stiffened. 'I will not –'

'Trent, wait.' Emily held up her hand, turning towards her boss. 'Is this about Zara's biological father? Didn't she make contact with him recently?'

'You know about him?' Caesar said quickly.

Emily shook her head. 'Not much, only that Charlotte doesn't really want him anywhere near her family. Isn't he a criminal or something?'

'Yes,' Caesar said softly. 'He's now suing for custody of Zara. Unfortunately, the hearing is in seven days. Charlotte needs to sort out representation soon. That felon didn't give her much time. '

'I knew she didn't sound right on the phone.' Emily nodded and turned to her ex-boyfriend. 'Trent, you have to help her.'

'But –' he blustered.

'If you love me at all,' she insisted, 'you'll help her.'

Trent looked at her for a long moment. 'Is that what you want? Proof of my devotion?'

'No,' Emily said quietly. 'I just want you to consider for a moment being a decent human being. Coming to someone's rescue because you're the only one who can.'

Will would do it.

'Fine,' he nodded. 'I will consider your proposal *if*,' he added as her face lit up, 'you will consider mine.'

Yikes.

Chapter 27

Will

Well, that sucked.

Thanks, Trent, for ruining my life.

He knew that in good conscience, at this point, he had to take a step back and wait. If he was to have any sort of relationship with Em, she had to make the choice to reject Trent on her own *without* his influence. Of course, there was no guarantee that that's what she'd decide. Trent had just offered her the one thing that she'd been waiting for all along. Now that she could have Trent, would she still want him?

He did a hundred sit-ups trying to burn off the stress. It didn't work. If he were a fly, he'd be on the wall in her unit, listening to exactly what was going on. As it was, he was stuck here with the noble obligation of giving them both some space.

It was late when the knock came on his door but he was still up. Sleep was not going to come easily to him that night, so why even try? He flung open the door hoping it was Em, but knowing who it would be instead.

'Will.' Trent clasped his shoulder in a kind of half-hug before walking in. 'How's it all going?'

'Er . . . good. How have you been?'

Trent rubbed his hands. 'Fantastic.'

'Listen,' Will turned around, running his hands through his hair, 'sorry I didn't stay earlier at Em's to see you.' He walked further into his unit, expecting Trent to follow. 'I thought you guys might have needed some space to talk.'

He turned back when he reached the living room and saw that Trent was looking at him with a rather arrested expression on his face.

'You were over at Em's place tonight?'

'Yeah.' Will raised his brows. 'Sorry, I just assumed she told you.'

'No.' Trent looked stern. 'She didn't. Didn't mention you at all.'

Will's gut dropped heavily like a wet sponge. Probably didn't even notice that he wasn't in the living room when she'd returned there with Trent. Too distracted by the proposal, no doubt. He rubbed his temple. Had he really expected her to say, 'Sorry, Trent, I'm in love with Will now'?

'Is there something bothering you, Will? Because I'm here if you need to talk about it.'

He looked up, guilt firing his bones. This was exactly the place he'd been trying to avoid. If Trent knew what he'd done behind his back, their friendship would be over. When Trent had knocked on Emily's door she'd been practically naked and in his arms. She still would be there if Johnny-Propose-Lately hadn't turned up.

'No, no,' he mumbled, looking down. 'I'm fine.' He was only now appreciating the futility of his situation.

He'd exchanged no promises with Emily. They'd made no declarations. Clarified no long-term goals. Their encounter was one of two people who had given in to a crazy impulse.

An impulse that probably never would have happened if Trent had still been in the picture.

'You were there when I proposed, weren't you?' Trent demanded.

Will realised for the first time that his friend was looking angry rather than concerned.

He held up his palms. 'Just barely. I pretty much got out of there as soon as I heard what was going on.' He looked at the ground, flicking the edge of the floor mat with this big toe. 'So what did she say?'

There was a moment of agonising silence while he waited for Trent's response. And then it came like a knife through the heart.

'She said yes of course.'

His head jerked up as pain sliced through his body. 'She did?' His voice barely made it out of his voice box.

'Aren't you going to congratulate me?' Trent eyeballed him.

'Congratulations,' Will said dully, and then, because he knew it was expected, gave his friend another half-hug.

Surprisingly, Trent didn't appear to notice his lack of enthusiasm. He was all news and plans as he went to make himself comfortable on the couch. 'It was a long time coming, wasn't it? But you know, Will, it was inevitable. We've been together five years. There's too much history there.'

'I guess so.'

'So I'll be staying at her place for the week while she wraps up a few things here. Then we're flying off to Brisbane.'

'Brisbane?' Will repeated weakly.

'Well, her R and R is due and we've got wedding plans, a ring to pick out and lost time to make up too. Seemed like a good idea to take a holiday together.'

'Right.' Will's throat was as dry as jerky. He'd lost her again, only this time it was worse.

Much worse.

'When's your R and R coming up?' Trent asked.

Will was barely listening. 'I don't know. I think it's this week.'

'You should take it then,' his friend exclaimed. 'Give yourself a break, Will. The shippacker is in now, right?'

'Shiploader,' Will corrected him and also sat down, resisting with an effort the urge to drop his head into his hands.

'Yeah, whatever.' Trent waved it away. 'The point is, you should take a break while you can. Not that I'm trying to get rid of you or anything.' He laughed. 'How about we catch up for dinner one night next week? You, me and Em can go into Mackay to celebrate.'

Celebrate?

The suggestion made him feel physically ill. He didn't give a damn about the shiploader or whether the time was right for him to have his R and R. What he did care about was that Trent and Em were going to be living as a couple a mere three doors down from him. Sleeping in the same bed, talking weddings and expecting him to smile about it. He couldn't watch them moon over each other for a whole week. He'd been through that once before and it had nearly killed him. Not to mention that this time there was the added complication of the awkward conversation he knew he and Em had to have. The one where she said, 'You know the other night? It was a mistake. Can we forget it ever happened?'

Yeah, he'd much rather not hang around for that.

'Actually, Trent, I think you're right. I really should go on R and R while my workload is low. There'll be plenty of time to, er, celebrate with you and Em when you guys get back from Brisbane.'

'I completely understand,' Trent assured him. 'Well, listen, I better get back to Em. She's probably wondering where I am. I was only supposed to take out the rubbish.'

'Yeah, yeah. No worries.' Will was eager to see the back of him too. 'Tell her I said congratulations, won't you?'

'Sure, mate.' Trent clapped him on the shoulder. 'Sure.'

Chapter 28

Charlotte

Charlotte passed the next five days in a kind of emotional haze. Mark continued to remain in the background. He checked in at least once a day whether at work or at home. It was funny how when she saw his stern, uncompromising face a feeling of safety seemed to wash over her. He never uttered a loving word or even took her into his arms. And yet, whenever he was there, she felt at peace. Like everything really was going to be okay – they just had to get through it.

Trent, the lawyer they had hired, came to visit her every day to discuss what evidence Dennis was bringing against her and how they should counter it. It was a matter of law that both parties had to disclose to the other any evidence they had gathered prior to the court date. She read with disgust the documents that Denis had found to support his case, including her sister's letter. In the meantime, Trent also proposed papers they could use to support their argument. Unfortunately, these would take a little time to procure.

Trent always came while Zara was at school and so in this

way she was able to keep the entire ordeal a secret from her sister. The last thing she wanted to do was scare her. Zara had only just found out what her father had done and that blow had been crushing enough. She did not want to put this on her as well. In any case, children under the age of eighteen were not allowed to testify or even attend a court hearing concerning them. Luckily, Trent said he could build a good case without Zara's testimony.

Otherwise she mainly passed the time cleaning and preparing the guest room for her brother to stay in while she was out of town. On the third day, when she went to her mother's room to collect her dirty laundry out of the wicker basket, she noticed that something was sitting on the bottom of it under all the soiled clothes. She reached in and pulled out a sealed envelope. There was nothing but the words *To Emily* scrawled in a not very neat handwriting on the front. She could only assume that her mother must have picked it up somewhere in her wanderings. She was known to take a fancy to things and just put them in her pocket.

When Trent came around that afternoon she showed it to him.

'I found this note for Emily with my mum's laundry. I'm not sure how long it's been there. Could you pass it on to her?'

'Sure.' He nodded and took it from her hand. 'Did she tell you she's decided to come with us to Brisbane?'

Emily had actually told her the day before. The young woman had turned up in the evening with a DVD and a box of chocolates.

'Just here to cheer you up.' Emily had smiled. But Charlotte got the feeling the need was actually pretty mutual. She'd heard that Will had very suddenly taken his R and R and wasn't going to be back on site again till next week.

'So,' she drawled conversationally, 'Trent's visit! That was a big surprise.'

Emily groaned. 'Tell me about it.'

Charlotte pressed her lips together. Given the lawyer was staying in Emily's unit, she had to wonder where things now stood, especially with Will out of the picture.

'What's that look for?' Emily demanded. 'We're not back together if that's what you're thinking.'

'It's none of my business.'

Emily rolled her eyes. 'The truth is, he probably would have left by now if he wasn't doing this case.'

'Oh cripes.' Charlotte put a hand over her mouth. 'You're putting up with him for me, aren't you? Why didn't you say so?! I'll give him his own room. No charge.'

Emily smiled sheepishly. 'If you don't mind, that would really make things a little easier.'

'Of course.' Then after studying Emily's averted face for a couple more seconds she added shrewdly, 'You haven't said much about Will recently. Did you tell him how you feel?'

'Nearly,' Emily grimaced. 'The night after the shiploader went in. We kissed . . . and *kissed*.' She blushed. 'But then Trent arrived and proposed.'

'Proposed!' Charlotte exclaimed. 'That's a little sudden!'

'Yeah, I didn't see it coming either,' Emily nodded. 'But he did and Will was in the other room. He must have heard everything because he bolted and then I made the huge mistake of not calling him till the next day. By that stage he'd already left.'

'On R and R.' Charlotte scowled and couldn't help but compare it to when Mark had walked out on her in exactly the same way. 'Have you tried calling him?'

'Incessantly.' Emily looked absolutely miserable. 'But he won't answer my calls. He just turns off his phone as soon as he sees my caller ID. I did get this one text message, though.' She took out her phone, scrolled through her messages and then showed it to Charlotte.

Don't worry about me, Em. I'm fine and I understand. We should never have crossed that line. Now you can have what you've always wanted. Just be happy. And I'll be happy for you. xo

'Ouch,' said Charlotte.

'Yep.' Em dejectedly tucked her phone away. 'He just wants me to get on with my life with Trent. I've ruined everything, including our friendship. Why else would he be avoiding me?'

Charlotte put her arms around her friend as the girl bravely, if not effectively, held a sob in check. 'Oh, I'm sure you haven't lost Will,' she said soothingly against her hair. 'He probably just needs a bit of distance for a while after what happened. He'll always be your friend. That's just the way he is.'

'But everything's changed now. Even if he will be my friend, that's so much less than I want. It would be torture.'

Charlotte bit her lip, unable to find a comforting thing to say in this instance. 'Plenty of fish in the sea' seemed rather callous at this point.

Emily chuckled weakly. 'Look at me crying on your shoulder when I came to take your mind off things.'

'You have taken my mind off things,' Charlotte assured her and then mused, 'So I take it you've refused Trent's proposal?'

'Technically, I've agreed to think about it,' Em revealed. 'At least until your court case is over. He wants me to come to Brisbane with him, but I'm not sure.'

'I can understand that.' Charlotte nodded. 'You want to be here when Will comes back.'

Emily frowned. 'Or do I? He was pretty clear in his message that what happened between us was a mistake. When he gets back things will be awkward. Perhaps I should just give him the space he obviously wants.'

'That's up to you.'

Emily smiled wryly. 'What about you? How are you holding up?'

'I've been better.' Charlotte shrugged. 'It's a strain hiding all this from Zara.'

'Tell you what,' Emily straightened, moving out of Charlotte's arm, 'I'll come to Brisbane, not with Trent, with *you*, for moral support – for the both of us. My R and R is due and it would be good to get away and regroup. What do you reckon?'

'Perfect.'

Just then there was a knock at the back door. She felt her face heat as she realised who it might be.

'Oh,' Emily's eyes widened, 'I didn't know you were expecting company. I should go.'

'Oh no, that's all right, I'm not,' Charlotte quickly denied as Emily stood up.

'No, it's okay. We can watch that movie another time.'

There was a knock at the door again and Charlotte quickly hurried over to answer it. Sure enough, her first instinct had been correct: it was Mark standing there, with windswept hair and some sort of document in his hands. Her heart skipped a beat. She barely registered Emily say a quick hello to Mark before stepping around him and leaving.

'Good evening, Charlotte,' he said rather formally.

'Good evening, Mark,' she responded and wanted to laugh at how stiff they both sounded. The other night, when he'd stayed for dinner, you would have thought they'd get a little closer. But he had been there for her only in the literal sense. Running some of her resort errands, serving her dinner and keeping Zara occupied while she tried to process everything that had happened that day. Like a sentry, he'd mostly just watched her and they'd hardly spoken at all. It was no wonder their conversations remained stilted.

'I brought you this.' He held out the paper.

'What is it?'

'Flight itinerary,' he replied shortly.

She took it from his outstretched hand and glanced briefly over the document. 'You didn't have to do this; I was going to book it myself tomorrow.'

'Rest easy, I didn't. Ann did.'

'Still, it's not your responsibility. How much do I owe you?' she said as her eyes fell to the page.

'You'll have to ask Ann.' He turned to go, but she had spotted something else she didn't like.

'It says here she's booked two seats and two hotel rooms.'

'Yes,' he nodded, 'I'm coming with you.'

She started. 'Why?'

A muscle worked in his jaw. 'I need to go on a holiday.'

Her eyes narrowed on him and then she repeated his words slowly and succinctly in case he hadn't heard how ridiculous he sounded. 'You-need-to-go-on-a-holiday?'

'Yes, it's on my To Do list.'

What's with this bloody To Do list? And why couldn't he just be straight with her? Tell her the real reason he baked cakes, adopted turkeys and went diving. The real reason he wanted to go on a date with her? Until he let her in, how could she have any sort of real rapport with him? She couldn't have a relationship with a man who continued to speak in riddles. Riddles that insulted both her intelligence and her dignity. '*Right*,' she said crossly. 'And this hasn't got anything to do with the fact that I rejected your offer of a date last week.'

He raised his brows. 'Are you suggesting, Charlotte, that I'm trying to take advantage of you?'

'If the shoe fits,' she retorted before she could check herself. 'I'm surprised you had two rooms booked instead of one.'

He seemed surprised. 'Why? Is that what you'd prefer?'

'Of course not,' she snapped but he ignored her denial.

'I hate to disappoint you,' he murmured, with eyes downcast and hands behind his back, 'but that is not my intention at all.'

She was immediately angry at herself for overreacting. She didn't want him to know that she often thought about that day he'd asked her on a date, especially in the quiet moments just before sleep, and wondered why he didn't repeat the offer or at least try again.

'I'm not disappointed,' she growled, chest heaving. 'Just surprised, that's all.'

'No need for an apology.'

'*I wasn't apologising!*'

'Well, good,' he nodded. 'I'll see you at work tomorrow.'

And then, to her complete and utter fury, he turned and walked out, leaving her with his travel plans in her hands.

Chapter 29

Mark

He knew in some mysterious way he'd botched their last conversation, which was probably why she'd given him the silent treatment for the balance of the week and most of the flight over. That or she actually preferred the mindless babble of Emily Woods and the self-serving conversation provided by the lawyer. Honestly, if that man wasn't as good as he claimed to be Mark was going to make him sorry they'd ever crossed paths. It was funny how his conversation with Chub about Kathryn had only been a couple of weeks ago. It felt like much longer. The truth was, thoughts of his late wife no longer hurt. She seemed so far away now. By contrast Charlotte was too agonisingly close.

They got into Brisbane at about seven-thirty that evening and he invited them all to dine with him at the hotel restaurant. Charlotte excused herself saying that she was too nervous to eat and would probably order a bowl of soup in her room. At her decline, Trent and Emily also said they would have meals in their rooms.

Later that night, though, he heard giggling in the room next door to his. It was clear the girls had got together anyway for a private dinner. The only consolation he had about the snub was that it had probably put Trent's nose out of joint as well. He could tell the man was trying to do everything in his power to impress Emily but his efforts were going dismally unnoticed. He couldn't help but wonder what Will's role was in all this. The Boy Scout had decided to take his R and R rather abruptly on Thursday morning. Not that he had a problem with that. The shiploader was in and the boy's time off was due.

'I'm surprised you don't want to wait and take your week off when Emily has her R and R,' he had said to Will when the boy had come to ask permission. 'I was sure the two of you would have run away together to the Whitsundays.'

Will had cleared his throat. 'What makes you say that, sir?'

He sat back in his chair with reluctant patience. 'The two of you have been inseparable since she got here. I take it things haven't gone according to plan?'

'According to what plan, sir?'

He folded his arms and looked down his nose at the boy. 'Very well, I see no reason for you to take me into your confidence. But let me give you one piece of advice.'

'What's that, sir?'

'Women never say what they mean.' He sighed at the melancholic nature of the thought. '*Never*.'

As he recalled the conversation, he couldn't help but reflect mournfully on his final statement and how fundamentally it applied to Charlotte Templeton, who was like a closed book to him. Every time he tried to build a bridge between them he failed. What did she want from him? What did she expect him to say?

He slept fitfully, as fear and regrets troubled him. Fear for Charlotte and Zara and regret for the relationship with Charlotte he could not seem to grasp.

They all awoke early the next morning, had breakfast together in the hotel and then took a taxi to the Harry Gibbs Commonwealth Law Court, which was situated quite centrally in the city. The multistorey gloomy grey structure seemed to reflect his mood exactly. But when he climbed the steps at the entrance, he happened to glance over at Charlotte and catch an unguarded expression as it flitted briefly across her face before she absorbed it back into her mask of calm.

She was terrified.

He knew it and a fist closed around his heart at his own helplessness in this instance.

He and Emily took their seats at the back of the courtroom in the public gallery, where they were allowed to sit to view proceedings. Charlotte went to the front with Trent, who was now fully robed. Trent sat at the left-hand side of the bar table, facing the judge's bench. He began ordering his papers, placing some on the small lectern in front of him. Charlotte sat directly behind Trent at the end of a long bench.

Dennis Mayer showed up not long after them, entering the courtroom from the right in the wake of a blonde woman in her late forties who was no doubt his lawyer, as she was wearing the same attire as Trent. Mark took in her hard face and ringless hands and was immediately put in mind of a woman who had sacrificed everything else in her life for her career. With considered efficiency, she prepared her side of the bar table, sparing Trent no more than one contemptuous glance. Dennis Mayer looked serene as he took his seat at the other end of the long bench on which Charlotte was seated. Mark had to admit there certainly didn't look like there was anything untoward about him. Dressed in a grey suit and tie, he radiated 'respectable businessman with family interests'.

Mark's focus immediately snapped back to the front of the room as the clerk of the court addressed them. 'All rise.'

As everyone stood up, the judge and his associate walked in, seating themselves in large black leatherbound chairs to face their small audience. The judge was a rather short, heavy-set man with a generous belly. The lawyers bowed and then the clerk announced, 'Court is now in session.'

After a few more formalities, where the female lawyer was introduced as Ms Pylforth, they all sat down.

Ms Pylforth remained standing. 'Your Honour, this interim application brought by my client, Dennis Albert Mayer, seeks parental responsibility and residence for his daughter, the child Zara Jane Templeton. The basis for my client seeking such orders concerns the physical and mental incapacity of the mother, Virginia Templeton, and also the precarious nature of the mother's financial situation. As your Honour will note, the application is fully particularised in the father's application and in the father's supporting affidavit.'

'Yes, I have seen them, though I admit I have not read them in any great depth,' the judge confessed. 'I have also briefly reviewed the respondent's documents. From what I understand, Ms Charlotte Templeton has been Zara's informal carer since her mother's deterioration. Given Mr Mayer has not participated in the care of his child for fifteen years I could not comprehend why he would think it feasible for him to be suddenly granted full custody now.'

Good.

Mark nodded approvingly at this rather promising beginning until Ms Pylforth shifted her client's position.

'Your Honour, my client would be the first to acknowledge that the circumstances of this case are unusual. That is why you will note that the father's application has alternative propositions for your Honour to consider. In the alternative, my client would move the court for a reduced parenting order, such as partial residence or visitation rights and also some legal say in matters concerning the child's education and medical care. My client currently believes that in relation to these issues his daughter's requirements are not being adequately met due to the Templetons' financial situation.'

The judge gave a derisive honk. 'You are trying my patience, Ms Pylforth. That is a rather broad statement. How can your client be so sure of this when he has not been in his daughter's company since her birth? From the papers, it appears he has not even met her.'

'Your Honour, if it pleases the court, I would like to read Annexure 1 from my client's affidavit, which is a letter from his daughter Zara Templeton dated five weeks ago.'

'Proceed,' the judge nodded.

'*Dear Mr Mayer, you don't know me. We've never met. But I'm writing to you because I've just found out that you're my father. I am so relieved to finally have a name to contact. My name is Zara Templeton and my mother's name is Virginia. I have always been curious about you and your history. My family has kept this from me, which I think is very unfair otherwise I would have written to you sooner. I would love to get to know you and be part of your life. I want to see if we have anything in common. I know that your hands are tied but I feel that I have missed out on a lot of things because I never had a father. My older sister, Charlotte, mostly raised me. Mum has been very sick for many years and needs to be taken care of herself. Often, my sister is too preoccupied with looking after her and our failing business to pay any attention to me. I feel like I am just a nuisance to her, always in her way and holding her back. I'm sure, in fact, that she would be quite relieved if it was one day possible for me to come and live with you. I was wondering if we could at least make contact so that in the future, when this might be possible, we will already know one another. What do you think? Yours sincerely, Zara Templeton.*'

Mark's jaw ached as he gritted his teeth.

'I see,' the judge remarked as Ms Pylforth looked up from the letter. 'That adds some complexion to things.'

Chapter 30

Charlotte

Charlotte's stomached flipped as Ms Pylforth read Zara's innocent words. Even though she had seen Dennis Mayer's affidavit including the letter before, the effect of it being read out loud was like hearing it for the first time. She closed her eyes in sorrow as she heard her sister describe herself as a nuisance. How blind had she been and how thoughtless! Her fingers gripped each other tightly in her lap. She should have paid more attention to what Zara was going through. If she had been a better parent, none of this would be happening. It was all her fault.

'It is clear from the child's letter,' Ms Pylforth went on to say, 'that Zara Templeton would benefit from having a father figure in her life. My client does not believe his daughter is being mistreated as such, but the child's letter, in her own words, demonstrates that Charlotte Templeton is finding it difficult to maintain her duties as a single parent, a struggling business owner and full-time carer to an invalid. The letter shows, your Honour, an insight into a lonely child reaching out to a lost father. In these circumstances, it is no reach for your Honour to conclude that Charlotte Templeton would benefit from some help from my client. Your Honour, my client submits that such an outcome would be in the best interests of the child. She did, after all, reach out to him. My client is merely responding to that call.'

'I understand your submission; it has some merit.' The judge nodded.

Charlotte's fingernails dug into her palm. She could not bear it if this monster got even three minutes' access to her sister. It was unthinkable!

'But only superficially,' the judge continued. 'If this is your client's only evidence it is not enough to make a ruling today.'

'My client,' Ms Pylforth straightened, 'has done some research into the Templetons' financial situation and has evidence to suggest that their business is one step away from insolvency. This is also contained in my client's affidavit.'

Charlotte's jaw clenched.

The judge opened the file in front of him. 'One moment, please.' The court gave him pin-drop silence while he read Dennis's so-called evidence. It was all Charlotte could do not to scream out, 'I'll sell the business if I need to!' But she had to wait her turn.

'Curious.' The judge's mouth twitched. 'It appears that a year ago, Ms Templeton had her resort on the market and Mr Mayer posed as a potential buyer.'

Charlotte's lip curled. She was glad that the judge was going to highlight what a creep Dennis had been getting the information. She still couldn't believe herself that he'd already been in their lives for over a year and she hadn't even known about it. A sudden chill ran through her and she shuddered.

The judge looked down from the bench over Ms Pylforth's head. The light seemed to catch the Commonwealth emblem above his head. 'Mr Mayer, please step into the witness box. *You* will explain this to me.'

Dennis's lawyer turned and nodded to him.

Zara's biological father stood up, entered the witness box and was sworn in. He addressed the judge. 'Er . . . yes, your Honour. That's true. As part of due diligence I was able to obtain financial records from the Templetons' agent showing the dire circumstance under which the business was operating.'

'I do not wish you to explain to me how you obtained the evidence,' the judge said sternly. 'That much is already clear. What I do wish to know is why you were snooping around their business at a time that pre-dates the receipt of your daughter's letter.'

Charlotte turned narrowed eyes upon her foe.

However, Dennis did not even blink. 'I am a successful businessman with friends in Mackay. I was looking to expand my business portfolio. Virginia Templeton is an old friend, as you have probably guessed. At the time, I did know of Zara but I thought that she was Charlotte's daughter. When I saw Virginia's business for sale, I took an interest. At one point I even hoped to rekindle our . . . er, friendship, until I found out that she had Alzheimer's disease.'

Friendship . . . yeah right. Perhaps when he found out her mother was an invalid, he considered revisiting his old victim less interesting. Charlotte tasted bile in her mouth.

'Very well,' the judge said. 'Is there anything further you wish to add to your case before I go on, Mr Mayer?'

'Just to say, your Honour, that I am a family man. I am married with one stepdaughter already, who is two years younger than Zara. I feel she would fit well into my family. I am distressed that I have already missed so much of her life. Her mother, Virginia, deliberately and purposefully kept the knowledge of our child from me. I have been robbed of my rights as a father and feel that I should at least be compensated for that. I am a partner with my brother in a well-respected pharmaceutical business, which we both inherited from my parents. I earn good money. I know that I will be able to pay for private schooling for Zara, give her top medical insurance and ensure that all her needs are met from a financial point of view. Respectfully, I believe I deserve this chance to be included in her life, especially when it's what she wants as well and she can only benefit from my involvement.'

The judge nodded. 'Is there anything further you wish to add, Ms Pylforth?'

'No, your Honour.'

'Then I will ask Mr Townsend to respond.'

Trent stood up beside her and she had to brace herself. Now it was their turn.

Please, please. Let us make an impression.

'Your Honour, in this case, I represent both Virginia Templeton and her daughter, Charlotte Templeton. As you know, Virginia Templeton has Alzheimer's disease and her daughter Charlotte has been the guardian of her estate and the informal carer of her youngest daughter Zara Templeton since she was diagnosed eight years ago.'

'Thank you for the recap, counsel, but I would prefer you cut straight to your response to the applicant,' the judge instructed.

Trent raised his chin. 'Charlotte Templeton wishes to apply for parental responsibility and residence for Zara Jane Templeton in Mr Mayer's stead with no rights granted to Zara's biological father at all.'

The judge raised his eyebrows. 'Tell me, Mr Townsend, how is that in the child's best interest given the financial aid her father might provide? Not to mention the fact that Zara asked to be part of her father's life.'

'My client requests this parental order on the grounds of the likely psychological damage to Zara if she is forced to be involved in her father's life.'

The judge pursed his lips. 'To be honest, Mr Townsend, I find your client's affidavit to be rather ineffectual in supporting such an argument. If you propose to continue in that vein, I will have to stop you here.'

'Your Honour, please excuse our incomplete material. Mr Mayer gave us a mere seven days to prepare our case.' The judge's glare swung to Dennis's hung head as Trent continued talking. 'Despite this, however, we have managed to secure a police report and also a statement from Zara's clinical psychologist for examination today. They have been annexed to appropriate affidavits.'

The judge's gaze returned to him. 'You understand that I will have to call a thirty-minute adjournment to allow Mr Mayer's lawyer time to read these documents.'

Trent inclined his head. 'I understand, your Honour.'

'Very well. Mr Mayer, in the circumstances, you are released from the witness box.' Trent reached into his materials and passed a copy of each of the new documents to the judge's associate and then across the bar table to the scowling Ms Pylforth.

The judge then nodded to the clerk of the court, who proceeded to announce the adjournment, adding, 'Court will resume at eleven am.'

The judge and his associate filed out, taking the new documents with them. Charlotte resisted the urge to bite her fingernails. Thirty minutes of limbo was going to be pure agony. The last thing she wanted to do was sit around and speculate on what was about to happen next.

'I'll be right back,' she said to Trent and walked out of the courtroom, making a beeline for the ladies. After splashing some water on her face, she felt only marginally better. She hid in there for as long as she could, but it wasn't long before Emily came looking for her. After that, it was back to the courtroom and she didn't know whether to be anxious or relieved.

When the judge and his associate were seated again, Trent stood up to make their case.

'Your Honour, any contact between Dennis Mayer and Zara Templeton would be psychologically damaging to his daughter. It is my client's case that Mr Mayer sexually assaulted Virginia

Templeton. Zara Templeton was conceived as a result of that sexual assault.'

The judge sat back further into his chair. He looked around the courtroom in a brooding fashion before focusing on Trent once more. When he spoke again his tone was grave.

'This is a very serious allegation, Mr Townsend, and not one for this court.'

'I am aware of that, your Honour,' Trent acknowledged. 'However, my client feels it is an issue that must be raised. The letter from Zara Templeton previously read by Ms Pylforth was written, as stated in the letter, at a time when Zara did not know her father's history. She has recently found out he was jailed for three counts of rape and has also been told that the relationship he had with her mother was non-consenting and that she was the product of this one sexual assault. Zara Templeton was deeply disturbed by this knowledge and has since been receiving counselling from a therapist in Mackay. It is my clients' understanding that at this point it would be more damaging to her mental health to be threatened with living with her father.'

'Objection,' Ms Pylforth stood up. 'Your Honour, this is all hearsay from the bar table. My client was never convicted of the rape of Virginia Templeton.'

'Nonetheless, counsel,' the judge looked at her rather crossly, 'your client is a convicted rapist who has served time. That information should have been declared in your own affidavit. Why wasn't it?'

Ms Pylforth lifted her chin. 'Your Honour, as you have just said, Mr Mayer has served his time and has been a model citizen for two years. He is no danger to anyone, including his daughter.'

The judge snorted. 'You are in no position to guarantee that, Counsel, and nor is such an assertion any excuse for the lack of disclosure. Sit down, Ms Pylforth. I will hear again from Mr Townsend.'

Ms Pylforth, much to Charlotte's delight, shrank into her seat.

'Although Mr Mayer was never convicted of Virginia Templeton's rape,' Trent continued, 'he was convicted of the rape of three other women and so any contact with Zara Templeton is not, according to my client, an acceptable risk. At this point, your Honour, I think it prudent that my client address the court directly.'

'Very well.'

At the judge's nod, Charlotte stood up, moved around to the bar table and was sworn in. She knew that everything she said was crucial to their winning, and pressure gathered on her head like magnetic filings on the point of a needle.

'Your Honour,' she croaked and then hastily cleared her throat, 'in my opinion, I do not think my sister would benefit from a relationship with her father. Her distress at finding out about his past was extremely hard on her. In lieu of her presence, I have a letter from her therapist, which accords with my own opinion, and also a copy of the police report my mother filed after she was raped sixteen years ago. If you would like me to read them to the court, I can do so now.'

The judge shook his head. 'That will not be necessary. Is there anything else you wish to add, Ms Templeton?'

Her breath caught and her mouth dried. Did he need more information? What had she left out? She wracked her brain and could think of nothing. She gripped her hands together; she could make promises at the very least. 'Only that, although our financial situation is not ideal, Zara has never wanted for anything. And should we need to sell the business at a future date to make ends meet, then that's what we'll do. I will always make Zara's well-being my top priority.'

The judge nodded and then turned to the room at large as Charlotte resumed her seat. 'The applications before me present a number of serious concerns and while I don't propose to reserve my decision, I do intend to take a recess to gather my thoughts and we will reconvene after lunch at two-fifteen pm.' He turned to his associate and the clerk of the court who immediately said, 'All rise. This court is adjourned until not before two-fifteen pm.'

Without further ado, his Honour and his associate walked out.

Charlotte released a long shaky breath. It was now in their hands. Trent turned to her with a smile. 'You did well.'

'Did I?' she asked, her fingers cold and trembling. She had to clasp them together to stop them shaking.

'Very well.' He nodded optimistically. 'Let's go have lunch.'

Without even glancing at Dennis Mayer or his lawyer she got up and filed out of the courtroom after Trent. To be honest, she did want to get out of there as quickly as possible even though she wasn't the slightest bit hungry. How could she eat while the judge deliberated over Zara's future? Her stomach was churning far too much already.

In the hall, Mark and Emily were already standing there waiting for them. She met Mark's solemn eyes over Emily's shoulder as the girl immediately stepped forward to give her a hug. Although he said nothing, she took both strength and comfort from his steadfast gaze.

She knew she had feelings for this man. Deep feelings. Feelings that she didn't want to think about because if it was love she must be crazy. There was nothing lover-like about him. He was blunt, abrasive, rude and obnoxious. The number of times he had insulted her were no longer countable. Yet, here he was. By her side, in this time of need. Like an anchor, keeping her in safe harbour – cocooned in his care, however distantly he gave it. He'd bought her airline tickets, paid for the lawyer and the accommodation . . . even come along. But what was she supposed to do with all that if he would admit nothing? When she had challenged him on his motives, he'd pushed her further away. In fact, he completely refused to acknowledge feelings for her at all – if there were any. Perhaps it was a bloody big assumption on her part. He could just be a man who took his position as an employer very seriously.

The wife he had lost coloured his life to the point where he'd let his grief take control of it. If she could not break through the barrier he had set around himself then what future could they have? She would not be part of a relationship that included a ghost.

'I saw this great little place down the road on our way here,' Emily was saying. 'Do you want to go there for lunch?'

'Sure.' Charlotte again tasted sawdust in her mouth at the thought of food, but this time she didn't know whether it was because of Mark or Zara. Maybe both.

Two hours later after a very lacklustre lunch at a little café called Noel, the four of them returned to the Family Court to receive the judge's decision. Charlotte shivered as she walked into the room and sat down even though she wasn't cold.

Just tell me what I want to hear. She repeated the words like a mantra, keeping her eyes firmly on the front of the room rather than on Dennis or his lawyer.

'All rise,' said the clerk of the court. They all took their places.

Charlotte had to purposely make herself not hold her breath as she resumed her seat.

'The applicant has made a solid case for custody, however, on balance I cannot, at this time, grant him even partial parental responsibility or residence for Zara Templeton.'

Charlotte could not stop the smile from stretching across her face or relief from swelling her chest.

'Although it is not a matter for this court to decide whether relations between Virginia Templeton and Dennis Mayer were of an unlawful nature, there have been some very serious issues raised with regard to Zara's current mental health. And it is clear that it is not in her best interest to change her home life at this time. Given that Zara has been in Ms Charlotte Templeton's care for the last fifteen years without mishap I do grant her parental responsibility and residence at this time. However, I will state that Zara is of an age now where she is capable of making some of her own decisions. If her mental health were to improve and she wishes to seek a relationship with her father then, if necessary, this matter can be brought back before me and we can assess other issues such as whether it is an acceptable risk to have Zara partially in his care.'

And then, in a flurry of final formalities, the judge gave a nod to both parties. 'Court adjourned.'

It was all Charlotte could do not to scream for joy as the judge and his associate filed out.

She heard Dennis Mayer's chair roughly push out and hit the bench behind him. She looked up as he slammed his file shut. Their eyes met for a brief moment across the room, and she received the full blast of his fury. She braced herself against it. It didn't matter. He couldn't touch her now. Even as she finished the thought, he turned to Ms Pylforth, who was trying to reclaim his attention. 'I'm sorry, Mr Mayer. I thought we had a better chance.'

He seemed to pull himself together quickly enough, an oily smile slicked across his lips to match the sheen on his forehead.

'Would you care for a debrief over a drink, Ms Pylforth? I know a good pub nearby.'

Charlotte shuddered as the two of them walked out.

Suddenly she felt a hand cover hers and realised that she was still sitting there at the desk in a kind of stupor.

'Are you okay?' a gentle voice inquired.

She looked up to find it was Mark who was addressing her. Trent had moved away to speak to Emily.

'Definitely.' She smiled radiantly at the remembrance of her win. She turned her hand over to grip his. For a moment, just a moment, he stood there and she sat there, holding hands and gazing into each other's eyes, a perfect bubble of triumph and bliss. And then, as she knew he would, he withdrew his hand and put it into his pocket.

'Well, Charlotte, I guess your holiday is over. Time to get back to work.'

Ah, the insensitive remark that always followed. 'How lovely of you to remind me.' She stood up briskly, pushing in her chair and straightening her jacket. 'Shall we go?'

'I thought you'd never ask.'

They went out into the foyer, where Emily and Trent looked like they were having an argument. As soon as Emily saw Charlotte she spun around in relief. 'You know what we should do?' she exclaimed.

'What's that?' Charlotte inquired lightly.

'Go shopping,' Emily suggested with a tad too much enthusiasm. 'I've never been to Brisbane before and it'll be a great way to kill the rest of the afternoon.'

'Sounds good.' Charlotte smiled watching the way Trent's mouth opened and closed. She knew he'd been hoping to spend the afternoon with Emily himself but he could hardly invite himself along to 'shopping with the girls'.

Neither could Mark. However, the project manager did not seem as put out by this – merely mildly amused. She didn't know whether to feel relief or pique that he didn't care whether he spent the afternoon with her or not.

Trent finally cleared his throat. 'Well, we should at least celebrate this win, tonight. All of us, together. For dinner.'

Charlotte glanced at Mark, who was silent. After her snub the night before it was clear he wasn't going to second the invitation but merely wait and see the outcome. She supposed there was no point in being churlish, especially considering he had been so kind financially. She nodded her head. 'All right, dinner tonight in our hotel's restaurant. Seven pm.'

'Agreed,' Emily added.

'I'll be there,' Mark murmured.

So they split up and she and Emily jumped on a ferry to see Brisbane. It was actually a very enjoyable few hours exploring this river city. They shopped, they had coffee, they walked along the south-bank foreshore, enjoying the parklands and the artificial lagoon. It was a gorgeous day, warm and bright, and she felt so much lighter. The angst of the week before was gone. Everything was how it should be. Except for one thing.

Mark.

'You've gone awfully quiet,' said Emily as they waited at the ferry station to catch their ride home. 'What are you thinking about? Or should I say, who are you thinking about?'

Charlotte sighed. 'Is it that obvious?'

'Actually, not until recently.' Emily looked thoughtful. 'Not until you told me he was coming with us and that he'd paid for everything. But even then I wasn't one hundred per cent sure. He's not very . . .' She trailed off.

'No, it's okay, you can say it.' Charlotte's lips turned up wryly.

'Affectionate,' Emily frowned. 'To be honest, he's actually rather cold.'

'Like a freezer,' Charlotte chuckled. 'But you're wrong. We're not together. We're just . . .' She groaned. 'I don't know what we are.' She decided it was best to change the subject. 'What about you and Trent? You seemed to be arguing when I came out of the courtroom today.'

'I had to reject his proposal again and he didn't take it too well the second time either.' She bit her lip. 'The problem is, he thinks he hasn't had enough time to persuade me, and that I might still change my mind. Why is it that all men think that women never say what they mean?'

Charlotte rolled her eyes in empathy. 'I have no idea.' But speaking of Trent had put her in mind of something. 'Say, did he give you that letter I found the other day? I hope it wasn't urgent.'

'What letter?'

'I found a letter with my mother's things addressed to you. I gave it to Trent to pass on.'

'He didn't give me anything.'

'Well, maybe ask him about it when we get back to the hotel,' Charlotte suggested.

Emily nodded. 'Sure, I will.'

Charlotte dressed carefully that evening in a conservative black cocktail dress that she hadn't taken out of her closet in years, a light but fresh application of make-up and her auburn hair styled in a loose twist. She never wore dresses any more. Jeans and T-shirts were her staple. But she'd thrown it into her suitcase at the last minute on impulse. They were going to the city. No point in being underdressed if they went out. She was pleased now that she'd brought it with her. Even more pleased when she noticed the way Mark's eyes followed her entrance from across the restaurant without breaking contact once.

He stood up when she reached their table. 'Hello, Charlotte.'

There was no kiss on the cheek. He didn't even take her hand. He just stood there drinking her in like she was the last sip of water on a desert island.

She cleared her throat and averted her eyes from the intensity of his gaze. 'Er, hi, Mark.' She pulled out her chair and quickly sat down.

'How was your afternoon?' he asked innocuously.

'Fine,' she said, equally so, and then bit her lip at the silence that ensued. 'Listen,' she said finally, 'I want to thank you for everything you've done for me this last week. I couldn't have got through it without you.'

He nodded. 'I know.'

She blinked at his short response and tried again. 'You've been so supportive, paying for everything, organising everything, and getting Trent to represent me. You really didn't need to do all that.'

'I know.'

Her lips pulled into a thin line at his averted eyes. 'I will pay you back, by the way. Every cent. We'll work out a payment plan or something. What do you think?'

'No rush.' He took a sip of water.

She gritted her teeth. Was there no entry to the rock-solid cave Mark had encased himself in?

For a while they simply sat there, looking at their menus, drinking water and making small talk that flowed as easily as sludge. Time passed slowly. First fifteen minutes, then half an hour while they waited for the other two to show up. At last, Charlotte's phone buzzed as a message came through.

She dived into her handbag and pulled it out. The message was from Emily.

Sorry, I'm not going to be able to make it tonight and I doubt Trent's coming either. Something has come up – will call you later.

'Damn.' She clicked the phone off and looked up at Mark's raised eyebrows.

'Bad news?' he inquired.

'Apparently,' she smiled sweetly, 'you'll be able to cross something else off that list of yours.' She tilted her head, a challenge in her eyes. 'Looks like we're on a date.'

Chapter 31

Will

He had never endured such an unrestful R and R. It was made all the worse by the fact that he didn't feel like he could confide in anyone back home in Perth. How could he speak to his family and friends about what he was going through, when they were all about to be recipients of Emily's 'wonderful news'? Instead, he had to find a way to grin and bear it as he had five years ago.

Getting through this was his top priority – if not for his sake, then for Emily's.

It's not like he wanted to lose their friendship on top of everything else. He just hoped she didn't ask him to be her maid of honour like they'd joked about at Lena's wedding. That would kill him.

As the week progressed further, however, no announcement was made and doubt nagged him.

Why hadn't she contacted all their friends? It wasn't like they were eloping or anything.

Oh crap! Are they?

He couldn't be sure. Emily had certainly phoned him a lot but he didn't trust himself to answer. He didn't know if he could be 'supportive' just yet. He sent what he hoped was a reassuring text message and was rewarded with stone-cold silence. He hadn't thought his message was rude – he had just wanted to give her the green light, in case she was worried about his feelings. That obviously wasn't the case. She'd taken his 'go ahead' literally and dumped him like a tonne of bricks.

His return to site at the end of the week was also disappointing. If he had hoped to catch Emily before she left for Brisbane with Trent, that hope was dashed when Ann informed him that they had left the day before.

At that point, he did the only thing he could do. He buried himself in work. When he got sick of Nova's teasing, he took a roll of drawings and went out to inspect the drive tower. Anything to get away from the draftsman's less than subtle prodding about Emily.

Unfortunately, even solid steel reinforcing bars could not protect him from the curiosity of his men. Spooks and the usual suspects hailed him within minutes of his arrival. First asking how his R and R had been (for politeness's sake) and then shamelessly delving straight into the guts of the gossip they were trying to collect.

'So how's Emily?'

'I have no idea,' Will retorted. 'I've been away, remember? You've seen more of her recently than I have.'

They all guffawed and Spooks slapped his own leg at the joke. 'I seriously doubt that, Boy Scout,' he said, chuckling.

Will did not like the sleazy note in his tone and looked up from the drawing he had been pretending to study. 'What are you talking about?'

'Nothing.' Spooks's eyes were too wide to be innocent.

In resignation, he re-rolled the drawing. 'Spit it out, Spooks, I know you're dying to tell me.'

Spooks spread his hands cajolingly. 'All we're after is a little bit of confirmation, Boy Scout. There's a lot of money at stake here and everybody's waiting to find out who gets paid.'

'Confirmation about what?' Will demanded.

'Who won the bet, you or Dipper. Are you with Emily Woods or not?'

Will gazed at him slack-jawed, anger bubbling just behind his eyeballs. This was all he needed. Why couldn't these guys just get out of his face and leave Emily's love-life alone? Didn't they have anything better to do with their lives?

'No need to prevaricate,' Spooks said slyly, misinterpreting his silent rage. 'We know something happened.'

It was all he could do not to grind his teeth. 'You've got a lot of nerve, Spooks,' Will spat at him. 'The fact is, you don't know jack shit. If you did, you wouldn't be asking me, would you? Besides, that's none of your damn business anyway.'

Spooks's eyes seemed to sparkle at this challenge. He rubbed his dirty hands together and licked his lips. 'That's where you're wrong, Boy Scout. We do know *something*.'

'For Pete's sake –'

'We know,' Spooks interrupted his next tirade, 'that on the afternoon the shiploader was installed someone bet a thousand dollars you'd win.'

'Like I care,' Will threw at him. 'Take your casino elsewhere, Spooks.'

'Even if the highest bidder is Emily Woods?' Spooks said slowly and succinctly.

Will halted in the act of turning away. '*What did you say?*'

'I'm *saying*,' Spooks smiled like a dog with a juicy bone, 'that Emily Woods bet a thousand dollars that you'd win.'

'Why would she do that?'

'Well,' Spooks shrugged a little too casually, 'I don't think it was about the winnings.'

It was like the lights came back on after a prolonged power blackout. 'You're not joking about this, are you?' he whispered.

'I never kid about money or football,' Spooks said seriously.

'The afternoon after the shiploader went in . . .' Will murmured, not even realising he was speaking out loud. *The night we kissed.*

And then realisation struck him. *The night she seduced me!*

So it hadn't just been just one of those things. Or because she was tipsy or needy or confused, as he had thought. It was premeditated and planned. She had known exactly what she was doing. He didn't know whether to laugh or to cry. Emily had made her choice and he hadn't even realised it. Was that why she'd called him so many times the next morning?

He groaned as he remembered the text message he'd sent. But why did Trent say she'd accepted his proposal? . . . *Unless he'd lied.* Something wasn't right here. Before he knew what he was doing, he was turning around and walking off, completely ignoring the men, who were still waiting on a response from him.

'Boy Scout,' Spooks called out, 'where do you think you're going? You haven't answered our question.'

He laughed again as hope made his chest swell.

'Brisbane,' he said over his shoulder and doubled his pace.

Chapter 32

Emily

When Emily returned to the hotel after her afternoon out with Charlotte, her jaw ached from smiling. She was so sick of putting on a brave face, pretending everything was great and that she was enjoying this break from work.

If she didn't feel like Charlotte needed her support, she would have flown to Perth this morning. Trent was annoying the hell out of her – putting the pressure on like nothing on earth and all she wanted to do was just get away from him.

How could I have contemplated marrying that guy? He was a complete control freak and if she tied herself to him permanently she would become the puppet she had been turning into just before they'd broken up. He was nothing like Will. Nothing like beautiful, generous, kind-hearted Will . . . who only wanted to be her friend.

She blinked back the tears that threatened. Now was not the time to feel sorry for herself. She'd just finished putting on her make-up for their celebratory dinner. Though, if she had her own way, she'd just stay in her room tonight. But she knew snubbing Trent twice in a row was just going to set his back up and make him redouble his efforts. No, what she needed to do was get through dinner and then have a firm chat with him afterwards. Tomorrow morning, she'd book the first plane to Perth and take the rest of her R and R there, which was what she should have done in the first place. She had thought a new city would take her mind off things, but that wasn't happening with Trent nagging in the wings.

There was a knock at her hotel-room door and she walked out of the bathroom to answer it. It was Trent.

'I thought I'd walk you downstairs.'

'You shouldn't have bothered.' She turned away from the door but didn't shut it so he could follow her in.

'Why are you making this so difficult?' he asked after closing the door.

She spun back. 'Trent, I think we need to have a serious talk.' She might as well do it now.

'Okay, I'm listening.'

She clasped her hands. 'I appreciate what you've done for Charlotte. Thank you for taking on her case at such short notice. But in terms of you and me,' she drew in a deep breath and then let it go, 'you're holding out hope for something that's never going to happen.'

He frowned. 'So you only came on this trip with me for Charlotte?'

She put her hands on her hips. 'I told you that before we left. So why you would think any different is beyond me.'

He chose his words carefully. 'You seemed like you needed to get away. And I was happy to be here for you.'

She sighed. 'Maybe there is some truth in that. I did need a distraction and I thought a new city would be exciting enough to make me forget –' She cut off her own words, her hand going to her temple to rub a knot of pain there.

'This is about Will, isn't it?' he said finally.

Startled, her gaze snapped to his. *How does he know?*

'Don't bother denying it.' He ground out the words. 'I've had too many hints along the way.'

When she said nothing and simply stared at him in wonder he added, 'I guess I always knew he had a soft spot for you. Even on the day we met, I was aware I had to act fast if I wanted to knock him out of the running. I just never thought he'd double-cross me like this. I mean, he's Will,' he shrugged as though that said it all, 'sacrificial to a fault.'

'He didn't double-cross you.' She immediately jumped to Will's defence. 'I went after him. He doesn't even know I like him that way.'

'Come on, Em,' Trent scoffed, 'don't be stupid. He took advantage of you when you were at your most vulnerable.'

'No.' Emily squared her chin. 'That's what *you* did. And I didn't quite realise it until Will showed me how to spread my own wings and fly free.'

He laughed contemptuously at her passionate announcement, making her blush. 'Now you're being ridiculous.' He smirked. 'Tell me, did he make you any promises?'

She was silent and folded her arms against a sudden chill in her bones. 'I think I'd like you to leave now, Trent. You can make my excuses to Charlotte and Mark. I'm not coming to dinner.'

'Emily,' his tone turned cajoling and soft, 'don't be like that. Come to dinner. We'll sort this out after.'

'No.' Emily shook her head. 'Tomorrow I'm flying to Perth without you.'

Trent's face took on a rather ugly expression. 'You saving yourself for him now, are you?' He sighed as one about to address a wayward child. 'When I told Will we were getting married he didn't even blink an eye, Em. In fact, he sent you his congratulations. Is that the behaviour of a man who wants you? Don't be dumb about this.'

She gasped. 'You told him I accepted your proposal?'

Trent seemed to realise belatedly what he had revealed and blinked at her.

'What else have you lied about?' she asked and then recalled her conversation with Charlotte that afternoon. 'Charlotte said you had a letter for me. Where is it?'

His eyes narrowed on her harshly for a moment. 'It's in my room.'

'Why haven't you given it to me? Is it from Will?'

'If I give you that letter, Em, there's no going back,' Trent shot at her. 'It'll ruin everything.'

'Maybe for you. I want it.' She lifted her chin.

He watched her darkly for a moment before spinning on his heel and stalking out. He returned seconds later with a crumpled envelope that had already been torn open. Her name was written on the front in Will's sprawling handwriting.

She bit back a gasp. 'You read my letter!'

'He betrayed me.' Trent shrugged. 'All bets were off.'

'Get out!' Emily pointed at the door.

'You can tell him,' Trent said as he backed away, 'that I never want to see either of you again.' On these words, he walked out and slammed the door behind him.

With trembling fingers, she retreated back to the queen bed in the centre of the room and sat down. She withdrew the single-sheeted letter. The handwriting was so messy it was almost a scribble. But she didn't care. The envelope fell to the floor as she devoured the words on the page.

Dear Em,

I need to tell you something. Something I've been keeping a secret from you for seven years.

I love you.

I've always loved you.

I love the way you laugh. I love the way you smile. I love the way your hair gets fuzzy when it's humid. I love it how the tips of your ears go redder than the rest of your face when you're embarrassed. I love how you walk. I love the sound of your voice. I love how you never give up when you don't get something. I love it that you cry in both sad and happy movies. I love it how you always want to make a good impression. I love it that you'll listen even when no one else will. I love it that you're modest. I love it that you're shy. It makes me happy just to be around you.

I love you.

Always,

Will

By the time she was through reading his magical words, tears were rolling down her face.

Oh Will, how blind I've been.

Even as the thought entered her head, a new one replaced it. She jumped up, crossed the room to her suitcase and began throwing stuff in it.

I need to get back to Hay Point.

As soon as possible.

Chapter 33

Mark

Somehow the triumph of sitting across from Charlotte at a fancy restaurant seemed less than sweet. After everything they'd been through together, over-priced food, elevator music and shallow chitchat just seemed out of place.

She looked gorgeous. There was no doubt about that. The black dress she was wearing accentuated every curve of her exquisite form. But he would have liked her just as well in an old T-shirt, preferably his, lounging on the couch in front of the telly. Talking seemed to do him more of a disservice than anything and so he spent most of the meal in silence, broken sparingly by comments about the wine or the food.

It was excruciating.

Finally, the waiter brought around the dessert menus and when she declined hers he began to grow desperate and tried the first topic he could think of. 'I was wondering,' he cleared his throat, 'about Augustus.'

She looked up. 'Your turkey.'

'Well,' he shrugged, 'I think he's just as much Zara's turkey as he is mine. He certainly seems to enjoy her company more.'

'I wouldn't go that far.' She smiled. 'Augustus has a . . . lively respect for you.'

'All the same,' he nodded, 'he's nearly better now and with the project wrapping up in a few short months, I'm thinking about releasing him back into the wild. Unless Zara wants to keep him.'

Her hand, which had been reaching for her half-full wine glass, recoiled. 'Yes, I suppose when the project finishes,' she croaked, 'you won't be able to keep him any more.'

'It will be strange not having him around,' he mused. 'I've actually grown rather fond of him.'

'Really?' she repeated stiffly.

'Certainly enough to miss him if he wasn't with me.' He swirled the contents of his wine glass with a grimace. 'I hope he won't think I've abandoned him. He's a very sensitive bird. Takes offence to just about anything.'

'Is that so?' Her voice had taken on a rather shrill quality. 'It's great to hear how profoundly sympathetic you are to your turkey's needs.'

'Er, thank you,' he said slowly, not trusting the vibe he was suddenly getting from her. 'Charlotte –'

'If you don't mind,' she opened her purse and then put some money on the table, 'I think I might call it a night now. I'm pretty drained after today's ordeal.' She stood up.

He did mind very much. They couldn't halt the conversation at this point. Not when he was nearly one hundred per cent certain she was mad at him again.

'Charlotte, wait.' But she was already making a beeline for the door. Swearing under his breath, he threw a few more notes on the table and raced after her, only catching up when she was standing in front of the lifts.

'What did I say wrong?' he demanded.

'You didn't say anything wrong, Mark.' Charlotte pressed

her lips together. 'You just basically didn't say anything at all.'

'About what?'

'About us.' She turned to look at him, drawing in a swift shaky breath. 'If there is an us. Who knows, really? You can't speak about your feelings, can you? Except in riddles.'

'Riddles?'

'No, no,' she lifted a finger, 'I'm being unfair. After all, you did just tell me how much you're going to miss *your turkey* when the project's over.'

An octopus began stretching its legs right in the middle of his stomach. 'Charlotte,' he licked his lips, 'what do you want me to say?'

She looked at him in disbelief, coloured with some dignity. 'I'm not going to spell it out for you. Besides, as you've so clearly implied, when the project is over, you're going back to Perth. There's no point in discussing something that's already over anyway.'

The lift doors pinged and swung open and she stepped in, jabbing the button of their floor. He stumbled in after her, barely making it before the doors jammed on him. 'Charlotte,' he said urgently, 'I want to discuss it.'

'Really? Are you *really* sure?' She turned to face him fully and then stepped right into his comfort zone, causing him to immediately jerk back. 'There, you see,' she said with some satisfaction. 'There it is.'

'There's what?' he demanded.

'You recoiled from me.'

'I did no such thing.'

She put up a hand to touch his face and he caught her wrist before her fingertips could graze his skin. A line of fire roared up his arm, as they stood there in checkmate, her mouth a delectable pout that made him shudder from head to toe. But she didn't notice. Instead she said, 'Do you really want to deny it now?'

The doors swung open and an elderly couple in the hall cleared their throats. He released her.

'Good evening.' She smiled at them before stepping out. He didn't spare them a second glance as he struggled to pull in his scattered wits. The old man and woman entered the lift and pushed the ground-floor button. His stupor finally broke just in time for him to dash out of the lift before it closed. He saw Charlotte several metres ahead, strutting with purpose down the corridor. Thank goodness it was a long one. He ran to catch up. 'Please let me explain.'

She shook her head. 'You forget, Mark, that I studied psychology. I know what you're going through. I realise you're angry. I know you feel guilty. Denial is only the first step. But it's okay. I love you.' She stopped walking in front of their rooms and turned back to face him because he had halted a few steps behind. 'Yes. You heard me correctly. I love you.' She touched her heart. 'More than I can bear and because of that I cannot and will not share you with a ghost. It would just eat me up inside.'

'Charlotte, I don't pull away from you because I feel guilty about Kathryn,' he rasped. 'To be honest, I haven't thought about her since I got back from Perth. My head is too full of you.'

'Mark –'

He held up his hand. 'No listen. You're the first person I think of when I wake up and thoughts of you stay with me all day. When we first met I was in a dark place and I didn't want to come out. But you're like the sun. You're brighter and warmer than any black hole can contain. You make me want to live.'

Her eyes filled and she lifted a hand to dash away her tears. 'Wow. When you don't hold back you really don't hold back.'

'I'm sorry if I've seemed withdrawn and reluctant. I just . . .' He swallowed hard. 'I'm just trying to be careful.'

'You're afraid I'll hurt you?' she whispered.

'No.' He shut his eyes with a wry smile at her self-blame. 'You see, Charlotte, there's something you've got to understand about me.' He sucked in a deep breath before opening his eyes again. 'Everyone I've loved has died.'

'Oh, Mark.' She closed the distance between them, taking his face between both her hands. This time he didn't flinch as they drank in each other's faces, nose to nose.

'Not this time, Mark,' she said softly. 'Not this time.'

He bent his head to take her lips and their first touch was like balm to his battered soul. He wrapped his arms around her, holding on for dear life, one overwhelming thought crystallising in his head.

'I love you,' he said against her mouth.

'I love you too,' she replied, fitting her curves more securely into the crevices of his body.

There was no holding back after that. The tide of emotion swept them both away to a place he had thought he'd never see again. Where the sun always shone brightly and life stretched out before you, like a smorgasbord of happiness waiting to be sampled.

The following morning, he and Charlotte rose late and ordered breakfast in his room. They sat eating it together on his balcony, in thick white hotel bathrobes. The view from this vantage point was spectacular. Tall silver buildings winked in the sunlight as the glassy Brisbane River wove gently through the foreground. It was picturesque, like the opening credits in a feel-good film that was now his life. He couldn't stop his mouth from stretching across his face.

'I love it when you smile,' she remarked. 'You don't do it often enough.'

He turned from the river to direct the smile at her. 'I'll remember to do it more.'

'But seriously,' she said, 'what are you going to do when the project finishes? I mean, I don't want you to get bored at lazy Salonika Beach.'

'Do you honestly think I'll get bored?' he murmured and she blushed a delightful shade of pink before averting her eyes and tucking a strand of hair behind her ears. She gazed out at the view now cupping her steaming coffee in both hands. 'I just think, you know, that you should have a plan.'

'Bossing me around again, Ms Templeton.'

'I suppose you think I'm being pushy,' she growled at him, though she didn't really have an angry expression on her face. 'I just want to make sure you're happy, that's all.'

'I don't think I could get much happier than I am right now.'

Her perfect brow wrinkled. 'Seriously?'

He sighed. 'There are many things I could do. I could get a job in Mackay or help you out with the resort for a few years.'

'Well, I'm sure Zara will love having you around. She thinks you're great.'

'She thinks you're great too. Remember that,' he said softly.

'Well, she's certainly been opening up more to me lately. I really think she's going to be okay.' Charlotte breathed deeply. 'Though I'm definitely not going to tell her anything about what went on yesterday for at least a year or so.'

'Good idea.'

'In the meantime, I'd like to focus on Mum. I'm sure there'll only be a few more years left. She's not getting any better.'

He reached across the table and took her hand. 'Don't think about that. Live for the present. That's what I'm going to do from now on.' He cleared his throat and then looked over at the pastry plate he had been avoiding since he sat down. 'And I'm going to start by having one of these delicious almond croissants.' He took one and bit into it. It was sweet, crunchy, buttery, magic. And yes, it made him think of Kathryn. But in a good way.

He realised that Charlotte was staring at him rather closely and he smiled at her again. 'Kathryn used to make these.'

She nodded carefully.

'She used to say they were the food of diplomats and would always make a batch when faced with a very ticklish problem. I remember once, she made a whole stack and gave them to our elderly neighbour Mr Watson with a note attached.'

'What did the note say?'

'*Please close your blinds when you get dressed.*'

She laughed and he laughed too and it felt wonderfully easy. Charlotte picked up the coffee pot and tried to pour herself another coffee. 'Oh damn, we're out. Do you want another cup? 'Cause I'll order some more.'

'Sure.' He nodded and she went back into the room to get on the phone.

He stood up and went to lean against the balcony railing, enjoying the gentle breeze on his face. He reached into his pocket and withdrew Kathryn's list. Opening it, he read the final item.

Talk to someone about me – the good memories.

It was done and she had been right. He had needed her to find himself again. Even in death she had looked after him. Very carefully, he refolded the paper and then tore it into tiny little pieces that flew off his fingers with the barest breath of wind. He watched them swirl and then descend towards the river, until he could no longer see them.

Goodbye, Kathryn, and thanks.

He heard a clink and turned around to watch the most beautiful woman in the world putting down a pot of coffee on the table. She looked at him and her smile made his heart leap.

'What are you thinking about so intensely?' she asked.

'New beginnings,' he said and opened his arms so that she might walk straight into them. 'What's on *your* To Do list?'

Chapter 34

Emily

After much negotiation with a Qantas representative at the airport, she managed to book herself the last seat on a flight from Brisbane to Mackay at ten-fifteen that night. The flight was only approximately an hour and a half so she would arrive in Mackay close to midnight. That would make seeing Will first thing in the morning possible.

The flight seemed to take forever and she didn't sleep a wink of it even though she was tired. The magazine she'd bought to while away the time remained open on the second page as she reread Will's letter instead, over and over again.

He loved her!

He'd always loved her.

The knowledge was like firecrackers in her head. She just wanted to explode with joy.

Finally, the plane touched down in Mackay and the gorgeous tropical air hit her skin as her feet touched tarmac. The airport was much smaller than the Brisbane one so there were only two carousels upon which her suitcase could appear and these were located right alongside the area where people were checking in. Thanks to this, it was also impossible not to notice Will, who was handing over a suitcase at a Qantas counter.

'Will!' she called out, lifting her hand in delighted shock.

He turned around, his gaze distractedly scanning the airport lounge as though his ears had deceived him. 'Em, is that you?'

His eyes finally found hers and for the very first time she saw there what she had overlooked for the last seven years. Her breath tore from her throat as he yanked his suitcase off the belt, threw a quick apology to the Qantas representative and hurried towards her. Abandoning the carousel, she ran to him.

He dumped his bag just before their bodies collided. She threw her arms around his neck and he lifted her off the ground.

'I was coming to Brisbane to see you,' he explained breathlessly. 'Why are you back?'

'Because I love you!' she said. 'And I just had to tell you that, *immediately*.'

'You do?' He put her down again, gazing hungrily into her eyes.

'Yes, I do.' She nodded, pushing her fingers into the hair at the nape of his neck. 'Trent lied to you, Will. I didn't accept his proposal. I've been miserable this last week thinking about how much I've screwed up everything.'

'You didn't screw anything up. I screwed it up with that dumb text message.' He touched his forehead to hers, closing his eyes in regret. 'I love you, Em. I've always loved you.'

'I know.' Her voice trembled at the emotion inherent in his words. 'I got your letter.'

He lifted his head at that. 'What letter?'

Her voice faltered as she fished it out of her pocket. 'This one.'

He opened the folded piece of paper and glanced at it in

surprise and then mirth. 'Bloody Nova. I think I was drunk when I wrote this on that night he came over.'

Emily's lips parted. 'So it's not true?'

'No,' he shook his head, 'it's true all right. Drunk men don't lie.'

Emily breathed a sigh of relief. 'Thank goodness!' And then she stood up on tiptoe to claim his mouth. But he grabbed her face just before their lips met.

'No. This time, I'm kissing you.' He captured her mouth with all the pent-up emotion and passion of more than half a decade, enveloping her in a world that contained nothing but the two of them and this beautiful moment that would change both their lives.

'I can't believe this is happening to us, Will,' Emily said when they finally pulled apart. 'This is the most amazing surprise I've ever got in my life.'

He brushed her hair behind her ears, smiling at her so tenderly her heart felt like it would burst. 'So,' he drawled tentatively, 'does Trent know about the letter?'

Emily felt her joyful smile droop slightly. 'He not only knew about it, he also concealed it. He lied to both of us. I don't think we'll be seeing him for a while. Not that I would want to.'

Will's eyes shone with both regret and resignation. 'I guess so. Perhaps one day he'll come round, but if not, I have you, don't I? . . . My *best* best friend.'

He picked up his bag and, with an arm slung across her shoulders, led her back to the carousel, where her luggage was now the only bag doing the rounds on the conveyor belt. She pulled it off and they walked to the car park together.

'So tell me how the job's going,' she said enthusiastically. 'What's been happening on site?'

'Well,' Will said, tugging her suitcase out of her hands so that he was now holding both his and hers, 'somebody bet a thousand dollars you and I would get together.'

'Really?' Emily blushed rosily. 'Fancy that.'

Two weeks later

The bar and restaurant at Silver Seas resort was packed with happy FIFO workers sharing a drink at her expense. Not even the quiet presence of their project manager Mark Crawford dimmed the revelry. Their leader seemed to have mellowed and quietened somewhat ever since he'd returned to town with Charlotte Templeton on his arm.

He was seated now at a table across from Emily and Will with Nova and Spooks on his right. He didn't say much, Emily noted, but he smiled more and it was an expression that transformed his entire face. It had certainly reduced the fear his men had of him. Nova was currently pushing a full jug of beer in his direction.

'Go on, I would kill to see you pissed tonight.'

Caesar raised his eyebrows. 'I never knew you were such an ambitious man, Nova.'

As Nova opened his mouth to respond, Fish stumbled up to their table, the perfect example of 'After' if Mark could be considered the 'Before'.

'I've gotta hand it to you, Boy Scout,' he slurred over her shoulder. 'You play a very deep game. I had no idea you were even interested in . . . what's your name again, girl?' He squinted at her.

'Emily,' she grinned.

'In Emma,' Fish waved a floppy hand, 'until Spooks announced you won the bet.'

Will said nothing, but he did squeeze her hand under the table. She felt a lovely comforting warmth creep up her neck and she turned slightly to send him a secret smile. Fish, however, was not walking on. He slammed his empty glass down on the wooden table, recalling their attention. 'I mean, you could have said something. Could have put a little hint in my ear.'

Will chuckled. 'You had your money on Dipper, didn't you?'

'The man brought her a toilet.' Fish wobbled precariously on his feet. 'What was I supposed to think?'

Just then Charlotte came up, removing his glass and giving the table a quick wipe. 'Calm down, Fish,' she reprimanded him gently. 'You might break something.'

He merely snorted and tottered off.

Mark put an arm out and grabbed her around the waist, pulling her to him. 'Stay awhile. I can help you with that later.'

'Well, I must admit,' she smiled at Emily from the circle of Mark's arm, 'it was very generous of you to put all your bet winnings on a bar tab for the boys. You didn't have to do that.'

Emily returned her grin. 'Well, I did kind of have an unfair advantage. I didn't feel right about keeping the money.' She glanced at Will. 'It was all about making a point, not making myself rich.'

'And what a lovely point you made, Casino.' Spooks toasted her and then drained his glass. 'If you'd like to place any other wagers, I'd be more than happy to receive them.'

'Ah-huh,' Charlotte drawled, widening her eyes at Emily. 'You've got a nickname now, I see.'

Emily nodded enthusiastically. 'I quite like it.'

'Well, it's better than being called the Shrink.' Charlotte rolled her eyes. 'It's a shame we can't come up with our own.'

'Where's the fun in that?' Spooks demanded and then whipped off his leg and put it on the table. Several men pushed back their seats at the sudden appearance of a human leg from knee to boot sitting in the middle of their drinks.

Emily shrieked and leaped into Will's lap. Her newly minted boyfriend laughed but generously put his arms around her all the same. It was only then that Emily realised, on closer inspection, the leg was a prosthetic one.

Clutching Will's T-shirt, she glared at Spooks. 'You scared me half to death!'

'Gave you the spooks, did I?' he chortled. 'I was saving that for just the right moment. Congratulations, Casino, you're now a real member of our team.'

'Yes, Emily,' Mark remarked dryly, 'and I believe the correct felicitation at this point would be *Break a leg*.'

'Mark Crawford,' Charlotte exclaimed, throwing an arm across his broad shoulders with an expression of feigned shock on her face, 'I do believe you just cracked a joke.'

Caesar looked first stunned and then supremely pleased. 'Yes,' he agreed. 'I suppose I did.'

Author's Note

The majority of this novel is set at the port of Hay Point on Queensland's coast, thirty-eight kilometres south of Mackay. This port is one of the largest exporters of coal in the world. There are actually two separate coal export terminals in this location. One is the Dalrymple Bay Coal Terminal and the other, the Hay Point Services Coal Terminal. In my story, I call my terminal the Hay Point Wharf, which is loosely based on the Dalrymple Bay Coal Terminal.

It was not my intention to capture the Dalrymple Bay terminal structure exactly but to give readers a general overview so that they can get a feel for what it's like to work on a job like this, rather than getting bogged down in details.

I was fortunate to work on an expansion of this wharf as a young engineer back in 2002. We were constructing a new berth and installing a new shiploader. It was a very exciting time, particularly witnessing the arrival of the new shiploader, which is the size of a ten-storey building. This project also forms the basis of employment in my narrative. Again, much detail has been omitted to focus on characters in this environment.

I have also ignored a lot of the port operations and the shipping schedule in favour of the construction project. This would have played a large role in interfering with the project. It is also important to note that Barnes Inc is a fictional company and so are all its personnel depicted in this work. Similarly, Silver Seas Resort does not exist and was created for the purposes of this story.

It has been wonderful writing a novel that shows off one of Australia's most picturesque landscapes and also the Great Barrier Reef. Many readers may question whether the coal export facilities in the area are a danger to the reef. While shipping accidents, i.e. oil spills, are a concern, the probability of this happening is low. Commercial shipping routes are carefully planned and heavily regulated, whereas climate change and fishing represent a greater ongoing threat to the reef's survival.

When I was posted in this area many years ago, exploring the Great Barrier Reef and the surrounds was the best fringe benefit of the job. I think it is our duty as Australians to protect it for future generations.

I really hope readers enjoy Emily's and Charlotte's journeys.

Acknowledgements

Third book out, you like to think that you're becoming a bit of pro and you don't need as much help as you used to. There's nothing further from the truth. As usual, I've had to call upon a whole swag of helpers from a vast variety of locations.

Firstly, I'd like to thank my critique partners, Nicola E. Sheridan, Marlena Pereira and Kym Brooks, whose thorough and critical eyes helped shape this book from dirty draft to final manuscript. Ladies, where would I be without your insight?

I would like to thank my long-time friend, Kristen Johns, for her diving expertise so that I could get those scenes on the reef just right. Hugs.

My gratitude to Penelope Giles, who was so generous with her time regarding the final court case scenes. Her expert knowledge really helped me make these chapters more authentic. If there are any mistakes concerning the law in the text, they are mine, not hers, and she never saw them.

Thank you also to Sharon Johnston from Dalrymple Bay Coal Terminal Pty Ltd for doing her best to answer all my questions and giving me a more thorough picture of the location and the surrounds.

My appreciation also to anyone else I called or spoke to as part of my research, no matter how briefly, including that poor woman at Woodford Correctional Centre whom I chatted to about giving out inmate details. There are so many people I have thrown random questions at. I am very grateful to you all for your assistance.

Apart from the nuts and bolts of the story, there are people I actually needed just to get me seated in front of my computer. My mum, in particular, has been an angel, taking the kids every Wednesday so I could write. Our nanny, Rebecca Laing, for doing Fridays. My mother-in-law Shirley, for those times she stayed overnight with us to free up my time from home duties.

I must also thank Clare Forster for being such a great agent. Your enthusiasm for my work has kept me motivated. Also to Beverley Cousins, my wonderful publisher, who makes me love writing more and more every day. My publicist, Jess Malpass, for her work with regard to promotion, and the rest of the team at Random House who contributed. Thank you all for your efforts.

And last but not least, to my four beautiful children. Mummy loves you very much. Thank you for your patience. And my husband, Todd. I love it when you talk about my writing because I can see how proud you are of me. You are the rock on which I build everything. Love you.

If you enjoyed *The Girl in the Yellow Vest*,
read on for a taster of Loretta's new romantic novella

OPERATION: VALENTINE

'Once upon a time, there was a young girl called Sarah Dubert who needed to fall in love in six weeks . . .'

Thanks to food poisoning, broken dates, airport malfunctions and even death, Sarah Dubert has never had a boyfriend on Valentine's Day. However, this year she's determined to break the curse and snare herself a man before the Big V. Signing herself up to the online dating site soulmates.com, she begins eliminating possible candidates through dates at her favourite bar, The Blue Saloon . . .

Owen Black, the handsome new owner of The Blue Saloon, likes his women fast, experienced and temporary. A woman on a mission to find love – particularly one with a six-week deadline – would normally have him running for the hills. So why is he *so* uncharacteristically interested in Sarah's search? And, more importantly, the success of her dates . . .?

Available as an ebook from February 2014

Week 1, Day 1: Strategising

'Okay, ladies.' Amy, the brunette with the pixie haircut, raised her wine glass. 'It's the first week of January. What's your New Year's resolution?'

'Buy less clothes, save more money,' her friend Mia immediately announced, causing the third girl at the table to groan.

'Wasn't that your resolution last year?'

Mia flicked her long blonde hair over one shoulder and said with a sideways look, 'Last year I'd just started a new job, Sarah. I needed to look good. We all knew it wasn't going to happen.'

'Mia, you work at a bank,' Sarah protested, lifting her own glass and taking a sip. 'You have a *uniform*.'

Mia stuck out her tongue. 'All right then, Smarty-pants. What's your New Year's resolution?'

Sarah set her wine glass on the table with a smile that also lit her wide blue eyes. 'To have fun, like we're doing right now.'

It was a Thursday night after work and the three women

had chosen to meet at their usual hangout and favourite bar in Perth, The Blue Saloon.

'Come on,' Amy scoffed. She was, by far, the most opinionated in the group and was not going to let an opportunity to have her say go by unused. 'That's too easy. It's not a real resolution unless you're changing something about yourself.'

'Seriously?' Sarah dropped her chin in her palm. 'Well, I suppose I could start exercising more.'

'Bor-ring.' Mia sang the word in mock disapproval. 'Besides, it's not like you need to lose weight or anything. Your wardrobe could use some TLC though. Want any help?'

Sarah chuckled. It was clear that if this year Mia was buying less clothes for herself then she was going to require someone else to get her fix.

'Okay.' Sarah held up her hands in mock fear. 'Stop looking at me like a new project. Besides, slimming down isn't the only reason people exercise, you know. I might want to improve my fitness.'

Mia snorted. 'They all say that. But it's not true.'

'Forget exercise,' Amy interrupted. 'What really needs a shake-up is Sarah's love life.'

Sarah coughed. 'What love life?'

'Exactly.' Amy poked her. 'Why not make it your New Year's resolution this year to fall in love.'

Sarah rubbed her arm where Amy had jabbed her but didn't say anything. As much as she hated to admit it, the thought of falling in love sounded wonderful. She hadn't had a steady relationship for a couple of years straight and independence was starting to feel more like loneliness every day.

'Maybe,' she said finally. 'But isn't falling in love more to do with luck and chance than premeditation?'

Amy blew her fringe out of her eyes. 'Not if you're continually dating all the wrong men.'

Sarah winced. 'Okay, so I'm not that good at meeting guys. But a New Year's resolution is not going to fix that.'

'No . . .' Amy's dismal expression didn't take long to brighten. 'What you need is a structured plan!'

Sarah blinked. '*A what*?'

The problem was, Amy had graduated from the University of Western Australia as a mathematician. She worked for the Australian Bureau of Statistics and often considered life a series of numbers and equations waiting to be solved. 'Your problem,' she said at length, 'is that in the past you haven't looked further afield than your own friendship group, your acquaintances and the bars you frequent. At the bureau –'

'*Here we go*.' Sarah nodded to Mia, who unfortunately turned out to be listening in rapt attention. Sarah sighed.

'*At the bureau*,' Amy said again, 'we collect data from a broad variety of sources. If you keep going back to the same place and the same lousy demographic, you'll get poor results. It's a fact. You need a bigger pool but a tighter net.'

Sarah rolled her eyes. 'And how am I supposed to achieve that, Doctor?'

'I have one word for you,' Amy announced triumphantly. 'Soulmates.com.'

'An internet dating site?' Sarah gasped.

'Bingo, baby.' Amy clapped her hands cheerfully. 'Why leave love to chance, when you can tailor your next date by occupation, hair colour and height?'

Sarah raised her empty glass and eyed it with dissatisfaction. 'I need another drink.'

'Internet dating,' Amy continued informatively, 'has worked for heaps of people and made many a happy marriage.'

Sarah glanced at Mia. 'You're not buying this, are you?'

'Well,' Mia tapped one shiny pink nail to her chin, 'I heard on the radio this morning that one in three couples who were married last year met online.'

'*Mia*, you can't side with her. You've known me since high school. She only came into the picture at uni.'

Mia shrugged apologetically. 'I'm sorry, I can't help what I heard.'

'The statistics speak for themselves.' Amy punched her fist into her palm.

'What I want to know,' Sarah scoffed, 'is how this went from me meeting a man, to me needing a husband.'

'Falling in love is all about meeting the one, isn't it?' Mia responded with a slight air of dreaminess. 'Why aren't you open to that?'

Sarah coughed. 'What makes you think I'm closed to it?'

'Well, take Valentine's Day for example,' Mia pointed out. 'Didn't you tell us last week that this year you're planning on working through it?'

'That's different.' Sarah folded her arms and pursed her lips.

'How?' Amy demanded.

'You know Valentine's Day is a completely different ball game. On that day, I'm cursed.'

In the dysfunctional universe that was Sarah's love life, Valentine's Day represented the black hole. She'd never actually had a date for it before.

Like *ever*.

From high school through to university, she'd always spent the day solo.

Always.

Even the years when she'd had a boyfriend had been lonely.

Travis, the cheat, had dumped her two days before.

Brett had been caught in a snow storm in Alaska and couldn't get a flight home.

And Jake . . . Poor, unfortunate Jake had caught swine flu and *died* a month out.

Mia rolled her eyes. 'Oh, for goodness' sake, you are not *cursed*!'

'Hello!' Sarah protested. '*Somebody died*.'

'Come on, Sarah.'

'No.' She held up her hand. 'For the safety of the male population of Perth, it would be better if I just stayed out of it.'

In fact, she had thought herself very cunning to have scheduled the Penwick Pty Ltd Inaugural Charity Ball for Valentine's Day. When their auditors had raised the issue that the company culture wasn't doing them any favours, it had been her idea to host a variety of well-publicised charity events to boost their image.

As the public relations manager, it was her job to show the media and their employees that, in actual fact, Penwick Pty Ltd was community orientated, environmentally friendly, sympathetic to those less fortunate and concerned about incurable diseases.

What a laugh!

Nonetheless, so far they'd had a bike marathon, a wine-tasting day, a fair and a concert. This ball was going to be their most lavish event yet and a lovely distraction for her. Thanks to her job, she didn't have to buy into all the Valentine's hype *except* in the name of Cancer Research fundraising.

Alleluia.

'For the record,' Amy tapped French-manicured fingernails on the table top, 'Jake was always a very sickly person. He was allergic to just about everything and anaemic as hell. When you were dating him, he had the mumps and whooping cough before he got swine flu. I'm surprised he didn't die earlier.'

'*Amy.*'

'I'm sorry, I meant no disrespect.' She clasped her hands together and looked heavenward. 'May his soul rest in peace.' Her gaze returned to Sarah. 'But to me, this only reinforces my previous point.'

'Which is what?' Sarah demanded.

'You choose all the wrong sorts of guys to date. None of them have had any staying power.'

'And by that you mean . . .?'

'Commitment value.'

'You're making this sound like a mathematical problem again.' Sarah shook her head. 'I don't believe it's as easy as that.'

'You're right, it's simpler,' Amy gasped excitedly. 'We could add your Valentine's Day problem to your New Year's resolution and achieve two outcomes at the same time.'

'Now you're definitely talking crazy.' Sarah folded her arms again. The conversation was rapidly descending into a place she just did *not* want to go.

'Valentine's Day is in six weeks, right?' Amy asked Mia who nodded. 'That's more than enough time in the dating arena to pull this off.'

Sarah threw up her hands. 'Pull what off?'

Amy lifted her hand as though writing the words across the skyline. 'I call it Operation: Valentine.'

Sarah dropped her head in her hands. 'I call it *dumb*.'

But Amy was in her element. 'Once upon a time, there was a young girl called Sarah Dubert who needed to fall in love in six weeks. So she gets onto soulmates.com, finds her prince and together they break the evil Valentine's Day curse and live happily ever after. See?' Amy looked around at her friends for kudos. 'It's a fairy tale waiting to happen.'

'It's brilliant,' Mia breathed.

Sarah's head jerked up. 'Are you high?'

'Maybe a little tipsy,' Mia conceded. 'I've had two glasses of wine. But I still think this plan could work. Obviously there are a few kinks to iron out.'

'No, no kinks.' Sarah made a cutting motion with her hands. 'No plan either. I'm not getting on soulmates.com. Period.'

Her two friends, who had clearly been getting excited by this idea, turned to her in dismay.

'Why the hell not?' Amy demanded. 'It's foolproof.'

'Yeah, like a bucket with six holes.'

'Oh, for goodness' sake, don't be a spoil sport.' Mia swatted her hand. 'It's much better than picking up men in bars. Besides, we've already established you're no good at that.'

'Speaking of picking up in bars,' Amy drawled. 'Look who's at it again.'

Mia and Sarah slowly lifted their eyes and followed the direction of her hungry expression.

He was dark-haired and olive-skinned. The white shirt he was wearing, with its unbuttoned collar and rolled up sleeves, only seemed to accentuate a strong muscular upper body. His eyes, the colour of a short black without the crème, were currently trained on two ladies at the bar whom he appeared to be chatting up. At least that's what Sarah had to assume, given they were hanging on every word that fell from that sumptuous mouth of his.

Sarah sucked in a breath. '*Man*, is he gorgeous.'

Amy sighed. 'Tell me about it. The bad ones get all the looks.'

'I found out his name the other day,' Mia informed them both with a certain amount of pride to be the only one at the table with the scoop. 'It's Owen Black.'

'Ooooh, Owen Black,' Amy repeated lazily. 'I like it.'

'Yeah, so does every other woman who walks into this bar,' Mia replied. 'He seems to do very well for himself.'

Amy nodded. 'Have you ever seen him not pick someone up when he's working a shift?'

Sarah shrugged. 'I'm just glad he hasn't made any changes to our bar since he took over.'

'I'll say,' Mia agreed.

Sarah and her friends had been using The Blue Saloon as their meeting place for every crisis, catch up, commiseration or congratulations between them for the past three years.

They loved the place.

The décor was comfortable yet eye-catching. A long traditional polished timber bar ran the length of one wall. An array of polished circular tables populated the floor in front of it. The windows were large and framed by huge royal blue curtains that were never closed. There was no dance floor but a number of blue couches dotted the corners for those quieter, more relaxing nights. The food was excellent, the music tasteful and the booze flowed freely as long as you paid.

When they'd found out the old owner Mr Martinelli was selling they were devastated. The last thing they wanted was for new management to make a stack of changes to their favourite haunt. But when Owen Black had sauntered in a few weeks later, the only thing he seemed to be taking out was the ladies.

One by one.

Amy nudged Sarah. 'Why don't you ask him out?'

'Are you mad?' Sarah squeaked. 'I've just made a resolution to fall in love, not get my heart broken. Owen Black is a player. Any girl with half a brain can see that.'

'Woohoo.' Amy gave her shoulders a squeeze and said to Mia, 'She's made the resolution. Now all we need to do is get her on soulmates.com.'

With a helpless laugh, Sarah shrugged off her arm. 'Don't you ever give up?'

'Not when I believe in something.'

Sarah shook her head. 'Now I really need that drink.' She pushed out her chair and stood up. 'You guys want anything from the bar?'

'No, thanks.' Her girlfriends shook their heads and she walked away from them in relief. She hoped the conversation would turn as soon as she left them.

As much as she appreciated Amy and Mia's support, sometimes their first instincts were a little out of whack. Not that she had anything against internet dating. She was sure that it had helped a lot of people find love. But the thought of putting all her personal details into a computer database so it could spit out a name and contact number just seemed a little too clinical for her.

Sarah had always been a romantic at heart. Her idea of meeting true love involved glances exchanged across a crowded

room or a misunderstanding that leads to lunch. Even hitting it off in a supermarket checkout line seemed more romantic than surfing the net. Dating websites just took all the fun out of it.

Better to stick with traditional methods.

They were slower but safer.

She drummed her fingers on the bar as she waited, pleased with her own sense of purpose. This year she was going to fall in love. She just needed to be a little more careful about it.

A little more choosey.

As though mocking the thought, a shadow crossed her body, causing her fingers to stop drumming. She looked up and to her dismay was unable to stop heat from infusing her face and goosebumps from rising on her flesh.

With eyes like that, Owen Black was even more dangerous up close. She swallowed hard and tried to smile, hoping her News Year's resolution was more solid than butter. He returned her gaze with his own lazy, seductive appraisal.

'Now what can I get for *you*?' he purred.